THE FINAL DRIVE

Other Books by the Author
THE BLACK PHANTOM CHRONICLES
The Savage War
The Eternal Struggle
The Island Siege
The Final Drive

THE FINAL DRIVE

THE BLACK PHANTOM CHRONICLES

BOOK FOUR

BY

ESTHER WALLACE

EMERALD LAKE
BOOKS
Sherman, Connecticut

The Final Drive
The Black Phantom Chronicles (Book 4)

Copyright © 2025 Esther Wallace

Cover design © 2025 Emerald Lake Books

Cover illustration © 2025 Emerald Lake Books

Books published by Emerald Lake Books may be ordered through your favorite booksellers or by visiting emeraldlakebooks.com.

Library of Congress Cataloging-in-Publication Data

Names: Wallace, Esther, author

Title: The final drive / by Esther Wallace.

Description: Sherman, Connecticut : Emerald Lake Books, 2025. | Series: The Black Phantom chronicles ; book four | Audience term: Teenagers

Identifiers: LCCN 2025007875 (print) | LCCN 2025007876 (ebook) | ISBN 9781945847851 (paperback) | ISBN 9781945847868 (epub)

Subjects: CYAC: Fantasy. | Quests (Expeditions)--Fiction. | Kings, queens, rulers, etc.--Fiction. | Orphans--Fiction. | LCGFT: Fantasy fiction. | Novels.

Classification: LCC PZ7.1.W3527 Fi 2025 (print) | LCC PZ7.1.W3527 (ebook) | DDC [Fic]--dc23

LC record available at https://lccn.loc.gov/2025007875

LC ebook record available at https://lccn.loc.gov/2025007876

For those scared
For those world-weary
For those searching
And for those who have stumbled home

Cast of Characters

Abby . . . . A tavern maid of the Cedar Apple.

Alexander Maxwell . The older brother of Evan Maxwell and heir to the throne of Ansky while he lived.

Almec, Abbot . . . . The Anskonian abbot of the monastery outside of Castle Ansky.

Andrew Dalacort . . The cousin of Evan Maxwell, son of Wilber and Lorene Dalacort, and heir to the throne of Evfel.

Arnacin . . . . Our islander. Son of Bozzic and Lady Talliaha and brother of Charlotte and William.

Brimstone . . . . . . Stallion of the Ice Woods.

Carrie . . . . Lisya's daughter.

Charlotte . . . . . . The sister of Arnacin and daughter of Bozzic and Talliaha.

Christina. . . . . . . An Anskonian villager and the wife of Martin.

Clare . . . . Formerly, Queen Lorene's handmaiden, and now a maid within Castle Ansky.

Cyril . . . . An Anskonian footman.

Darkfire . . . . Evan Maxwell's stallion.

Erik. . . . . An Evfelian knight.

Evan Maxwell . . . . True king of Ansky.

Felleno Topaz . . . . An Evfelian slave, in service in Arieh.

Gwenre . . . . An islander from Arnacin's village and Tevin's wife.

James. . . . . Twin brother of Thomas and adopted son of Lisya.

Klement, Sir. . . . . An Anskonian knight from the Fortress Tyhoronous.

Lazarus . . . . An island fisherman from Arnacin's village.

Lisya . . . . The enchantress of Enchantress Island and creator of the Ice Woods.

Lorene Dalacort . . The queen of Evfel and Evan Maxwell's aunt. Sister of Ansky's deceased King Phillip.

Malachi . . . . The youngest of Lisya's adopted sons and a refugee from Evfel.

Martin . . . . An Anskonian villager and husband of Christina.

Matalaide . . . . . . An island weaver from Arnacin's village.

Michael . . . . Lisya's son.

Newton . . . . The cousin of Evan Maxwell, son of Wilber and Lorene Dalacort, and the youngest prince of Evfel.

Phillip Maxwell . . . The father of Evan Maxwell and former king of Ansky.

Quincy, Lord . . . . Formerly, an Anskonian knight, and now a lord from Castle Ansky.

Radnor, Sir. . . . . . An Anskonian knight from Castle Ansky.

Raymond. . . . . . . An island hunter from Arnacin's village and a close friend of Arnacin's family.

Reginold, Duke . . . A duke and regent of Evfel.

Talliaha, Lady . . . . The mother of Arnacin and Charlotte and widow of Bozzic.

Taylor Magree . . . Owner of the tavern, The Sky Haven, in Ansky.

Tenacius . . . . The son of Arnacin and Valoretta.

Tevin . . . . An islander from Arnacin's village and one of the group of boys that used to play with Arnacin when they were children.

Thomas . . . . Twin brother of James and adopted son of Lisya.

Valoretta . . . . The dethroned queen of Mira, wife of Arnacin, and mother of Tenacius.

Vilo . . . . An islander from Arnacin's village, known for his skill with music.

Vincent. . . . . Tavern keeper of The Cedar Apple, in Arieh.

Wilber Dalacort. . . The king of Evfel, husband of Lorene, father of Andrew and Newton, and uncle to Evan Maxwell.

Wolflin . . . . An islander from Enchantress Island, known for his skill with poetry.

YEARS AGO, Arnacin of Enchantress Island set sail in search of a destiny greater than shepherding. But what he found instead was the darker side of human nature—betrayal by kings, the insatiable greed of pirates, and the despair of those crushed by corruption. Scarred and disillusioned, he sets course for home, but not before rescuing one of his last remaining friends and, in order to protect her, marrying her.

Valoretta was heir to the throne of Mira. But when she inherited it, there was little of her country left to save. With time slipping away, she helped as many of her people escape as she could before becoming a captive of her kingdom's destroyers until Mira's Black Phantom reappeared to carry her to safety. Yet such was hard to find in a world set on using her to claim the right to her throne. When she becomes pregnant out of wedlock, she marries her phantom to hide her trail and returns with him back to his homeland, Enchantress Island.

Meanwhile, Prince Evan Maxwell, robbed of his birthright, challenges the usurper King Wilber of Evfel to a duel for Ansky's throne. Though he wins, his mercy proves costly—Wilber, burning with hatred, amasses an army to strike back. Outnumbered and outmatched, Evan's only hope lies in a handful of untrained islanders and an enchantress's family.

But fate is about to intertwine his path with that of Arnacin and Valoretta—and the battle for their futures is only beginning.

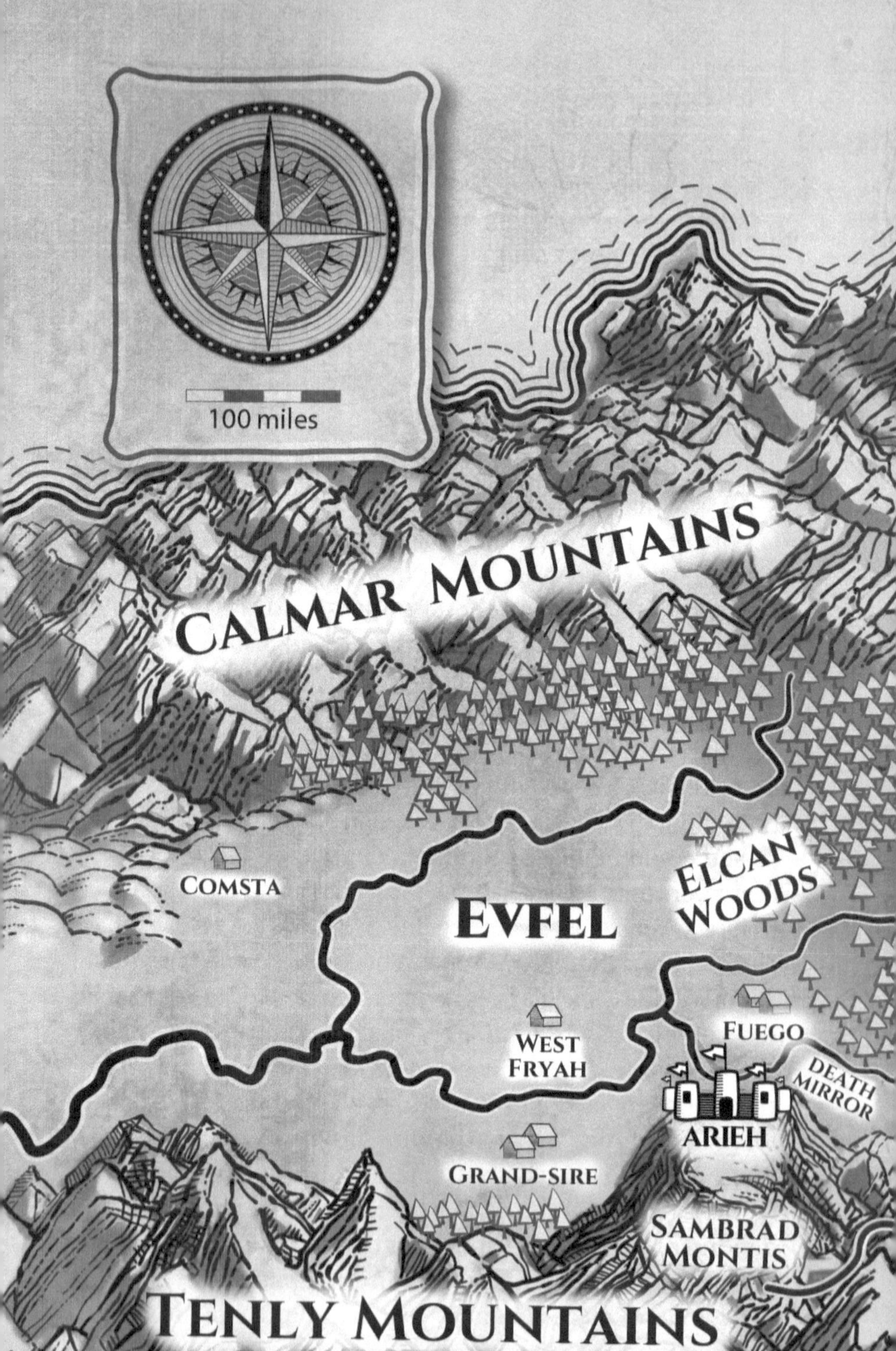

100 miles
CALMAR MOUNTAINS
COMSTA
EVFEL
ELCAN WOODS
WEST FRYAH
FUEGO
DEATH MIRROR
ARIEH
GRAND-SIRE
SAMBRAD MONTIS
TENLY MOUNTAINS

ENCHANTRESS ISLAND
SUMMOS VALLEY
CALMAR MOUNTAINS
PENELOPE PASS
WOODELL
ICE WOODS
RIVER GOLD
FORTRESS TYHORONOUS
ANSKY
SANGUINEA GORGE
CASTLE ANSKY
CYRA
TENLY MOUNTAINS

Prologue

Like many of the fortifications within and around Castle Ansky, the dungeons had received the special attention of the masons under King Wilber of Evfel. Even imagining escape was now impossible. But if there was one positive thing to say for it, there was much less dampness and decay—practically none, in fact.

And yet, that was far too generous.

Pulling his thin blanket over his scrawny shoulders, Sir Klement looked up from where he was sitting on the floor as feet clomped down the corridor outside. As he did every afternoon—the only marker of the days—the jailer, Apulion, entered the cell with a bowl of what he called soup. Starved, the prisoner never refused the slop.

The chain connecting Klement's wrists clanked its familiar complaint as he reached up to accept the rough vessel. Blobs of fat and carrot ends bobbed in the greasy-smelling water, but someone had included an actual piece of meat among the scraps. Klement did not know if the meat was included on purpose, but he sipped the soup gratefully while the jailer settled onto the bench he had dragged just out of reach. Chains prevented the prisoner from taking more than three steps in any direction.

"Well?" Apulion asked, folding his arms across his chest. The question was old, but Klement awaited it every day with eagerness. It brought with it company and speech while he drew his meal out as long as possible.

On this occasion, the jailer's lips twitched smugly.

Wondering at the smirk, Klement nevertheless replied, "No true-born Anskonian will ever yield to Wilber of Evfel. Yes, I know his reasons for seizing control again after Radnor died last winter, but submission to Evfel is no better than Prince Maxwell's supposed affiliation with magic." He hid his contempt by taking another sip from the bowl.

The smug smile broadened. "They will in order to protect themselves from hell. Maxwell just disappeared into the Ice Woods without falling."

Choking, Klement looked up at the jailer. "What?" As Apulion stood to thump him on the back, he shook his head. "It must be a lie."

Shrugging, the jailer returned to his seat. "Is it? His claims last fall, forced through Dalacort lips, came with the islanders' backing. And we cannot ignore the Evfelians that never returned, strangled to death by blades of grass."

Klement kept his lips sealed, even though he lacked a counterargument.

"And this time," Apulion continued, "there are too many witnesses for debate. You yourself should remember the commotion down here just this past week. Summos Valley alerted us that Prince Maxwell was on the way back—"

"Why are they involved?"

"I could not care less, but that is beside the point. Wilber decided to capture him and finally hold an actual trial, one that reveals Maxwell's true allegiances. The capture was easy, but the stallion ran away. Still, I locked our traitorous prince up myself, I did. According to King Wilber's orders, I put him in our most impenetrable cell, chained so as to be unable to move."

The jailer paused, letting those words linger. "He vanished."

Klement shook his head. "Someone helped him."

"The castle gates were immediately barricaded. But, very well, let us assume he escaped with help before anyone could act. Except..."

Impatiently, Klement pressed, "Except what?"

"We had an extra Anskonian knight at that time. He was as untrained as all the rest from town, but no one could remember when he was drafted. In the hunt for Maxwell, no one thought too much of this knight. He was at least ten years older than our prince, brown-eyed instead of blue, blond-haired rather than brown, taller, broader and so forth. The only thing that made anyone pause was that he had a vibrantly red-haired boy as a companion and could ride King Phillip's untouchable horses.

"Now, maybe he was just one of those animal-tamer types. Or so we thought for a week. But when there was no sight of Maxwell, Wilber finally ordered the gates to be opened and a search party to move out. A hundred men rode forth, Evfelians and Anskonians alike. Among them went the animal tamer, for if Maxwell was spotted, no one could ride better than he. Wilber personally selected the party."

Again Apulion paused his story. After a moment, Klement started to rise in frustration. Naturally, he could never reach far enough to shake the other, but he wanted to.

Laughing, the jailer said, "Have patience. I will tell. So, we waited back here. Hours later, ninety-nine men and a hundred horses returned. The animal tamer was gone, and the host was pale as albinos. They said they were in the midst of the valley when one of the knights broke away. Only, it was no longer the animal tamer. Every feature had changed. His blond hair became brown. His build was slighter. To put it bluntly, he had transformed into Maxwell.

"He turned his steed—one of his father's—not toward the mountains, but toward the Ice Woods. As they neared them, they saw something leap from the gate—the stallion stolen from Wilber last year. Maxwell leapt off the horse he was riding, was picked up by that demonic beast, and together they disappeared into the woods. They never slipped once."

Leaning back, Apulion regarded the transfixed prisoner. "Now, if you find that unbelievable, let me tell you about his red-haired companion. Know that no one left after that host. Wilber had the gates closed immediately behind them, but everyone has combed the castle for Maxwell's companion. No one has seen him since the prince left."

A long silence followed. Klement knew his heart beat, yet it seemed detached from his chest. No, he could not believe Maxwell had allied with the evil forces in the Ice Woods.

As if reading his thoughts, Apulion sighed. "The facts are, sir, Wilber has been telling the truth all along. The supposed confession forced out of his lips was the lie, and Maxwell has joined in with evil spirits."

Slowly, Klement looked up. "But why? What would even prompt him to make such a pact? And if the horse is a spirit of the Ice Woods, is it perhaps not more likely that Prince Maxwell was put under some spell when he was trying to tame it?"

Apulion sighed. "You are scratching at the bottom of the barrel. Anyway, it appears to me, sir, you might have until Maxwell is brought to justice. I assume the king is being pressured by Ansky to grant you a second chance, but if you still refuse to accept Wilber as your rightful ruler when he calls for you, it will be the rope that brings your end. To make matters worse, you will have betrayed all of Ansky in your refusal to aid it against a traitor. If our onetime prince succeeds, no matter the cause for his conversion, all of Ansky will fall to the creatures of darkness dwelling in the woods. I would suggest you think about it."

Chapter 1

SHEPHERD OR NOBLE?

ENCHANTRESS ISLAND rose above the small ship sailing toward its eastern shore. The late afternoon sun shone in glimmers, setting behind the tree-topped mountain in a slow descent. Light burnished the peak and flashed across the wind-blown ocean waves. The island itself burned beneath the sun like an emerald emerging from the sea and was no less wondrous than it looked. After five agonizingly long years, Arnacin would be home once his unusually sluggish ship reached the shore.

A light creak of the cabin door, followed by soft footsteps, told him of someone's arrival, yet he did not turn. Joining him at the bow, Valoretta whispered, "You're trembling, Arnacin."

The islander said nothing. No words could untangle the fluctuating web of joy, relief, fear, anticipation and self-doubt.

She waited a beat, then asked, "Are you still concerned about what your family will think of you, a husband and father, without their knowledge of either?"

Finally turning toward Valoretta, Arnacin confessed, "I don't dare ask myself." Beneath her hood, her pale blue eyes met his, and he changed subjects. "Is Tenacius asleep?"

"For now. When will we reach shore?"

"Not soon enough." His words came out in a sigh.

Valoretta said nothing for a long moment. Then she lightly touched his arm. "You should help me with Tenacius when he wakes in another ten minutes, or it's going to be a long afternoon."

Arnacin shook his head. Nothing could rip his focus from his home at that moment.

Valoretta's gaze remained fixed on him. "When we arrive, I'll stay here with Tenacius until afterward." She had no need to define *afterward*.

Arnacin did not take time to lower his sail or drop the anchor. As soon as the water turned shallow, the islander jumped over the bow. While the wind pushed his flat-bottomed ship onto the sand with a deep grinding hiss, he raced into the village along the shores of Alleluia Lake.

Now, as he approached the dancing water, the fact that the lake was really only a medium-sized pond was jarringly obvious. Once upon a time, he had thought it immense and second only to the ocean. Still, despite its actual size, it drew the eye, and its familiarity buoyed his spirits.

Before reaching the village, however, he slowed. No sounds of chatter or children greeted him, no yapping dogs, no boys splashing each other in the pond. As he entered, he noticed that half the doors were shut despite the summer humidity. Not only that, but he thought he remembered homes in different places than they were now. Though a few women sat in the distance, working outside their doors, they did so in silence.

As a dog wandering down the street suddenly perked its nose in the air, took a sniff, and then growled softly, Arnacin pulled his hood up against the deep cold that seeped into him. The soft patter of paws followed him before apparently losing interest and wandering away.

Reaching his home, Arnacin stopped. Its wood appeared unweathered and the door was shut, as was that of the neighboring home, which had been Raymond's. Yet Raymond had never been inside, and *still* he had never shut the door.

Quickly turning back to his home, the islander knocked. No response came. As his heart stopped for a beat, Arnacin numbly pushed open the door. The house was dark, and the curtained alcove that had once given privacy to his parents' bed was no longer there. A flat wall stood in its place, fresh and subtle and giving no hint as to the family who had once lived inside. The only signs of occupancy were a single pallet, a small table, one stool, and a pot and ladle hanging in the dead fireplace, though a light dust spoke of the owner's absence.

Slowly, sensations returned. Wind from the water rushed through the open door, around the room, and passed him—a mournful, cold and dying sigh.

Arnacin's skin crawled. Studying the barren scene only a second longer, he shut the door on the darkened interior with a snap. The sun's light suddenly became thick and depressing.

Pushing aside his dread, the islander trudged down the street, searching desperately for something, anything, that would put his greatest fears to rest.

Back past Alleluia Lake, where some of the homes sat on their legs three feet above the ground, past hundreds of memories that now snickered at him, he wandered until someone carding wool under her eaves captured his attention. "Matalaide!"

Matalaide's head snapped upward at his relieved cry, yet she stared at him without recognition. Then, abruptly, she leapt to her feet and strode over to him. She did not greet him or smile. Seizing his arm, she yanked him toward her hut.

She nearly threw him inside and shut the door behind them. "What do you have to say for yourself?" the weaver finally barked.

Catching himself on the loom, Arnacin whirled back toward her. "What's happened?"

Anger flashed in Matalaide's eyes. "First, you leave in the dead of the night! You desert everyone, every responsibility, and then you dare return?"

"I had to!"

"Oh, ho! Is that your take on it? I would think five years was long enough to come up with a good apology."

The weaver still stood with her back pressed against the door. Trembling, Arnacin expected the hut to begin shrinking in on them before waking to find it all the worst nightmare yet. "Matalaide," he whispered. "What happened?"

In the dim light of the nearby candle, he saw tears appear in the weaver's eyes. As if realizing how clearly he could see her pain, Matalaide fixed her gaze on something not far from Arnacin's shoulder. Cautiously taking his gaze off her, the islander glanced that way and then froze. Silk lay over the back of a chair—deep blue silk with some emblem in the middle and fire along the bottom. The exact insignia was unclear. Only black lines faced him, but it would not matter if those lines depicted angel wings. It was a mark of nobility.

Matalaide approached it and ran her finger along the brilliant blue cloth. "There was a battle on our shores, Arnacin. All the able-bodied men who survived have gone to help finish the war. Your mother left with them." When Arnacin didn't respond, the weaver added, "I'm sorry to say your brother and sister are dead. Will died two years ago of food poisoning—at least, that's my assumption—and Charlotte died of an arrow in the battle. She wasn't supposed to be there, but..." Matalaide shrugged. "She was Charlotte."

The air buzzed sharply in the ensuing silence until Arnacin forced some response from his tongue. "None of those things ever happen here!"

"Call me a liar, then!" Matalaide whirled back toward him. "Face it, boy! You needed to be here, and you weren't!"

Arnacin shook his head in horror, and the weaver sighed. The pity on her face was far worse than her flash of temper.

"Many things change in five years." As she pulled the banner off the chair, a dark, fiery horse revealed itself in the falling folds. "And it is likely we have claimed a king. Charlotte herself deliberately took the arrow meant for him."

"No!" Arnacin dashed through the door and fled for the mountain. Yet his denial had been automatic. He knew, by the blue standard alone, that Matalaide spoke truly. Charlotte was not wandering the mountain, nor would she ever again. His nightmares were reality. The island had lost itself.

Far away, loomed the forest known fearfully to Elcan as the Ice Woods—treacherous hoarfrost and black abysses. Inside, Enchantress Island's chosen king, Prince Evan Maxwell, leaned against the wood's sole cottage, Darkfire the stallion by his side. Both youthful and aged, Evan appeared, scarred by war and yet too young for lines of deep weariness.

He did not turn when the door opened behind him and a man stepped through it. As the newcomer placed a hand on Evan's shoulder, however, he glanced over with a sad smile. "Raymond."

"Do you intend to attack Ansky immediately?" the island's hunter inquired in the same softness of tone.

"The sooner, the better. Yet you and the other islanders have more right to call the time than I if you truly mean to act as my army."

"We intend to see it through until the end."

"There is very little possibility of survival for any of us."

"So be it" was Raymond's steadfast reply.

"I am not sure I am—"

"And what are you going to do if we don't? Hide within the four walls of Lisya's home?"

Evan shifted but could not respond.

In the prince's continued silence, Raymond nodded. "We all go to war for the same reason you do. And if we die, if the mission never succeeds, it doesn't matter. In the long run, we're not fighting for this world."

"Oh, no?" A reluctant grin spread across Evan's face. "Yet I was born with the responsibility for Ansky."

"No, you weren't." Raymond's gray eyes glinted in laughter. "Your brother was, and *he* died."

Shaking his head with a puff of amusement, Evan sighed in submission.

Riding behind his father, Prince Andrew Dalacort couldn't decide if he felt fear or exhilaration as the troop rode for the Ice Woods. This was the first time he would see any action. In that, Maxwell had long since passed him. His insides boiled at the thought.

How dare his cousin earn the title of adult? He was only Andrew's elder by four... well, five years. Regardless, that title would soon make no difference. The troop was headed to burn the Ice Woods to the ground. If that failed, they would find another way. Elcan was going to bring Maxwell to his justly deserved end.

There would be no markers to prove Matalaide's tale. Enchantress Island lacked the space to dedicate to a graveyard. Instead, holes were dug where people died or bodies were slid beneath the ocean's waves. A few families buried their loved ones deep beneath their dirt floors and scratched their names into the wood of their homes. Those were the only markers of past lives.

Knowing that, Arnacin ran straight up to the grassy knoll of Castle Mound, where the westerly sun ignited the ground in glowing viridian and allowed the crumbling remains of the castle walls to shadow each other in sorrow.

There, the islander collapsed, the storm in his chest stealing his breath and overextending his throbbing ribcage. He knelt in the grass, propping himself up on shaking forearms, until a stone caught his attention.

It was more chestnut-colored than those around it, positioned to look like a support post for the deteriorating wall nearby. Yet sunset shadowed indentations around its sides.

Forcing his weak legs back under himself, Arnacin approached, his skin growing colder with each step. The stone was made of reddish clay, every side covered with names beneath the inscription: "In memory of those who fell fighting against Evfel."

Long lists of individuals, specified by their parents' names, followed. And there, blazing brightly on the western-facing side, was "Charlotte, daughter of Bozzic and the Lady Talliaha."

For the second time, Arnacin's legs gave out beneath him. Seeing Charlotte's name shaped into the clay felt different from hearing Matalaide's story. This sensation was like the deep thrum of a large tolling bell, as hollow as that instrument, and with it came the hated, unwelcome tears.

Those days in which a black-haired nymph had still lived, rushed through his memory as he traced the inscription. His sister, companion, rival, adviser, nemesis and friend. She would never again call him every kind of fool or berate him for leaving and taking so long to return. She would never smile that crafty smile of hers or build a ship when he needed it. Charlotte was gone.

The cursed king of Mira had claimed only a god could have preserved Arnacin's life through all that had happened. Thinking back over the past five years, there was no doubt Miro was right. Time and again, someone had always appeared to keep him alive right before the end, allowing him to make it back to the island. All for what?

So his nightmares could become reality. His family dead or absent, the island's life and freedom stolen by a king.

"Then take me too!" he cried. "Finish it! You've had your fun! End it!"

Not even a brush of breeze answered, and Arnacin rested his forehead against the memorial. Slowly, its warmth cooled in the gathering night. No insects brought their songs, not up on Castle Mound. To islanders, night among the ruins was a time for death to take shape and dance with mortals.

"Take me," Arnacin pleaded again. Yet, despite his island's fear of the mound, he continued breathing.

Or did he? His insides were all gone, his last bit of life stripped away. His body was merely a cold husk, condemned to remain behind.

Ever since the ship had ground onto the rocky shore of that frigid land, Valoretta had waited. Hours had gone by, and still she waited, brushing the silky black wisps of hair off the forehead of her five-week-old son as he lay in her arms. "He'll return," she whispered to the child. A happy snore was the only reply. Apparently, he did not share her chill. Then again, her emotions could add to her senses. It was summer here too, after all, even if it hardly compared to the summers she'd known back home.

Finally, feeling she could wait no longer, she gently laid her son on the wool blanket in the middle of the cabin floor and stole onto the deck. A glorious pink and red sunset met her, lighting the wood of the ship and the green mountaintop directly ahead.

The village lay silent, seemingly serene, slumbering on the sandy rise, but none of the view matched her expectations of Arnacin's homecoming. Would not the whole village be in a joyful uproar over his return? Yet no hubbub met her ears—no barking dogs, no laughter, no chatter, not even the sound of happy crying drifted toward her.

Glancing back at the cabin, Valoretta paused enough to remind herself she would not be gone long. Then she tossed a rope over the side of the ship and slid down. With a wince as sharp rocks met her bare feet in the low tide, she limped toward the smoother shoreline.

She had not yet reached the village when an older woman approached her. "You appear a fine disaster," the woman chided.

Remembering she was wearing pants beneath her cloak, Valoretta blushed. However, she met the woman's gaze. "Have you seen Arnacin?"

Something flickered in the woman's sharp gray eyes. "I have. Who are you?"

"Is he with his family?"

The woman crossed her arms. "No. He would have to throw himself off a cliff somewhere. Who are you to Arnacin?"

Valoretta stumbled backward a step. "Arnacin's family is dead?"

"Answer me first. Who are you?"

It was a stalemate. Arnacin had the right to answer that himself, but it seemed the women were at an impasse without that fact cleared. "His wife. Now, do you mean to tell me Charlotte, his mother... They're all dead?"

The woman froze. Her gaze took in Valoretta from head to toe, reevaluating. "All but his mother. Now, do *you* mean to tell *me* Arnacin is married?"

"Arnacin." The word blew from Valoretta's lips in heartsick sympathy. Still, the woman studied her, and the Miran let her gaze drop. "I'm sorry you didn't hear it from him."

The woman responded with a sigh. "Come to my home. It's growing dark. Arnacin will be back when he is ready."

"Matalaide," Valoretta asked while feeding her son, "is your mountain a gentle slope all the way up? I mean, there aren't any drop-offs, are there, where someone could... fall off?"

The weaver's hands paused in her tub of dinner dishes. "What are you asking? Arnacin would never be so foolish."

Slowly, Valoretta shook her head. She glanced at Tenacius beneath the blanket over her shoulder. "He has nothing anymore, Matalaide—"

"Don't be ridiculous, girl," Matalaide sniffed, turning back to her soapy dishes. "He has both of you. Are you not his heart, the one he was so impatient to wed he didn't wait for his family's blessing?"

More like the yoke around his neck, but she could never breathe a word of that. Instead, she admitted, "I never had high hopes for a long life for him. He's been through too much. His home, as it was, and his family were what gave him his drive. He has little strength left for this blow."

At last, the weaver paused, her head cocked in consideration. Then she shook her head. "You don't know your husband if you think he'll quit. That family is too stubborn for their own good. He'll come back, and I hope he'll have gained some sense up there."

Hopelessly, Valoretta shook her head. "If you won't go find him, will you take care of Tenacius while I go?"

With a sigh, the weaver's face lost some of its bluster. "He needs time, Valoretta. Leave him alone. That mountain has always belonged to his family alone among the islanders, but it's not safe so close to Castle Mound by dark." She shuddered. "Let alone for someone who is new to the island. I, myself, would never approach the mountain by night, and I've lived here all my life."

Although Valoretta had argued no more, she could not sleep. Dressed now as an islander in a three-layered gown Matalaide had given her, she pushed the light blanket off her legs. In the complete darkness, she shoved her feet into the soft shoes the weaver had stitched together that evening just for her, found a lantern, and grabbed a shawl to wrap around her head and shoulders. Matalaide would hear Tenacius if he woke. Hopefully, he would take goat's milk. Valoretta had to at least try to find Arnacin.

Once outside, she lit the lantern and set off for the woods at the base of the mountain. Just beneath the cover of the leaves, a cool wind whipped at her. Was she imagining whispered words? What was it about the mountain that scared the islanders so? Was the weaver's fear simply affecting her imagination?

Holding the lantern higher, she looked ahead, but only the unusual emerald leaves, flickering in the light, met her searching gaze. She did notice, however, there was no path; at least, not where she had entered. Despite having spent weeks trekking through the woods beside Arnacin, she did not feel comfortable going farther inside them by night without an obvious trail.

Feeling hopeless, she called out, "Arnacin?"

There was no sound but the whispering of leaves in the wind.

Hesitantly, the Miran took another few steps deeper into the trees, but with each one, she knew how foolish she was being, trying to travel in the woods without the guidance of stars or light. While at sea, she had memorized the constellations, but the canopy above her head was too thick for that.

As a low patter of four feet sounded before her, she spun back to the village and Matalaide's hut. Losing her way or being killed by wild animals would never help Arnacin, nor Tenacius.

It was dinnertime in the Ice Woods when Evan noticed the enchantress grow still. If it were possible for any living being to become actual stone, she did so. The light winked out of her all-seeing, bluish-gray eyes and the color seeped out of her skin. No breath moved her chest. Then, the pitcher in her rigid fingers trembled slightly as a roar of wind rattled the walls of the cottage.

"Lisya?" Evan asked. He found he was whispering, even as ice began pelting the roof. "What is happening?"

Strangely, even though the room held four hundred islanders, plus those few from Elcan, it did not feel cramped. Evan suspected the enchantress's cottage could subtly shrink and grow as needed. Be that as it may, the rustle of people was as loud as one might expect. Between that, the happy chords of the reel Vilo was strumming on his instrument, and the pounding of the ice storm, the enchantress's reply was lost, even though Evan was standing at her elbow.

Glancing around at all the faces turned in their direction, the prince paused at the two for whom he searched—silent Carrie and red-haired Michael, the enchantress's children. Their eyes held as much surprised concern as everyone else, and Evan turned back to Lisya. Carefully taking the pitcher from her gray fingers, he led her outside, where the arch of the doorway protected them from the violence of the whirling storm. Darkfire himself was a shadowy figure in the sleet, now joined by the blurs of the herd.

"Lisya, what is wrong?" Evan tried again, feeling his skin chill at the sight of the enchantress's pallor. A slight flush colored her cheeks. As she leaned against the doorframe, she looked like she could actually faint. "Lisya?"

Carrie came out of the door. As she ran her hand down her mother's arm, the enchantress took a deep breath. "They are attacking... with fire."

Evan did not need to clarify who *they* were. Instead, he asked, "Is there any danger of them succeeding?"

Lisya shook her head, yet her eyes were closed. "They do not harm the forest first, Evan." Her meaning was clear. With her connection to her creation, the attack unintentionally struck her before causing any harm to the woods.

"What will happen to you?"

Her eyes finally met his. Strength shone in them despite the signs of pain. "As long as the storm's ferocity remains, you will know they have not harmed me."

"Is there anything I can do?"

The enchantress shook her head. Meeting Carrie's dark eyes, Evan read his concern mirrored in those doe-like depths.

In that instant, a deep creak and sizzle sounded from the woods around them, as if the ice itself was complaining about the attack. The hail fell so fast and thick even the dark blurs of the herd were lost to view.

"Actually, there is something you can do," Lisya said, taking Evan's hand. "Go back inside and tell them all shall be well."

"Will it?" Evan asked skeptically.

"Whatever the outcome, all shall be well. There is no possible way they can force their way into these woods. Should they succeed in ripping apart its strength, its death throes would eat them alive before they could make it to this cottage. Know that, Evan. But even without knowing it, always deny fear—for yourself and those you command. It is a terrible enemy."

As Carrie rested her head on her mother's arm, Evan bowed.

Chapter 2

Attack on the Ice Woods

As Andrew watched the soldiers emptying even more buckets of oil onto the boulders in the catapult, he complained to his father, "It appears to be doing nothing!"

The king barely glanced at him. "That is to be expected at first." Although his words didn't invite further questions, there was sure to be more.

Shivering beneath his cloak, Andrew shoved his hands farther into the warmth of his arms. After another minute of silence, however, he pressed the subject. "Then what are we doing? That is almost all of our winter's supply of oil."

King Wilber sighed. "Those boulders will hit the bottom of the abyss in large clusters and their intense heat, however short-lived, will melt the ice at the bottom of the trunks. With the melting below, the weight above will snap the trees."

"But we would have to topple only those trees that shield their fort. Those boulders will never be enough for every single tree in that nightmarish wood, and just felling trees will not allow us entrance, either. How are we ever going to know if we take down the correct trees?"

A smirk, half annoyed and half proud, crossed the king's face. "The nest of evil should reside in the very midst of those trees toward which we set our trajectory. Unfortunately, there is no infallible plan when dealing with this accursed *magic*, but we cannot allow Maxwell and his gang of witches to think we are intimidated by their disgusting evil."

For a long moment, Andrew said nothing, staring into those woods towering above the army. That black monstrosity howled on its own, defying the light of the sun striving to break through the top. It flung a horrible winter of snow and ice at them in the middle of summer's heat. Had they not pulled their troop back when the fury grew, many would have walked blindly into the great abyss.

It was terribly easy to picture a large, boiling pot hung by chains over a raging fire in the deep darkness of the woods, hissing black figures stooped over it with Maxwell beside them.

Forcing aside these images, Andrew contented himself with watching as each fiery boulder flew overhead, smashing through those ice-covered boughs.

Perched as an eagle atop the trees, Michael watched the enemy scurrying below. When the occasional ball of fire forced him to spread his wings, he merely hopped to a safer branch and continued to watch. Curse Evan for asking such service of him because he was born innately able to transform into an eagle.

Still, Evan did not bother him half as much as the cries of "Witchcraft" and "Demon worshippers" he heard echoing from the army below. Clacking his sharp beak, he growled, "We are enchanters, *humans*. We are born with magic running in our veins. It is as natural to us as walking is to you. I should condemn you as demonic followers merely because you use your feet."

Keeping his disgust in check, Michael remained there, even as his copper eyes glinted in the light of the fire hissing past him. As night fell, the assault lessened and the wail of the woods decreased with it. Then, right before dawn broke, the attack halted. The woods returned to their normal gentle fall of ice and snow. Wilber's force had depleted its supplies.

Exhausted though Andrew was, he forced himself to remain on his feet. As they used the last of their projectiles, Wilber's forces halted the catapults in defeat.

Glances passed from infantry to knights to Lord Quincy, granted his new title just that winter. He, in turn, approached King Wilber, who stood beside their prince a safe distance away. Sweat soaked the Anskonian lord's face despite the ice clinging to his clothes and hair. "I guess we lost this one. I have not heard even a single crack from those trees."

It was not fear or defeat that sparked in Wilber's gaze as he stared at the woods, hands clasped behind his back. What it was, Andrew could not decide. There was challenge there, yes, but more than just that. It most resembled a man seeing his future and his choices while refusing to accept that possibility.

But then Wilber dipped his chin without looking away from the woods.

Andrew spluttered. "How can we just surrender? Is there not some way we can know we at least wounded them? What if someone were to crawl over those boughs on his stomach? It would be less slippery."

"No," the king snapped. "It has been tried before. All have died." His hand landed on his son's shoulder. "Cease your concern, Andrew. Maxwell won this battle, but he will never win the war."

Before the prince could ask how anyone could possibly know that, Wilber ordered the army to load up. They would return to Ansky and await a new day.

With a satisfied ruffle of feathers, the red eagle that was Michael flashed into the dense woods as the last of the attackers disappeared.

Despite the dawn, the cottage slept. Even the herd stood with their heads hanging in slumber behind Lisya's home. Only Evan and Darkfire remained awake, the former leaning against the latter's strong shoulder, running his fingers through the thick, tangled mane.

As Michael alighted, transforming, both heads turned in his direction. "Wilber retreated," the boy reported with a mock bow. "Is there anything else my liege wants before I take my well-deserved sleep?"

"Come on, Michael. I thought those of enchanter blood did not require sleep." Weariness edged Evan's playful words.

"Huh. That is the worst thing about humans. Using us simply because we do not need to sleep. It is purely inconsiderate to order others to stay up the whole night while you lie in bed." Yet Michael knew just from the exhaustion in the prince's face he had not rested himself, standing guard through the entire night beside Darkfire.

As a small, hopeless laugh escaped from Evan, Michael could not prevent the slight upward tilt of his lips. "How is Anwae?" he asked, using his and his sister's name for their mother.

"She did not appear too weakened a few moments ago when she went to bed."

"Anwae went to bed? She must be unwell. In the nearly fifteen years of my life, I cannot remember a time when she took to her bed."

There was no way to tell if the prince had heard him since his eyelids had closed and his head rested against the stallion's neck. Darkfire merely passed Michael a knowing glance.

The boy shrugged. "Then again, no one has ever been dumb enough to dare attack her. Evan, I have decided your family is made up of fools. It does not bode well at all for your kingship."

Evan sleepily replied, "One battle at a time, please, Michael. Sleep well."

Giving the prince one last wicked smile, Michael slipped inside.

For two days, Valoretta waited for Arnacin's return while Tenacius grew increasingly unsettled. Perhaps her son simply missed the waves lulling him to sleep, but regardless of the reason, he remained awake, fussing most of the time.

Then, on the second day, as she walked along the riverside, comforting her son, she spotted Arnacin emerging from the pine trees at the foot of the mountain. But it was not her islander.

His gaze never strayed to her as he swept past, heading toward the village. Valoretta sighed. In his appearance and aura, she saw again the phantom who had arrived in the dead of night to take her off Mira—once more shrouded by the coldness she could not bridge.

Wordlessly, Valoretta followed the islander back to Matalaide's home.

The weaver sat on a bench under the eaves of her cottage, pulling thistles out of a basket of wool. Without any greeting, Arnacin stopped before her. "Where in Elcan did the islanders go?"

In her typical style, Matalaide did not even look up and her fingers continued to slide through her basket. "To wherever Ansky is. Beyond that, I haven't the foggiest notion."

Arnacin did not pause. "How much would it cost to secure passage on the train?"

Valoretta shifted, glancing at the sail across the beach, billowing limply on its mast. Odd that he asked about the train. Were there no harbors for a ship on Elcan? Or was he guessing there were no safe ports to leave his trusty vessel? He was sure to have considered sailing to the mainland. Whatever the case, Valoretta left her questioning thoughts unspoken.

The weaver finally looked up at the family standing before her, glancing between them. Her gaze paused on Tenacius. "I doubt you two own a scrap of anything valuable, even if you were to put all you possess together."

Arnacin glanced at Valoretta, who pursed her lips. Between her gold signet and his Tarmlin blade, they could have afforded multiple trips, yet neither were to be traded. Knowing Matalaide was watching them, Valoretta quickly turned away from her by kissing Tenacius's cheek to soothe his fussing gurgle.

"If you will take a simple weaver's suggestion," Matalaide snorted, "stay home for once and learn to be a man."

Valoretta's eyebrows rose at the insult, but she kept her lips shut.

To her surprise, Arnacin reacted. "At twenty years, I have already endured more than a hundred men!"

Shifting Tenacius to free a hand, Valoretta brushed her husband's sleeve.

He sighed. "Matalaide, I have to go. Do they take wood? What if I disassembled my ship?"

"Phaw." For a minute, Matalaide said nothing more, instead gathering all her work. "I can tell that you don't care at all for anything I have to say."

Arnacin held his tongue.

At his silence, the weaver started for her door. "As you know, Elcan doesn't make ships itself and would find no use for wood that has been used for such. No matter how much you feel you have to go, you have no choice but to stay. That is, unless you take that thing of yours around to whatever harbor Elcan has. I don't know if there is any accessible coastline to enter by, other than the tracks. Even if there were, you likely don't want to flaunt your ship away from this island."

When Arnacin looked toward the shore, Matalaide sighed. Her tone gentled a bit. "Stay here, retrieve the sheep that should be yours, and do what you ought to have done years ago. Elcan and those on it are out of our control." With that, she whisked inside.

In the weaver's absence, Valoretta met her husband's icy stare. Whether they liked it or not, Matalaide's last words were probably true. Events in Elcan were out of their control; his mother beyond their reach. Their only choice was to make a home out of this place that now belonged to neither of them.

But Arnacin's gaze turned again to the line of the ocean, his eyes only growing more distant. Then, without a word, he started down the shore.

Valoretta began to follow, then stopped uncertainly. Instead, she watched the islander cross the stony beach and scale the side of his ship with enviable ease. He dropped to the deck after reaching the rail, disappearing from view. Nothing else moved on the vessel, save the wind through the sails no one had lowered, constantly blowing it into the shore. It was the very image of a ghost ship, which so many had claimed it to be.

Trusting Arnacin would not leave for Elcan without at least telling her, Valoretta turned away from the cool breeze with their son and stepped inside the weaver's hut.

Only a few moments later, Arnacin returned to Matalaide's home with a black bundle under his arm. Stopping before the weaver, he tugged the cloth down and it fluttered to the ground. "Will this suffice?" Candlelight struck the orb the black covering had hidden and fiery rainbows shot in all directions of the room, turning it into a cavern of orange.

Valoretta's breath caught in her throat. Her gaze was trans-fixed by the flickering light bursting from the stone cupped in the islander's hands, a brilliant rock the size of and nearly as round as a child's head.

How long had she slept within the same space as that, never aware of its existence?

Matalaide's scream broke the stillness. "Cover that! How dare you think to use it for trade? Do you want Summos Valley to think we are laden with treasure?"

A dark glint had entered Arnacin's eyes as he obediently retrieved the black cloth at his feet and rewrapped the stone. The glow blinked out. Suddenly, the hut seemed oppressively dull.

"Do not show that to them!" The weaver's hand pressed into her chest.

"I *must* go to Elcan."

"All right! I'll pay for your passage. Just toss that thing into the ocean and take the banner and all that other blue silk with you into Elcan for me."

With a cold bow, Arnacin turned, vanishing out the door with the stone under his arm. Watching him depart, Valoretta wondered if Matalaide had just reacted exactly as Arnacin had planned.

Matalaide met Arnacin as soon as he returned from the shore. "The train will not be here for five days. So, what are you going to do in the meantime? Don't think I want you idling around underfoot."

"I am quite capable of disappearing, Matalaide, if my presence irks you." Without waiting for the weaver's response, he turned away, but a hand dropped onto his arm.

"For once, why don't you help instead of hinder?" Unlike the weaver's usual tone, soft compassion tinted her voice. "I'd be willing to share my workload with you. It will help the wait pass more swiftly."

Although Arnacin's eyes flashed, he inclined his head in submission. Valoretta noticed he did not yank himself out of Matalaide's loose grasp.

Four days passed while Arnacin helped with the weaver's sewing. Valoretta assisted some, but primarily took care of Tenacius. By day, her islander sat, ever silent, on Matalaide's bench outside the cottage door. By night, he vanished, perhaps to rest but more likely to wander the dark woods that were once his home.

On the fourth day, Matalaide beckoned Valoretta near. "Tomorrow, the train comes. Does Arnacin expect you to accompany him?"

The Miran shrugged. "I intend to, but we haven't talked much since arriving."

"For his protection, I believe that is the right choice."

Valoretta paled. "For his protection? Who would harm him?"

Matalaide's gaze pierced her. "A male islander might be seen as a threat to Evan's opponents, but a family with a baby is not as likely to be traveling for that purpose." She paused, tilting her head to the side in appraisal. "Although *you* might attract a few stares."

"Surely they have red-haired women there."

"*Noble* ladies traveling without an escort?"

As Valoretta stared warily, the weaver's lips quirked. "From what I understand of nobility, it's in your bearing, your mannerisms, your way of speaking, and the particular skills you lack. I would have felt more certain sooner, but for Arnacin having married you. In fact, until your eyes suddenly withdrew, I was not sure. But I still know this: Arnacin is too wild for any noble, and none would give a shepherd their daughter. Did you elope?"

"Absurd," Valoretta breathed. "Could you truly imagine Arnacin wanting to elope with a noble?" When Matalaide merely sat back, a grim smile on her lips, the Miran shook her head. Any possible response, however, was cut short by Tenacius's wail.

"Ignore my probing, Valoretta," Matalaide sighed. "I think you should give your son a wash before the journey. The stream is warm enough at this time of year for bathing a child."

Gratefully, Valoretta scooped up Tenacius. As she passed Arnacin just outside the door, she wondered how much he had overheard. He did not look up from his needle, however, so she could not guess.

Barely had Valoretta left for the stream with her son before a young woman approached the house, her hair veiled as a sign of her married status. Gwenre, Arnacin recalled, was a featherheaded, unremarkable girl in her youth and had likely remained so. Dismissively, the islander bent his head over his sewing and let her sweep past into the weaver's home.

"Good afternoon, Matalaide," Gwenre said.

Arnacin tuned out the rest of her words with the weaver. That was, until he suddenly stuck his finger with the needle when Gwenre said, "His fault or not, I'll throttle Evan if Tevin isn't home by the time our child is born."

From outside, Arnacin heard no response. The only real question, of course, was who had been the bigger fool in the marriage, Gwenre or Tevin? She may have been one pathetic female, but he was an extremely immature troublemaker. Either way, they'd both made it onto Arnacin's list of those he considered unqualified for marriage.

Shaking his head, he gave up on the question. Yet even as he did so, the conversation inside the hut changed direction when Gwenre asked, "By the way, since you are so often outside, do you know anything about the ship just sitting there?"

Again Arnacin stilled, his heart beating faster.

The weaver's only reply, however, was a short "No." The islander slowly let his breath out.

"You sound as if you've no interest, Matalaide!" Gwenre protested, ever the gossip. "It wasn't shipwrecked, but there have been no foreigners. Thank goodness!"

"Have you ever seen a shipwreck?"

"Of course not, but—"

"Then it could very well be one."

"Matalaide, you know something you're not telling us. And while we're at it, who's your new assistant?"

"I doubt you want to know all the things I know. As for my *assistant*, if you will, he's not staying. Anything else you want to know must come from him. I wouldn't repeat the treacherous tale for all the pay on this island."

"Matalaide! He could hear!"

"Then he could hear your questions as well. As for my opinions, I haven't held them back. If he dislikes hearing my thoughts, he has not said so. Did you come here to order clothes for the child or for the local gossip?"

Feeling a grim smile cross his face, Arnacin returned to his task, forcing himself to tune out the rest of the conversation. A moment later, Gwenre swept past without even looking in his direction. Footsteps followed her, then stopped behind him. He slowly looked up to meet the weaver's crafty hazel gaze.

Leaning against the doorframe, Matalaide nodded, crossing her arms. "Very well, Arnacin. It seems you are to keep your secret for now. Heaven knows you don't need to deal with any condemnation at the moment. For now, they are so convinced of your death, they can't see the obvious, though it will come."

"They can think what they like."

Matalaide studied him for a moment. "I never thought Talliaha could ever have more than one Charlotte, but you sound and look much like her in your bitterness. Don't you see how you've destroyed yourself?"

Arnacin merely turned his face toward the ocean.

"I don't know why you want to go to Elcan," the weaver continued, "Anyone can tell you would rather commit suicide than help a foreign king. However, if you insist, I'll not stop you."

Thankfully, the weaver did not wait for a reply. Her feet pattered back into the dimness of her hut. There was no answer Arnacin could voice. Yes, he would prefer death before entering Elcan's fray, but somehow he was choosing the opposite. Without wincing, he drove the long needle into his palm until it pricked through the other side.

The soft tread was his only warning. He yanked out the needle just as Valoretta stopped beside him. "Arnacin?" As he turned to her, she held out Tenacius, wrapped safely in blankets against the breeze that blew through his wet wisps of hair.

Pausing for only a second, Arnacin accepted the bundle, knowing as he did the Miran would not fail to notice the spot of blood his palm left on the white wool. Wondering, pale blue eyes stared up at him from inside the blankets, and the islander clenched his jaw.

To think he had ordered the heavens to strike him dead, when here, in this precious bundle, was someone who needed him—to say nothing of the child's mother. The thought did nothing to alter his wish for something to end the emptiness of his heart, but it worsened his self-condemnation.

"I'm sorry," Valoretta whispered, joining him on the bench. "About what?"

Despite his low growl, the Miran did not retreat. "Your family... Everything you've lost."

"You're not sorry. Is this not the very thing you wanted, your deepest wish? Here, with sole familial claim on me—"

"Arnacin! Stop it." Despite her firmness, her voice was gentle. "Just open your walls. I know the extent of your pain by their presence alone—pain that's so intense and trapped, you must stab yourself just to give it an outlet."

He shifted, yet said nothing.

Valoretta exhaled. "Cry. I won't think any less of you, and you shouldn't either. You weren't even able to... to hold them one last time."

Images Arnacin dared not let himself entertain leapt into his mind, but he shoved them away. At last, he changed the subject with a sigh. "You're not coming to Elcan."

Valoretta's expression instantly cleared, as if she had no idea what he meant, yet he continued. "Don't think I didn't hear your conversation with Matalaide."

"As she can probably hear ours now," Valoretta hissed. "And for that matter, I refuse to debate this with you until Tenacius is asleep."

"Arnacin," Valoretta called up to the ship's deck late that moonless night. "Arnacin, I am coming with you tomorrow."

She sensed him approach the rail only a few feet above her. "You forget I have no respect for royal orders, my lady. You and Tenacius are staying here."

"This is not an order, Arnacin. It's a statement, with which Matalaide agrees. If you don't let me come with you, I will follow with Tenacius alone, whether I know the territory or not."

There followed a soft sigh. "I'm going into a war, Valoretta."

"Naturally. Don't say I've had too much of it. You've had too much yourself. Some things simply must be done."

"And what about Tenacius?"

"Your mother went. There must be somewhere safe in Elcan."

"My mother would not consider her age nor her protection when she has nothing left to lose. There might not be any safe place."

"As a mother with her baby, Matalaide assures me I will be much more secure than you. And with me as camouflage beside you, she thinks you will also be safer than you would be by yourself."

"Valoretta—"

Cutting off his argument, the Miran insisted, "I love you, Arnacin, whether you believe it or not, and I know you must do this. If I can support and protect you, even just a bit, I will. I also *must* go."

"I can't go armed, Valoretta, not through a place *looking* for that. If something happens to you or Tenacius, do you think I should care any less than you?"

"Should, Arnacin?" Valoretta whispered, whirling away knowing she had won—he would not ask such a question otherwise. "No, but I'd bet everything that you would."

Chapter 3

The Last of Enchantress Island

"Do you have anything with which to conceal these?" Matalaide asked, holding out the folded layers of blue silk. "Word is that Summos Valley, where the train stops, now pays tribute to Evan Maxwell's enemy. You'll be instant targets should someone realize you carry this."

Arnacin's eyes flashed upon looking at the pile, yet he only nodded in answer. It was Valoretta who asked the obvious. "Do they currently recognize this as your king's emblem?"

Though Arnacin shifted at the combination of "your" and "king," Matalaide did not even blink. "I wouldn't trust them not to put the pieces together, should they see it. Ansky's emblem has long been the horse, and it is probably well known that we of Enchantress Island are his only supporters. A single family coming off a train is not an attack force, but be wary."

"Don't worry. I *don't* support him," Arnacin growled, grabbing the pile of blue silk and sweeping out toward his ship. The vessel had carried him in relative safety across the world. It had been built by a family that was no more, and its deck still had wood that came from his grandfather's hut, which once rested on the mountain of Enchantress Island.

Retrieving a sack from the hold, Arnacin emptied its contents across the deck and began stuffing the silk inside.

Partway through, he paused, his gaze going to his cabin as his thoughts traveled to the thing he had again hidden there.

With a final glance at the sack, he stole to the cabin. He paused only once at the door to look guiltily over his shoulder, then ducked inside.

Sliding panels, carefully crafted to look almost seamless, revealed the storage space beneath his bed. His family had constructed it that way, not to hide anything, but for the aesthetic. However, it had been useful for camouflage over the years.

Now, pushing an arm through the panel's opening, his searching fingers found his short sword first. He paused when its etching pressed into his palm, dredging up memories. His Tarmlin blade, its gold-covered sheath engraved with the emblem of Lord Carpason's city—a marketplace canopy above a crane in flight.

Despite its symbol of peace, and what it must have meant to its lord, it was a sword that had been given to Arnacin, as Carpason had once promised, "with no intention of retrieving it," and it had defended the islander in many a tight place. Leaving it behind was challenging, given what he feared lay ahead.

With a sigh, Arnacin shoved the blade and his memories of Carpason aside.

Pulling out the stone from under the bed next, he sat back on his heels and unwrapped it. Was there even a place where it would not cause trouble? Of course, Matalaide was right. He should throw it into the ocean. Yet he still could not make himself do so.

Why? He might never know. Watching the rays of sunlight coming through the door play off the orb, his heart felt lighter in his chest. In the stone's depths, another world danced. Maybe it was the enchantress's birthplace he felt, but he had never imagined that realm to be a nice place.

Sighing, he shook the silk back out of the sack and wrapped the rock within the center of all the blue. Once done restuffing the sack, he turned to leave his cabin forevermore. In the doorway, he paused yet again, his hand going to where his compass rested beneath his shirt—an item no person from Elcan, or even the island for that matter, would possess.

Slowly, he slid it over his head. There it lay in his hand, its glass surface and spokes gleaming in the morning light. Chipped, battered and worn, in that moment, it looked completely forlorn. Or was it actually his heart that suddenly felt bereft?

Had he longed to return home, to the livelihood of shepherding? Firm ground without the peaceful rocking of the ocean beneath one's feet? At least, the wild sea was still nearby, with the crash and whisper of waves just outside the door and the tangy scent of salt on the breeze. The habitations of Elcan were all inland, as natural a tomb as existed.

Without actually deciding to do so, he slipped his compass back over his head, tucking it inside his shirt. Then, knotting the sack closed, he shut the cabin door behind him with a gentle snap, leapt to the ground, and strode away. He refused to look again at the ship he suspected would sit in the sand until decay turned it into the shipwreck it had never been.

The trip up the mountain was torturous, winding ever southwest toward where the tracks had been built when Arnacin was young. It was not the roughness of the path that made the trek so hard, but the memories—this time knowing he was leaving even the link to his past behind.

While Matalaide and Valoretta, carrying Tenacius on her back, toiled over the remains of the old stone steps, Arnacin strode ahead quickly to block out the familiar sights. Yet, due to the others' slowness, even that proved impossible. He was forced to halt time and again while Matalaide complained about "Youth!"

Still, he avoided Old Horns, the stone bust of some long-forgotten notable person. Weeds now entangled the statue, but he had never been fully neglected. Long before Arnacin was born, the children of Alleluia Lake had given him his name and wreathed him in new flowers every spring while they skipped around him with songs of how the powerful fell.

That spring tradition was now a mockery. The island had chosen a king who would build new statues for the powerful and ruthless.

To avoid Old Horns, Arnacin went so far as to leave the usual trail briefly. Behind him, Matalaide puffed. The sound of her feet stopped, as if she was trying to decide whether to follow him or not. Her feet finally resumed along the trail, Valoretta's beside her.

Despite his meandering route, Arnacin made it before the others to a knobby tree a third of the way up the mountain. There, he paused to let them catch up, his gaze traveling to the oak's numerous upper branches. Its bumps, limbs and protrusions had made it perfect for the boys to climb. They had been entertained for hours by that tree.

When Arnacin led the children's play, he spun stories of floods and bold islanders who would brave the current to bring people to the tree before it was too late. Others would pretend they had a secret fort and were making plans against evil rulers.

Charlotte, however, hated the tree. Sometimes, she would watch the boys playing from the thicker part of the woods, but her parents had always told her she should only climb trees, if she must, when there was no one around to see up her skirts.

Running his fingers along one rough lower knot, Arnacin sensed Valoretta stop at his elbow. Matalaide's location was heralded by her gasping as she ascended the mountain.

His whisper slipped out before he could stop it. "Why is it that humans are such fools—to be drawn to touch things of their past as if the sensation will somehow bring back that time?"

"Are you so drawn?" Valoretta's tone was laden with sorrow.

"No." Arnacin barely allowed Matalaide to join them before striding up the path.

At last, they reached the train. "Finally!" The train conductor from Summos Valley unwittingly echoed Arnacin's impatience. "We have been here since this morning. Where is all your trade?"

"We also have quieter months," Matalaide replied, with her usual waspishness. "However, if you want my trade, I would suggest some courtesy. I'm not young myself."

"Very well. What would you like?"

Ignoring the man's gesture toward the laden boxcars, the weaver opened her satchel, revealing the pure, soft contents within. "I want passage for this family. If you take them to Summos Valley, I'll give you all of this wool."

Every man's gaze fixed on Arnacin and Valoretta. "What do they want with Elcan?" the first man asked after a moment.

Matalaide effortlessly avoided the truth. "With the long-standing trade between our shores, we have made some friends, if not many. It should not concern you if they wish to see them. If I'm willing to make an exchange, I don't see that you have much to quibble over."

For a moment longer, the men stared at the family. Arnacin coldly returned their stares. Seeming to cower, the conductor surrendered. "Very well. All the wool you have with you for their passage."

As if testing him, Matalaide slowly passed the man her satchel. Their gazes locked for a moment before he dropped his own.

Whatever he thought, however, all he asked was, "Did you see anyone else coming, or should we leave now and stop wasting our time?"

"No one else is coming to my knowledge." Matalaide's tone was disinterested. "As far as wasting your time, that's for you to decide."

"Load up," the conductor barked to his men. "You!" He turned to Arnacin. "Take your family onto that boxcar before we leave you behind."

As the islander turned toward the indicated boxcar, however, Matalaide touched his arm. "Arnacin, make sure to give them no cause to notice you, else I fear they may kick you out in the wild lands long before Summos Valley. I have heard a person can become lost in those mountains for life." At his questioning look, she added, "There was an accident with the train last year, and they have made it clear they think we should freely hand over our goods in payment for the repairs. Our response is that they care about the trade, not us. Should they become disagreeable, we will simply destroy their tracks again."

Arnacin nodded.

Once more, she halted him, holding out a small sack. "Food and water for both of you."

"Matalaide—"

"I would have gladly helped you retrieve your sheep and resettle here. My offer stands when you return with the rest."

After Arnacin accepted her gift, she drew back her sleeve to loosen two strips she had wound around her wrist. "Now, I also have these lengths of leather for you to sew onto your sack. That will keep you occupied for a bit and make travel a little more comfortable. Remember, the needle is not a weapon." As Arnacin withdrew his gaze, she finished, "Take care, and God be with you."

With a sigh, the islander accepted the gifts. "There's still food in my hold. Use anything you want."

As Arnacin stepped away, Valoretta kissed the weaver on the cheek. "Thank you."

"Oh, get along with you," Matalaide huffed. "I won't be able to stand another second with you three underfoot."

With a tight-lipped smile, Arnacin led Valoretta onto the car. A groan of releasing brakes announced the beginning of the journey, and the train clacked slowly around the small loop encircling the empty space where there would usually have been a market. Straightening out on the main track, it gained speed.

As Matalaide shrank into the distance, she raised her arm in farewell. Standing in the still open doorway, Arnacin nodded in reply. Then the track shot over the edge of the spur that faced Elcan and they were in the air, racing over the wide strait separating the mainland from the island. Slowly, even his home shrunk, and Arnacin stood staring at what could nevermore be his home.

Still as an emerald, far more beautiful than any real gem, the island glimmered under the sun. The trees on the mountain—Charlotte's mountain—shifted from green to blue to purple and back again as the ocean breeze coursed through their leaves.

His sister's words from their last parting seemed to whisper. *I have the feeling I will never see you again.* Whatever salty breeze had informed her of that, he had not paid it any heed.

When the island disappeared from view, he slipped to the floor against the wall, burying his head in his arms. He jerked away at a light touch on his arm, but that was all the movement he made.

"How much longer until we reach this Summos Valley?" Valoretta asked, three days into their journey.

Arnacin's gaze remained on the rock formations the train was racing past. "It is said to take a week altogether. I don't know personally."

Smiling, Valoretta recalled his original stance on Elcan. "'It's possessed by four kingdoms who have nothing better to do than war over each other's thrones,'" she quoted. "Matalaide said there were only two."

The islander shrugged. "She would know. One of them belongs to her *king*, after all."

"Well, as long as you don't intend to murder him to return the island to independence..." Valoretta's words trailed off when Arnacin finally turned to her. Her smile faltered as she met the pain and disgust in his gaze.

"In all likelihood, they'll do the murdering themselves once they realize what they've done." At least some life showed in his tone. "I have no intention of becoming the tiniest bit involved."

Yet there was authority in the way Arnacin carried himself, in every tilt of his head—a shrewdness in his eyes that saw every secret of the earth and heart, or convinced people it did. The cold, scarred and wary shields over his features and stance only served to make his air of nobility stand out more harshly, so even the blind could see it.

"That will be a trick," Valoretta mumbled, ignoring the glare she received. "You always possessed a royal air, from the day I first saw you. I think it must have been your naivete that kept me from wondering if you were exactly as Father suspected at times—a royal spy for some foreign country."

The islander's spine straightened in defense against the unintended slur as he turned back toward the scene speeding past the open doorway. He had once again closed her out.

Sighing, the Miran turned her attention to the outside world. The train now ascended a hill, having curved inland, and a valley skittered away below. There, the deep green grass danced, a vibrant color unique to Elcan and Enchantress Island from what she'd seen. Despite the otherworldly appearance, their struggles were very real, even though Arnacin and Valoretta had both hoped otherwise.

The first view of Summos Valley was a small, golden city nestled in an oval-shaped hollow in the mountains. A waterfall poured into a small pool to the east before taking off into a river that cut a course through the southern mountains. From above, it appeared as peaceful as a city could exist. But once the train stopped in the marketplace, reality could not hide.

The cries of merchants hawking their wares filled the humid air, crisp and enunciated despite the speed at which they spoke. Alongside their clamor rose the enraged protests of indignant women, the deeper shouts of equally unhappy men, the heavy pounding of hurried feet, and the sharp squealing of animals. Even so close to the river, the covetous excitement drowned out the water's soothing rush. Despite the gold latticework on every building—all two stories high with balconies—and the stone-paved roads without a patch of dirt, not a single face appeared content with anything.

"Is this the *lower class*?" Valoretta whispered, crushed against Arnacin's shoulder. "Many of them are wearing silk."

How poor Mira looked in comparison. Grinning, Arnacin shook his head. "I have no knowledge beyond the fact this is the home of the train. Remember, Matalaide told us the silk she used came from here."

"Yes, and Elcan is—"

"Made of four kingdoms," they finished together.

Neither spoke again until the throng around them lessened a little. Then, Valoretta admitted, "I don't think I would trust anyone here to tell us where Ansky is located, or how to go there."

With an appraising glance at the people nearby, Arnacin nodded. "I bet a bit of gold might earn all the answers you want."

"Which is one reason we can't trust anyone."

As if on cue, a merchant hailed them. "Hey, Islanders!" He beckoned them over. With a cautioning glance toward his wife, Arnacin approached.

"You look a little lost there," the merchant continued once the islander stood in front of him. "Could I help you find yourself?"

"For what price?" Arnacin replied knowingly.

"Well." The man's tone dropped confidentially, his words keeping their clear definition like everyone else's speech here. "Information for information is fair, right? Is the legend of all those mines deep inside your mountain true?"

With a wicked grin, Arnacin shrugged. "I certainly have never come across any mine, and I also don't own a coin to credit such a story."

Suspicion filled the merchant's face. "Do you lie, boy?" His face reddened, and he took a threatening step forward. "I do not *have* to help you."

"I didn't ask for your help."

Despite the warnings, Arnacin did not stop the man from roughly shoving him. After slamming into someone who shrieked, he landed on the stone street with a hard thwack.

"I do not help insolent beggars!" the merchant snapped. Swiftly turning away, he again began shouting his patter into the air.

"Arnacin," Valoretta sighed, holding out a hand to help him up. "When will you learn some tact?"

"Curse Elcan," he hissed, brushing himself off. Several gasps sounded from the crowds.

"Apparently, they take that seriously here."

"Let them." Turning to leave, Arnacin nearly ran into a man leading a donkey.

Unlike those who had drawn away, this man held out his hand. "I am on my way to Ansky if you wish to accompany me."

The islander took a step back, and the man dropped his hand with a small smile. "I am not looking for gold. I just over-heard you mention you want to go there, and so I stopped."

He could have overheard more than that, including a foreign accent. Still wary, neither Arnacin nor Valoretta replied.

The man shrugged. "I make a living by taking the trade from here to Ansky. You would be no burden if that bothers you. At least, you could not surpass Jezebel here." He gave the donkey's lead a slight tug.

Slowly, Arnacin relaxed. "We would be very grateful if you could tell us how to go there ourselves, and we won't slow you down, risk our son keeping you awake, or anything."

With a smile at the baby, who was staring wide-eyed over his mother's shoulder at the hubbub, the man nodded. "As you wish. If you follow the River Gold, it will take you through Penelope Pass. The entrance is very narrow, so people wade through the river to enter the pass. There is no bank. Beware: the edge is slippery, and if you are pulled into the center, it is both deep and swift."

Valoretta paled.

"Is there no other route?" Arnacin asked.

"Not from down here. The Calmar Mountains are impossible to scale on this side." The man threw out his arm to take in the view outside the city. "You can see their height and how they travel almost straight up, although..." His voice lowered. "It is said Maxwell's stallion ran down them into this valley, without falling."

After staring at the cliff faces surrounding them for a second, Arnacin shook his head. He could not see any horse running down those sides without perishing. "Obviously a complete fable."

"I would not scoff at it so quickly. Strange things go on in Ansky, and Maxwell is in the thick of it. I have heard he hired demon worshippers to help him regain his throne."

Arnacin's breath hitched. Yet Elcan believed the islanders had received magical power through submission to the lord of evil. It was very likely he, himself, was considered one of this man's demon worshippers.

Valoretta, however, had lost all color, though she was not shivering. Her spine straightened and chin raised despite her round eyes, she was an alabaster imitation of prey that ran out of room to escape and turned to fight its hunter to the last.

For a second, Arnacin wondered if pursuing the topic of demon worshippers would give them any real information, but most likely the man had only heard rumors himself. Any further discussion was likely to lead to all sorts of absurdities. After all, the train's crew had been blathering ridiculous things for years, such as the man who boldly asked if the islanders changed their skin tone to look more human while dealing with Summos Valley.

Instead, the islander returned to the point. "Where do you go after entering the pass?"

"It opens into Ansky, but if you want one of the villages, you must travel east a bit and then enter the mountains again. They have roads and markers for that portion of the Calmar Mountains, but do not stray from the markers. The Ice Woods slumber east of the pass, and that is a place to avoid above all else."

He shuddered, but controlling himself, he pointed south. "If you are asking for the capital, however, there is usually a small track pressed through the valley this time of year. It will lead you to the town of Ansky itself."

"What are these Ice Woods?"

"You will know when you see them. The trees *are* ice. I do not think there is any actual substance beneath their cold cover. The woods are evil, believe me. They have killed many a man throughout their short history."

"Thank you." With a nod of parting and gratitude, the islander drew Valoretta away with him.

Behind them, the man called out, "If it is not an intrusion, may I ask what islanders want in Ansky?"

The Miran's eyes shot toward Arnacin's, a clear sign she also saw the danger. Taking a deep breath, the islander turned back around and simply answered, "I have relatives down there that I haven't seen for years... I mean, one relative." He could not prevent the pain from edging into his voice.

Nodding, the man raised a hand in farewell. "God keep you."

"Arnacin," Valoretta asked as soon as they had left the city, "if Ansky is that cold, how are we supposed to survive?"

"Ansky isn't that cold." The response was resolute.

"It's apparently cold enough to form such thick ice on trees that men don't think any wood exists."

"It's summer."

"He made it sound as though the Ice Woods are there now."

Stopping in his tracks along the riverside, Arnacin sighed. "He said it was evil, Valoretta. That doesn't come from natural elements."

"Of course it does. The natives back home thought earthquakes were their gods alighting on Mira. And it's already so cold here."

Giving her an exasperated look, the islander reminded her, "Elcan does not believe in *gods*. They all say there is only one god, and then live as if He never existed at all."

"Just because you have not heard of all the beliefs on this continent does not mean no others exist."

Arnacin exhaled. "The man is traveling to Ansky, and he wasn't wearing any winter garments, nor was his donkey carrying anything bulky." With that, he resumed walking.

Frowning, Valoretta studied him as she followed. His posture was at its straightest; his expression when he glanced at her was cloaked and wary. Her lordly phantom was back, hiding pains and secrets alike. "What are you not saying?"

"Only guesses."

"You are avoiding my question, Arnacin."

"I am under no obligation to answer you, my lady." He did not even look at her.

Huffing in frustration, she fell silent.

Over the next days, they followed Penelope Pass through quite a few turns, but there remained only one direction forward. Everything else stood blocked by high walls of stone, and Arnacin felt it strange that such an oft-used highway lay so still. It was not until two nights into the pass that he started to see camps, and he shared nods with a few watchmen. No one seemed to think the small family was a danger. They passed unhindered, although a few people asked the lonely travelers to stop and share a meal or just to rest a little.

Both Arnacin and Valoretta declined offers of food since they had their own, but they briefly agreed to join some folks around a fire, for Tenacius's sake.

It was after leaving one such group that Valoretta asked, "Everyone's speech here is so enunciated. They don't even use contractions. Is that how everyone speaks in Elcan?"

Arnacin shrugged. "How—" A sly grin spread over his face before he finished. "Elcan has four kingdoms."

Controlling her smile, Valoretta raised her chin. "I refuse to encourage such behavior."

A chuckle actually escaped the islander.

In three nights, the little family had reached the end of the pass, finding grass again. There, they set off to the east to view the frightening trees of ice. At dawn's light, they reached Ansky's wonder. A monstrosity towered under the sun, howling mournfully.

"How did you know?" Valoretta finally breathed, standing in the safety of the taller grass. At her feet, the ground cover abruptly shortened, as if the cold from the woods made it impossible for the greenery to grow.

Arnacin's only answer was a slow shake of the head. He stared into the blackness between the ice trees until the

Miran suddenly seized his hand and turned southward. The islander did not resist her guidance, although he could not take his gaze off the unearthly woods.

Only once the last shimmer of ice was out of sight did Arnacin whisper, "We may be seeing it again."

Valoretta shuddered as they returned to the beaten trail. "What have you not told me, Arnacin? Isn't the island's name simply poetic?"

At last, they had come to it. Sighing, the islander admitted, "Carpason warned me to tell no one else what I had told him."

"What did you tell him?"

"Our island's name comes from the fact that it was conquered by enchanters and that they held it for hundreds of years."

"Enchanters, like the natives' mediums?"

"No." Arnacin's tone was soft. "Both much worse and much better."

For a long moment, he studied Valoretta where she had stopped, appraising her unflinching gaze. No fear shone there, no signs of hesitation or bias. She stood as the queen she was, open to the unknown, with the insight to sense the implication behind Arnacin's words.

To that serene gaze, the islander dared say, "Somewhere beyond the sea, perhaps in a place impossible to sail to, there at least *was* a land… naturally magic, I suppose. I've never met anyone from there to ask for details. To my knowledge, only one still exists, but she left the island long before I was born. And as far as I know, she has never been seen again, at least by us."

"And you suspect those dark woods are hers? Is she evil?"

Despite years of believing in the goodness of the last enchantress, the woods, combined with his distrust, gave Arnacin only one answer. "I don't know."

"Yet, you expect us to return to those woods?"

"Have you not put it together, Valoretta? To the older island-ers, the enchantress Lisya is practically their queen. Should she support a king of Elcan and tell them of her fealty, they might accept it without question. You heard yourself that this Evan Maxwell has hired demon worshippers. Of course, Elcan would look at an enchantress as a supernatural evil because they could never fathom a being for whom magic is as natural as breathing."

Valoretta remained impassive for several moments, her gaze on the rich, waving grass surrounding them. Then she glanced warily toward the islander before looking away uncomfortably. "And you, Arnacin? Are you a magical descen-dant of these enchanters?"

Arnacin could not hide his amusement. "Would you not know if I were?"

"Not if you were only so in a small way, diluted by human blood." At last, Valoretta faced him. "You have always had a mystical aura about you, and you've survived the impossible."

Her fingers were neither trembling nor sweating as he gently took her hand in his. For that, he was glad. "I survived for other reasons, ones I don't understand—and don't want to. I have no enchanter blood, I promise."

Despite his assurances, Valoretta turned back to their path with only a light squeeze of his hand before pulling away.

Ansky was the quietest town Arnacin had ever come across. As they approached it in the afternoon of the next day, the castle towers and what could only be an abbey or church spire dominated the sky. All the rest of the buildings jutted up from the ground, the majority of them single-story with a few slightly taller structures, mostly barns, dotted here and there.

Birds fluttered from the church tower, and people toiled away in the nearby fields. The sounds of birds and the humming of conversations occasionally drifted on the wind toward the travelers, along with the lowing of draft animals.

Once they were closer, the islander saw that the castle walls tilted slightly outward instead of rising straight up. A single tower stood before a dry moat, its archway guarding the path of the drawbridge. Less than a foot of ground protruded from the castle's side before the wide gully.

The walls in particular forced Arnacin to give a dark nod of respect. He knew the angle was purposely planned. Very few climbers in the world would be able to scale that wall.

The islander glanced at Valoretta. Her expression was unreadable, and he was not about to talk architectural strategy while in the middle of a potential enemy's territory. Leaning close, he whispered, "Don't say anything that makes them realize you're not from Elcan. I suspect our secrecy will be the difference between life and death."

"You'd best do all the speaking, Arnacin. My accent could never pass as native here, but yours is closer to theirs, so long as you remember to pronounce all your syllables."

"We hope," Arnacin muttered. That hope was all they had, however. So, shifting his pack higher over his shoulder, he led the way down the main street of the town.

The sight of an inn, identifiable as such by the tables and counter visible through the open door, stopped them in the middle of that street. Proudly, the two-storied stone building bore a swinging sign in the shape of fluffy clouds with light streaming upward. Thick lettering covered the bottom. Although the characters were close to the island's, they were foreign enough that Arnacin gave up trying to decipher them after a moment.

Sometimes, there was nowhere better to ask for information than a tavern. Taking a preparatory breath, Arnacin stepped into the dim interior. Barely had he done so, Valoretta at his shoulder, when an older man greeted them with a wide smile. "Travelers, welcome! Take a seat, please. We are not rich with either food or drink, but we will supply what we can."

Only extreme distrust kept the islander from returning that smile. But Valoretta's wariness did not go so far. Her face lit up in response.

The man blushed and waved them to an empty table. Thankfully, it was the one closest to the open door, still within the square of light that covered the floor.

Accepting the offer, Arnacin plopped his sack against the table leg. To hide its value, he paid it no more attention, instead pulling out a chair for Valoretta.

With a glance of gratitude, she slid Tenacius's cradleboard off her shoulder before sitting. The walk had rocked the baby to sleep, but as his parents loosened his wrappings, his blue eyes snapped open with his typical look of wonder.

The innkeeper stood aside, awaiting their request. As Valoretta lifted her son into her arms, Arnacin met the man's gaze at last and pulled a chair out for himself. If he left it so his legs were not under the table, most would think he was just drawing his seat closer to his family. It was as good an excuse as any.

The innkeeper did not seem to notice his unease, at least. "So, what may I do for you?" the innkeeper asked, wiping his hand on a cloth tied about his thick middle.

"I regret to say we have not a coin between the two of us. We were hoping just to sit for a while," the islander informed the man.

To Arnacin's surprise, the innkeeper laughed. "I am not the least bit surprised at your lack of funds. Very few of us have any around here. Do you see those men over there?" He pointed toward the back of the inn, where a few sat around the cold fireplace. "They come here just to talk politics and put their feet up."

Yet tankards and bowls sat between them on the table. "But they have food?"

"Listen. By your accent, I have no idea where you come from, but when you live in a community, you find there is much more to gain from an open hand and pocket than a closed one. That is one lesson from King Phillip I hope we never forget." The innkeeper sighed. "Sure, I feed them. They give what they can, I give what I can, and we all know we will always have each other, though the rest of the world burns."

Arnacin caught Valoretta's glance and licked his lips. If their king had taught them that, he had some morals at least; perhaps more than enough to stop a foolish power struggle. "Is Phillip the king at war with Evan Maxwell?"

The innkeeper burst out with such laughter that it appeared for just a minute his heart might stop. His face grew red from the lack of air. His guffaws quickly turned into choking coughs, and he dropped into the chair opposite the family.

One of the men who had been sitting near the hearth stepped over with his tankard, handing it to the innkeeper. He commenced patting the keeper's back until his breathing returned to normal. Then, without a word, he slipped back into his seat.

After a sip from the tankard, the innkeeper wiped his brow. "My! Where have you come from?"

"We traveled from Summos Valley. Who are *you*, and where did you come from?"

"Now, do not take offense. I am Taylor Magree, of course, and I ask out of curiosity alone. If you have some secret, you may keep it. Perhaps your ignorance is simply a front. I will not press. In case you really do not know, King Phillip Maxwell is Evan Maxwell's deceased father. Evan Maxwell declared war on Wilber Dalacort of Evfel last year, and we have all been suffering since."

Again Valoretta glanced at Arnacin. This time, he looked away. Yes, if Evan Maxwell was the son of a decent king, the islanders might be pardoned in their support, but there were too many unknowns. What he did know was the new King

Maxwell had stolen their freedom, killed his sister, and ripped islanders away from home to fight in a bloody war.

In the long silence, Taylor hesitantly asked, "Is there something with which I may help?"

Sighing, Arnacin whispered, "We are looking for friends. We were told they passed this way."

"You are the first travelers I have seen. They say Maxwell returned this way, but he is the only one, and thankfully, I myself did not see him."

It was time to take a chance. "If you loved his father so, why do you not support this Evan Maxwell?"

Predictably, the innkeeper sobered. "Evan Maxwell was orphaned at four. Since then, no one knows exactly what happened to him, but he is not a person anyone would support. Maybe the pain of that terrible day never left him. Maybe he blames us for destroying his family. Someone here brought the sickness that killed them.

"Regardless of the reason, he hates the world, hates people, and hates love. While he lived here, he hibernated as much as possible. Then, one night, he raced off on his demonic stallion and disappeared to that island of witches who enchanted grass to strangle Evfelian knights. Some say he was seen entering and leaving the Ice Woods before that night, and that in them he had already met and made a pact with the enemy of all humans, the devil himself."

Arnacin's eyes widened slightly, but Taylor pressed on. "Wilber Dalacort may or may not be a compassionate king, but he is human, and he is the only person between us and the gates of hell."

The islander could hardly correct the man's misimpression. No one from his home could enchant anything. Instead, he asked, "What is so significant about entering the Ice Woods?"

"Why, even the most cunning and dreadful animals shun the place! Earth ends there. Only an abyss is left. Those thick branches twist together into spiderwebs of dark paths. And the whole wood grew up in a single night.

"Moreover, no one, not even the most skilled ice flier, has ever pierced their midst before. The woods kill everyone long before they even reach the barricade of branches—the gate, as we call it. Does that mean nothing to you?"

"Apparently, they didn't kill *everyone*."

"You look like you have never heard *no*, but there are some things that, unless you are invincible, you cannot conquer. Do not try. Find your friends. Maybe they are still on their way. But stay away from the woods unless you crave your own death. The only way Maxwell could have entered was through a pact."

Tapping his thumb on the table in thought, Arnacin glanced at Valoretta. She seemed lost in studying the wood grain beneath Tenacius's slapping hand.

"Have you heard of anyone by the name of Lisya?" the islander asked after a second.

"Is that the name of one of your friends?" When Arnacin remained quiet, the innkeeper shook his head. "Unfortunately, I have not. If you heard they went to Ansky, I would try the mountain villages. More travelers go through there."

"Thank you." With that, Arnacin stood, picking up his sack.

"Can I at least give you something for your journey?" Taylor quickly asked.

"Keep it for someone who can return the favor." With that, the islander whisked his family out the door.

Chapter 4

Evan Maxwell

It was not until they stood before the Ice Woods early the next morning that Valoretta spoke her mind. "Arnacin, I don't care if you hate my commands or not. I forbid you to try entering."

The islander's gaze did not waver from the ice-slicked path stretching before his feet as he stood at the border between safety and that great abyss. "They're in there, Valoretta. You can be sure of that."

"I don't care. Obviously, the people in there were either allowed to enter or knew the secret it takes to do so safely. Neither is true for you. If you so much as try, you'll die."

The islander's spine straightened. Futilely, Valoretta tried to position herself in his line of sight without stepping too close to the abyss—not with Tenacius. "Arnacin, I'll beg, order, ask—don't do that to yourself. If the other islanders are in there, let them come out."

Ignoring her plea, Arnacin pushed a foot forward, testing the path, then quickly yanked it back as it slipped.

Perspiration beaded on the Miran's back. "Arnacin! Why are you such a stubborn fool? You're not even listening!"

The islander had now sat down in the grass and seemed ready to straddle the path.

Was she that helpless to convince him? "There is nothing good in those woods. If the islanders are in there—" He was now sliding very carefully over the ice. "Arnacin, listen! I don't trust this Evan Max—!" Her words ended in a shriek as Arnacin slipped over the edge of that traitorous bridge.

From the sky, something red plummeted.

Valoretta hastily but gently slid Tenacius in his cradleboard onto the ground, then dashed to the edge. Even those few steps she took toward the forest brought such a strong wind that it buffeted against her, throwing so much of her shoulder-length hair into her face that she almost didn't see the small rust-colored eagle with its talons latched into Arnacin's shoulder as its wings beat furiously.

But the bird's strength and the islander's struggle to find purchase could not last long. Dropping to the grass, the Miran ripped at the hem of her skirt intent on giving Arnacin something to grab onto. The trembling of the ground made her pause and look up again.

Something large leapt from the dark interior of the woods—a giant reddish horse. In a second, it stood over the struggling pair, dipped its powerful neck, and clamped its teeth around Arnacin's arm. It ripped him off the ice and, without letting go, steadily trotted toward Valoretta, where it deposited him in a trembling heap.

Valoretta was beside her husband at once, and she noted new, blood-stained talon holes in the left shoulder of his shirt. His ashen face showed no pain, however, and she wordlessly helped him to his feet.

Before them, the eagle touched ground. As it did so, human toes appeared and its form began shooting upward. In less than a second, a boy of around thirteen stood there, his hair the color of the eagle's feathers, hands on his hips as he looked at Arnacin. His copper gaze briefly flicked to Valoretta and then to Tenacius, wailing a few feet away, before returning to the islander.

Without comment, the boy stepped over to the stallion, firmly standing on the ice as if it were normal ground. The horse did not look sinister, yet the woods' wind whistling through its mane added to the majesty of the upward arch of its head.

"The idiot," the boy muttered to the horse as if it could understand him. "No family would try entering. Not unless Wilber is behind it."

"Why would Wilber ask a family to try that?" The question came from the horse, its mouth moving in time to the words.

Valoretta's breath caught in her throat, but she dared not turn away from the creatures while their gazes were firmly planted on her and Arnacin. The islander's hand, scraped from the ice and warm and sticky from plasma, found hers briefly, squeezing once in assurance—of what, she had no idea. All the same, it soothed her.

"Why else would you find a family here?" the eagle-boy continued. "Anyway, I will not risk it. What with our rescue, he will have plenty to take back to Wilber if he did hire them."

"What do you intend to do about it? Kill him?"

"Do not be absurd. He goes in with us, and so do they."

The horse's eyes glanced toward mother and then baby. It shook its head. "I am not the one being absurd. I cannot possibly take them all at once, and we cannot leave the mother and baby here alone. What if they are innocent and some-one comes across them? They will be instantly regarded as islanders."

"Hush," the boy commanded, scrutinizing Arnacin.

As casually as she could, the Miran stepped over to her son and picked him up, sliding the cradleboard back over her shoulders while the islander had the creatures' full attention. For just a moment, both groups appraised one another in silence, each ready and waiting for the other to move.

It was Arnacin who broke the stillness, his usual distrusting tone carefully controlled. "Do these woods belong to the enchantress, Lisya?"

The boy's copper eyes hardened. "Come!" he snapped, closing the gap between himself and the islander. "Any resistance will be met with force, and I have *plenty* of force."

Had the boy not just been an eagle, the sight might have been comical. Arms akimbo, he faced Arnacin, even though the islander stood a head taller.

To Valoretta's surprise, the islander's air of authority dissipated as he exhaled in submission, stepping toward the horse and sliding his sack off his shoulders.

Barely had the boy turned with him, his attention wavering just slightly, before that sack slammed into the side of his head. He collapsed as if hit with a rock, while Arnacin pivoted toward the mountains with a glance at his family.

Yet before the islander could do anything else, the stallion moved in a surge of pure muscle. Valoretta only had time for one shout of warning before the horse rammed into Arnacin's shoulder. With a cry, he flew to the ground, facedown. Unsympathetically, the horse shoved him deeper into the grass and dirt, placing a hoof between his shoulders.

Valoretta pushed all her weight against the beast, but it did not budge. It took no notice of her or her glare; craning its neck toward the boy as he painfully shifted on the ground.

In a fit of temper, the Miran slapped the horse across the nose, as she had seen handlers do with troublesome beasts. "Move!" Her command brought only a brief flicker deep in the eyes, but even that was more like a volcano's laughter.

Beneath the horse's hoof, Arnacin stilled and struggled for breath. It was that sound that prompted Valoretta to look directly into the beast's eye. "Move. Can't you hear him? He can't breathe!"

Finally, the horse turned its head toward her, and she took a step away.

"If he really cannot breathe, you can be sure I have no power over it." The authority in the horse's tone stilled her—wise and somehow compassionate. "I am not pushing that hard. Should it be an act—and it would prove a good one—I cannot fall for it."

"That rat!" The sudden exclamation from the boy stopped their debate. Shoving himself to his feet, he strode toward Arnacin. "I warned you."

Stopping at the steed's tail, he snapped strands out while muttering darkly under his breath. "Next time you wish to convince someone you came from the island, pay attention to more than just accent. Any of the knights could tell you their males wear their hair short."

Bristling, the Miran exclaimed, "Arnacin *is* an islander! Now, order your horse to release him."

Braiding those snapped hairs together, the boy snorted. "Sit, before I kill him here. I am very interested in where you gathered your information. Unless you prove too much trouble, I will find out."

Warily, Valoretta studied him. He was probably serious, with his nimble fingers that could so effortlessly transform into wicked, ripping talons. Glancing at Arnacin, still captive underneath the horse's hoof, she lowered herself to the ground. "If you want us inside those woods, just tell us how to enter. We'll go."

"You lost that opportunity," the boy huffed, moving around to the beast's side. He then proceeded to wrestle Arnacin's hands behind his back and used the finished rope to bind them. "Horseback is the only way in or out for you humans."

The Miran's gaze locked with that of the horse. No natural beast could enter the woods, she was sure. Once in, there was no escape, not unless they could sway these creatures into allowing them to leave. No compassion showed in their eyes, however.

Hopelessly, she watched as the boy angrily snatched up Arnacin's sack. Only then did the horse lift its foot.

Arnacin slowly curled into a ball, his breathing evening out once more.

Paying close attention to that sound, Valoretta heard only the last bit of conversation between the boy and horse. "...over the gate, then we will slide back on," the boy was saying.

"What about the other two?"

"If Anwae does not know about this now, it will just have to wait until someone can make a return journey."

"She sent me."

"Then she knows. Our job is to take this troublemaker in before anything else happens." With that pronouncement, the boy threw the sack over his shoulder and hauled Arnacin off the ground.

The horse meekly lowered itself to its knees before the boy and captive, allowing them to mount it.

Then, in seconds, the steed was galloping across the ice with its riders. It stopped by a gnarl of twisted branches that must be what they referred to as the gate. There, the boy dragged Arnacin onto the top of the blockade. While the horse leapt over the pile, she saw the islander jerk against his captor once, but the boy simply leaned forward, whispering something, and Arnacin stilled. Then, all three were gone into the darkness of the woods on the other side of the gate.

Tenacius's wail called for Valoretta's attention. As she slid him off her back, a soft light filled the air. The softest sigh of grass sounded behind her.

Gasping, the Miran whirled around and came face to face with a... It was not a woman. The figure before her was tall and slender. Silver hair framed an ageless face, but it was the glacial blue eyes that captured her attention—seemingly all-knowing, yet warm.

Under their piercing gaze, Valoretta dropped her own. There was only one thing to say. "You are Lisya."

"Come." Even that one word sang with music.

Slowly, the Miran looked back up. No longer did the being stand there, but a great white horse with powerful wings. Only its eyes remained the same.

Valoretta stepped back. The beautiful creature of dazzling white followed her, and as it neared, it tucked its head into her shoulder. Peace and courage rushed through the Miran's bones. Its nose did not move against her collarbone, but she heard its thoughts. *There are other ways home, but for the safety of your little one, this way is likely the best. My gait shall be smooth, my leap a feather's glide, and my hair warm enough to block all cold.* The music of its tone was now tinged with a note of celestial laughter as the creature's head tossed up and down. *You will be only the second queen and little son I have borne home this way.*

Valoretta jumped slightly. However, no fear followed. She stood still as the creature bowed, offering its back. Shyly, she slipped between those great wings with only a moment of hesitation, still clinging to Tenacius.

There was no jolt of movement. The sensation of the creature standing and turning toward the woods was more like gliding. Using its wings, it passed the gate as if it did not exist and lit the darkness as it ran.

However the woods usually appeared, they sparkled during that journey, as warm as a pleasant day on Mira. The creature's passing caused the ice to dance the way sunlight shimmers on the base of trees near brooks; the snow and sleet glimmering with rainbow colors. Snowflakes and ice puffed upward as those shining hooves touched ground.

Like Tenacius's eyes frequently shone in awe, so now did Valoretta feel her heart hammer and beat faster.

It was not until she saw a cottage ahead that she asked, "Why did you allow them to take Arnacin away like a criminal? You could have come for all of us. I doubt he would have the same distrust of you."

Again, the musical voice sounded amused. *Arnacin and Michael have many a road before them, roads they will travel together. They must learn to understand one another without my interference.*

Valoretta could not think of a suitable response.

It was almost dinnertime in the cottage. Lisya had excused herself from her soup pot an hour ago while Carrie took over. Lorene, Talliaha and Lazarus sat around the table talking, while Raymond perched on its edge, peeling potatoes. Each scrap fluttered to the floor or onto the queen's skirt.

As Lorene brushed yet another wayward peel from her lap, Lazarus quipped, "I hope you're going to clean that up!"

"Of course," the hunter laughed.

With that, the conversation seemed to dry up. Lorene returned to cooing at her six-month-old son, Newton, as he lay in Talliaha's arms. Lazarus was left watching the latter three.

"Evan, stop pacing." Lorene's sigh brought Evan to a guilty stop before the fireplace, where he had been slowly wandering in tight circles, twiddling his fingers.

"Michael is late," the prince explained, sliding onto the bench beside Lazarus. "Something must have happened."

"Lisya would know."

Without looking up from his task, Raymond commented, "Have you considered using the information Michael brings to kidnap Andrew instead?" He shrugged when Lorene stared at him. "Wilber should be willing to trade anything for him."

Laughing, Evan shook his head. "Wilber would not keep any promise he made. No, he, himself, must be our target."

Lorene absorbed herself in her interactions with Newton.

Raymond shrugged. "What happened to your chosen regent, anyway?"

Instead of answering, the prince looked to his aunt.

She sighed. "In short, he died." Despite her explanation, everyone continued watching her as she ran her hand through her son's fine hair. "All Wilber had to do was wait. Once again, people played into his plans. Radnor was not happy. He took to drinking more than he should. Although I cannot think of a time he particularly acted drunk, his tongue was looser, and the one thought on his mind was how the ground itself had defeated them on the island 'at Evan's command.' It was no wonder no one believed the tale about Wilber's manipulation and dreaded the return of summer, when the prince would come back.

"Then, in midwinter, Radnor died in his sleep. Our healers said his heart gave out, possibly due to drink. Wilber stepped into the void, and all of Ansky breathed a sigh of relief. He easily gained almost everyone's support for raising weapons, building better defenses, and plotting a snare for their true king's return. It was that simple."

In the following silence, Talliaha asked, "What made you think differently than Ansky, if I may ask?"

Lorene shrugged. "I am not certain I thought any differently of Evan until I met Lisya. It was more that I realized Wilber was as... manipulative as he had admitted to being. Everything I had always questioned about Evan fell into place. No matter who he had turned to, I knew Wilber had pushed him there." She brushed angry tears off her cheeks. "Realizing that, I had to ask myself how he would shape Andrew and Newton, what he would make of them as men. There was nothing I could do for Andrew, not as things stood, but I had to leave with Newton if possible.

"Lisya appeared the very night I was trying to escape the castle. Every sense told me to trust her, but..." She paused, shrugging. Evan smiled slightly at her inability to explain why she had struggled to believe the enchantress.

After a moment, Evfel's queen continued. "She told me later it was the power in the mound itself that had murdered the men, not any islander or Evan; that its power could not touch the islanders or those of Ansky. Even Quincy had once promised himself to a greater master. As for Wilber, Lisya thinks he was left alive for other sinister reasons. I believed her. Somehow, she—"

A sudden hush fell over the room, and everyone turned toward the door. Michael had entered, pushing a stranger ahead of him. In Lisya's cottage, it was common knowledge that everyone who passed through her door was trustworthy. This entrance belied that, yet there was something about him...

An image pushed at Evan's memory as he regarded the stranger, yet it remained elusive. Despite the guardedness in the young man's dark blue eyes, they flickered with the ready ability that rippled throughout his stance and movement. He bore a quiet air of strength, though even the bulky layers he wore hung from his bones. The browned skin beneath his black hair and sun-bleached clothes spoke of the intensity of the weather he had seen, but neither the fading of the fabric, the many old stains spotting his attire, nor their raggedness could hide their once-fine material and elaborate design.

He might well have been a cast-away ruler like Evan himself, only with a harsher story if one could judge anything by his appearance—particularly considering the depths of his eyes.

"Arnacin!" Talliaha's cry echoed in the silence. Hastily handing Newton back to Lorene, she raced to the stranger, flinging her arms about him.

Raymond's knife clattered as it hit the floor, and he also shot to his feet, although he did not immediately move forward. Around the room, other islanders were leaping up in stunned silence as well, but Evan's attention returned to the reunited mother and son, tears soundlessly sliding past their closed lashes.

By all accounts, the sight should have brought joy, but the prince felt only cold. Charlotte had thought him dead, had died with that pain. Talliaha had walked away from her empty home believing all her family buried, and Raymond had slaved away to fill the aching pit that this black-haired young man could have alleviated.

A hand on his shoulder caused Evan to turn. Lisya stood there, her eyes wreathed with sorrow but also with deep fondness. "Why do you frown so, Evan?" she asked, her low tone meant to reach only him.

She undoubtedly knew, but Evan shrugged anyway. "The years of pain he put them through. Charlotte is dead—"

Gently, the enchantress interrupted. "Do you think his presence would have changed the outcome? Charlotte chose alone, and it was love that made that choice, not heartache. Give Arnacin a chance. He is not the adventure-seeking boy that thoughtlessly left his village, and his heart aches worse than yours at his sister's death."

Sighing, Evan patted her hand as he spotted Michael. The boy leaned against the doorway, his arms folded and a glare directed at the prince. With one more glance at the islanders slowly gathering around Talliaha and her son, Evan slid out from the table. Playfully, he shoved their spy back outside and shut the door behind them. "Yes, Michael? I am at your disposal."

"Good! I will dispose you directly."

At Evan's smile, Michael sighed and began his report.

A few moments before, Valoretta had entered the cottage beside the enchantress. Only the red-haired boy they had met outside the woods noticed her entrance, giving her a curt nod as she passed him where he leaned against the door-frame. The room was completely silent. A crowd far bigger than should have been possible filled it, but they still had a comfortable amount of space. The enchantress's home must have been much larger than it looked.

At the moment, every eye was turned to Arnacin, stand-ing only a few feet from the door. Then a cry came from the right, and a seemingly middle-aged woman rushed toward Arnacin. His arms opened for her, and she clasped him tightly, tears running down her cheeks. "You're alive," she breathed. Valoretta could not say which of them trembled more.

Feeling her own eyes moisten, the Miran dropped her gaze, turning her attention to Tenacius's peacefully sleeping face. Around them, a small group of men gathered, respectfully waiting for mother and son to part. Three of every five of them bore the same aura of wisdom and authority as her islander, likely arising from years of self-government. And yet, unfathomably, they had surrendered their right and freedom to a king.

As the moments passed, neither mother nor son moved from their embrace. Valoretta could just imagine their mixture of relief, disbelief and joy. Was her islander's heart melting, all his scars feeling as nothing in that moment? Did his mother fear that if she ever let go of Arnacin, she would wake up and realize it had been a dream? Was she thanking her God with all her might for the return of her son? Her tightly clenched fingers, wet cheeks, and trembling were the only clues.

With a few ragged breaths, Arnacin finally pulled away from his mother. Almost as if to escape the fact his eyes were puffy, he wordlessly turned to the young man at their left. As they embraced, chuckles rose from the rest of the men—their own display of joy.

Another young man stepped forward. "Well, you're not a ghost, Arnacin. If you were, you'd be younger and less sickly. You should still be a child."

An unexpected laugh escaped Valoretta's islander. She had forgotten he was capable of such a sound. "You're one to talk, Tevin. In actions, you were always the youngest of the group."

"Shh, I'm married now and soon to be a father. That's the past, and you should forget it."

"How could we?" the curly-haired man asked, slapping Tevin on the back. "With times such as the apple rob—"

But Tevin launched to cover the speaker's mouth. Gales of merriment burst forth around them. Wickedly, Arnacin finished, "The time you stole apples and doled them out to all your friends without telling us how you acquired them? That time?"

"Arnacin, you're ruining my reputation!" Tevin squealed in protest. Nodding toward the young man he had tried to silence, he added, "But if I'm the troublemaker, Raymond here's the madman, wanting to wed the witch."

The laughter on Arnacin's face blew out like a candle.

Tevin paled. "I'm sorry. I mean… Well, Arnacin, you can't blame us that your sister was… *unkind* to most."

Arnacin gave a conciliatory smile, yet the boisterousness did not return as others from the island either shook hands or hugged their long-lost friend.

After the last of the villagers had extended their greetings, Arnacin turned back to his mother. He opened his mouth, then shut it, dropping his gaze to the floor.

With a smile, his mother held out her hand. "I don't want any apologies, Arnacin. You're alive, and that's all I care about."

The islander took her hand, squeezed her fingers, and then let go, lifting his head again. For a moment more, he faced her without a word. Then, biting his lip, he turned to Valoretta. For all that he had seemed not to notice her, he had known she was behind him.

She could not prevent her heart from racing, however, when he joined her. Without a word, she handed Tenacius over. A sleeping grin covered the baby's face, and a gentle snore escaped him as he changed parents.

His innocent happiness brought a smile to the Miran, and she looked up to see her emotion matched by Arnacin's expression as he cradled his son.

Complete silence filled the space around them as the islander returned to his mother. Ever so hesitantly, he offered her Tenacius.

"Arnacin!" his mother exclaimed, her elated gaze flicking from the baby she accepted to Valoretta and back to her own son. "He's beautiful!"

How gracefully she had received the news! But the men's faces had stilled. Some eyes grew wide. Arnacin's friend Raymond paled.

It was he who broke the tension, however. "Well, Tevin, you can't be the only one who's married in five years." As laughter again filled the silence, his gray eyes found Valoretta's.

As the other islanders drifted back to their groups, Arnacin's mother turned to the Miran, holding out her free arm for an embrace. Hesitantly, Valoretta stepped into it, yet the feel of lips on her forehead caused her to jump.

The lady, Talliaha, swiftly dropped her arm. "I'm sorry. Tell me the story in your own time, but I thank you. Thank you for being such a companion for Arnacin."

Both Arnacin and Valoretta absorbed themselves in studying their son. A shadow shifted across the Miran, however, and she looked up to see Raymond extend his hand in greeting.

Gratefully, Valoretta took it, meeting his wise gaze.

"Don't worry," he said. "The others will ask more once they think of things to say. Words sometimes only come after—when we think of something meaningful. At least, for those of us who don't possess many words... I'm afraid I'm one of them."

"You do not seem to have much trouble."

"Well..." An impish smile danced in his eyes. "I have a burning question." He gently led her a few feet away and then lowered his voice, nodding back toward Arnacin. "You fell in love with *him*?"

Valoretta laughed. There was no way she would fall for that. Instead, she quipped, "I thought every girl fell in love with Arnacin. It was only a question of which one he picked."

With a nod, Raymond acknowledged her rebuttal and pressed no more.

Dinner was served by three boys—the youngest, Malachi, and the twins, James and Thomas. Fighting his instincts to distrust any food not prepared by his own hand, Arnacin forced himself to eat. He stopped once he caught Valoretta watching him with laughter in her eyes as she blew on her soup and took a sip.

As soon as the meal was over and groups were reforming in conversation, the enchantress approached Arnacin. "Will you speak with me and my children in private?" she asked.

His first reaction was to refuse, but before he replied, he met her gaze. Instead, he nodded, and Lisya led him into the back room. Half the space was a garden with glowing plants lighting most of the area and stretching up to the roof along that side of the enchantress's chamber. Moss gave way to a wooden floor, marking the divide between garden and a living space that held a loom, bed and bureau.

There, in the center of the wooden floor, beside a deer-like maiden, the red-haired boy stood holding the stone the islander had rolled into his sack the previous week.

Fear shone in the maiden's ebony eyes as she regarded the orb. In contrast, something almost like greed flickered in the depths of the boy's gaze. Greedy or not, however, he held out the crystal to Arnacin without the slightest sign of hesitation. "Why do you have this?"

"It's not mine," Arnacin admitted, not moving to touch it. "But I'm uneasy leaving it far from me."

"What do you intend to do with it, then?" the boy asked. Beside him, his sister scrutinized the islander. Her gaze penetrated deep, and her lips compressed into a thin line. Not once did she speak, as invisible to most as a silent guard.

There was no use searching her for the answer he didn't have. Instead, Arnacin looked at Lisya, who smiled and shook her head.

"It is yours, Arnacin. I will not tell you what to do with it."

"Then I give it to you. Somehow, I know you will not use it for ill, nor will anyone be able to steal it from you."

Although something furtive seemed to pass through the enchantress's eyes as she glanced at the stone, she nodded. "Very well, Arnacin. I accept the gift."

"Just promise me you won't use it to fund this Evan Maxwell." When only an amused silence met him, the islander surrendered, asking instead, "He is here, isn't he?"

"Yes," Lisya replied. "He is here."

Nodding, Arnacin turned to go. At the door, he paused to look back at the enchantress. "If I please, can I leave the woods? You won't keep me here?"

"People are never kept here against their will, Arnacin. If you wish to go, there will be someone to escort you out. Should you have been the sort of person I could not trust to leave, I would not have sent Brimstone to meet you and Michael at the gate."

A dead silence fell, but after a second, the islander looked at the boy still standing with the glimmering stone that was shining whitely. "I... We both trust our mother," Michael replied as his sister nodded in agreement. And with that, Arnacin exited, shutting the door behind him.

While Talliaha played with her grandson, the other islanders of Alleluia Lake sat around the table with her, telling stories of the past five years and, mostly for Valoretta's sake, of things farther back than that. "He looks like he'll be just as energetic as you were, Arnacin," Vilo said with a nod toward the baby, who was trying to catch his feet in the air.

"He is energetic," the Miran insisted. "With the same sort of quietness as his father."

Arnacin remained silent, his chest tight as he watched his mother bounce Tenacius gently—a black-haired babe, currently untouched by the awareness of loss. He had never before noticed the similarities between his son and William.

Maybe it was just the presence of his mother, but they were there all the same, stabbing him with sharp memories.

Tearing his gaze away, he noticed Raymond's wordless scrutiny of him. The gray eyes dropped as soon as their gazes met. Whatever questions he had or whatever things he noticed, he was keeping them to himself, along with the story Arnacin had not heard anyone share—the tale of Charlotte and Raymond.

In fact, no one talked about Charlotte or William at all. For their seeming consideration, the islander was thankful, but as for the lack of mention, he could not decide what he felt.

"Evan," Lazarus exclaimed. A hush fell over the table as a stranger joined them, the length of his brown hair marking him as a denizen of Elcan.

Beside Arnacin, Valoretta excused herself, taking Tenacius with her. Her islander merely straightened, closely studying this Evan Maxwell his kinsmen had chosen to follow. There was nothing tall about the king's frame. Anyone might describe him as small, although he was not—unnerving approachability created that impression. In fact, there was nothing regal about him other than his upright posture. Even his clothes looked much like those of any villager from around Alleluia Lake.

However, his eyes were his most striking attribute. Brilliantly blue, they were alive with unconcealed feeling—weariness, sorrow, care and humility. Yet as those gentle eyes flicked toward Arnacin, the light in them extinguished. For just a second, they filled with bitterness. Without a word, however, the king turned back to the others around the table. "Michael *insists* I ask you what you think of a full attack on Castle Ansky."

Lisya's children—Carrie, Michael, James, Thomas and Malachi—joined the group at the table. The enchantress stopped by the dying embers of the warm fire, cloaking herself in shadow. No one spoke.

As the silence wore on, Lazarus asked, "What do *you* think of it?"

An ironic smile crossed the king's face and he glanced briefly at where Michael stood stonily. "In keeping my promise, I refuse to say until someone besides Michael shares their thoughts."

"None of us is trained for war strategy," Raymond reminded him. "I gave you my thoughts earlier. No, I don't think a full attack is wise, but I can hardly say that's sound advice."

Michael folded his arms, his fingers tapping his elbows. His glare remained fixed on the king. "Do not think you will win this argument just because they refuse to assert their opinion. Their lack of an answer does not equate to assent."

Curious despite himself, Arnacin turned to Vilo, now on his right after Valoretta's departure, and whispered, "How many men does Wilber have in Ansky?"

Startled, Vilo glanced his way, then relayed the question to Evan.

The king did not respond immediately, appraising Arnacin. When he replied, his gaze did not waver. "Through the winter, Wilber has pulled in an army just over one thousand strong between infantry, guards and knights. Their skill is mixed, although every day it improves."

Arnacin could not recall ever having shrunk from any stare, but Evan Maxwell's was too knowing, too aware by that one question of the islander's experience, or at least some of it. Biting his tongue, Arnacin sat back. He could not add that a mere four hundred or so had little to no chance against a guarded fortress with the fully equipped fortifications he had noticed in Ansky. Not only had the foolish islanders picked a king, they had entered a losing battle.

Michael did not think the same. "A full attack is far better than trying to capture Wilber. I can lower the drawbridge, kill the guard. If you give me permission, I will also slit Wilber's throat. That will subdue any argument."

The king sighed. "It will also forever set up a kingdom forged by murder and magic. Without that foundation, you will be slaughtered in a full onslaught."

"You know you have to kill him. He left you no other option," the red-haired boy insisted.

With one long look at him, the king turned to outline his own plan. Michael would help one person infiltrate the castle by night to find Wilber, then wait fifteen minutes. At that point, he would open the gate to the islanders. Their distraction would help the first infiltrator escape with the captive Evfelian monarch. Andrew could still be relied upon to keep his word, while being young enough to care sufficiently for his father to agree to terms and old enough to order Evfel back home. His youth would create vulnerability in Evfel that would keep the country in chaos until Ansky could regrow and strengthen. Wilber, they would keep—in good health. Although Andrew would only know his fate as long as their terms were met.

"When you speak about a distraction to let the abductor escape, you refer only to us," Raymond said, at last. "Where will you be?"

"I must be the abductor."

Arnacin's head jerked back up. Instant protest broke forth. Someone even pleaded, "Lisya, say something!" Yet, she did not move.

The king was insistent. "Only I know the castle enough to find Wilber quickly. If he is not captured at precisely the right time, the plan fails and many die."

"We came fully prepared to die," Raymond reminded him. "We have all told you as much."

"But I am not prepared for you to die. And Wilber's forces hardly signed up for their death. If all goes well, perhaps the casualties can be minimized."

No other words could have given Arnacin as much pause. He studied this Evan Maxwell anew.

In the ensuing silence, the king closed the meeting. "Tomorrow afternoon, we will set out by the coastline so as not to be seen and arrive in the darkness of night." His gaze went once more to Arnacin, aware of the scrutiny. Then, with a nod, he left.

Since Lisya's cottage consisted only of the main room and the enchantress's chamber, the male islanders spread across the floor to sleep. Somehow, they all fit in a sea of lumps, each with their own blanket. Even three of the five beds were shared—Talliaha, Lorene and Newton in one; the blond-headed Malachi with Michael in another; and the twins James and Thomas in a third. The maiden, Carrie, had moved into the back room, leaving her bed for Evan Maxwell. The last one was offered to Valoretta and Tenacius, which she reluctantly agreed to accept. Arnacin took the floor space alongside the Miran's berth.

The mattress was as soft and warm as when her Sara had tucked her in every night; the blankets, the perfect weight. Thus, despite her cares, Valoretta fell almost instantly asleep. She woke only once, to feed her son and pass him to his father, then pulled her covers over her shoulder and drifted back into a dreamless sleep.

Much too quickly, dawn's light warmed her cheek, slowly rousing her. Strange that Sara had not woken her earlier to fuss her about hair and clothes... Maybe it was one of those insignificant days that her nurse decided to let her rest?

But that wasn't right.

With a jolt, Valoretta pushed herself up to her elbows. Tenacius had not disturbed her since his first feeding, nor was he next to her.

Despite the lack of windows in the cottage, light shimmered in rays across the many sleeping forms covering the floor. Carefully, so as not to disturb anyone, she leaned over the side of her bed.

There, Tenacius lay on Arnacin's slowly rising and falling chest. Both slept, and Valoretta reached down to run her fingers through her son's silky hair, so soft and cool in that moment it was like brushing the surface of water, its blackness contrasted against his father's white shirt.

Her fingers stilled. White shirt? Not since Mira had it truly been white. But now, although still tattered, it was fresh and clean—as was Arnacin himself. Nor was it just him. Valoretta too was no longer travel-stained.

In the enchantress's home, a night's rest seemed to restore one. Who knew what other effects it might have?

A slight movement beneath the baby caused Valoretta to freeze. Hesitantly, she met Arnacin's alert blue eyes. There were no dark shields in them. Like the morning silence, his gaze was serenely at peace.

Shyly, Valoretta returned her attention to their son. "Did he not wake after the first time?" she whispered.

"Not once."

"When did you fall asleep?" She took his silence to mean he must have only done so recently. Quietly, she asked, "Does Evan Maxwell still concern you as much after meeting him?"

Arnacin sighed. "It's worse after meeting him. I'd almost prefer the Ursan king and his peaceful dungeon."

Valoretta could not keep herself from chuckling. "Surely, you jest."

The islander smiled ruefully, but then shook his head. "The Ursan king was predictable, if wilier than some."

"And this Evan Maxwell is not?"

The sudden stirring of others around them, however, ended their conversation.

Despite Arnacin's inclination to have nothing at all to do with the war, everyone's focus was on helping the islanders prepare for battle. Soon, he found himself filling quivers next to Raymond at the table. Neither said anything as they tested the soundness of every arrow before approving it. Arnacin's childhood friend might or might not have changed much in five years, but he had, and he found no words to bridge the gap that had formed.

Talliaha's approach broke the uncomfortable silence.

"Arnacin," she said. "I know you haven't had me around to advise you for five years, but I think you should stay here tonight."

Arnacin smiled grimly, without comment.

Shifting, Raymond said, "I agree with your mother. You're thin and pale. Honestly, you look like you should join Evan."

Arnacin glanced toward the beds along the wall. Despite the preparations all around, the young man in question still lay beneath the covers, deeply asleep.

"Is he well?" Arnacin wondered. "He wants to leave by noon?"

Raymond's gaze also went to the only occupied bed, and he shrugged. "I wouldn't be surprised if Lisya's involved there. Most of the time, he's outside lately, and I don't think he's been sleeping. While Carrie doesn't speak much, even she insisted he needed the rest tonight."

Shaking his head, Arnacin muttered, "It's an insane plan."

"You're changing the subject, Arnacin," his mother interjected. "Please stay here. I fear you don't have the strength for it, and I can't bear the thought of losing you again."

"As you wish, Mother. I'll stay."

Kissing him on the cheek, Talliaha moved off to help Carrie inspect bow strings.

Raymond was studying him. "I can't be sure," the hunter said, "but it feels like you gave in too fast." When the islander's only reply was to start filling quivers again, he insisted, "Arnacin. Did you intend to stay?"

Finally, Arnacin met his friend's gaze. "I can't support your king, Raymond."

"Why not? We support him. Is it too much to ask you to support us?"

No, it was not too much to ask. But he could not assist them to their deaths, which is where their current choices would lead them.

After a moment, Raymond sighed. "I'm sorry. I can imagine what it was like to hear how we're sacrificing our freedom, about..." He trailed off, and with the barest shake of his head, shifted his attention back to his work. Softly, he concluded, "It was just the right thing to do."

Arrow feathers bent beneath the anger in Arnacin's fingers. "Right thing to do," he growled, discarding the arrow. "Tell me that five years from now, or a month, or even tonight, when all of you lie in Castle Ansky with your blood soaking the courtyard. Because it will, all for a worthless battle over thrones."

Raymond was silent for a long moment, his own hands still as he appraised his friend. Then he took a breath. "What happened during your travels, Arnacin?" He paused, seemingly on the verge of saying something more, yet he never spoke.

The islander had no answer anyway.

As if to prove Lisya's involvement, Evan awoke just before the sun reached its zenith. While most of the islanders filed out the door, she took the king into the back room. He emerged with the enchantress's gift, a long black cloak. Arnacin acknowledged its usefulness for camouflage but shuddered at the symbolism of death.

Valoretta did not seem to notice her husband's unease, instead attempting to walk a cranky Tenacius to sleep. With no way to help her, Arnacin instead followed Evan outside. Talliaha, Lorene, the boys—James, Thomas and Malachi—and Carrie stood along the wall to say farewell. Unlike Tenacius, Newton had remarkably fallen asleep while crawling about in the midst of all the noisy preparations.

Leaning against the doorframe, Arnacin surveyed the press of horses, massively tall and strong. With a complete lack of grace, islanders scrambled onto the impressive creatures.

Tevin was halfway onto a mare when he slipped, landing in the dirt with a thud. Passing by at that moment, Evan helped the troublemaker onto the horse's back before continuing in the direction he'd been going.

Quickly turning away, Arnacin found his attention caught by a stallion standing alone. It was the tallest of all the horses, and Arnacin had never before seen independence in anyone like what shone in the dark stallion's eyes. Unyielding and sharp, they revealed the story behind all the thin lines along its body, gleaming in the cottage's light. Someone had whipped its hide to shreds in a war for submission. And by the erect cock of its head, it had clearly won.

Yet as Evan stepped near that stallion, concern and love filled its rebellious eyes. Arnacin's skin grew cold, watching. The steed's great head lowered, its mouth moving in soft speech. The prince patted its nose soothingly and slid around to pull himself up with much more skill than the islanders.

"Is everyone ready?" Evan asked, king of even the untamed horses. To the chorus of "Yes," he nodded. "Then, God willing, we will return tomorrow with good news."

Seemingly by its own volition, the stallion turned, leading the other mounts into the thick darkness of the woods. Just before the leaders disappeared from view, the red enchanter-eagle lightly dropped onto Evan's shoulder, settling there.

It was just one more strange thing about the Anskonian king—suspicious, overbearing Michael was willingly playing the part of his domesticated raptor.

Slowly, most of the group watching turned back toward the cottage's warm interior. As if prying himself out of quicksand, Arnacin followed them. The analogy was probably a good one. He might wish to believe otherwise, but he doubted he would ever see any of them again and there wasn't anything he could do about it.

Inside, the enchantress stood before the fireplace, staring into the flickering flames. Approaching her, Talliaha asked, "Lisya, are you alright? Did you not wish to see them off?"

With a smile, Lisya turned. "I saw them off."

"Do you know something about tonight?" Worry creased Talliaha's brow.

"That, I cannot say."

"Won't," Talliaha softly contradicted. Yet, with an understanding smile, she returned to where the boys dispiritedly watched Valoretta pace with her wailing son.

"Don't feel left out," Arnacin joked to lighten the boys' mood, walking past to take Tenacius. "Taking care of a child is tiring, believe me."

With soft laughter, the boys dispersed. In the following silence, Talliaha asked, "Would you tell us some of your adventures, Arnacin? We have a whole quiet day."

Glancing at him, Valoretta sealed her lips, and Arnacin sighed. Pulling his compass out, he avoided his son's fingers. "Well, I learned more about ocean travel than I ever cared to."

He handed the compass to his mother. "That needle always points north. Many sailors use it to guide them, even when the stars are clearly visible."

With a small laugh, Talliaha said, "It looks quite abused, Arnacin, though it's still beautiful."

"It is well loved." Beside him, Valoretta glanced down, and Arnacin wondered if she was keeping a secret regarding the compass.

His mother's smile turned sorrowful. As she passed it back, she asked, "Your ship returned in one piece?"

At least five answers passed through his mind, but looking down at Tenacius's sky-blue eyes, all he whispered was, "Yes, they built it well."

"It is the best ship on all the seas," Valoretta said. "You should be proud."

"I am proud of its builders," Talliaha said softly. Something in her warm tone made it feel as if Charlotte and Arnacin's father were not that far away.

Chapter 5

The Real War

As evening came, Arnacin assisted the enchantress's children in making dinner. The three remaining boys seemed all too glad to busy themselves in the absence of so many, but Carrie chopped vegetables with slow preoccupation. Talliaha, Lorene and Valoretta clustered nearby on the floor, while the babies entertained each other in their mothers' laps. Over Newton's happy squeals, the ladies discussed the trials and joys of motherhood. Valoretta kept her own tales silent, only asking questions to prompt the other two to share their experiences.

Was birthing painful for them? How well did their children eat and sleep? With an impish delight in her tone, the Miran particularly asked how difficult it had been to birth and raise Arnacin.

Talliaha didn't fail to notice the intended audience. Smiling at her son, she answered, "Quite challenging, for his energy alone."

Arnacin was spared from hearing more when Lisya approached the cooks. James looked up as she neared. "I think our stew needs something," he informed her.

Without hesitation, the enchantress turned to the islander. "Arnacin, will you gather some herbs with me?"

Once again, there was no refusing her. As Arnacin passed off his task to James, Lisya tapped Thomas on the nose. "Try not to distract yourself and burn it, Master Stirrer."

"Hey, Carrie burned it last time!"

Laughter erupted from the other boys. Carrie blushed, never looking up from her chopping, and the enchantress led Arnacin into the back room, then toward the half that was a garden. Stepping into it, however, was like stepping into another world. Light emanated from the depths of some of the plants and reflected off others.

Passing by a vine bearing thin, spear-shaped leaves of emerald green light with glittering blue veins, Arnacin cautiously ran his fingers along one, watching his skin glow green against it.

"Do you like my fallyo?" the enchantress softly asked, nodding at the vine. "It is a precious plant."

"How do they grow?" The question was unintentionally spoken aloud. "It's dark in here."

Lisya's nimble hands carefully broke some thin leaves off a low plant. "Many things grow in the dark. It only needs the smallest amount of light."

"But outside, the sun exists even at night."

"Not always. Some darkness is much deeper than night. Your own island knew that darkness for a long time. A very long time."

Slowly, Arnacin nodded and turned his attention to a tomato plant. "Seven hundred years."

"Yet it survived. Plants grew, children were born, and life went on. They had light."

"But not enough. Candlelight alone doesn't make a difference."

"No, Arnacin, light is in love." The enchantress never paused in her task, gathering leaves and needles from plants whose names only she knew. "That is what everything needs to grow, to live. We bring it or devour it."

Shifting, the islander cast a sidelong glance at her and quickly flicked his attention back to the bright yellow tomato before him.

But his silence did not save him. Lisya softly asked, "Arnacin, may I ask why you cannot trust?"

From anyone else, Arnacin would have avoided the question. But under the enchantress's clear blue gaze, alone with her as she picked herbs, he could not. "I have trusted too freely and seen where that takes men. I have blindly stepped into so many traps, surrendered simply..." His chest tightened, and he broke off.

Instead of him finding words, Lisya whispered, "...given love simply to have your heart sliced open all the more through betrayal."

He did not deny it. She knew anyway.

Standing, the enchantress focused on the islander. "No one can deny all that you have been through, all that has taken everything you hold dear. But understand this: only you can actually destroy it. Every moment, every time you choose to lock your heart away or refuse love and trust through fear of the agony betrayal brings, you betray yourself. You deny others the chance to give you more than you ever imagined, deny your own being the thrill and exhilaration of all that love entails. There are many people who need you, Arnacin, and there are people you need just as much."

"I don't need Evan Maxwell!"

"No one mentioned Evan."

"You know full well he is the one I am refusing to trust."

"No, Arnacin, you refuse to trust your family—*all* the islanders, in fact. Have they not chosen to fight for Evan themselves? How could you know better than they what is best for them? Have you been home to know what has led them to this?"

Darkly, Arnacin responded, "I know better than the blessedly ignorant what is best for them. I have seen what happens under the rule of kings. No one needs that. *Starving*, they are better off without a king."

"On the contrary, the only thing that can help them is a king, a king that no mortal has ever known, yet of whom they have all heard."

Ignoring the implication, the islander insisted, "I don't want a king."

A small smile passed across Lisya's face. "No one ever does, Arnacin, myself least among them."

And looking at her standing there, framed in the light that seemed to shine from her very being, the islander saw everything. Here was a being powerful enough to command the stars to fall from the sky, the waves to roar, the mountains to crumble, all at a word—a being born capable of placing the entire world beneath her authority, and some would say with the birthright to do so.

But also a being with scars in the depths of her eyes.

Her voice calm, she put words to the things he had seen. "I failed to succeed on my own, as does everyone. Did you keep your purity through all those years of war? Your love? Did you not accuse yourself of being a monster? You, Arnacin, possess a god's strength of will, but was it enough? Can you deny the Eternal King is the only way?"

Arnacin buried his answer alongside his toes as he pushed them beneath the garden's cool soil.

For a minute more, Lisya watched him. Then her voice broke. "In an easy life, one could avoid the answer. I almost pity those who live so carefree—blind to reality due to the sun overhead."

Fearfully, the islander raised his head to meet her sparkling eyes. His throat was closed, but he had no need to worry. She pushed no more for a reply.

Once the cottage lay in the silence of sleep, the enchantress returned to her room, shutting the door behind her. A lock softly clicked. Sitting at the table, bouncing Tenacius on his knee, Arnacin involuntarily shuddered at the sound.

"Anwae has red in her hair." The hesitant, musical voice came from the corner, and Arnacin met the ebony eyes of Carrie.

"I wasn't sure you spoke at all," was Arnacin's only response. In the following silence, however, he asked, "Lisya? Why shouldn't she have red in her hair?"

Never taking her gaze from the door, the enchantress's daughter slipped onto the bench opposite the islander. After a moment, she said, "*Anwae*—our word for *mother*—uses very little of her talent, but when she locks her door, we know." There was another silence, and then she breathed, "She has the ability to end this war her way."

Despite the fact she had not truly answered his question, the islander nodded. "I know."

Finally looking toward Arnacin, Carrie declared, "Should she, all of Elcan will burst into flames."

"Why?"

"This is not a war over thrones. It never has been. It is a war driven by lust and hate on Wilber's side. Ansky does not yield to anyone they cannot love, and the closer Evan comes to us, the more they hate him. Should he win by Anwae's authority, the war will never end. Yet, this war tempts her terribly."

After a long pause, Arnacin asked, "Was that why there was fear in your eyes in her room yesterday?"

Carrie at first shook her head, but then she nodded. "Orbs of that size hold their own power, of which only enchanters know. But that power is great, whatever it is."

"You don't know what it is?"

"I refuse to touch it, but even should I, I have stayed away from learning the depth of power that might be required by it. That knowledge presents temptations that restrict the ability to help anyone." She met the islander's contemplative stare. "If you need proof, look no farther than these woods."

Seeming to anticipate his reply, she added, "Yes, Anwae has found some individuals to rescue, yet there is more isolation than not and too many deaths."

"Deaths of the idiots who have tried to enter?"

"Yes."

Glancing back down at Tenacius, who was sagging in sleep, Arnacin asked, "In other words, I should have kept the stone."

"It is safe from all that was causing you concern."

The cottage's unique morning light crept over the place, and still Carrie sat watching her mother's door, which had not opened once. Arnacin was just tucking Tenacius in beside Valoretta when he heard the rumble of hooves in the distance.

Carrie beat the islander out the entrance. Before his horse slowed as it reached the cottage, Lazarus leapt off its back. Urgency filled his face. "Where's Lisya?" the fisherman hurriedly asked, stopping before Arnacin and the enchantress's daughter on the doorstep.

"What happened?" Arnacin demanded. As the returning force entered the yard, not a steed appeared without a rider, and not one rider looked the least bit injured. Yet when Michael fluttered to earth and the stallion cantered up, his back empty, it became clear there was no real need for the question.

It was Raymond who answered. "Evan called the retreat, and we thought he was with us."

"Did anyone see him when the order came?"

"No." Even as Lazarus spoke, Michael looked away. No one seemed to notice his reaction, however, and the fisherman stepped up to the door. "Where's Lisya?" he repeated.

"I think she is out," Carrie replied. "Her door is locked. If she were here, she would be before you now."

"Does she know what happened?"

"Her door has been locked all night," Arnacin replied. From inside, he heard the ladies and children shifting. All but the enchantress hurriedly came through the door, and Arnacin took Raymond aside.

"What happened?"

"I don't know, but we attacked on time. I can't even say if Evan found Wilber or not. Just as we crossed the first curtain, we heard him call the retreat. I thought he was with us, but then…"

Something in the pain etched in Raymond's face stopped Arnacin from expressing his lack of surprise or how foolish he had thought the mission was from the start.

In the silence that followed, other conversations drifted their way. "Evan's dead, you can be sure of that."

"I guess there's nothing for it but to go home and burn the tracks behind us. It doesn't affect us one way or the other, really."

"But Ansky—"

"Is not our responsibility. Evan would want us to go home anyway."

"Hush!" Lazarus commanded as he reemerged from the cottage with Talliaha. Silence fell in the yard. "Until we know for certain what happened to Evan, there is no need for all this commotion. And only Lisya will be able to tell us."

"Are any of you injured?" Talliaha looked at each of them in turn. When no one spoke, she said, "Then come, we'll make some breakfast. Lisya will return in her own time."

Raymond nodded to Arnacin in parting, then the crowd entered the cottage, and the herd drifted into the woods. Arnacin found himself alone with the stallion and Michael, who was whispering, "There was nothing you could have done, Darkfire. Know that. I am sorry I lied to you."

"What did you really see?" the stallion growled. "You said—"

"I said, 'I see him,' and I did! If you had not moved, none of them would have. You would all be dead."

"What did you see?" The light swirling in Darkfire's eyes in that moment fully lived up to the stallion's name.

Even Michael flinched beneath their stare. "Once he called the retreat, he fell from an upper keep window after his escape rope was cut. He landed—" Shivering, the boy looked away, no doubt wishing to avoid the sight his words brought to memory. "Ask after we hear from Anwae, please." He received no response, but took that as acceptance and slipped inside.

Slowly, Arnacin dared to approach the stallion. "Is he so foolish a king as to not know this would be the outcome?"

That fire grew livid. For a second, the stallion and islander faced each other without a word. Neither submitted. At last, Darkfire dipped his head regally. "As a newcomer to Elcan, I will forgive you. Know this, though: there was no other way. The wretch gave him none. If Wilber were other than what he is, he could keep Evfel. It is his by right. But, being that he is not, this was the only option to grant him any mercy at all. His death will not heal Ansky's hearts. Only mercy will do that."

With a wild toss of his head, Darkfire took off into the woods. In the settling dust, Carrie's words from only hours before echoed. *This is not a war over thrones. It never has been.*

Arnacin shivered.

Since Tenacius still slept, Valoretta helped serve breakfast. Yet she noticed no one touched their food. All eyes remained fixed on the closed door in the back of the room. When Arnacin finally entered the cottage, his mood did not appear much lighter than the others. The only difference was that his gaze was fixed on the floor.

In time with Tenacius's wailing, Lisya's door opened and the enchantress emerged. A hush fell over the cottage. Meeting their worried gazes, she announced, "Evan Maxwell lives, if only just."

"Will you rescue him?" Lazarus asked.

"You must do that, Larry."

"Lisya," the fisherman protested. "There isn't a feasible way to—"

"You must do it!" The enchantress suddenly appeared to tower over them, her head raised, a different energy blasting from her, tense and yet tired. Then she closed her eyes, letting her shoulders slump slightly. "I will help where I can, but you must know this is not one of those times."

"Then Evan is as good as dead," someone said. "The only reason Wilber would leave him alive is to trap us. How are we supposed to even enter, let alone safely take an injured captive out of a castle with only one entrance? They will have doubled their watch over it. Only four people can walk abreast over their drawbridge, or two horses. They'll cut us down for sure."

"I know how." It was Arnacin speaking, his tone beaten. Every gaze whipped around to where he had settled himself beside Raymond.

Valoretta studied him. He continued to stare at the floor, seemingly memorizing the wooden pattern. Though he did not look happy about his words, the Arnacin Valoretta had come to know would never have volunteered his knowledge, particularly for a king.

"What would a shepherd like you know about entering castles?" one of the islanders finally asked.

"He's hardly a shepherd," the muttered reply came from the opposite corner.

It was that comment that caused Arnacin's head to rise in pride. "I *am* a shepherd." Beside him, a smirk filled Raymond's face. Arnacin kicked him, but that only caused the smile to broaden. Valoretta hid her own amusement by turning her attention back to her son.

"Very well, Arnacin," one of the men, who Valoretta recalled was named Vilo, said. "How would we do it?"

"You enter in two places. By the route they expect and by a siege tower with its own drawbridge. It could be balanced by a counterbalance on the opposite side."

"They'll have it up in flames before we can even pull it there," Lazarus commented. "You can't move a ninety-foot siege tower up to a castle without anyone noticing."

"They won't see it if you move on a moonless night—not at first. As for their flames, saturate the wood with water. There's nothing more you can do."

"Well," Raymond sighed. "It's not foolproof, but there's a chance it will keep them occupied long enough for us to enter. When is the next moonless night?"

"In a week," Lisya answered.

Valoretta did not know whether the enchantress meant in the moon's natural cycle or something else. She hadn't paid attention to the moon's recent phases to be sure.

"You may enter the castle," Lorene spoke up, "but, assuming Evan remains alive for another week, what will prevent Wilber from killing him instantly once you are inside?"

"I will make sure the swine dies first," Michael growled.

"Then know they took him to his old room and not the cells, intending to trick you," Lisya said.

"Who will capture both the interior and exterior gatehouses if Michael is rescuing Evan?" Raymond asked.

"The first people inside can secure the outer gatehouse to open the main gate," Arnacin replied. "I heard your king was able to enter the inner yard through the stables. Once we're in, I'll go through there to open the interior gatehouse."

Valoretta raised her eyebrows, but if her husband noticed her astonishment, he made no sign.

"Arnacin?" Talliaha protested, but then, biting her lip, she looked away.

The islander's resigned gaze left his mother and returned to the enchantress. "Is there a safe forest from which we can obtain wood?"

"You will have all you require here, Arnacin," Lisya replied.

Valoretta had no words as she watched Arnacin join forces with Lazarus to lead the construction of the siege tower. With Lazarus's talent and belief that joinery worked better than nails, he led the careful design of cutting wood and notching beams together. Meanwhile, Arnacin made sure the original design and every change produced a fully balanced tower.

On the second day, the Miran was joined in her watch by Michael, who stepped through the door to lean against the entryway with his arms crossed. He looked neither impressed nor hopeful.

After a moment of silence, Valoretta casually asked, "Where are you originally from, Michael?"

He shrugged. "Here. Isful. I never knew the land of my ancestors, but this is better anyway."

"I thought this was named the Ice Woods."

The boy scornfully glanced her way. "That is Ansky's name. These woods were given the name Isful at their creation. You would have to ask my mother if she intended any meaning behind it. Regardless, we have long been the Isfullen, we of the woods."

Valoretta nodded thoughtfully. "Are the islanders also considered Isfullen in their own way, then?"

Michael's eyes softened. "As far as Elcan is concerned, if you can leave Isful alive, then, yes, you are Isfullen—allies of the enchantress."

The evening before the moonless night arrived. Valoretta stayed up after putting Tenacius to bed and found Arnacin sitting by a bag of tools on the second landing of the tower as Lazarus tested everything. Jumping on one level, the fisherman called down, "If I go through, just give me a good burial."

"I'll give you a good burial if you find any more changes," Arnacin muttered. But after a pause, he called up, "Larry, if this tower becomes any heavier, that counterbalance might as well be the size of Ansky."

Laughing, Lazarus replied, "It has room to grow, Arnacin. Don't worry."

As Arnacin knocked the back of his head against the beam behind him, Valoretta sat nearby. With a small smile, her islander whispered, "Or I'll just let you figure out all the calculations. You remember them, don't you?"

Smiling sarcastically in return, Valoretta nodded. "I wouldn't trust myself, though."

After a moment, Arnacin asked, "Are you not tired, Valoretta? You've been rather busy this week."

She studied him, then softly asked, "Why are you, of all people, leading your kinsmen to more war and reinforcing their slavery to a king? According to you, anyone would be proud to defy the nobility, or the devil, or whatever it was." When Arnacin only looked down, she insisted, "Honestly, you would help your family more if you didn't aid in this. I heard them say they would just return to the island and destroy all routes to their home."

For a long moment, the only sound was the soft *thump, thump* of Lazarus's feet on the tower above them as Arnacin fiddled with his fingers. Finally, he sighed, "Maybe I have to."

"Why?"

Darkness glimmered in her islander's gaze as he turned his face back to her. "Because their king *gave* them that choice."

"So you would refuse freedom just because it's granted by a king? That hardly sounds like the Arnacin I know."

"What Arnacin do you know?" His snapped words seemed to echo. Above them, the sound of Lazarus's feet stilled. More quietly, he sighed. "If they are too blind to realize the future they chose, I can't force freedom upon them."

"It's not force to simply stay out of it!"

Slowly, the islander stood. "It is when I... They think they love him, and he did just put their safety above his own."

"Which could be pure arrogance, particularly for a king upon whom the whole country depends. And you could just as easily be forcing your home into slavery with your choice."

Without replying, Arnacin stooped to pick up the tool bag.

Valoretta sighed. "But perhaps I'm actually not concerned for them. You've made your distrust of nobles plain, and we have no real reason to believe this Anskonian king will be any better. Miro had good intentions as well. Arnacin, if you do as your island wants, you'll kill yourself, one way or the other. I want you to be able to heal."

But Arnacin slung the tool bag over his shoulder and turned toward the cottage. "Arnacin can't heal, remember? He's dead, as you pointed out. 'I'm everything he stood against.'" With that, he stepped into the cottage and shut the door behind him.

Hearing footsteps above her, Valoretta looked up as Lazarus descended the ladder to the level she was on.

"Is there anything I can do for you?" the fisherman asked.

Turning back to the view of the cottage's glittering shingles, the Miran shook her head with a sigh.

An hour before daylight found Arnacin still at the table, while the enchantress began breakfast preparations. "Lisya," he said, "I have to see the dawn."

"Come, my sailor," the enchantress whispered. She set down the bowls she had taken from a shelf and led him outside. "For you, there will be dawn in the east." She pointed to their left where the snow fall slowed. Already, a pinkish glow was starting to form among the trees in the distance.

Without answering, Arnacin watched as the light intensified, reflecting through every icicle. In his yearning for the open water, his chest tightened.

Beside him, Lisya asked, "Is your structure finished?"

"You know it is." He paused before inquiring, "Why do you back Evan Maxwell when you can see the future?"

"I only see possibilities."

"At the least, you see his thoughts and heart."

Lisya laughed. "So do you. Your pain might color your insight, but you can also sense a heart's leaning." When the islander again said nothing, she changed topics. "Did you know Raymond intends to hold an archery tournament today before you leave? He thought you could all use the practice and entertainment."

"I've heard Raymond discuss it, but I don't think there will be time. We have to leave by noon."

"Arnacin, find the time. All of you need it." With that, Lisya turned back inside and a single drop of melting water plopped to the ground at the base of the stoop. Such was the gift of sunrise.

Lisya had her way. As she oversaw the war preparations with Talliaha, Lorene, Carrie and the occasional islander, the rest took turns shooting a piece of wood Vilo had erected after marking a target on it. The only rule Raymond gave was, "If you split an arrow, you lose and you go help with the war preparations. We need our weapons."

"But, Raymond," Tevin asked, "what about the ones we send into the woods?"

"Michael will retrieve those," Raymond replied with a wicked grin toward the red-haired boy.

Guiding Valoretta in some archery of her own, Arnacin tried to ignore the group's laughter as they jeered Lazarus's clean shot, clapped him on the back, laughed over an arrow from Tevin that bounced off the target, and cheered on the more tentative competitors. Somehow, Arnacin knew he could never again be part of that. It was too innocent, a life of camaraderie for those without scars.

"Arnacin," Raymond eventually called out, "we're running out of time. Show us how rusty you've grown."

It was just the right sort of comment. With a wicked grin, Arnacin asked, "You have the most points so far?"

"We haven't been counting."

"Very well." Accepting the bow offered him, Arnacin took two arrows, stuck one in the ground at his feet, and nocked the other. In one fluid motion, he fired the arrow, switched hands, took the other, fired it, then tossed the bow back to Raymond. Both his arrows stuck out from the center, one angled upward to share the space.

In the stunned silence that followed, someone muttered, "Braggart."

Shaking his head, Raymond patted his friend on the shoulder before stating, "All right, we have to be off."

To everyone's dismay, Darkfire volunteered to pull the tower. While the stallion submitted to the process of being attached to the front with a makeshift halter and lines, Michael described the layout of Castle Ansky to Arnacin as Lisya outfitted the islander with a jerkin embossed with Ansky's horse and some boots in order to make his way safely into the inner bailey alone.

At last, they were under way, through the eastern side of the forest. As Darkfire's great shoulders pulled at the soft ropes, the islanders and Michael pushed from behind. They traversed a thawed pathway that had not been there before, the trees opening and closing to allow them to pass.

Halfway to the castle under the afternoon light, Arnacin called out to the enchanter, now in eagle form, "Michael! Fly ahead and make sure they don't kill your king as soon as they spot us."

With a diving swoop, the eagle took off. On the fastest winds, he was above the town of Ansky within moments. Humble buildings clustered within the shadow of its abbey, with the castle brooding on their outskirts. Once upon a time, it may have guarded those bustling below to finish the last of their chores before darkness fell, but now its fortress mocked their efforts. Inside the monastery's walls, the brothers were no less active, tending to their edible plants and bedding down their animals in the little barn.

Quietly, Michael descended, landing in the church's tower. There, he waited until dusk, then winged his way to the castle. Of course, the window he wanted was latched, but he saw guards were playing a game at a table just inside the door and Evan's still form lay in the bed.

Drifting passed the nearest opening, Michael heard one guard say, "We should just finish him. I doubt you can kill those Ice Wood..." The words trailed off as Michael flew out of range and then into the castle.

There, he transformed back into his human form, found his way to the right door, and knocked on it.

"What is it?" a voice barked from inside.

"I have a message from the king," Michael called. "Do not make me shout it through the door. It must not be overheard."

As the door creaked open, Michael transformed. Faster than either guard could move, he sunk his talons into the first man's throat. That guard collapsed, and the second instantly yanked out his knife, diving for Evan. Michael launched himself at the man's neck, snapping his spine.

Again transforming, the boy bolted the door before settling himself on the edge of the bed. Evan had not moved during the skirmish. The only sign that he still lived was his labored breathing.

"Evan," Michael whispered, cutting through the rope around the captive's wrists. As far as the boy was concerned, pure spite had bound the prince. Regardless of the reasons for it, Evan had still not moved when the boy finished.

Feeling the prince's burning forehead, Michael tried again. "Wake up. You have to help us rescue you."

To his relief, Evan turned his head away from the boy's hand. Slowly, eyelashes parted, although Michael was not sure how much the eyes beneath them saw. "Evan," he insisted for the third time. "Can you at least make it to the window?"

"They're waiting for you, Michael," Evan weakly responded after a long moment.

"We know. Just answer the question."

"Maybe. Promise one thing."

"Anything, Evan."

"Kill me yourself before you are all captured."

"I changed my mind," Michael growled. "Now, come on."

By this point, it was completely dark outside. Briefly springing from the bed, Michael blew out the candles to avoid being seen at the casement. In the pitch blackness that ensued, he tripped over one of the guards' bodies. Wincing, he picked himself up, inched to the window and opened it.

Standing at the edge of the dry moat, Arnacin's position marked the place where the tower's wheels would stop. On guard, Raymond stood beside him. As one of the islanders began to turn the wheel that would lower the drawbridge from their siege tower, an alert sounded through the castle.

"Keep going," Arnacin commanded. With a wince-inducing bang, the tower's drawbridge slammed onto the battlements.

Above, lights were springing up along the parapet. To the west, Arnacin heard the answering thud of the castle's drawbridge. Either Michael had secured his charge enough to spare a moment to dispatch those in the guardhouse, Wilber's forces were coming to meet them, or it was a trap. Either way, they were pressing on.

"Come," Arnacin ordered. Then, he began the ascent up the tower, those behind scrambling after him.

Halfway up, Talliaha's son froze as the first missile, alight with flames, struck only an inch from his foot. While the blaze didn't catch in the soaked wood, he cast a quick glance over his shoulder all the same to check on the others. A few rungs below, Vilo urged him forward. With a nod, Arnacin kept the line moving.

A scream from above told the islander one of Raymond's archers had struck a mark. A body flipped over the parapet and plunged into the moat.

"Where did islanders learn siege warfare?" Quincy asked, standing at Wilber's shoulder as they watched from the inner ramparts. Before them, they could see Maxwell's forces pouring over the wall and streaming through the gates.

"Maxwell's trained them quite a bit, it seems," Wilber replied before turning to a guard beside him. "They have taken the bait, even if we haven't caught those spies in their act. Go kill the hostage."

Bowing, the guard turned down the stairs. Beside him, Quincy pointed. "That fat better boil fast."

Islanders were now spilling across the courtyard, and still more were coming through the gates. They had taken the gatehouse and blocked the entrance.

"They still have not reached the inner wall. Send someone to guard the stable door as an extra precaution."

Letting the invaders slide past him, Arnacin took the corridor leading underneath the parapet to the inner wall. Defending troops neared at a run, however. "Quick," he snapped, pointing back the way he had come. "We need reinforcements! Their siege tower is not burning!"

As the guards rushed by, Arnacin took off once more, thanking the darkness.

After cutting across the ward and finding the outer door to the king's stable, located in the inner bailey, the islander tried the handle. Locks could not stop him. He had trained himself long ago to pick them.

On the other hand, the sound of shifting feet on the opposite side of the door was another story. Arnacin cringed as the releasing lock clicked, however softly. His Tarmlin blade lay far away, and everyone knew close-range fighting meant death to an archer.

With little choice, the islander kicked the door inward and rolled into the stable. The abruptness of the move enabled him to pass the two men standing there. As they turned, swords raised, Arnacin dove into the darkness of the nearest stall.

The guards paused. "Islander," one of the men taunted him, "there is no escape from there. Come out."

For a second more, Arnacin remained crouched in the corner. Then he vaulted over the stall's stone wall into the next one. Its occupant shied away from him.

Movement outside told him the men outside the stall had seen him go over, and he leapt another wall. His only hope was to gain enough distance to draw his bow.

Height would also have helped, but the loft stairs were on the opposite side of the building.

"Go raise the alarm. They are coming through the stable. So far, we only have one."

Those words spurred the islander to throw himself back into the main passage, arrow nocked. The first man fell silently, a shaft in his throat. The second man dove into a stall nearby.

Drawing another arrow, the islander waited. A moment of stillness followed. Then, the guard tried to vault over the walls as well. Yet Arnacin was ready. The motion of the guard's leap carried him up and his arrow-pierced body flipped into the other stall.

On either side, horses pawed the ground and tossed their heads. Ignoring them, Arnacin brushed past into the inner ward.

Above, the ramparts crawled with men, all watching the outer bailey. Ducking his head, the islander ran to the inner curtain's gatehouse, which stood closed and fastened.

Pulling out another arrow, Arnacin kicked the door in and hastily flattened himself against the wall. As he'd expected, two guards rushed to the opening. As they appeared at the door, Arnacin shot them down.

"Look out!" Raymond cried from the base of the tower, seeing knights lift a cauldron onto the parapet. A cry rose from the islanders still on the siege engine. Despite their fear, no one paused. Fluidly, they broke away, those closer to the bottom dashing downward as fast as possible while those above scrambled upward.

Raymond shot an arrow at one of the men tilting the cauldron. As his target collapsed, the stand it was on slipped. Scalding fat and pot both plummeted over the edge. A flaming arrow flashed through the cascade, and fire leapt across it.

Yanking the nearest islander to the ground, Raymond felt intense heat wash across his head and shoulders as a million screams rent the air. With a resounding clang, the cauldron smashed through the tower's bridge and support.

Pain washed over him. The last thing Raymond saw was their burning siege tower crumbling and crashing into the dry moat below.

Chapter 6

The Isfullen

As Michael pushed all his weight against the pounding door Wilber's men were trying to force their way through, he gasped, "Darkfire, come soon!"

Behind him, Evan lay crumbled on the window bench. Glancing at the still figure, Michael clenched his jaw. No one would lay a hand on Ansky's rightful king while he stood guard.

The door splintered and the first four men stormed through. Drawing Resplandecer, the glowing white sword Anwae had made for Evan, Michael launched himself at the attackers. Although the boy was practically without skill, the sword's light pierced the vision of those men, strengthening his offense.

A clarion call split the air through the open window. Darkfire had arrived at their agreed upon meeting place in the inner bailey.

"Evan!" Michael snapped. "I tied a rope to the window. Use it!" There was no response.

Stabbing another guard and kicking the body into the others, the boy wheeled about, stuffing the sword through his belt. Then, seizing Evan about the middle, Michael hauled him out the window. As they fell, the enchanter grasped for the rope and they jerked to a stop. Michael's shoulder screamed, and he let them slide swiftly downward. With a thud and a gasp, they landed across Darkfire's back.

The stallion instantly wheeled as Michael scrambled to latch his free hand onto that flashing black mane.

As they reached the inner gatehouse, guards were still falling to Arnacin's bow. "Arnacin!" Michael shouted. "Take him back! I have the gatehouse!"

Instantly, guards whirled on Darkfire, but those flashing hooves avoided their blades. As they swarmed him, Arnacin leapt onto the stallion's back. Michael launched into the air as he changed back into an eagle, then shot into the gatehouse, where he sank his talons into the soldier bent to the portcullis's wheel.

Outside, the sound of battle disappeared into the outer ward. Quickly, Michael took wing to join Vilo and Lazarus at the outer gatehouse. Beneath him, Darkfire raced through the battlefield, while Arnacin clung on with his legs, wrapping his arms around Evan. A cheer burst from the islanders as Darkfire passed beneath the outer portcullis and over the drawbridge, then raced toward the Ice Woods.

Islanders swiftly followed. The eagle was the last of those retreating that night, staying behind to scratch a note into the outer gatehouse door: *Beware the Isfullen.*

Waiting for the others to return to the Ice Woods, Arnacin stood beside Darkfire, the boys, Carrie and the women as Lisya tended to Evan's still form in one of the beds. Over the night, as he was borne back, he had almost stopped breathing.

Without looking up, the enchantress spoke. "He will live. Please, stop hovering."

A general flurry ensued from all but the stallion and Arnacin, both of whom remained, studying Evan's pale features. The prince seemed so young, so... unlike a normal king. Yet if he died, what then? It made no true difference to the island.

Even telling himself this could not change the leaden weight of the islander's heart. Hopefully, that had more to do with his own treachery in trying to rescue Evan, who would keep the islanders embroiled in bloodshed over thrones, rather than with any misplaced care for the young king.

"Darkfire!" Lisya laughed as she bumped into the stallion's nose. "When the others return, there will be no room for you here. Go."

With a gleam in his eyes, Darkfire obeyed. Only then did Arnacin ask, "What is wrong with Evan?"

"They poisoned him."

A commotion outside stopped Arnacin from saying anything more. He rushed to the door. The rest of the islanders had returned with the herd. Many of the horses were double laden, however. Atop Brimstone, Lazarus held Raymond in front of him, draped over the stallion's shoulders. White blisters covered the hunter's exposed skin.

War had come to the people of Arnacin's island, and the full reality of that poured into the yard before him. Here a sliced open arm, there a bleeding side. Cracked heads, burns... The variety of casualties continued.

As figures dashed by, Arnacin numbly helped Lazarus lift Raymond and carry him into the cottage. Carrie was already laying out blankets. Thinking back, the islander remembered she had been doing that since leaving her mother's side by the prince.

Raymond shifted in pain as he was lowered from Brimstone's back, but there was no other sign of consciousness. Arnacin clenched his bottom lip between his teeth. With nothing more to do, however, he turned back to help bring more of the wounded inside.

Lisya stood at his elbow, a filled jar in her hand. "Do not fear, Arnacin. All will live, and under this roof, even the scars will disappear quickly."

Over the next month, Lisya cared for the injured and sick. When one week had passed, everyone was better except for Evan. The enchantress had left him to heal more naturally, claiming her medications might conflict with the poison used. Although Arnacin suspected she was not being entirely open, he let the matter slide.

Returning from a scouting trip, Michael reported that there were seven islanders no one could heal. They had died when the siege tower fell. "That is a small number. Wilber lost over a hundred between injuries and those that died that night."

Despite the bitter truth in that, the fallen were islanders, torn from their lives of freedom for Evan Maxwell. War-hardened or not, Arnacin's heart grieved for them, even though he had never really known them in life. All the islanders from his village who had traveled to Elcan still lived.

Nor could he dismiss the whisper that, while Evan had managed to keep all of them alive, if not for Lisya's medications, he would have killed nearly a quarter of Michael's Isfullen.

Tenacius, who had started an early form of laughter, prevented Arnacin from feeling too dead. Meanwhile, he learned quite a bit about the Dalacorts over that week.

Overhearing Michael report to his mother that three footmen had been promoted to knights since the prince's escape, Arnacin looked up from where he sat at the other end of Lisya's table with his son. "Wilber promotes his footmen?" he asked.

Michael shrugged. "Some of them. Wilber divided Ansky's recruits from the start according to potential talent."

"Does he not care about their bloodline?"

"Why would he?" Michael asked. "The Dalacorts have long honored skill, not bloodline. That is their strength and their undoing. They know well that, should they lose their family's strength, a stronger one will topple them. So, they drill for life."

"It is also said that no king will allow himself to grow old," Malachi whispered. "That when a king deems his heir strong enough, he loses to the younger in a tournament, and in his death, declares the strength of his chosen king."

Valoretta's eyes grew wide. "That's…" Yet she apparently could find no words to communicate her disgust.

Malachi just shrugged, hunching over as if to disappear.

A warning flickered in the Miran's gaze as she glanced at her husband. What warning, he had no idea, but his own eyes drifted to Evan's bed.

Lazarus was sitting there, talking softly to the prince. Evan seemed only partially conscious, but he was obviously responding a little. It was an improvement, at least physically.

Perhaps it was time Arnacin actually met Evan.

The next afternoon, Arnacin settled on the edge of the prince's bed after having convinced himself of the need to meet his island's chosen king, if for no other reason than that of knowing an opponent.

Deep blue eyes blinked open as the mattress sank slightly. For a long moment, they appraised each other.

Evan broke the silence first, with a shaky whisper. "Lazarus tells me I have you to thank."

"And I hear you might not be thankful since Michael says you wanted to die."

Amusement brought a tint of pink to that white pallor. "Regardless of gratitude, I have questions."

"Why not ask directly?" If the islander thought to avoid revealing anything about himself, he suspected he would fail.

"Sometimes gratitude succeeds where normal questions seal lips."

Sighing, Arnacin submitted momentarily. "I've seen castles, studied their strengths and weaknesses, the means to infiltrate and exit them." He could not restrain his growing bitterness. "And I know of the *people* they hold. In some ways, Wilber seems twice as clever as many."

Quietly, Evan studied him. When Arnacin's gaze faltered under that scrutiny, the prince asked, "What do you want?"

"I don't know. I wanted to be home, but I will never find it, and even if I did, I don't know that I would truly be happy." It was strange he was admitting it, and he couldn't suppress a small shudder. Perhaps it was because Evan's eyes, like Lisya's, suggested he knew everything already and was just waiting for the truth to come out—even if, unlike Lisya, he could not possibly know everything.

Stifling his discomfort, Arnacin continued. "I hate adventure, and I hate monotony, so…"

Evan weakly tried to prop himself up a little higher on his pillows. All hints of color drained from his face. As he sunk back into the bed, his eyes closed.

Sighing, the islander straightened the blankets. "Wait until you're actually ready."

With a tight-lipped smile, the prince placed his hot fingers over Arnacin's wrist, still on top of the bedding. "If you know where to look, Arnacin, I think you will find home. It will probably not be what you thought you wanted, but… maybe it's better. At least, that is what I found."

"You found," Arnacin scoffed, pulling his hand farther away. "I doubt any king knows what a home is."

Although Evan's eyes crinkled in amusement, he did not answer. Perhaps he did know.

There was one way to find out. "Where were you born?"

"In the castle."

"And raised?"

Silent laughter again sparked in the prince's eyes. "In the castle. My uncle raised me… or…" His laughter snuffed out and his gaze grew distant for a time. Then, he whispered, "Or I raised myself. Possibly, my father's horses raised me. I guess I will never know."

It made for quite the image: a crowned baby surrounded by shaggy horses. Despite half wanting to laugh, Arnacin shoved the mental picture aside. "Do you still have noble family outside these woods?"

"Yes."

"Yet your uncle is not supporting you?"

Evan's lips curled upward as he regarded the islander. "Wilber Dalacort is my uncle."

The room seemed to sway for a moment. Had the islanders chosen the protégé of a grasping, twisted tactician as their king? The man whose queen herself had escaped? "You were raised by him?"

"He married my father's sister. After everyone in my immediate family had died from the plague, Ansky's nobles were afraid to take me for fear of jealousy. He became the logical choice."

"Did he marry her in order to conquer Ansky?"

"Maybe."

"How long ago did your family die?"

"I was four." Evan's eyes again closed. Minutes passed. Despite the stillness, Arnacin doubted the prince had fallen asleep. He knew too well the ability a lost past had to wound one.

As if from a distance, the prince finally sighed. "My parents took my siblings with them. I wandered the corridors for years, wishing I had been buried with them."

There was no way to deny the humanity in that pain—the realness. And there was also no way not to sympathize. And yet, Arnacin refused to. "You will never be happy with kingship?" he demanded. "With authority?"

Evan's eyes flicked back open. "I need to be. I thought I wanted—no, I *do* want to leave for the mountains and raise a herd of horses there. They would run over the highlands with the wind. By night, we would listen to the song of the frogs and..." He trailed off, pulling his blankets a little higher. "I need to stop dreaming," he breathed. "It will never be, and if I choose discontent, I betray myself and those for whom I am responsible."

"I don't think you can just choose happiness."

"Not with *my* strength alone, no."

Sighing, Arnacin dropped his attention to his fingers, fiddling with the blanket's edge. "I want to doubt everything you've said," he whispered at last. "Perhaps the last part, most of all. But I can't."

With a soft smile that understood far too much to be comfortable, Evan said, "When I asked what you wanted, I actually meant that. What reward did you seek that you would help in my rescue? I am everything you yearn to hate."

A shudder passed through the islander. "Yes," he breathed. "I hate kings. I don't care if they burn." There was no reaction to his statement. Not yet able to surrender, he pushed harder. "I *want* them to burn."

Still, Evan's understanding gaze betrayed no wrath.

Arnacin was forced to sigh. "But you don't act like one, and until that faith is broken, I can only treat you like a person."

"And if that faith were ever broken?" Just the slightest note of trepidation entered Evan's tone.

"It depends on how much I cared previously. Assuming I cared at all, I would at first hate you. In a few hours, that hatred would take turns with heartache. Within a couple of years, I wouldn't give it any more thought. At least, most of the time."

"You speak from experience."

"That is for me to know."

Laughter returned to the depths of Evan's eyes. "Why? Do you have something to hide?"

"I hide everything. But if you're asking if I care to lie, no. There are only two understandable reasons to lie. The first is to protect someone in terrible danger. The second is if you are ashamed of your thoughts. I am never ashamed of my thoughts—" He paused and then had to nod. "Until later, or sooner, or..."

As the islander quickly compressed his lips, Evan laughed. It was a weak sound, quickly turning into an even weaker cough, but it was laughter.

"You should sleep," Arnacin muttered as he stood.

Whether due to frailness or a lack of pride, Evan immediately shifted beneath his covers and closed his eyes. With one last appraisal, the islander slipped off.

Evan lacked the patience for his slow recovery, but finally, he was able to sit up for a couple of hours at a stretch before the world started to heat and sway. In those better periods, one of the boys would join him in a game; he would listen while Vilo and another islander, Wolflin, composed tunes to go with a piece of poetry the latter had written; or Lorene would lay Newton down between his legs.

Then the fevers left. He was still growing tired after long stretches of sitting or when someone helped him to his feet for a bit, but at least the temperatures and chills were gone. With that bit of improvement, it was time to start making plans again.

Evan called the enchantress over. "How long has it been, Lisya, since we returned?"

"Three weeks."

The prince studied her, fiddling with his fingers. Then he asked, "And how much of summer remains, if any? What does it look like outside the woods?"

"Golden." The enchantress settled herself on the bed. "Autumn has returned. The nights are cooler, the fields and trees are lit with color, and the sky is filled with the cries of migrating birds."

There was likely no one who could remain stony faced after hearing that description, particularly coming in the enchantress's voice. Evan knew he was smiling broadly. "You make it sound beautiful. I always just thought of autumn as the year's ending, before winter settles in."

Lisya's gaze dropped. "Yes," she sighed, "and so I am named."

"What do you mean?"

"In my language, the word for autumn also means death. I was born in the autumn, and so I was named. So I became."

Angrily, Evan took her hand. "You are not death, Lisya. Far from it."

With an ironic smile, the enchantress looked back up. "Yet, I was their death. I am the 'midnight glow,' the messenger long prophesied in my homeland to mark the end of their entire world."

"You *were* just the messenger."

Lisya laughed. "Thank you, Evan."

When she said no more, the prince asked, "Did the names of the other seasons also have other meanings?"

"Everything but summer. Winter is in stillness or wasteland, and spring is in life, but the closest thing to summer is in endurance. And that, only if you want to force it."

"Winter alone wins the title of endurance."

"In Elcan, nothing endures as much as winter, but it is not always so in other places."

"Was summer the longest season in your homeland?"

"Yes, and it was growing ever longer."

"How did it do that?"

The enchantress's smile was distant. "When I came to be, light and shadow shared everything so perfectly that you would consider the view alone magical. Every color shone. There were rich blues and greens, and the *moonlight*, Evan... I have never seen its equal."

"But then?"

"The land's very veins were magic, and such things so reflect the heart... The darker the heart became, the more the world died. Our home became oppressively hot every year. I was fifty the year we first had to struggle to breathe.

All the plants wilted long before autumn could kill anything. We made new plants, forged not from the world's veins but from ours. While the enchanter lived, so did his plants, but not even our commands could shorten the summer. When I left, only summer existed."

She smiled wanly. "Do you now wonder why I choose to keep my woods wintry?"

Chuckling, Evan shook his head.

For a long moment, they were silent. Then, as the enchantress stood, the prince asked, "How far away is Evfel?"

"A season's journey from here to its capital of Arieh, should you go by foot."

"Then we would need to leave now."

At his beaten tone, Lisya again sat down. "Before you decide anything, let me tell you something about that place.

"In Ansky, people have a freedom unimagined by those in Evfel, whose cities are crowded with the homeless and the criminals, while those who own homes also starve just to keep those roofs over their heads.

"The most prosperous in the cities are the *charities*, places like the orphanage that beats money out of their charges to give to the ruling class. In return, they are allowed to keep some and are granted a small amount of authority in the streets."

Again she stood. "You will find only two types of people in Evfel. Those who would betray instantly for a reward, and those who shrink in terror from everything."

As she left, Evan spotted Arnacin leaning against the wall, listening. The islander's eyes burned black.

Although uninvited, Arnacin followed Lazarus and Vilo into the back room with the enchantress. Behind him, he heard Valoretta's soft patter. Lisya only nodded to the foursome as she shut the door behind them.

"Evan will not be well enough in time," the enchantress said, turning to the fisherman. "Reluctantly, he has asked that you, Larry, lead the Isfullen to Evfel, with Vilo as your second."

"When are we to go?"

"Early tomorrow or you will never make it before winter is upon you."

Lazarus nodded, seemingly taking the news in stride. "Very well. How do we get there?"

Instead of answering, Lisya turned her attention to the floor. Hundreds of tiny trees sprang up, stretching from their feet across the floorboards, all covered in ice but only as high as their knees.

Valoretta gasped.

The enchantress cast her a soft smile before turning again to the others. "Westward you will travel from these woods until you reach the Sanguinea Gorge. That is the only way to Evfel without going through the mountains—a longer and much more treacherous route."

Following her words, the woods rushed past them to where a jagged crack split through the mountains. Wind moaned through it with a ghostly wail. Arnacin wondered just how tight and muggy the real gorge was.

As if echoing his horror, Lazarus whispered, "What does that mean, 'the Sanguinea Gorge'?"

"Although Evfel has long forgotten the old tongue of the original possessors of upper Evfel, it is the gorge 'where blood trickles down the walls.' Or, as the common folk of Ansky simply put it, 'the Bloody Gorge.'"

It was very easy for Arnacin to see those jagged outcroppings along the gorge dripping with blood. Without taking his eyes off the shimmering landscape at their feet, Arnacin saw both Lazarus and Vilo shift uncomfortably beside him.

Feeling Valoretta's shoulder touch his, he passed her a wicked grin, prompting her to find her courage.

"Why do they call it that?" Vilo spoke up. "I ask just to rid us of wild imagination."

"You may do better not to know," the enchantress warned. "Yet if you do so choose, the last battle to determine the boundaries of Evfel and Ansky took place inside this gorge long ago."

Watching the gorge now, somehow paralleling Lisya's words, Arnacin saw knights clashing together closer to Ansky's borders. With some relief, he noticed that six horses, if not more, could stand abreast from cliff wall to cliff wall.

"The ground served Ansky well at first as they forced Evfel deeper into the heart of the gorge. Yet they left the carnage of battle scattered from one end to the other, and neither kingdom could win. Then winter struck. In the cold, both sides withdrew slightly, occupying the gorge simply to deny their opponents entrance into each other's kingdoms. Still, they continued their bloody harassment. It kept them warm in the sharp wind, but within a short time, ice had filled the gorge. Whether that forced them into stillness and made them freeze to death or for some other reason, all anyone knows is that by the time either kingdom could send reinforcements with the thaw of spring, only the dead covered the gorge.

"Since then, no king, no matter how greedy, has ever dared try expanding his border through it again. Many still believe that to even try would bring the Watchers of the Gorge down on them, the spirits of the dead knights."

Lazarus was the first to break the silence. "Great. So what joyful trail do we follow from there?"

With a laugh, the enchantress said soothingly, "Fear not. Even should their superstition bear truth, no harm will come to those simply passing through." Again, the gorge shrank to a bird's-eye view, away from the winter scene of death and battle. "The gorge ends at the Elcan Woods, the largest forest known to those of either Ansky or Evfel. Once there, you will travel southwest, uphill, until you arrive at the summit, at Evfel's capital of Arieh."

At their feet rose the summit of the highest mountain in Evfel, where a massive castle loomed on its peak, separated from its city by a cleft in the mountaintop. Even with that security, the stronghold's outer walls were at the same angle as those of Castle Ansky. The city itself was only accessible by a single trail clinging to the western cliff before it branched off into many roads lower down the mountainside.

Turning quickly to the enchantress in disgust at the Evfelians precautions and skill in so doing, Arnacin asked, "Why would that need to be our destination? Would not a more accessible city suffice?"

"Suffice for what cause, Arnacin?" Lisya asked. "To make trouble for Evfel, yes, I should say any city would suffice. But to strike at the very heart of Evfel and the Dalacorts' might, is it not necessary to aim for the seat of power?"

"No one could attack that castle without wings."

"Castle Dalacort prides itself on its invincibility, yet are not words more powerful than the sword?"

"If one desires to charm them into crumbling from the inside, the snake would just as well lie in a more accessible city and poison another noble house first."

With a smile, Lisya asked, "Do you wish to go? Doubtless, you could work in the more accessible areas first."

"This is not my war."

Although the enchantress looked down at the shimmering map, which vanished then, Arnacin suspected laughter was dancing in her eyes at his insistence. However, none showed when she returned his gaze. All she said was, "I believe others will have more effect in Arieh itself. Revolt is already strong there—the banner of all Evfel's tyranny. With that platform on which to stand, perhaps this war need not continue too long."

The first step—agreeing to go—was the easy part. Then came the planning, the preparation, and the debate.

In Lisya's cottage, Lazarus and Vilo had shifted a bench from beside the table to Evan's bed and sat on it. While they discussed plans, others came by to listen and offer their own thoughts on the matter.

Obviously still too sick for the process, Evan slid deeper beneath his blankets and dropped his arm across his face. "Forget it, Lazarus. I'm sorry. The journey is too long. Winter's blizzards come much faster here in Elcan than even on your island."

"Shh." Lazarus lay a hand on the prince's shoulder. "The idea is good, and there may not be another chance."

"If you are that concerned about the time, Evan," Vilo commented, "we could ask Brimstone if he and his herd will take us as far as the gorge entrance."

The prince lifted his arm to raise his eyebrows at the minstrel. "You want to take a mounted force across the valley unseen?"

Vilo shrugged. "I didn't say it was a good idea, just that we could."

Passing by at that moment, Tevin stopped with one of his cheeky grins. "Who said anything about a force? We could go a few horses at a time."

"You risk an ambush or blockade if you try to go in small groups. Someone is eventually going to notice the activity from here before everybody makes it into the gorge." The words came from Arnacin, sitting on the floor at the foot of the bed, playing with a top for Tenacius's benefit. His son's bright blue eyes stared at the whirling toy while he lay on the woolly green cloak spread out beneath them. "It would be better for you to make one trip if you are going to ask Brimstone's herd to take all of you that far."

Tevin shrugged. "Well, I have a different issue anyway. Michael is fully ready to title us all, 'the Isfullen.' I'm an islander and don't belong to the Ice Woods to be called an Isfullen."

Vilo groaned softly. "I don't care if we're called 'Drowsy Quaffs.' It won't make any difference if we can't remove Wilber from Ansky." He shot Lazarus a glare as the fisherman laughed aloud.

Coughing, Evan shook his head. "We might as well be an Isfullen, Tevin. It is a banner we can all fall under that will make enough sense to Wilber's side that they may refrain from branding us instead 'Maxwell's Witches' or some other such slur on our connection with Lisya."

"I still don't think much of the Isfullen as our collective name," Tevin mumbled, crossing his arms.

Whacking him aside, Vilo ordered, "Shoo, you're tiring him out. We're Isfullen, and that's that."

As Evan pulled the covers over his head, probably to hide his smile, Tevin obediently went back to whatever it was he had been doing.

Lazarus sighed. "Well, Max? It's your choice in the end whether we travel to the gorge on foot or by horseback. The tall grass will probably shield us a little if we go on foot and give the fortress a wide berth, but then we risk winter catching us."

Evan flung the blanket back off his head. "No, if I am not to go, the choice is for the two of you—and if not you, Brimstone. He has to agree to endanger his herd if you decide that is necessary. And..." His frustrated tone hissed out as all the remaining color drained from his face. "You need to decide the rest. Lisya refuses to let me go."

Smiling sadly, Vilo shrugged. "Well, there's no use arguing with her. She knows things none of us could comprehend."

Yet Lazarus sat silently, stroking his whiskery chin. At last, he nodded, as one coming to a decision. "I'll ask Brimstone how far he'll go before settling on a plan."

With that, he lightly flicked the edge of the cover back over Evan's head. "Now sleep. You need it." No one debated with him as he turned for the door and stepped outside.

Brimstone was not comfortable risking that the herd might be cut off from returning to the woods by Fortress Tyhoronous should they be noticed, and so the choice was made. As the only Evfelian, Malachi volunteered to go with the traveling Isfullen. James and Thomas instantly did the same. To Arnacin's amazement, Lisya did not refuse them, instead sending them to bed with the rest of those following Lazarus the next day.

Once they were asleep, the enchantress swept Arnacin and the women into helping pack for the journey. The islander had not volunteered to go, and no one thought he would. Despite his reluctance, remaining behind was a clear sign he was no longer part of the group.

At the moment, that sense just left him feeling drained, but not upset. After all, he had already known the fact. He might like to deny it, but he would never again truly be an islander.

As Lisya passed him what looked like dried meat to wrap, he paused. "You don't serve meat here."

The enchantress smiled, taking the strips back and rolling them in cloth herself. "Who said anything about meat?"

"Then what is that?"

"My version of it. They will need it." She pushed a bucket closer to him that was filled with more of whatever it was and tied off her first bundle, setting it on the table before them.

Sighing, Arnacin lent his help. The enchantress returned to her pot and the food bubbling in it for the journey.

For just a moment, the islander paused, regarding her again—the enchantress named after autumn and death. Resuming his task, he said, "I agree with Evan Maxwell when it comes to this season."

"Indeed." Lisya continued crumbling herbs into the broth, but her silence was somehow inviting a response.

"Autumn is nothing if not death's companion. Everything withers, crumbles and then turns to dust. Even the grass browns and dries, until the wind, hoping to revive it, breaks the thin strands left and sends them tumbling away over the lifeless land. As autumn gives way to winter, it moans over the unrepeatable past."

Lisya only smiled. "Your talent for speech, Arnacin, could rival the greatest manipulators of my kind." Those wise and gentle eyes seemed to pierce him. "Now, you must learn to use it in the correct way, to bring not guilt and despair, but life. Autumn is also made by the only Creator."

"Yes," Arnacin growled, leaving to fetch the blankets Carrie had stacked for packing. "The only honest thing He made."

When he returned, the enchantress changed the topic. "Have you decided whether you wish to go with the Isfullen or stay?"

"This is not my war, Lisya. I've already aided more than I thought I would." Arnacin paused, methodically folding one of the blankets. As he set it aside, he relented. "Yet I know I must go this time, regardless of what I feel. They're my home, my family." His gaze flickered over the sleeping forms about the floor and beds. "If they wish to support their king in life and death, I have no choice but to support him also, or betray that last spark of meaning in existence."

Patting his shoulder, Lisya advised, "Then go rest. Light and harshness shall come all too soon, I fear."

As if hearing her, Carrie joined them to take over Arnacin's job. But before leaving, the islander inquired, "It has been on my mind, Lisya. Is not Lorene afraid for Newton, should Evan Maxwell win Evfel?"

"Lorene has come to trust her brother's son. At great risk, he gave the whole family, including Wilber, the chance to leave in peace. He is certain to grant life and more to his innocent—and sure to be faithful—cousin."

"What if he's not faithful?"

The challenge was plain, yet the enchantress only said, "You knew the mercy that would be offered before you asked about Lorene."

With a nod, Arnacin retreated.

Standing out in the yard among the horses as farewells were made, Valoretta and Arnacin watched as Evan embraced each traveler. The fevered flush had returned to his cheeks.

"He's been on his feet since we woke for breakfast," the Miran whispered. "And now he's in this cold. He'll likely be sick again tomorrow, not just weak. I can't blame him for feeling guilty about staying behind, though." Darkfire must have thought similarly about the prince's frailty. While the other steeds milled around the edges of the yard, waiting to escort the three hundred ninety-eight travelers outside the woods, the great stallion trailed his chosen master at a respectful distance.

Arnacin said nothing regarding Evan's health, or lack of it, his attention caught by the sight of Malachi. The boy was trembling, clinging to Lisya as she bid him farewell. She gently took his right hand, brushing her finger over his thumb. For a minute, light sparked from it, then it faded. The boy looked a little stronger, however.

Valoretta sighed, "I know they need you to go, Arnacin, so I won't say anything. I wish I could go as well."

"Tenacius would not make the freezing journey."

The Miran nodded. Finally looking up, she whispered, "Promise you'll keep your compass close."

There it was, the significance of the compass. "Just because you gave it to me?"

"Yes." She blushed. "Your mother wears a polished wooden ring. She told me it represents her marriage. That is what the compass means to me. It was my promise to you, long before I thought that possible." She quickly glanced away. "I suppose you'll leave it here now that I told you what it symbolizes to me."

Gently, Arnacin turned her toward him. "I promise, if circumstances force me to remove it, I'll find a way to send it back to you."

Valoretta studied him quietly, her eyes guarded. Slowly, he leaned in to kiss her. But, losing his courage, he pecked her on the cheek instead. "I don't intend for you to raise Tenacius alone, I promise."

A movement beside him jerked Arnacin's attention back to the Isfullen. Raymond stood there with Evan. The prince's face was almost as white as the snow fluttering down, and he was trembling despite how well Lisya had bundled him up.

As Arnacin faced him warily, Evan slowly dropped to the ground, his strength fading. Behind them, Darkfire shifted as if holding back from insisting the prince go back inside, then and there. Raymond's lips were tightly compressed. "You're the last in line, Arnacin."

Sighing, the islander knelt beside the prince. "I don't want the island to claim a king, Evan. I never will." He paused, then dropped his gaze. "But what I've observed in you are all the makings of a great one. Keep that, and you will make a better leader than I ever could."

"I already know I will fail, Arnacin. I have failed. You could be just as good, or better. It really only matters on whom we rely."

The islander studied Evan. "How old are you, really? Sometimes you appear as knowledgeable as an old man, and then you are as innocent as a small child."

When the prince did not answer, the islander pressed him further. "Twenty-what?"

Laughing, Evan said, "I wish I *was* a small child instead of the unwilling thief of Alexander's birthright." With that, he wrapped his arms around Arnacin, who tensed like a bow. The islander could not find it in himself to pull away, however.

As Darkfire came forward to support Evan, the islander joined those climbing onto horseback. Brimstone took the lead with Lazarus atop him. Watching over his shoulder as the small group huddled in the doorway, Arnacin returned Valoretta's nod of farewell.

Chapter 7

Into the Bloody Gorge

THE ISFULLEN AGAIN CREPT OUT of the Ice Woods through a temporary path created by Lisya to hide their exit. Once on firm ground, they tumbled off the horses and threw their packs over their shoulders, waving goodbye to the herd and setting off to the southwest. The autumn days were still comfortably warm, and the few trees they passed were mostly green.

While Michael kept watch from above, Arnacin urged Lazarus to push them at a harsh march through the first night and into the next day. But as the pre-dawn glowed against the sky, James snapped, "We have to stop! Malachi will not make it!"

"The valley is a dangerous place to stay for any amount of time," Arnacin insisted. Yet, as he looked at the smallest boy, leaning on James's arm, he shook his head. "Bringing children on such a trek," he grumbled. But still, he knelt down so Malachi could clamber onto his back.

"I think we all need the break, Arnacin," Lazarus said as they again set off.

"Tonight, we'll stop." Arnacin hoisted Malachi a little higher. "I fear resting while the valley's awake."

Beside him, Raymond was smiling, watching his friend's care for the boy.

"Malachi," Arnacin growled, "If that grin grows any larger, hit him for me."

The boy laughed, but otherwise made no comment.

Arnacin refused to admit it, but he felt relief when they stopped that night. Malachi was already asleep, his weight hanging from the islander's shoulders. Even thirteen-year-old James had ridden for the past three hours, while his twin brother had insisted he was fine and stumbled along, almost blindly.

No fires were lit—most of the islanders fell instantly asleep as soon as they touched ground. Taking a spot beside Raymond, Arnacin pushed his palm against his right shoulder, burning from his old injury.

The stars directly above twinkled as Michael's black form swooped across them. Raymond shifted in the grass. "Ironic, isn't it?" he whispered. "You married the woman of your mother's imagination."

"What?" Arnacin asked in surprise.

"She told me she had imagined a daughter with auburn hair and sky-blue eyes." Raymond's voice was tinged with a hint of laughter. "Little did she know she was imagining her daughter-in-law."

"Why would she ever imagine that? Our family has always had black hair."

That shadowed head finally turned. "She was one of Lisya's closest friends and pictured a daughter looking like her. The enchantress's hair was that color—all the colors of the autumn trees."

"Yes," Arnacin whispered. "Did you know she was named after this season?"

"No. Why are you asking?"

"You said her hair had all the colors of the autumn trees."

Raymond rolled onto his side and rested his head on his hand. "How would you describe that color?"

"Yellow-red."

"No, really. If it were Valoretta, what would you say?"

Arnacin sighed, watching Michael's wings flicker over the sky. "The stars are brighter at sea," he finally commented.

There was no answer, yet Arnacin had the feeling his friend was studying him in the darkness. Finally, Raymond whispered, "Arnacin, may I ask—"

"No."

Yet Raymond pressed forward anyway. "Why couldn't you wait to marry Valoretta? Did she rid you that much of love for your family? We would've liked nothing better than to support you." When Arnacin continued to stare up at the sky, he added, "What's worse is that I don't see any evidence for that story. Sometimes, it seems like you two are not even aware you're married, if that makes any sense. I'm not asking to pry, really. I'm just concerned." He looked down, pulling blades of grass apart. "And hurt."

Arnacin closed his eyes. For just a moment, he considered revealing the truth. But the moment slipped by. Not even he or Valoretta knew what had happened when they were prisoners in the dungeon of the Eyrie. Everyone would look on their tale as a lie. By all rights, it had to be. Tenacius could not be his. Yet there was no other explanation for their similarities, either.

Finally, he whispered, "If you wish to help, Raymond, go to sleep. We need to leave this valley."

After three days, the Isfullen had reached the opening to the Sanguinea Gorge without incident. The crack was only a dark shadow in the rock wall, slowly enlarging into the gorge itself as they approached. High above them, the mountain sides glowered.

Bringing up the rear of the group, Raymond followed Thomas into the opening. Yet, he paused just inside. Arnacin was no longer beside him. Turning, he spotted the other islander twenty feet back, still and colorless. As their gazes met, Arnacin's expression closed and he strode past into the gorge, head lowered.

Silently, Raymond resumed his pace. The ground beneath their feet turned rocky, with patches of wispy grass poking up around them. With the walls pressed so close, the sound of the group's whispering echoed around them and the lack of conversation became oppressive.

It was Arnacin who had always been the talker. Not anymore. He was now stone silent.

After a while, however, Raymond asked, "I imagine the storms were much larger on the ocean, when they happened. Were they frightening?"

Arnacin turned to him, but there was no comprehension in his gaze. If he was the same as he had once been, then Raymond would have thought he was just refusing to acknowledge his fear.

Lightly, the hunter punched his friend in the arm. "Prideful pup, you know what I'm asking."

"Pup!" Arnacin protested, yet the laughter that had been missing since their meeting in Lisya's cottage bubbled in his voice. "I'm anything but a puppy!"

"All right, piglet or ch—"

"Hurry up, you two!" Lazarus called out. "We need to make it *before* winter!"

"We'll just settle down in the closest city," Arnacin muttered, his laughter gone, the window closed.

Sighing, Raymond scuffed his feet through the dust and dirt powdering the ground. "I'm glad there are some things that have remained the same about you, even if it is your pride."

Arnacin's lips twitched. "You may be eating those words. Remember how I could never be wrong?"

"I couldn't possibly forget. I credit any humility I possess to those fights."

Arnacin's smile dropped guiltily.

Determined not to let the conversation die, Raymond insisted, "I don't think you can talk about 'could never.' Your opinion seems just as strong when you come out with it, and you still can't even answer a simple question about storms."

The wry smile returned. "That's not due to pride. Honestly..." Distance grew in Arnacin's eyes; a distance Raymond had long associated with storytelling—the gaze that meant Arnacin was seeing things far beyond the physical world. This time, however, pain filled the edges of that expression. "I loved them. It was more like watching a volcano explode while at a safe distance..." He dropped off, as if noticing his friend's blank look. "Or a blizzard from inside your door, although that's a really poor example."

"Describe it then."

Sighing, Arnacin surrendered. "The waves seemed to tower higher than the peak of Castle Mound. Maybe they did. At their tops, they foamed in white, disturbed spray, much like a dragon would spew fire, only crystallized. And at night, the lightning would bring out veins of deep greens, dark blues and purples amid all the black for that brief second during which the bright flash of white lasted. Then the light would disappear, only to flash back. Others probably couldn't see it. There are people out there who are almost blind in the dark."

He paused his storytelling, the echoing sound of whispered conversation growing loud again in the silence. With a glance at Raymond, he continued, "And then there was the thunder. No one could hear anything, even if someone screamed directly in their ear. But some say they imagine hearing waves smack into the ship, even over the noise, as if trying to break it into a million pieces. I never did."

"Then you have never been afraid?"

Arnacin turned quickly away, yet Raymond had already glimpsed the answer in his eyes. Indeed, he had seen it before that moment. It had been there when Arnacin paused outside the gorge, and it lurked in the shadows when he looked at Evan.

Fear prowled like some great beast in the depths of his friend, almost old and comfortable where it lay controlled, scarred over and beaten—yet still alive. Although Arnacin guarded it like the rumored treasure in Castle Mound, Raymond wondered how many islanders failed to see that fear in their friend and how many, like himself, were waiting for it to emerge so they could help.

Certainly, something terrible had happened. Raymond wondered, at times, if Valoretta was involved.

As if reading his thoughts, Arnacin whispered, "I'm sorry, Raymond. I'm sorry I promised I'd tell you everything. It was the promise of a stupid child, dreaming of adventures. In reality, there are things I don't know if I can ever talk about, and others I never want the island to know."

"Perhaps you will find we already know those things," Raymond replied, equally softly. "Evil is not unique, Arnacin, and we will never be as innocent as you pretend." He paused, then added, "You've mistaken a joyful face and a caring soul for naivete."

Arnacin made no reply. Cautiously, Raymond slipped an arm across his friend's shoulders while they walked. It was not shrugged off.

The wind changed direction, now blowing straight down the gorge. In the freezing cold, Arnacin again insisted the Isfullen march through the night, yet the wind did not abate, yanking hoods off and hissing sharply past red ears. Before long, many of their party were too tired to continue.

"If we don't stop," Lazarus whispered as he and Vilo dropped back to walk by Arnacin, "I fear some will die. We can't keep up this march."

Shivering, Arnacin shook his head. "We can't stop until this wind stops or changes direction."

"If we rest during the day and all huddle together, we might make it," Vilo suggested, readjusting his instrument slung on his back. "Lisya packed wood. Hopefully, that will help. If we keep going like this, some of us might die while walking instead."

Arnacin laughed bitterly. "There's not a fire in existence this wind won't blow out."

"And there's no natural wood that comes out of the Ice Woods," Vilo said. "We don't know what this wood will do."

Vilo and Lazarus won. To Arnacin's surprise, the wood burned despite the wind. It was somewhat amusing to watch so many people bundling as close to it as they could. Strangely, the twins and Malachi hung in the background, balling their feet in their cloaks.

Joining them, Arnacin asked, "Are you not cold?"

"Of course not," Thomas insisted, although his twin jabbed him in the ribs.

"Lisya makes her cloaks warmer," James said. "They are more weatherproof, and others are likely colder than we."

"Michael is probably the least cold," Malachi muttered, shrinking into his cloak.

Arnacin looked up to where the eagle happily perched on the cliff above them, resting. "If you believe you're warm enough," the islander advised, "try to sleep."

"I am too cold to sleep," Malachi insisted, yawning all the same. "But I am too tired to keep moving."

Hesitating only a moment, Arnacin wrapped his arms around the boy. "Is that better?"

"Yes, thank you."

Tucking his nose into the warm cavity between his cloak and arm, Arnacin felt sleep briefly creep across him.

He awoke as a particularly strong blast of wind beat against his back. The noon sun dispersed all shadow from the gorge. Beyond where James and Thomas slept, doubling their cloaks around each other, the islanders huddled like a mound of crocodiles.

Malachi, however, was still awake, running his fingers against the side of his palm.

"What's wrong?" Arnacin asked.

"We're going back to Arieh," the boy whispered. "What if they recognize me?"

"Who?"

Sighing, Malachi looked up. "I was a kitchen boy in Castle Dalacort until they caught me stealing food." Arnacin said nothing, and the boy held up the hand he had been fingering. "They branded me a thief and told me they would hang me."

"But Lisya came?"

The boy nodded. "She just appeared in the cell. Then we were home, and even the brand was gone."

"How long ago did that happen?"

"I was seven. I am eleven now."

"Then don't worry about it. Boys change quickly in four years. I was full grown when I left my home, and they still didn't recognize me." Meeting Malachi's scared eyes, Arnacin added, "And they have so many thieves, they're never going to remember one from four years ago."

"You have never been to Evfel," Malachi muttered. Nevertheless, he relaxed. "You would not know how many thieves they had."

"By the time children have been driven to steal, a city is crawling with thieves."

Yet Malachi was already asleep.

As another gust of wind blew against him, the islander carefully tucked the boy into the folds of the twins' cloaks, adding yet another layer of warmth, and slipped off toward the fire.

The crocodile heap was not as tight as it appeared, but the fire had extinguished without the exhausted islanders watching it.

After gently shaking Raymond awake, Arnacin slipped away toward a crevice in the cliff. He heard his friend follow with a weary sigh.

The niche was slightly too tight for the two of them, but out of the wind, Arnacin could not care. He unintentionally jabbed Raymond several times while tucking his feet under the folds of combined cloaks. Only then did he cheekily glance upward. "Thanks."

Laughing slightly, Raymond shook his head, "You look cold enough to *be* frostbite."

"And soon, you'll look stiff enough to be a board."

They lapsed into silence, arms across their knees, staring out at the other islanders and at the dust swirling and scattering across the ground.

"What made you decide to help Evan?" Arnacin asked at last.

Raymond shrugged. "Lisya. And we shared a common goal, I guess. We both wanted Wilber off the island. But now, Evan is family. It would be like asking why we would help Lazarus."

"Family," Arnacin scoffed.

"Arnacin, he lived with us for a year."

"A year is hardly long enough to take in a king as family!"

Family! Family. Family... The word echoed off the gorge's high walls, stilling the two. It also wormed the guilt deeper into Arnacin that he was not being fair in his accusations against Evan, yet his fears and hurts could not allow otherwise.

As the sound trailed off, Raymond asked, "Outside of stolen independence, what is it about monarchs that sparks your hatred, Arnacin?"

Slowly, the islander exhaled. "All right, Evan is a decent person. No matter what anyone wants, they couldn't deny that. But even decent people deteriorate on a throne. Soon they are nothing but greedy, murderous beasts." Letting his chin rest on his arms, Arnacin avoided his friend's searching gaze.

Raymond did not probe too long before asking, "Were you told what happened to your siblings?"

The islander balled a little tighter, closing his eyes. He didn't know why Raymond had mentioned them and wasn't sure he wanted to know. But as the silence stretched on, Arnacin breathed, "William died of some unknown ailment..."

Raymond's gaze flicked downward, a little too quickly.

Ignoring that suspicious action for the present, the islander finished the thought. "And Charlotte died in battle."

"Then you know Charlotte would have been a 'greedy, murderous beast,' right?"

With a glare, Arnacin's head shot up.

Raymond sighed. "Did you know she would have become queen, were she still alive?"

"What are you talking about?"

"Oh, Arnacin." With those words of remorse, Raymond fell silent.

Seconds went by. At last, the hunter whispered, "Charlotte loved Evan. I couldn't say why. They had one argument, and the next thing any of us knew, she was slipping her hand into his."

"Not Charlotte—"

"Yes, Charlotte! The nymph who insisted she hated males. She followed Evan up to Castle Mound and purposely stepped in the way of the arrow that would have killed him."

Arnacin's face drained of color. Yet there was nothing to say. He'd once had a nightmare in which Charlotte was in love with a conquering king. Now it snickered in the back of his mind. Withdrawing from the conversation, he shoved his nose into his folded arms.

Raymond paid no attention to this response. "The truth is, she saw something in Evan that none of us wanted to accept. No, he's not perfect, but if you can look into those eyes full of love, compassion and even stubbornness and tell me he will change because of a throne, you might as well condemn your sister now."

"She died long before any such thing was possible," the islander muttered. "You have no right—"

"I loved Charlotte, Arnacin!" Raymond's grief sounded in his voice. "I loved her, and I spent months hating Evan because of her—months trying to keep it secret, because I had no doubt how wrong I was.

"You can accuse away, or say she wasn't really in love with him. Honestly, it was still too early for that. She wasn't 'in love.' But she loved him, and we all knew that if she lived, it would not be long before she *was* in love." Raymond's voice softened, beaten. "And Evan would love her in return. She would have been queen."

Arnacin could not look up, could not bear to see the expression on Raymond's face. Instead, he growled, "You can't turn a wood nymph into a queen."

"Can you turn a master horseman into a king? Evan's equally wild."

For just a moment, Arnacin had no response, but then he looked up defiantly.

Raymond was watching him. Before Arnacin could argue, the hunter blurted out, "I can tell you he wasn't. Whatever you're about to say, he wasn't trained for kingship. Evan's not the heir of Ansky by birth—"

"Alexander," Arnacin breathed, now understanding Evan's jest about being a thief on the day of their departure.

"Alexander, who died by plague. Being only four, Evan wasn't trained for kingship before his brother's death. Nor did Wilber train him after it, except a small bit to hide the fact he himself was after Ansky's throne."

In a gentle tone, he continued, "Have you noticed Larry calls him Max? Obviously, it's short for Maxwell, but that's just it. That was the name he gave when he first arrived on the island, trying to keep his identity secret. Evan can't act to save his life, so there's no use trying to use the political training argument."

Arnacin simply buried his nose once again.

Raymond sighed. "Yes, he's still a mortal being. He will be the first to admit he's acted selfishly many times, but he's not too proud to confess. He's too wise to fear retaliation for doing right, and… he cares too much to fail as thoroughly as you claim every monarch does."

There was no argument left. Not now anyway. They fell into silence, each left to their own thoughts. At last, Arnacin softly asked, "Did you ever tell her how you felt? Charlotte, I mean?"

"Yes. Long before Evan came, I asked her to marry me," Raymond whispered. "She refused."

After a miserable week while the Isfullen made their way through the gorge, sleeping only in the noon hours and traveling during the frigid night, the passage in the mountains opened in the distance. Red and gold trees filled the space beyond.

"The Elcan Woods," Vilo sighed in relief.

While many of the islanders seemed to relax under the clustered boughs, as if feeling a similarity to home, Arnacin was hauntingly reminded of other, more distant forests. Still, it provided some shelter from any sentry's eyes and the winter-like cold that swept through the gorge.

Since he was no longer needed in the air, Michael joined them, and as he changed form, he yanked his reddish cloak back into place. "Finally. I'm so sick of wings, I could—"

"Careful, Michael," Arnacin warned. "Your complaints might earn you a pummeling from at least three boys. Although Thomas won't have any excuse for it. He insists he wasn't cold."

Folding his arms, the red-haired boy scoffed, "You can't make me say I enjoy being an eagle."

"But you just did," Tevin laughed, lengthening his stride to join them. "You just said, 'I enjoy being an eagle.'"

"I said the opposite."

"No, the last five words of your sentence: I enjoy being an eagle."

Michael's eyes flashed. Laughing, Arnacin tugged him away. "Don't let Tevin irk you. He delights in doing so."

It was not long, however, before the woods thickened and traveling became ever more difficult despite the warmer temperature. In the lead, Lazarus called out, "We must have taken a wrong turn. Evfel can't use this part of the woods."

"We took what we thought was the most southwesterly trail from the gorge," Raymond mumbled beside Arnacin, trying to pull his cloak free from a thorn bush. "If it was actually a trail, it wouldn't look like this."

"Well, after four hundred of us break through, there *will* be a trail," Arnacin said. "And in the meantime, no one could possibly stumble across us."

"Oh," Tevin huffed, finally ripping himself free and bumping into Raymond with a resentful apology. "Somehow, that's not comforting."

With a smile, Arnacin glanced over to where Michael had again taken eagle form, now sitting on a branch while the Isfullen struggled to find a clear path. Other islanders gave the enchanter dirty looks as they freed themselves and pushed forward.

They trudged along for what felt like hours, without much progress. Arnacin could still see the same trees as when they entered the dense part of the forest. The passage of time was only marked by how spread out they had become. Some men had found an easier path and were much farther ahead, although they had encountered more overgrowth to slow them down again. Others were far to the right, attempting to use the course of a stream to press onward. The rest were scattered in groups throughout the woods, while Michael watched from the trees above.

A horrified cry came from those to the right.

Michael swooped around to find ten islanders stuck in what looked like mud. Every attempt to lift their feet only sank them a little farther into the grime. As they pulled with all their might, every muscle aquiver, the tension around them increased.

A few people reached out to try to pull their friends to safety. Instead, their feet slipped into the soft ground, and they couldn't lift them again. Their panicked shouts filled the air.

Quicksand!

Even Arnacin had never encountered any. Had it not been for the extensive writings he'd read in Mira's library, he would not have that word silently resounding in his mind now. Yet, with the panic around him, no one would hear his warning even if he gave one.

Instead, some islanders were dashing away from the floundering group. They did not make it more than six paces before lurching to a stop—their feet also stuck. They were surrounded by mires.

Arnacin acted. Drawing on the cold authority of the dreaded Black Captain, with which he had stilled hundreds of pirates, he commanded, "Leave them!"

Shocked stares turned toward him. Those nearest him took several steps back. Silence fell, but all had stopped moving.

Some gazes were empty, others filled with horror—the horror of one confronted with a murderer. One of the slowly sinking islanders, Wolflin by name, dared to spit in response, yet Arnacin met that anger, as he did all their reactions, with the same unrelenting coldness with which he had faced many before, the same coldness that caused flames to dance in Darkfire's eyes.

He did not know how long he held their frozen attention, never shifting for fear of breaking that spell—the only thing standing between them and complete chaos. While he kept them captivated, Michael quietly left and returned with strong vines.

Only when all the victims were free, temporarily in the safety of the trees above, did the islander release his command. Thankfully, their stillness had guaranteed not a single one died.

An explosion of angry accusations burst around him. "Who are you? What type of killer have you turned into? Were you going to let them die? Murderer! Do you not care at all?"

As those words smashed into some deep interior wall, Arnacin felt something splinter as he recognized Tevin among his accusers. "Of course I don't care!" Despite his fury, he could not deny the tears rushing down his cheeks, loosed from the dam he had built stone by stone after Mira. "Turn back time! Try to rescue them! Kill yourselves! I won't care!"

As if from a distance, he felt strong, gentle arms wrap around him, yet he was far too weak to push them away. "Shh, Arnacin," Lazarus's deep voice whispered. "We all know that's not true. You saved us in the only way you knew how."

"We're dead anyway! We're all but surrounded by this!" Arnacin railed.

A sigh seemed to pass through Lazarus's arms. "Michael," he softly commanded; by the volume of his voice, the enchantress's son must have stood nearby. "Find us a firm road, even if you must take us back to the gorge itself."

Another pair of arms briefly wrapped themselves around Arnacin, yet he felt them grow ever smaller and downier. Then, with a snap of wind beneath wings, they vanished. He did not bother to move or look as his own pain slowly dissipated into extreme exhaustion.

Back in the Ice Woods, Valoretta watched in thoughtful silence as Evan and Carrie cooked dinner. The prince was trying to tease words from the enchantress's daughter as he repeatedly passed her the wrong spice to add.

"You know, if you actually said what you wanted, I would not be confused." Evan threw up his hands as Carrie replaced the jar he had passed her. All he received was a stubborn grin.

Valoretta smiled grimly as she turned back to the silk standard she was helping Lisya sew between the double layers of Carrie's blue cloak. Had it been another time and place, had she not married Arnacin, she would have instantly liked Evan Maxwell as both a person and a king. However, she could not shake off her fear of what might happen should Arnacin be forced beneath anyone's rule.

Her gaze flicked across to Lisya. The enchantress had stopped sewing. No lights danced in those pale eyes; they were simply vacant windows. Not a breath stirred the enchantress's chest. Yet her fingers were perfectly curved around the needle, both hands still elevated around the cloak hem, her head tilted slightly. She seemed like a statue, or as if she were dead.

"Carrie," Valoretta squeaked. "Carrie!"

Every head turned toward her. Then Carrie sighed. Resting her stirring spoon on the pot's rim, she stepped over and placed a hand on her mother's shoulder. "Come back," she whispered.

As if those words were a magical order, Lisya shuddered. Instead of gaining color, her face whitened and her gaze swept the people standing about her before landing on Evan.

When she did not speak, the prince held out his hand. "What is it?"

Accepting his grasp, Lisya squeezed it as if it were a lifeline. "I am reminded again that I am not omniscient."

"What happened?"

The enchantress's gaze dropped. "Bogs."

As Evan glanced in confusion at those around him, Lorene gasped, "Did you not tell them?"

"I travel *over* the Elcan Woods, never through."

Valoretta's heart stilled. "They fell into bogs?"

Lisya's piercing gaze turned to her. "The victims were saved, but I fear the cost."

"What cost?" Valoretta was not sure if she said those words, or if Talliaha had. But Lisya shook her head.

A long silence filled the room. Then Evan was gently pulling the enchantress to her feet. "You did not know, Lisya." He smiled reassuringly. "And dinner is just about ready."

The Isfullen risked small fires and food only once they had put several miles between themselves and the bogs. When they camped for the night, a whole fire was left to Arnacin. Lazarus and Raymond were the only two willing to keep their silent friend company.

None of the three said a word, however. After their light meal, Lazarus dug out a knife and began whittling a stick. Raymond fiddled with the leaves about him, as Arnacin stared motionlessly into the flames.

As the voices from other fires quieted, Arnacin muttered a "good night" and curled up beneath his cloak. For a long time afterward, firelight sparkled in his friend's glassy eyes whenever Raymond glanced up. But, at last, those dark lashes closed.

It was impossible to hear Arnacin's breathing over the distant snores of others, the pop of fire, and the patter of falling leaves. Raymond waited some moments before softly breaking the silence. "Lazarus? Will Arnacin be alright?"

Glancing at the islander's still form, Lazarus shrugged. "I see no reason for this to mar him permanently. The rest will soon recover from their shock and recognize what he did."

Ripping more leaves, Raymond whispered, "I'm not talking about today. Arnacin *is* marred, Larry. The only difference about today was that... the crab decided to dig out of the sand. Do you think he'll ever recover from whatever happened out there?" In a beaten breath, he finished, "Or if he'll ever recover his compassion, at least?"

For a long moment, Lazarus remained silent. Finally, he asked, "Why do you think he's missing it?"

"Can you tell me you don't?"

"I don't know, Raymond." The fisherman sighed. "Real love runs deep in that family. And considering what he's done since returning, I don't think it's all dead. Even a spark can heal the rest, with time."

"But it can't heal if he continues stuffing it away. The difference is frightening, Lazarus. There wasn't a boy his age who cared more about helping others..." He trailed off. Smiling slightly, he added, "Or who was as proudly self-righteous about it, either. It's all gone."

"Well, I don't think you can complain if he's not the self-righteous boy he was."

Meeting the fisherman's fond smile, Raymond shook his head. "Lazarus, don't joke. I know he'll never be the boy he was, and no one even wants him to be. But how can we help him be who he's *meant* to be?"

"Raymond, I don't think any person can help another be who they're meant to be. But simple healing, patience, love and support can accomplish wonders. I have a feeling that whatever Arnacin witnessed was anything but that."

"Even considering that he married someone?"

"You keep asking me questions just to see if I have the same answers as you. Valoretta seems to be a wonderful girl, too wonderful to be conniving. My guess is that whatever happened, it was before he met her. By herself, I doubt she could bring the healing he needs."

Laughing slightly, Raymond said, "How easily Arnacin would label you naive... You do it purposely, don't you?"

"You would be labeled that as well, Raymond, if you'd stop worrying over things. It's in the best hands there are. Leave it there. Arnacin, heartless or not, will heal."

Over the next few days, Michael led the Isfullen across safe paths. As they continued south, the ground slowly rose, and the temperature dropped just as steadily.

Wishing Elcan was not the half-frozen place it was, Arnacin pulled his thin cloak tighter and trudged forward, now banished to the rear of the group through unspoken agreement. It seemed everyone except Raymond picked up their pace if he drew level with them.

Even their hunter had fallen silent, however, and Arnacin spent those days wrapped in his own seclusion.

But then, a week after the bogs, Tevin dropped back beside Raymond and Arnacin. Although the hunter nodded a greeting, it was some time before Tevin sighed. "Arnacin," he mumbled. "I'm sorry. I didn't mean what I said back there... I mean, not everything."

Unable to control his dark smile, Arnacin nodded. "Just most."

Raymond's eyebrows rose, but he remained silent, his gaze still on the muddy path those in front were breaking for them.

Tevin shrugged uncomfortably. "I was just... I've never seen anyone... Well, you know what I mean. I don't think anyone actually believes you're the wretch I charged you with being." He coughed. "Except perhaps those who were stuck. I heard Wolflin accuse you of betraying them, as a matter of fact."

Raymond sighed. "Do you ever know when to stop talking?"

Tevin's lips compressed, but Arnacin smiled slightly. Raymond might moan about Tevin's lack of control, but honesty was honesty, and it was a quality in need of more praise.

Patting Tevin on the shoulder, Arnacin increased his pace.

He found the brown-haired Wolflin to the middle-left of the Isfullen. There, he matched the man's pace and waited.

Although Wolflin threw the islander a glare, he did nothing to move away. Instead, his gaze wandered over Arnacin appraisingly. At last, he growled, "I suppose you want a confession. Yes, I know you were simply controlling a panicked crowd. Now, scram. I'm not about to listen to all the reasons you didn't have a choice."

"I had no intention of listing them. And no, I don't want a confession." Arnacin paused, just briefly. "Tevin told me what you said. I thought I should let you know, I agree. At the very least, I've betrayed... what I should have been."

"Tuh," Wolflin snorted.

"I should have done something else. I was too afraid to try." A grim smile crossed Arnacin's face. "And there's only so long one can hide the fact he's a monster."

Wolflin glanced at him, then huffed. "A panicked crowd is the worst type to control. There's no predicting what they'll do. You probably did the only logical thing." His expression soured. "There, I've said it. You tricked it out of me. Now go."

"I didn't want your acknowledgment," Arnacin growled. "I was trying to be honest, since I figured you deserved it." When there was no answer, he warned, "Eat those words before I ram them back down your throat."

Wolflin laughed, a strange sound breaking into the islander's anger. "You need to work on your stoniness, but I am impressed with your ability to lead. Mix some compassion into your hard shell, and men will follow you anywhere."

Those words spiked Arnacin with ice. Had he not done just that on Mira? Had Arnacin of Enchantress Island not died because of it? His chin rose as if against an accusation. "I will cling to my stoniness if it prevents me from being harassed into leading."

Wolflin shrugged. "Did you go to sea to learn how to command?" When Arnacin snorted in response, he murmured, "Regardless, you obviously did learn. No one who has not led large groups of men would be able to do as you did the other day."

"Exactly. Speaking from experience, no one in their right mind would want to lead."

"I think you would be throwing away the very path for which you were born, should you not."

"That's a wild idea."

Again, Wolflin chuckled. "I confess, I don't have much authority to know. You aren't someone I remember well from the island. I live on the west side, although undoubtedly we must have passed each other during the solstice festival. However, I am familiar with your family—the enchantress's friends. In fact… Well, let's just say your forefather, Yulcer, has become a local legend. Foolish, but a hero."

He smiled. "One story is that, as a young man, he was dared to kill a giant snake that had crawled down from Castle Mound. And, for pride's sake, he did it with his bare hands."

Arnacin gave him a long look, and Wolflin laughed again. "Yulcer is your great-grandfather, correct?"

"My grandfather, and I never knew a humbler man."

"Ah… That just goes to show how maturity can change people. Look at him or your father, who might not have been legendary, but was still a leader to those around him. And Lazarus, for that matter. They're leaders worth emulating, even if you are called to something more difficult."

Arnacin's gaze traveled ahead to where Lazarus was crunching along. He breathed, "I am not capable of emulating them. They are of a different world, trained for a higher leadership—the leadership of souls, never the leadership of four hundred troops."

That night, Arnacin heard the peaceful sound of contented sleepers all huddled together. But despite being snuggled beside them, he could not feel warm, could not stop trembling.

His clothes were thinner than those of the rest, and he knew movement was probably the only antidote for the cold.

Still, his body's warmth, whether he felt it or not, helped protect those next to him from freezing. Even after death, it would be some time before that heat left. With that thought encouraging him, he stayed where he lay.

Then, it seemed heat rose up his extremities and back. Alarm rang in his mind, yelled at him to move. He told himself it mattered little.

Slowly, sleep stole over him.

Chapter 8

Arieh

From the darkness, Arnacin sensed the cold return. Yet it felt both icy and hot, as if he was two separate entities. He jerked, choking, as something warm trickled down his throat. Fingers clamped onto his shoulder, supporting him until his breath returned.

He looked up into copper eyes. His head was in the crook of Michael's arm, the reddish folds of the boy's cloak wrapped around him.

"What I must put up with," Michael growled. "You've been a dead weight on my arm for the past ten minutes. Now quit shivering piteously and finish this."

He held a mug in his free hand, the rim of which he again placed against Arnacin's mouth. Warm broth slid down the islander's throat, and he could not find the will or strength to resist.

The pale light of dawn gradually roused Arnacin. Then he snapped awake. His arms were pinned!

His own cloak as well as another, a thick reddish one, and two blankets were wrapped about him as he would bundle

Tenacius in the cradleboard. Even his nose was covered by the folds of Michael's cloak.

His slow success in wriggling free woke those next to him and brought Michael back over. "Oh, you survived, did you?" the boy growled. "Had to make us suffer."

"Michael," Arnacin moaned. "Stop complaining. And next time, don't try to mummify me. I'm not dead yet." Shaking the last of the wrappings off, he pulled the red cloak from the bundle of cloth.

"I have no idea what 'mummify' means," Michael said, making no movement to take the proffered cloak. "You can keep that old thing. I hate it."

"Liar."

Michael only crossed his arms. "It overheats me. My fiery red hair is enough of a source of warmth. Keep it. If you return it to me, I *will* bind you into it."

Arnacin could not refrain from laughing slightly. "You're such an actor." Yet Michael had won. Feeling some comfort, the islander threw the long cloak beneath his thin green one. Despite the temperature, the cloak provided a constant feeling of having sat by a fire for hours. It was, after all, made by the enchantress.

As he turned, he heard Raymond whisper, "Thanks, Michael."

Humph was the only sound the boy made.

Despite the cold rain later that day, the Isfullen pressed on, knowing they could not waste the light. Shoulders hunched against the rivulets pouring down his neck, Michael led them over the path he had found.

Arnacin guiltily tugged the red cloak tighter around himself. Unlike wool, the long fabric repelled water, even after hours of being wet. Its inside remained dry and warm. Nor did a single thorn or briar stick in the fabric.

Indeed, Lisya had made it.

When Michael brought them to the edge of the immense Elcan Woods on a clear sunny afternoon forty-five days after their departure from the cottage, many sighs of relief sounded in the sharp air around Arnacin. Grassy brown mountainsides rose to their left, away from the red leaves of the forest. A few fields and houses dotted the view above and below them.

"Evfel really is very scenic," Vilo said, nodding to himself. "Despite its tyranny."

Arnacin could not prevent himself from snorting, yet in the rustling of feet in the leaves, no one appeared to notice.

Squished next to Raymond by all those trying to glimpse the mountain hills, Tevin said, "I don't care what it looks like. I'll just be glad to leave these woods."

"That, we shouldn't do," Lazarus warned from the front of the group. "According to Lisya, Evfel has many more settlements than Ansky. Should we leave cover, we won't be able to remain unnoticed, and it is not safe for us to split up."

"Do the woods go that far south?" Raymond asked.

"They go until the last rise of Evfel, where Arieh sits," Michael said. "There is a river in our way, though, the Death Mirror, and the city, Grand-sire, commands the nearest bridge across it."

"At this rate," Arnacin muttered, "it'll be frozen over by the time we reach it."

He felt Thomas shudder beside him. "We will never reach it," the boy whispered. "Our *bodies* will be frozen before then."

A chuckle escaped Arnacin, but he said nothing.

Before them all, Michael turned back toward the woods. "Take one last look at the view, men. This is the last you will see it."

No one moved until James broke off to follow the young enchanter. "Come on," he sighed. "We need some optimism around here. Of course, we will see it again!"

"You're right," Raymond said, dropping his arm across James's shoulders. "We'll enjoy the view when we leave the woods to cross one of those bridges."

"Because the river will not be frozen, of course," Thomas sarcastically muttered under his breath. In response, Arnacin pushed him forward slightly.

After a moment's silence, except for shuffling feet and rustling leaves, something occurred to the islander. "Michael, do they keep a watch on those bridges?"

"Naturally." The boy's tone was ominously dark. "This is Evfel."

"We better wait until the river freezes so we can cross there, then."

"If we can't find a safe ford," Lazarus said, "we'll split up and cross the bridges in small groups." It seemed no one wanted to repeat the river's ominous name.

"Unless they have tolls," Arnacin reminded him.

"Lisya packed a little money. It won't go far, but it should cover this."

Yet even that assurance did not soothe Arnacin. "It's fake."

"Lisya made it!" Lazarus insisted. "It will be identical."

"Fine... But how long are you going to wait before another group goes over?"

"Arnacin!" Seeing the fisherman's obvious annoyance, the culprit could not control his grin. Everyone on the island knew it took talent to irk their Larry. "We're not there yet! The river and weather will dictate the answer when we arrive and not before."

As Raymond impishly caught his eye, Arnacin glanced away. "Come on, Arnacin," the hunter lightly chided. "At worst, you could find some way to bribe the guards, and we can all cross at once."

"Why me? Shouldn't that be Tevin's job? He's the jester."

"Hey!" Tevin protested. "I've grown up, unlike you boys!"

As Raymond laughed, Thomas asked Arnacin, "What is he implying? Are you not the same age?"

Arnacin shrugged. "He's married. On the island, that makes him a man, whereas a bachelor doesn't earn the title until the age of thirty-five. Although at that point, it's just a title."

"Then Raymond is the only boy."

Raymond's sole response to Arnacin's grin was to shrug his sack higher onto his shoulder.

"To Tevin, I will always be a boy," Arnacin admitted. "After all, I'm still two years younger than he is."

"Alright." Thomas shrugged. "If you are not men, how old are… men when they are allowed to marry and what is that considered?"

"Ah, my friend," Tevin exclaimed. "You must not confuse adulthood with manhood. Adulthood, when one can no longer ignore taking on the responsibilities of his own occupation and household, comes for a boy at sixteen on the island. Manhood comes when the full maturity of having taken on those responsibilities catches up to one and that man is able to become an elder of his village if chosen."

"Of course, that assumes responsibility will actually mature one," Arnacin mumbled.

Tevin glared back.

Although it made no difference in the Ice Woods, there was no doubt in Evan's mind that winter was approaching. Autumn was very brief in Elcan, and he was fairly certain it had been at least four weeks since he'd been told the trees were changing.

More importantly, he knew the town of Ansky would dread Elcan's longest season as they had not for some time. With all the men Wilber had conscripted from there, they had a harvest they couldn't bring in and preparations that never would be made.

A soft thump of Lisya adding something to his mixing bowl brought the prince back from staring motionlessly into the fire. For another minute, he devoted his attention to the vegetables he was grinding into a purée for Tenacius. He could only push aside his thoughts briefly, however, before they forced themselves back to the forefront. "Lisya."

Beside him, the enchantress diced the soft vegetables to make them easier to crush. At the sound of his voice, she looked up.

"I am better now," the prince said. He waited for her to gainsay him, but she remained silent, so he pressed on. "I would've been in Evfel, if not for my health. Still, I am beginning to think it is best I stayed."

"Why do you say that?" The enchantress's melodious voice was soft, without a trace of foreknowledge. Yet Evan knew she only asked out of politeness.

"Ansky. Wilber's obsession with fortifying the town and manning it with troops has left it... very poor. Without help, its inhabitants might not survive the winter, not in the condition I saw it." After a pause, during which the only sound was the crackle of the fire and the soft pounding of the pestle, he said, "I need to be there to help them."

Though Lisya said nothing, a soft gasp sounded from across the room. "Evan!" Lorene protested. In seconds, she was beside them. "You will die the minute you enter the town! There is no love for you there. They will not give you a second to even try to assist them."

Meeting her gaze, Evan sighed. "They are my responsibility, dear aunt. It is high time I took on that duty."

"But not in this way."

"I think he's right." The soft voice made them all turn to Valoretta, who sat on one of the beds with Tenacius. "What is there to rule if they all die?"

"They cannot *all* die," Lorene insisted. "Ansky stretches all the way into the mountains, and Cyra is also technically Ansky's island."

"Pardon my bluntness," Evan said, "but I cannot sit back and view them as anything but individuals who are starving."

"It is not the task of a king to think of individuals. It is not a risk you can take."

"Then I'll go," Talliaha spoke up. "I'll help however I am able."

"You are an islander. They will notice the difference in your speech," Evan sighed.

Placing her knuckles on her hips, Lorene changed tactics. "What could you possibly do to help, anyway?"

"He will take the sack I just finished, from which food never disappears," Lisya replied, finally speaking.

"Lisya!" Lorene gasped. "You, of all people should know the impracticality."

A small smile crossed the enchantress's face. "I see many things, both good and bad, but I will never advise by that sight."

"But having Evan go to Ansky is impractical."

Slowly, Lisya dipped her chin. "There are only two things that win hearts, Lorene, and without them, this war is lost: love and self-sacrifice."

"But this war is lost if he dies."

"Aunt Lorene," Evan softly interrupted. "This war is for them, not for the vague 'people' to whom nobility refers. If it were not for them, as individuals, I would disappear into the Calmar Mountains and raise horses. As it is, whether I win this war or not is irrelevant. I must help them before they starve."

Three days later, Evan prepared to leave the Ice Woods. "I have made it harder for anyone to recognize you, but beware, Evan," Lisya said as they made their farewells inside the cottage. "Before you arrive in Ansky, the snow will turn into a blizzard."

"It will hide our progress, then," the prince said with a bow before he left, shutting the door behind himself.

Darkfire, however, pawed the ground. "I dislike this idea of leaving you in Ansky."

Soothingly, Evan patted Darkfire's shoulder, feeling the stallion's warm breath on the back of his neck. "It must be, Darkfire. There will be no disguising you, and although deep snow will keep the castle away from the town, your presence will sound an alarm."

"But if you are discovered, you will have no one. I am afraid I agree with your aunt. You should stay here."

Meeting those deep eyes, Evan sighed. "Darkfire, help me reach Ansky. Surely, you must understand. They need assistance, and I am here. Did you not sacrifice your kingship for the same reason?"

The stallion dropped his head over the prince's shoulder, in the semblance of a hug. Pressed into Darkfire's powerful neck, Evan heard the words reverberating from the stallion's chest. "My own life was the only sacrifice I made."

Pulling away, the prince again faced his friend. "That is all I am sacrificing too, Darkfire. Believe me, Wilber will never win Ansky. It has a spirit that calls no one king for long, except out of love."

At that moment, the door creaked open. Valoretta stood there, wrapping her cloak more tightly around her small frame. "Evan?" she asked. "I don't mean to interrupt, but may I ask a question?"

Evan nodded, regarding her thoughtfully. She might hide her sovereignty behind islander clothes and hesitancy, but as a vagabond king himself, with a dethroned stallion, he could not miss the hints that she too had lost a kingdom.

Judging by the look in her eyes, she also knew about his awareness of her royal status. Yet he would not ask about the peculiarities of her marriage.

"Are you related to Lisya?" she asked after a pause.

"No," Evan laughed. "Is that your question?"

She shook her head. For a moment, she seemed to struggle with her words. Then she asked, "Do you ever consider the kingdom as a whole, or is it always as individuals?"

"In short, am I even capable of being king?" Evan's question brought a small smile, and he slowly exhaled. "To be perfectly honest, I doubt I *am* capable, but there is one thing I have noticed. Rulers focus on protecting the land they govern, but as long as there are people to till it, they think the land is good. They cannot know otherwise if they are not out there themselves."

"But no one can do everything, and governing is so time-consuming that there is not a moment for anything else."

"Is there not, my lady? Do you never have a moment to pace, or even stand at a window? There may not be that much time, but I think it is only right to use every single breath for those you vow to serve in life and death."

Contemplation shone in her eyes. "It would be an early death."

"Valoretta," Evan sighed. "Are you aware Elcan is church-centered."

"Superstitious, you mean?"

"If you will. As that is the case, I believe God's rules come first, and those of kings second. That means the first rule is to rescue as many people from damnation as possible. Protecting nations is insignificant in comparison. Yet I have been given a throne. Somehow, those two things must meet." He shrugged. "Right or wrong, that means if I have a moment to dislodge a rock from a mule's hoof for a villager, I will. And if doing that kills me early, then so be it. I will have done my best to keep my duty as a monarch."

Valoretta simply stared at him.

Bowing, he pulled himself onto Darkfire and readjusted Lisya's precious sack onto his shoulder. With that, the stallion started off.

Valoretta, standing on the enchantress's stoop, faded into the distance. Slowly, even the cottage's light gave way to the darkness of the Ice Woods.

Arieh could only be reached by a winding path up the north-western side of the mountain peak. A week ago, the Isfullen had crossed the Death Mirror by moving a fallen tree across a narrow place. Afterward, they had pushed their makeshift bridge into the swirling current. They had crossed just in time. Barely had they reached the uppermost edge of the woods on the hillside when snow started fluttering from the sky. Now, it was almost impossible to see, causing them to hug the cliff face and keep a hand on the person in front of them.

In this manner, they discovered the tavern on the outskirts of Arieh. Leading the group, Vilo stumbled into the cave in the mountainside that served as the entrance to the establishment's stable. The rest of the Isfullen stumbled in beside him, and in the lantern light filling the place, they met each other's blue faces.

No one seemed able to move again. Having found shelter, their exhaustion was taking over. But Arnacin shook his head. "We can't stay here," he warned Vilo. "They'll find us, and with our numbers, it's going to look suspicious."

Sighing, the minstrel adjusted his instrument over his shoulders. "We'll slip in by groups of fours and fives as long as we can find the front door. If you're up to it, come with me. We'll take Raymond and Malachi along, and hopefully, I can distract them from noticing how many are out in this storm." He smiled winningly. "Perhaps I can even barter for a warm meal for all of us."

No one came to the door to greet them, so Vilo herded them to a table. Soon, a girl came by. "Welcome, travelers! How may I serve you? The Cedar Apple has the best mulled cider in all of Arieh." Her gaze surveyed their snowy cloaks with curiosity, stopping on Arnacin. Yet she said nothing.

Vilo beamed. "May I speak to the owner?"

The girl's gaze jumped back to the minstrel. Concern flickered across her face. "Is there something wrong?"

"No fear." Leaning closer, Vilo whispered, "The truth is, we are penniless, but I have come to play for your patrons and cheer them from the storm if the owner allows."

"He will not be hap..." As the girl spoke, however, her gaze returned to Arnacin, and her face reddened.

He quickly looked away, only to meet Raymond's laughing grin. Although Arnacin tried to keep his face neutral, he felt his expression darken.

Out of the corner of his eye, however, he saw the girl curtsy. "I will pass the message on, without revealing the fact you are beggars."

As soon as she had left, Malachi turned to Arnacin. "Why did she blush?"

"I couldn't tell you," Arnacin muttered, elbowing Raymond as his friend laughed softly.

"Arnacin causes a certain nervousness," Vilo said, swinging his instrument from behind him to tune it. "It can be like staring down a bear."

"Is that so?" the comment's victim growled. The minstrel said no more, however, and Arnacin's gaze was drawn to the instrument. He had never really looked at it before, but now he realized just how unique it was. It appeared Vilo had stretched strings over two large intersecting gourds.

"Does that thing even sound nice?" he asked.

Vilo proudly brushed his fingers over the strings, and a deep, soft echo rumbled. "With the double chamber, it's better than blowing air through a glass pipe." He glanced up at Malachi. "Can you sing?"

The boy had no time to answer, as a small, portly man strode toward them. "I want to make it very clear I will not accept any so-called minstrel trying to cheat a meal out of anyone. If you are actually skilled, I don't mind if you play for us and see what that buys you."

Vilo smiled. "You put such pressure on me already." The owner's face remained stony. Nodding, the minstrel stood. "Do you have a favorite song? I can play it if you can hum it."

The owner's eyes narrowed. "*Arieh Forever,*" he finally growled. "But I do not *hum.*"

Whether he did or not, a tentative humming started. Looking around, Arnacin noticed Malachi's lips compress. With a nod, Vilo strummed his strings.

Silence fell as that instrument gave forth a magnificent melody filled with pride and glory. Looking around, Arnacin noticed many had stilled, and all had straightened in their seats. As the song heightened in power, he marked the faces of those whose hands turned white around their tankards. Considering the rough guide Vilo had received, he had to be improvising, but it blended seamlessly all the same.

As the last notes sounded from the instrument, calls of "More!" burst around the tavern.

Vilo bowed. "All right, I will, yet this is my offer. Do not pay me. Find the first person next to you who has not eaten, and pay for that man's dinner. It can be as skimpy as you like. Just feed them. I will play anything you like in return."

More than one person shared an incredulous gaze with their neighbor. Raymond, however, stood. "That's the signal for more of us to slip in," he whispered.

Arnacin placed a cautionary hand on his friend's arm. "Do not be seen leaving or they will suspect Vilo's scheme, whether or not we all eat tonight."

With a nod, Raymond slipped out the door. Turning back, Arnacin noticed a few men were searching the room for people who had not eaten. One man came to Malachi, and sizing the boy up, he ordered a piece of bread and water.

"Wretch," Arnacin mumbled into his hands, but Vilo had already clapped the man on the back. "That is the spirit. What would you like to hear?"

"Colbra." An unkind smile crossed the man's face. "Do you know it?"

Malachi shivered but softly hummed it. Even in that incomplete form, it was a deep tune, its long-drawn notes filled with death. Vilo's gaze flicked from the man to Malachi, but with another bow, he again struck a chord, letting it reverberate alone before moving on.

There was something in the minstrel's instrument, as in Lisya's voice, that gave life to the sounds coming from it. This time, it filled Arnacin with the dread of the tomb.

He jumped as Raymond rejoined them by clasping Arnacin's shoulder. "What's this song?" Raymond asked, nodding toward Vilo as he resumed his seat.

"Colbra," Malachi whispered. "Do not ask about the story behind it. It is evil, and they say its monster still lives."

"Like the Black Captain." Arnacin could not prevent his dark grin.

A stiff wind and snow suddenly blasted into the Anskonian tavern, the Sky Haven. Looking up from polishing dishes, Taylor Magree saw a black-cloaked, snow-blanketed figure push against the door to close it, and he rushed to help.

As they latched it once again, the innkeeper spoke. "You were traveling in this! Are you insane?"

The figure pushed his hood off, revealing thick brown hair and brilliant blue eyes over an infectious smile. "I did not have much choice," he said, shivering.

"Come." Taylor hastily beckoned the stranger over to the roaring fire. "Warm yourself. I will be back with some spiced wine."

Wearily, the stranger sank into the offered seat. "Thank you."

In moments, the innkeeper returned with the wine and sat opposite the stranger. "I am sorry. I do not have much to offer. You have come to a place on the verge of obliteration."

"Why is that? Ansky was strong back in the day."

"There were not enough hardy men to work the fields after King Wilber came in and hired them for the army, and he takes more food than in previous years to feed them. For now, we are making do, but many of us have no hope for the future."

"Surely your king would not starve his own troops. If he lacks enough field workers, even the extra supplies he takes will diminish rapidly."

"King Wilber has also brought food from the mountain villages to feed the castle. We have too much to do here to make the journey. Now, winter has struck, and the journey is well-nigh impossible."

"You will survive," the stranger sighed, taking another sip of the wine.

"Even if you believe in God, that sounds like pride to me." Impishness danced in the blue eyes over the tankard, and Taylor added, "No one can know the future."

The stranger shrugged. "Sometimes, you can know portions. But say that is pride... Is not simply sitting here quitting?"

"We are rationing where we can, and doing things like that. Where are you from, anyway?"

"North. I am escaping family."

"Why?"

Leaning back until he was balanced on the chair's rear legs, the stranger shrugged. "We hate each other. I decided to leave before they killed me."

"You came at the wrong time. With the war..." It was Taylor's turn to shrug. "I hope King Wilber can catch Maxwell soon."

The stranger's gaze dropped to his lap. With a soft voice, he asked, "Are you certain you wish for that? I have heard things about Evfel, and it would be terrible if Wilber Dalacort had the complete freedom to create another such kingdom here."

"We will take one step at a time. Evan Maxwell is the danger that must be destroyed now, before the worst happens."

For a long moment, there was no answer. The stranger simply rocked back and forth on those two chair legs. Finally, in a voice barely above a whisper, he asked, "Are you sure this Maxwell even exists anymore? I keep hearing everyone say, 'I heard he did this, and I heard that,' but it seems no one has actually seen him. Does anyone even know what he *looks* like?"

Studying the stranger, Taylor said, "Careful, my good man. You try to push me into voicing treason."

"I am not afraid of treason, master innkeeper." Those blue eyes bored straight through Taylor. "Such fear is the destruction of freedom, and it was always my opinion that nothing would cause Ansky to sacrifice that."

"Pride again. Do you not understand that freedom is an insignificant thing when compared to the gates of hell Maxwell tries to pull open? Yes, we saw him last year with a few of those magical islanders of his. He forced Wilber to spin some bizarre story about Dalacort manipulation, but somehow left out how he took off with a horse he wanted, pretended to acknowledge his responsibility, and tried to force it on Sir Radnor instead."

The stranger winced. "My question is whether you have any evidence the gates of hell are opening, or if they were, in fact, invented to secure your slavery."

"Invented by whom? We all saw those islanders. We heard the stories from the knights who returned. And if Prince Maxwell's story was true—if he had just escaped assassination by way of the fastest horse—why did he not prove it by returning the stallion?

"No, whatever might have happened while he lived here makes no difference now. He has made a contract with spirits to assist his selfish desertion, and all we are left with is the choice between his demonic evil and Dalacort tyranny. Some of us have promised, if we do meet Maxwell, we will nail his hide to the butcher's wall for his betrayal."

All four legs of the chair slammed onto the ground. But placing his elbows on the table, the stranger only said, "I hope you will fight as hard for your freedom when the day comes as you would fight against such evil."

Taylor could not be certain, but he thought he detected sarcasm in that voice. "Physical freedom is hardly important in comparison to the eternal."

Studying the grain of the table under his folded arms, the stranger sighed, "No, it is not, but I would hate for Elcan to become an empire under the Dalacorts."

"Sometimes, we must let the heavens decide such things." Sighing, Taylor added, "I just wish King Phillip were still alive. None of this would have happened then."

The stranger's smile returned as he lifted his tankard into the air. "I am with you there. Perhaps you should just replace your current king with a commoner."

Although said in jest, Taylor sat up straighter and pushed his hair back. "I know just the man."

The stranger laughed. "You cannot tell me you would want that job?"

"Of course. Would you not want it?"

"I would never want that job."

Taylor paused at the complete seriousness in the stranger's voice. "Why not? Is it not great to know you are king?" Softly, he tried the word again. "King."

This time, the stranger's laughter was tinged with sorrow. "It is such thoughts of glory that differentiate good from bad. There is no real glory in kingship, to my understanding. If the king in question is good and beloved, he crumbles mentally from the knowledge of the many precipices waiting to bring about his people's demise. And if he is bad, he is hated. Where is that wonderful, soaring feeling in either of those choices?"

"You know," Taylor said, resting his cheek on his fist. "I think we should make *you* king. Between your insane boldness and insight, we could do much worse."

With a hearty laugh, the stranger replied, "I just said I would never want it. You will have to drag me there first."

The innkeeper chuckled. "I am Taylor Magree, by the way. Fool that I did not say so earlier."

"I was given the name Max in my travels. It suits me."

Shaking the stranger's hand, the innkeeper said, "Well, Max, welcome to your winter home."

Vilo played through the storm and into the next afternoon to make sure no one was unfed. In that time, he stopped only once, when Lazarus used Lisya's coin to buy him a meal under cover of Vilo's arrangement. For a short while, the minstrel chatted with the tavern's patrons about how he had come from the Elcan Woods, seeking fame and fortune.

Arnacin shook his head, but he could not help but chuckle.

Once the storm stopped, the Isfullen left to head to the center of the city. Hauling each foot through the snow into which they sank to the knees, Arnacin asked the minstrel, "Why do you bother trying to teach them charity, Vilo? They don't wish to learn. They weren't brought up to value it and so never will."

"It is only for us to try, Arnacin, not to know." Pausing in what would usually be a short ascent to Arieh, Vilo turned to the younger islander. "It is also my opinion that our task here is rather vague. Still, we will each try in our own way to accomplish it. My way is to call them to a higher life, to desire goodness over evil, and selflessness over selfishness. Whether Evfel simply changes its outlook or rejects its king, I will have accomplished my mission."

Bright sunlight glistened over the snow on the trail, angled around the sides of the wooden sign shaped like an apple identifying the tavern they had left, and bounced off the mountainside.

Arnacin sighed. "Yours is the fantasy, Vilo. Some may change themselves, some may desire to change the kingdom, but their very nature will prevent them from fully turning things around. The only way to weaken the government's domination is to fuel the people's selfish desires, or they will have no courage to take that first step."

For a long moment, Vilo studied him. Then he resumed his slog through the snow. "I fear the results of that path, Arnacin. And I do not feel that any result is worth encouraging people to debauchery. I'm surprised you do, actually."

"There is no result I think worth anything. I am here as support. That is all. I simply tell you what is impossible and what is not."

"Ah, but have you forgotten the very words you would have once insisted upon?"

Shifting, Arnacin took five more exhausting steps. "Yes, I have forgotten," he finally whispered.

"You would have once stood there with scorn in your eyes and your head held high to tell everyone within earshot that you work for the possibility of good, not so anything can come by it, but just so you do what is honorable and righteous."

Briefly meeting the minstrel's laughing expression, Arnacin felt a sad smile cross his own face. "That was another world, Vilo," he whispered. "That boy failed to realize honor is impossible to achieve. Selfishness is too strong, and his search for honor was just proof that even he was self-centered."

Softly, Vilo replied, "I think, all told, you have succeeded in your mission at sea."

"I left to find a direction, Vilo. I never found it."

The minstrel only glanced askance at him and remained silent.

Despite all the places Arnacin had traveled, Arieh was by far the largest city he had ever had to navigate—so large that it was divided into six districts. The oldest of these, taking up the middle of the city was known as the Montza District. Most of the wealthy settled in the southwestern-most section, the Sol District. Opposite that region, split by the city's largest street, Lion's Heart, lay the Governmental District. No one went there unless they were part of said government or when dragged into the courts and offices therein.

Everything in the northern part of Arieh, including its old dilapidated guard towers, was dubbed the Norlend District, the poorest and most rundown portion of the city farthest from the castle. That left the Glenvil District to the east and the Erado District in the west.

Perhaps most disturbing was that where King's Crossing—a road leading from the city center to the mountain path— intersected with Lion's Heart, it formed what would in most cities be the market. In Arieh, however, no one traded there. Instead, stocks and pillories lined the street.

More often, it was the stocks that were full, where those locked inside them by their hands and ankles were forced to sit for hours or several days on end rather than stand hunched over, like those in the pillories, with their hands and head restrained.

One large platform, lacking only a rope to make it a gallows, dominated the city center. Even though it caused Arnacin's skin to turn to ice, the locals were using it as a stage.

Malachi whispered that their greatest wish was not actu- ally to make money with their performances, but to appear valuable enough to be claimed as a slave. Coins tossed by the occasional viewer could never provide the same food and shelter as bondage.

"This city is sick," Raymond whispered as he, Arnacin and Thomas walked by the gallows, hunting rats for their dinner about a week after their arrival.

"I do not know how they can perform on that platform," Thomas added from Arnacin's other side. "All someone has to do is throw a rope arou—"

Arnacin seized the boy's arm. "Silence." Neither compan- ion questioned that low growl.

When nothing else happened, Thomas said, "You know, if all we keep turning up with is moldy, soggy bread, I think we will be sick by tomorrow."

"From lack of food or from the quality of it?" Raymond teased.

"Unless you want to sell yourself as a slave on that platform, I would suggest you find something else to complain about," was Arnacin's only reply, soft and deadly. He sensed the skepticism of the other two.

In the end, Thomas shrugged. "All right, we will freeze to death tonight."

"Will you just be quiet?" Arnacin sighed, watching without interest as one of their quarries scampered behind some barrels a few feet away.

Raymond nodded toward it. "Well, Arnacin. There goes our delicious dinner." Yet even Thomas hung back.

Arnacin could not prevent a dark grin spreading over his lips. "And you complained about hunger, Thomas. Apparently, you're not hungry enough."

"I said we would die by sickness or freezing, not starvation. Are there not any alternatives?"

Glancing at him, Arnacin quickly answered, "Stealing."

Raymond only trudged forward. "We'll catch the next rat."

Arnacin, however, could not resist quipping, "So stealing's not an option?"

The hunter did not look back. "With your reluctance to even look at the gallows, I'm surprised you dare ask. Even if we stooped to such a thing, our inexperience would find us all beneath the rope."

"Your inexperience, maybe." Arnacin only muttered that, however. Then he resumed his own trudge through the cold mud of the street, following behind the other two.

It was not a rat that caused him to halt abruptly, however. It was a middle-aged woman, bundled in rags, next to a prisoner in one of the pillories. With a soggy piece of bread, which she had rolled into a cup of sorts, she was feeding him what looked like gruel.

Moving aside—as much as the thick wood around his neck permitted—the prisoner rasped, "Eat the rest, Mother. I—"

Yet before he could finish, men wearing tabards blazoned with the Dalacort's emblem of the lion came down the street. One of them shoved the lady aside. She landed in the mud with a splat, her gruel spilling over her front.

Over the soldiers' mocking laughter, Arnacin heard a cry of protest from the prisoner. Yet no one paid attention. "Save your food for the living, woman," one of the men said. "This thief hangs tomorrow."

"If you call that food," another of the men exclaimed. With that, they walked off, laughing.

"Arnacin?" The sound of his name came from Raymond, who had stopped farther down the street with Thomas when they noticed he was no longer following. Sighing, the younger islander turned away from the condemned prisoner.

Curled up in a doorway in the southern end of the Sol District, Arnacin pulled Michael's cloak closer. Beyond him, the tight alley in which his alcove sat was filled with Isfullen crowded under blankets, some borrowed from clotheslines, others, brought with them.

Looking at the largest bundle, far in the back of the alley, Arnacin smiled slightly. They were so tightly packed together they looked like a single rounded heap in the darkness, warming the mud beneath them. They were out of the wind there, at least, and would likely sleep the night away with each other's heat.

Despite the small comfort of people caring for each other in a cold city, the scene that afternoon on Lion's Heart would not leave Arnacin alone. After another moment of sleeplessness, he pushed himself to his feet. A mother's love had convinced him.

Something swooped down from a window above, and the islander froze. "Is anything amiss, Arnacin?" Michael's talons clutched his shoulder. Warm feathers nestled against his right cheek.

Pushing the eagle off, Arnacin sighed. "Keep watch, Michael. I will be back before morning, I promise."

"You are planning something stupid, as usual. Fine, but I will not rescue you if you are caught."

Wishing Michael lacked the ability to speak as an eagle, Arnacin turned down the intersecting ally. On second thought, the enchanter would most likely make his thoughts known by screeching incessantly instead. But regardless of birds speaking or not, the islander had something he had to do.

Glass did not exist in Arieh, at least not in the city itself. Most homes did not even have windows, although a few had wooden shutters. The well-to-do had upper floors—their high windows left open in the servant quarters, gaping black holes that only the birds and bugs could enter.

Or rather, only the birds, bugs and Mira's Black Phantom. Finding an upper window in the wealthy end of the Sol District that looked wide enough to enter, Arnacin scaled the stone walls and slipped inside.

A short while later, Arnacin turned onto Lion's Heart. Walking casually, he still tried to avoid making a sound in the sucking mud as he passed several prisoners sleeping in stocks. He dared not ask, but from what he had heard, he wondered if the stocks were for culprits not meant for execution and pillories for those about to die. Whatever the answer, of the four prisoners on the street, only one was locked in a pillory— the man previously visited by his mother.

Although Arnacin had thought it strange no one was guarding the prisoners, he found that an excessive number of chains could keep everyone except an expert thief from freeing them. After picking the locks on the shackles around the condemned man's ankles, the islander stood, facing the now-awake culprit.

"Who are you?" the prisoner rasped.

Arnacin did not answer, instead picking the locks on the man's wrists, around the neck, and on the pillory itself. As the prisoner painfully stood, however, the islander shoved his stolen supplies into the man's hands. "This will take you and a small family to Grand-sire. They're not likely to chase you there. You're just another peasant to them, one thief among millions. Take all of your relations. Even if they fall under suspicion, at least they won't be here."

The prisoner continued to stare at him. "Who are you?"

This time, the islander could not find it in himself to refuse an answer entirely. "A shepherd from out of town."

"Let me help with your flock, then."

"They are no more." With that, Arnacin turned away, tensing as the prisoner grabbed his arm.

"Then you are in the city for more. I'll help."

The islander jerked away. "No. There are no sheep here. Go, now."

"Please, whatever you do, I want to follow."

"If you wish to help, then leave, but if you ever find someone you are capable of assisting, do so."

After studying the islander some more, the thief nodded. Arnacin waited only until he turned away, then slipped down the closest alley.

With his keen ears, Michael heard Vilo's chipper reel drifting on the breeze, and Lisya's son wondered how many people he was feeding this time, how many Isfullen had gone with him to eat instead of grubbing through garbage heaps or hunting for rats.

Two streets away, Malachi was in the middle of a brief washing job he'd obtained in the Erado District. It looked to Michael like the boiling pots in the yard were a comfort to the blue-faced boy. Although the enchantress's son had argued against taking the job for fear of the employer enslaving Malachi instead, his only option in the end was to stand guard. Watching for potential attackers, he flexed his long talons on the roof.

Yet he was not the only one who was guarding the boy. Arnacin was leaning against the open gate to the yard, talking softly with a hunched man with an eye patch. Considering the man's twisted grimace of a smile, Michael did not care to know the topic of that conversation. But he could guess, given the islander's tactic of increasing Arieh's hatred for its government.

From the distance came an angry clamor only a mob could produce. The eagle turned to look over the rooftops, toward its source. In the exact middle of Lion's Heart, three black-hooded men tied ropes to the gallows platform.

"Quick!" an excited call came from a ragged man who entered the yard. "A hanging!"

As all the doors flew open, Malachi and Arnacin were pushed along in the hurrying mass. Spreading his wings, Michael launched himself from the roof, keeping Arnacin's black head in view as the islander strove to hang onto Malachi. Fear filled both their faces, but Michael noticed Arnacin had turned slightly green as well.

Meanwhile, the crowd buzzed. "What was the crime?"

"Lying during interrogation."

"I hear someone helped the thief in the pillory escape."

"Did they catch them?"

"That is why they are hanging the others. They were brought to the Governmental District early this morning. When they continued to lie about whether they saw the culprit or not, the court brought them into the castle and the inquisitors there."

So the tittering went, often repeated across the expanse of people as newcomers joined the gathering crowd. In their midst, soldiers shoved three prisoners toward the gallows.

Michael saw Lazarus and Raymond also caught in the press, but the fisherman's bulk gave him an advantage as he fought through to Malachi and Arnacin's side. With those four together, Lisya's son momentarily risked losing sight of them to settle himself near the gallows. There, one of the culprits begged piteously for mercy, but his pleas were ignored.

One lady in the crowd scoffed, "It is completely indecent for a man to carry on so."

There was no decrease to the clamor of the crowd as the executioners bound the condemned from the ankles up.

Tugging on a man's sleeve, a small boy asked the question on Michael's mind. "Why are they tying so much rope?"

In a tone meant to fill the boy with awe, the man bent down and whispered, "Do you not know of the story of the acrobatic thief who wrangled up the rope meant to hang him?" The boy shook his head, and Michael could imagine the man winking during the split-second pause. "Well, he climbed up to the crossbeam, untied himself, and fled before anyone could catch him."

"Really?" The boy's eyes were wide.

"Well, that is the story, which is why..."

But Michael was no longer listening. The mob with Lazarus and Malachi in it had pushed itself onto the street. Arnacin and Raymond, however, had vanished.

Chapter 9

Wretches and Assassins

Trailing Arnacin, Raymond could not fail to notice how his friend trembled. Yet Arnacin did not break the silence or slow his aimless stride. Finally, Raymond asked, "Are you all right?"

"The whole city is revolting!" Still, there was no break in that long stride.

"You're not shaking because they're excited about an execution. That's not some horrible revelation to you. You've said all along this is exactly the type of people dwelling in Arieh."

"They should *all* be on those gallows." Arnacin's voice was a low hiss. "Every single one of them."

Catching his friend's arm, Raymond forced a halt. "Arnacin," he whispered. "What happened?"

Slowly, Arnacin turned to meet him, anger the only emotion readable in his eyes. Although his lips parted a few times, he said nothing.

He would have turned away again, but Raymond prevented him. "They are people, Arnacin, just like any other. Do you really think us any different on our own merit?"

Nothing shifted in that hardened glare, yet Raymond tried again. "They think nothing of this. They're trained into this

163

from before they can remember. Do you know how many children I saw in that crowd?"

Arnacin looked away as he softly sighed. Releasing the younger islander's arm, Raymond waited, counting their shallow breaths.

At last, Arnacin whispered, "I didn't want to come back to this sort of life. I thought I could just return home, that it *was* so different from the world's evils. I was wrong. The islanders are as scornful of and yet as foolishly blind as everyone else."

"Without an intercessor, yes."

Arnacin's dark eyes flicked upward, and he finally pushed past. Heaving a sigh, Raymond followed.

Shortly, they came out of the small side streets and back onto the north end of Lion's Heart, where it ended at the edge of the cliff in the Norlend District. The buildings lining the street butted against the sharp descent, while the view of the sky stretched unbroken before them. At their backs, the noise of the crowd on the street's southern side blew away in the breeze.

Arnacin hardly stopped as he walked directly to the edge. Just as Raymond's heart skipped in concern, his friend slid around the corner of the northernmost building. A thin lip of rock, barely seven inches wide, jutted from the structure before plunging down. So precariously hidden, Arnacin braced himself against the sun-warmed stone, his toes curling over the expanse.

Taking a breath, Raymond edged out.

Snow and ice glimmered below them. All of Evfel opened to their view from that perch, the Elcan Woods poking up along the mountain's rise. Far to the north, the hazy line of the Calmar Mountains rose again, their guarding arms wrapping themselves to the north and northeast of the Dalacorts' kingdom, where they merged with the Tenly Mountains to the east and south.

The winter wind blew unhindered, though thankfully southward, pressing them into the stone wall behind them. Pulling his cloak tight, Raymond wondered at his companion's insensitivity to the temperature, but his unvoiced questions wandered away as his eyes turned again northward to that faint tan ridge of the Calmar Mountains.

Far beyond those peaks lay their home. Its inhabitants would be snuggled down during their idle months before planting began again. People would be visiting neighbors, sharing food, hot drinks, concerns, stories and games. On warm days, they'd be outside, playing in the snow or foraging for fresh supplies.

Yet, most of those that would have been the largest part of his winters were no longer there. And as for Arnacin...

Raymond turned to look at his friend, but the wind drove black waves across the other islander's face, hiding it from view. As if reading the hunter's thoughts, however, Arnacin whispered, pain filling his voice, "The island is no more, Raymond. I'm not sure it ever was, but it's only a dream now, and never will be anything else."

"You can start again—"

"Never."

"The island has not changed all that much, Arnacin, I promise. Evan won't harm its way of life."

"Evan." A sound that could have been sarcastic laughter came from Arnacin, yet it died almost instantly. "Evan," he repeated, more musingly. "The truth is, I fear trusting him, Raymond, and I will never love him. I yearn to hate him. I want nothing more than to blockade myself behind the strength and safety of bitterness, yet..."

Finally, Arnacin turned his head toward his silent friend. Light shone brightly in his eyes. "Evan is the earthly king they need, as far as I can tell. One who will sacrifice all of himself for them. I don't have the desire to interfere."

Over the next week, Raymond stayed close to Arnacin, noting a troubled silence from his friend. Eventually, Vilo invited the two of them to the inn at which he was to play that afternoon, the Black Print in the Glenvil District.

With the thought of hot food and a warm room, Raymond readily agreed. Beside him, Arnacin merely nodded.

As Vilo entertained the inn's patrons while standing at the center of the tavern's floor, his comrades had only just settled down at a table when a stooped man with an eye patch lumbered over to them. "Ah, it is my young friend from the other day!" he said, settling into a seat at their table.

Glancing around to see who the man was addressing, Raymond's unease settled as Arnacin replied, "I did not think you had the funds for a tavern."

"Nor I you, but..." The man leaned closer to Arnacin; his head ducked over the tankard he carried. "Our regent, Duke Reginold, is a generous man, after all, even if he may not know it. He keeps his purse strings loose when he comes out into the city."

Grim laughter sounded from Arnacin.

Raymond leaned closer. "He is nothing of the sort. This city suffocates in his stranglehold."

The man slapped his arm. "Oh, you are a bold one." He nodded toward Arnacin. "This one says less, and him with the very air of a powerful man."

Raymond carefully avoided looking at his friend, but he could see him shift slightly. To keep the man's attention, Raymond straightened. "I have no fear of stating the truth. If they wished to hear otherwise, they would act differently."

For the first time in days, a small smile crossed Arnacin's face. The man made a low chuckle that echoed that grin. "Sonny, such a tongue will pay your pass to the gallows. Sneakiness serves better." He shook a bag at his belt.

Although Raymond had no trouble interpreting the action, he asked, "Sneakiness serves better in what fashion, pray tell? Cowering, stealing and lying only serve to generate more cowards, thieves and liars. And at the rate this city is producing them, we will all kill each other in months."

The man tapped his eye patch. "Goodness and truth serve no man in Evfel, sonny. Whatever the outcome of deceit, you do live longer with guile as your friend."

Despite the sad truth in those words, Raymond insisted, "What is the point of living longer under such circumstances? What could possibly be gained from such survival?"

The man's one eye fixed on Raymond. "Do you not fear death?"

"Yes," Raymond whispered. "It is something no one truly wants to face. But I prefer to live knowing I helped someone than to shy away from death. If such a choice forces me before a duke so drunk on bloodshed, he hates love, then so be it. I will tell him as much."

In the man's stunned silence, Arnacin muttered into his fist, "You are the sort of man any king would feel it his duty to execute, and he would feel even that was too good for you."

Raymond shrugged. The victorious twitch of his friend's grin informed him he was being harassed, but this was no place to dig further.

"You better listen to your friend, sonny," the man said. "He knows wisdom."

"Earthly wisdom only," a new voice boomed.

Vilo's music cut off.

Turning to find the speaker, Raymond beheld an aging man clearing a nearby table, with the lines of someone old long before his time.

Plunking the dishes he carried back down, the man approached Raymond. "Never change your views. We've long lived with the results of the other stance in this sorry kingdom."

"You were listening." Raymond's voice trembled slightly. How many others had also eavesdropped?

Before the aging man could answer, the owner strode from behind his bar. "What are you supporting, slave?"

The aging man took a hesitant step back. Still, he replied, "Charity."

"As long as you eat and sleep here, you have charity. You could have starved instead. Now, carry those dishes into the kitchen."

The slave straightened. "If that is your perspective, then I will take my leave and starve on the streets. I have had enough of your type of charity. Good day." He turned, and Raymond tensed as the tavern keeper pulled out a knife.

"You forget, under our agreement, your life is forfeit if you desert," the tavern keeper said. "Only I can give you permission to go."

The aging man did not even turn around. Without another word, the tavern keeper threw his knife. With a ping, the weapon fell to the ground before meeting its target. Raymond leapt to his feet as screams rose from the tavern's patrons.

It cut off midway. The slave still stood, although he had now turned back in alarm. No pain showed on his features.

Stooping, a patron plucked the knife from the ground. Five tables away, someone else scooped up a small stone. The tavern keeper's face turned red as he stared at the dagger, wordless. He was still only for a moment, then he rushed back to his counter. From somewhere beneath it, he yanked out another blade.

"Toss that, and it will be the last thing you do." The command came from a voice Raymond knew well, yet in that moment, it was alien to him. It was a voice he heard only once before, in the Elcan Woods, during the order to stop the Isfullen from sinking into the mires. This time, it lacked some of that heartlessness, yet it was no less that of the king unveiled.

Chairs scraped in the silence that followed, yet Arnacin remained seated. His gaze never left the tavern keeper as he rolled a small stone between his fingers resting in his lap.

An expectant hush filled the room. Even the intended victim watched the scene, a single step backward the one sign that he was considering escape. Otherwise, he scrutinized Arnacin himself. Only Vilo moved, carefully slinging his lute-like instrument back over his shoulder.

Finally, the owner spluttered, "Who are you to interfere?"

"Who are you to ask?"

As if trying to shake off a dream, the tavern keeper jerked his head once. "You have no authority here." A low whisper sounded throughout the room. "Had you, you would arrest or kill that slave yourself for his treason."

Arnacin's eyes lit up, as if a match had been struck behind them. "You did not give anyone the time to act. But, as you insist, I will take your slave away."

Beside Raymond, the man with the eye patch suddenly shot to his feet and vanished out the door as if afraid Arnacin might arrest him. However, the room was too tense for laughter at his hasty departure. Every person sat taut, like a drawn bow. All it would take was the slightest misstep for pandemonium to break out.

"You do not act like one of Reginold's men," the tavern keeper growled as Arnacin stood to go. "You sat by while I presume they discussed treason right next to you."

Arnacin did not even look back as he crossed to the slave. Barely had he touched the man's arm, however, before the room erupted. "Stop him!" the tavern keeper shouted. "For the love of Arieh!"

Raymond jumped into the surge of those following the tavern keeper's command, intent on reaching Arnacin. But a patron reached the islander first. Before the man's hands could close around his target, the islander whirled, striking with his fist. His assailant collapsed with hardly a sound.

Another was coming from the left. Raymond shoved a nearby chair into the new assailant. With a grunt, the man tripped. He was only down briefly, however. As Raymond passed, the man shot back to his feet and punched the hunter in the face.

The blow sent him back a faltering step, and the sound of pandemonium reached his ears. The owner's cry for assistance had brought the entire tavern to its feet, yet not all the fighting was directed against the islanders. Either the Isfullen had sympathizers who hoped the confusion would allow them to blend in as they struck out at potential attackers, or everyone considered any cause for a fight a good chance to take out their aggression.

Chairs flew. In the chaos that followed, one of the barmaids smacked her tray over a man's head, men shouted, and Raymond lost view of Vilo and Arnacin.

Moments later, an echoing boom of strings from one corner revealed the minstrel's location. Ducking yet another attacker's aim, Raymond fought through to the minstrel's side.

Vilo met him somewhere in the middle of the tavern. Despite the earlier protest of the instrument, it was still safely over the minstrel's shoulder. "Where's Arnacin?" he asked.

Shaking his head, Raymond replied, "I think we should leave. If he's not outside, we'll block the doors and make sure no one exits until he's with us."

Vilo nodded, but it was not so hard for them once they won through to the door. Arnacin was waiting for them right outside, the aging man beside him.

Pausing only to yank his friend to flight, Raymond took off. Three pairs of feet followed him. As quickly as possible, they twisted around alley corners until sufficiently beyond pursuit.

There, in a narrow street in the western end of the Norlend District, they all stopped, laughing and panting. Holding himself up by his knees, Raymond shook his head. "That won't go without repercussions."

"Yes," Vilo laughed. "Black eyes, sore jaws, bruised backs..."

Leaning against the wooden wall behind him, Arnacin grinned. "That won't incriminate anyone. Every person in that tavern is going to look the same."

His eyes still dancing, Vilo shook his head. "Oh no, they'll look worse. With how filthy we are, black eyes only improve our appearances."

"Thanks," Arnacin huffed, shifting to lean on his knees. "I'll stay ugly."

Before Raymond could laugh, a voice asked, "Are you actually nobles?"

Suddenly remembering the man collapsed in the mud beside them, the hunter turned and held out his hand. "We're most certainly not nobles. I'm Raymond. Our superb minstrel is Vilo." The indicated islander bowed. "And our advocate here is Arnacin, my adopted brother."

Shaking the offered hand, the man dipped his chin. "My name is Felleno Topaz. I see you actually do what you say."

Vilo offered his hand in turn. "We try anyway."

Felleno clasped the minstrel's hand in gratitude. "I thank you for your humility. I'm so pleased to meet you in person. All of Arieh takes heart from you. Your skill with your instrument is practically magical. Wherever you play, a crowd forms to listen. The paying ones flock inside, and those that can't fill the streets nearby. You would have been contracted early, yet no one will dare to take you as one of their slaves. I've heard my master grumble about the threat from all the other landholders if a single person tried to steal you for himself."

As Vilo shifted, the aging man swept a bow. "It is more than your renowned skill, though. You, of all of us, could be living quite well by now, even so soon after your arrival. But instead, you refuse pay, except for a meal for yourself and the few vagabonds you pass by and invite during a single afternoon. There are hundreds of homeless, I know—too much for you to truly make a difference in this city. But by your sacrifice, you have fed quite a few and helped their hearts even more.

We can't thank you enough. Until you came, I had no faith at all in humanity."

"I *don't* have faith in humanity. But never mind," Arnacin muttered dismissively, not offering his hand. "What are you facing now? Are you safe living in these streets, or is there somewhere else for you to go?"

No one seemed to notice Raymond roll his eyes. Felleno himself meekly replied, "My wife, Selywn, is a slave for the orphanage. I will not leave the city without her."

That gave the hunter pause. "Pardon my curiosity," he asked, "but how did you marry a woman you rarely see? I imagine slaves don't simply go visiting other people's slaves on a whim."

"We owned a farm before a couple of dry seasons ruined us. First, they took our son to work for the tax we had failed to pay. And then, when the farm failed another year, they took our land and tossed us into the streets. In order to survive, we accepted enslavement by whoever would take us."

Strangely, it was Arnacin who softly asked, "Do you still see your son?"

"Little Joseph?" Felleno whispered the name with pain. "They took him to Castle Dalacort when he was no more than two. It's why we came to this city when we were evicted. But we never heard a word, nor have we seen anyone who remotely looks like he could be our son."

Hesitating for only a moment, Raymond asked, "What would he look like, do you think?"

Those pale eyes grew distant. Then they briefly closed and Felleno sighed. "He would be twelve by now, but other than the fact he would have the softest blue eyes you ever saw, we know nothing for sure. As a babe, he had pale blond hair, a bit lighter than mine was, but Selywn's is brown, and I know some blonds change to brown later on. That's all we have to go on. We can't even be sure if he'll know his birth name, if he lives at all."

After a moment, Raymond offered, "If you refuse to leave the city, perhaps you would be willing to stay with us. We wander in small groups, but our numbers keep us warm at night, and our scavenging skills feed us, if minimally."

Felleno's eyes grew wide. "Numbers! What are you?"

"A stubborn lot determined to avoid slavery," Arnacin growled. "Unity is the only way to do so."

That answer extinguished the fear in the man's eyes. He nodded. "Very well, then. I will be pleased to meet your friends. God bless your endeavors."

"God bless them indeed," Vilo sighed.

The scuffle in the Black Print melted away as a group of knights strode in, their swords clicking and lion-bearing tabards rustling. "What is this?" the knights' captain snapped.

A man crawled out from under a table, coughing. "Alert the duke," he rasped. "There is a man... He is dangerous, I am telling you."

Laughing, the captain sneered. "I am dangerous. Where are the servers? Who is responsible for this commotion?"

Hurriedly, the man, seemingly the owner, scrambled over the counter as others began righting tables and chairs. In seconds, he had filled a tankard for every knight. "Take it for free, sirs, as my apology."

The captain leaned against the counter and took a sip before repeating, "Who started this?"

Trembling, the owner wiped his forehead. "There was this man in here—black-haired. He was inciting rebellion, sirs. I tried to stop him, and others from following, but he is dangerous, *trained*. I have no idea how many went with him."

"Trained, you say? In what way?"

"Every way." The owner gulped. "He knows politics, knife-throwing... Some people are convinced he is a noble himself, one of those Montiszian half-breeds trying to gather helpers before he brings out his own forces to attack. He has been in other places before now, but we only had suspicions."

"What did he do?"

"He prevented me, on pain of death, from punishing one of my slaves for voicing treason. When I resisted, this happened." He swept an arm about the wrecked room. "He was gone with the slave before anyone could say more."

Sharing looks with each other, the knights nodded. "You think people will follow him easily, then?"

"Most certainly. He has something about him. A… a power."

"Keep watch, then. What else marks him, other than his hair color?"

"He must sleep in the streets. Mud covers him, and his bones show. He lacks a beard, though, which is odd among the street riffraff, as you know. That is why people think him to be partly Montiszian, from the old kingdom…"

"Yes, we know what Montiszians are. What else?"

"His eyes burn."

"That is gibberish. What color are they?"

"I have no idea, but they burn, I tell you!" Huffing, the owner added, "He is most frequently seen with another young man. That one has curly brown hair and a stubbly beard. Not much, though."

Raising their eyebrows, the knights filtered out to report to the duke. True or not, if such a man existed, he was the type they would hang first and ask questions about after.

The town of Ansky had finally finished tramping down enough snow on the streets to make travel easy. With the birthday of Prince Maxwell—and thus the New Year—a month away, the townsfolk hoped no more blizzards would interrupt their ability to walk from house to tavern and back again.

When Max asked why they would bother keeping their current New Year, Taylor Magree shrugged. "We might accept the Dalacort's reign for now, but until *we* choose a king, we will not take up a new birthday as New Year's Day."

"Do you not fear Wilber will smash this celebration, though? It could be seen as siding with your enemy."

"With this weather? Not this year!"

And the conversation was left there. No one had any extra food to use on a celebration anyway, though two weeks ago, little piles of wood, animal fodder and staples had started appearing in front of people's doors—just enough to make it through that day. When some stayed up through the night to try to catch the donor, no food appeared.

In the Sky Haven tavern, Max had volunteered to keep watch for the secret giver; he too had seen no one, and no food had appeared at the door. After a few nights like that, people quickly gave up the attempt. Food and warmth were more important than curiosity.

Now, on a warmer day a month after Max's arrival, Taylor looked up to see another man shuffling through his tavern door. "Charles!" he exclaimed. Walking over, the innkeeper shook his friend's hand. "What brings you here at this time of year?" Without waiting for a reply, he steered Charles toward the backroom.

"We heard you were suffering, so our chapel priests organized gifts. I am just stopping here for some..." Charles abruptly stopped walking. "You are allowing me into the kitchen?"

Taylor gently propelled his friend through the doorway. "Until there are more people here, I am not using the wood for the fire. This smaller space is easier to heat."

Charles did not protest again. They found Max, melting snow in pails over the fire. After introducing his two guests to each other, the innkeeper said, "Truth to say, we have had some good fortune lately. For the past two weeks, food and wood have been appearing on doorsteps. My guess is that it comes from the church. They are the type to hide their generosity. It goes back to that clause of theirs about humility. But then…" He shrugged. "That also seems improbable. The price Cyra is asking for their wood is outrageous these days. When the war started, they tripled it." Sitting the traveler down, Taylor asked his assistant, "Max, will you fill a tankard of our best?"

Max nodded with one of his good-natured smiles and replaced the kettle.

While Taylor went to pull out jerky and a little fresh cheese, Charles asked, "So, you finally took on some help?"

"For now. Max is a wanderer at heart. I doubt he will stay once spring comes, but he has been great help since he arrived a month ago." Placing the small meal before the traveler, Taylor pulled up a chair for himself. "Did you walk?"

Charles laughed. "No. My mule is outside. We dropped off the food we brought to the church, and I thought I would stop in to see you before heading home."

Max returned at that moment, placing the tankard before the newcomer. "Did you want me to see to your mule? I was just taking water to Cormrick anyway."

Hesitating, Charles said, "I usually see to my—"

"Have no fear." Taylor slapped his friend on the back. "Your mule will be in very good hands with Max. In fact, Cormrick, the donkey out back, is a bully, so we keep him in solitude here instead of our city barn. But he acts like a kitten with Max, and so do all the headstrong cows. Hence, the cheese. We have been receiving nice, uh, thank-you gifts from the young ladies who appreciate Max's talent when they go to milk their cows."

The young man in question turned red, and Charles laughed. "Very well, thank you. I will be much obliged."

As Max left, Taylor pushed his chair closer to the table and rested his elbows on it. "How is it at Fortress Tyhoronous?"

"The Ice Woods are very still. Granted, we never saw that much movement, even when we heard their army attacked Ansky. We did notice an eagle on the move regularly." Charles leaned closer, whispering, "However, the eagle disappeared into the Bloody Gorge a while ago, after he spent around a week swooping over the valley. Our guess is Maxwell has taken his force to Evfel, and that was his eagle."

"He has an eagle? What does it do?"

The mountain villager shook his head. "Ever since Maxwell returned, there has been an eagle flying into and out of those woods. What it does is anyone's guess, but the timing must tie it to Maxwell."

"Does King Wilber know of this?"

Charles grinned. "Who cares? I hardly think it urgent. We all know if Maxwell tried to go to Evfel, no one would ever see him again. They say only Evfelians can survive the Elcan Woods, even if you do avoid the dangers of the gorge."

"I would not be too sure of his death, Charles," Taylor sighed. "Maxwell deals in magic. 'Course, I cannot say I care if he is loose in Evfel."

They looked up as Max reentered. "Your mule is happy," he informed them. "Would you like me to take your things to your room?"

Taylor laughed. "Pull up a chair, Max. You work too hard." Once his assistant had slung his cloak over the back of his seat and joined them, the innkeeper said, "When Charles is done eating, we can both help."

Max's infectious grin brought a smile to Taylor's face.

As the winter worsened, it became even harder to find food in Arieh. Then another blizzard struck, driving all the homeless into any public building available to them. Following suit, the Isfullen split up. Amid a crowd of people pushing into the smallest tavern in the Erado District, the King's Reward, Arnacin settled at the table nearest the door, nodding to the two men sitting there. Since most of the clientele shoved themselves around tables out of range of the wind blowing through the open entrance, the one the islander picked was spacious.

Pulling his cloaks tighter around him, the islander softly asked the two other men, "Do you not mind the cold coming in that door?"

"Huh," the dirtier of the two snorted. "There is more room to think here. I should wonder why you chose this spot. You shiver much more than do we."

Unsuccessfully trying to control any such signs of cold, Arnacin nodded. "You must know how to find food on these streets better than I do."

The cleaner of the two leaned forward. "Considering the circles I have seen you in, I am not surprised by your ignorance. You are very innocent, you know. You buy food off that minstrel you met and keep to garbage heaps, but you never beg or pretend illness before the younger ladies of means in order to steal their sympathy. No, you have yet to learn duplicity."

Arnacin could not prevent the dark smile that crossed his face. Leaning forward himself, he whispered, "I know duplicity, men. Yet I care nothing for 'sympathy.' After all, your 'ladies of means' never have any."

"In my experience, women and children cannot ignore their horror. The ignored wretch haunts them, howling in their dreams until they drop a coin, be it a small token, to assuage their conscience. Such coins have a way of piling up."

"I would much rather put my trust in the tyranny of the masses—as in today, when the tavern keepers will not kick us out because of how many desperate folk crowd their buildings."

"Force in numbers, yes," the dirtier one mumbled. "I hear things about you." As Arnacin pulled back slightly, the man smiled. "I hear about others as well, but they disappear better. You, on the other hand, are said to be a noble."

"Yet you are not concerned," Arnacin commented. "You're still sitting here, after all."

"You are Montiszian." At the islander's silence, the man nodded. "The old kingdom. Those the Montza District is named for, as the original part of the city. As you know, any nobility of theirs was thrown into the streets, and there they stay. No one who looks to be as much of their blood as you can claim Evfelian nobility."

Aware he was treading on dangerous ground by admitting ignorance, yet too curious to back down, Arnacin asked, "How do I resemble those of the old kingdom, and how would you know? They merged into Evfel ages ago. No man now lives who remembers that time."

"My great-grandmother prided herself on descending from the last king of Montisze. From her, we heard many stories long handed down. As for their looks, you can easily pick out the purer bloods here. They are marked by darker hair—generally black—fair skin, small bones, and their women are stunning beauties. Oh, to see a Montiszian woman…" The man coughed. "Yes, I saw one that was closer to a pureblood—a rich prostitute, unfortunately—before some wretch of a noble killed her instead of paying her for his *time.*

"As it is, you are not pureblood. Your height is Evfelian, though you are small in stature, otherwise. Another thing that marks the men, though, is that they are incapable of growing beards. You also have that to mark you."

"There is Montiszian blood in Evfel nobility, though," the cleaner man said, calling the other Evfelian's bluff. "Obviously, not all the old nobility were removed."

The dirtier man's eyes flashed. "Oh yes, they were. I don't count that half-Montiszian who was given a position of lord. In fact, I hate his very name." His gaze fixed on Arnacin. "And if you are related to him, I will kill you on the spot, as I would him if he still lived for betraying his country."

"Who?"

"Fromca, Evfel's 'legendary hero.' I have landed in a cell many a time for starting brawls over that traitor, the man who assisted in the fall of all Montisze."

"Why would he do that?" Arnacin asked.

"Revenge, although he had no right. His father was a Montiszian criminal, sent to the penal colony. Fromca was born there, but as he was not a condemned man himself, he was able to weasel his way into Montisze's trust. Legend goes that he played spy for Evfel, helping it annihilate Montisze."

Compressing his lips, the islander shook his head. "I am not related to him."

Their conversation abruptly ended as a man stumbled through the door, catching himself on their table. "Oh, oh, let me sit down." Slapping into an empty chair, he pushed a snow-laden scarf off his head. He was round-faced, though the usual starvation of the homeless had caused his cheeks to sink.

After a moment, he lifted a bag, pulling out a coin as he beckoned a serving man over. "A leg of mutton and a pint of hot cid—" he broke off, looking at the other men at the table. From one pair of eyes to another, both of which had lit at the mention of food, his gaze finally stopped on Arnacin, who was still trembling slightly.

"Skip the mutton," the newcomer sighed. "Four pints of hot cider, please." He closed his fist about his coin, jerking his hand out of the server's reach. Smiling, he added, "I came by enough fortune to share."

Snorting, the server tromped away, but he was back not too long afterward with the order, holding out his hand for the money. After the exchange was made, he plopped a tankard before each man at the table and turned away.

None of the three tablemates moved at first, so with a sigh, the newcomer lifted his tankard and guzzled a good portion of it. Rosiness appeared in his cheeks, heightening his pleasant smile as he plunked the tankard down and looked at them. Slowly, his smile faded. "You do not want the gift? Come, drink. It will warm all of you right down to your toes."

Arnacin hesitated for a few minutes as the other two accepted their own cider, their shoulders relaxing in the warmth. Such a denial of generosity could harm the Isfullen's plans, and he had no real reason for distrust at the moment anyway.

Giving in, he took a large sip of the steaming cider. Wonderful warmth seeped all the way down him, though he did not risk any more, as laced with alcohol as it was. Considering his lack of food lately and the alcohol's strength, that one sip was already a dangerous amount.

The newcomer was watching him. "Are you the undercover noble?" To Arnacin's blank stare, he leaned closer. "How is the rebellion going?"

"What rebellion?"

Looking around the table at the other two men, who were watching intently, the newcomer shrugged. "Just let me know when the fighting comes," he whispered. "I want to bash some knights' skulls."

"You would be the first," Arnacin laughed. As the others joined him, the conversation turned to the rough lifestyle of the street and the abuse inflicted by those with money. Mainly, the islander only listened, nodding his head in sympathy here and there.

Slowly, however, he felt his internal temperature rise feverishly. As the room began to sway, he cursed his stupidity for actually drinking any of the cider. When he thought about it, he could not recall the last time he had even touched alcohol, and here he was drinking it without a morsel of food to help. Of course, under current circumstances, his memory was hardly something on which he could rely.

His forehead pressed into his hand and his senses dulled. He only became aware of the real danger when he felt a vise-grip on his upper arm, pulling him to his feet. "The duke wishes to see you," a voice growled in his ear. Grayness was falling over the room.

Then he felt rough fibers tighten around his wrist, and he jerked backward as some alertness returned, some knowledge that no sip of alcohol could have made him lose consciousness like this.

As if in another world, he felt toes under his heel and yanked himself forward. The grasp on his arm disappeared, and he bolted through the door into the safety of the deadly blizzard.

As soon as the storm slowed enough to see anything, Tevin slogged through the deep snow to find Michael. The enchanter immediately took wing when he learned Arnacin had disappeared into the blizzard and that, as soon as clouds had rolled in, the duke had positioned men in every public house to catch their black-haired companion. There was no sign of Arnacin. If he had ducked into another shelter, he was most likely already caught and guards would be hauling him up to the castle soon.

With that thought, the eagle climbed higher, cautiously swooping around, watching for movement along Arieh's streets. Untarnished snow covered the usual mud, although that was sure to be altered soon by the number of the penniless streaming from the buildings as they were forced back outside.

The Isfullen gathered in clumps, then fanned out in their own searches. Meanwhile, those who had found themselves trapped outside the castle overnight, soldiers and tradesmen alike, returned, slogging up the streets to the drawbridge, which grudgingly lowered for them.

None of them had a prisoner, yet that alone did not calm Michael. Then, the castle gates opened and a battalion of armed men marched into the city. Quickly scanning the streets, the eagle located Raymond on its northern edge, staring down toward the forest, and plummeted.

"Be on guard," the enchanter warned as he landed in the snow beside his ally. "Castle Dalacort has sent out men. They might be looking for the rest of you."

No alarm passed on the hunter's face. Instead, weariness filled those gray eyes. "No sign of Arnacin, then?"

"Leave that to me," Michael growled, ruffling his feathers as he again prepared for flight. "You and Vilo are most likely to be next if they do catch that idiot."

The only sign that Raymond disagreed was a brief tightening of his jaw. He nodded, and the eagle took to the sky.

When Michael found Vilo, he repeated the warning he'd already shared with Raymond and, afterward, he returned to observing the city. Voices carried on the breeze soon informed him the Isfullen's opponents were also on the hunt for Arnacin. As good as that was, there was still nothing to indicate the islander's whereabouts, as armed men shoved their way over the homeless, into houses, and back out to the streets in their search.

Some of the penniless were leaving the city, trooping down the narrow path in the snow with pitiful bundles over their shoulders. How they thought they would survive the winter without the city's slim protection from the weather was anyone's guess, but go, they did. Laughing, Castle Dalacort's forces let them pass. Their only opposition was to place two men along the top of the sole trail leaving the city to check faces. It was probably a bad omen that their presence did nothing to stem the number of evacuees, who apparently sensed an approaching slaughter.

Four soldiers searched the Cedar Apple, located on the trail leading away from the city. Later, the two guards checking faces were called to join the hunt for the rebel leader. Duke Reginold's men had turned over enough of the south side; now they could start on the northern portion instead of controlling the trailhead to the west.

It was then that a girl started up the mountain path, a bucket clutched to her chest. A bucket. The Cedar Apple had its own water supply, never needing to use the few city wells. As far as Michael knew, their larders were packed for the winter—more than other taverns, at least.

Suspicious, the eagle swooped closer as the girl shuffled through the snow onto King's Crossing, stumbling against the people traveling in the opposite direction. She was dressed warmly enough, with odds and ends, marking her as a serving girl. At every corner, she peered around it before moving on, and at every person that passed, she glanced up.

As she turned into a smaller, less-used side street in the Erado District, Michael touched ground behind her and transformed. "What use is the bucket?" he asked.

With a squeal, she whirled around and lifted her bucket higher. "W-Water."

"If you want to avoid the authorities, you better try harder." As the girl shrank back, Michael added, "Or you could tell me why you need a disguise, and I may help you."

For a second, the girl remained quiet as she trembled and licked her lips. Then, the sound of a horse snorting caused her to flinch. "I need to speak to the minstrel." She spoke in a rush. "The one that has been playing for the local taverns."

Hearing hooves approaching, Michael did not press her. Instead, grabbing her wrist, he jerked her around the corner with a "Follow me" and then dragged her down several side streets.

Fifteen minutes later, they came to where a good portion of the Isfullen now sat around an alleyway in the Montza District that was filled with boxes and barrels. The street at their feet had already been tramped back to brown slush by the search parties. Slouching against one wall, Thomas was asking, "What if they found him?"

"Impossible, Thomas," Tevin sighed. "They're still searching, aren't they?"

"Maybe they are searching for us," Malachi whispered. "Who—"

They all straightened as Michael stopped the girl before the barrel against which Vilo was leaning. "She wishes to speak to you," the enchanter announced.

The girl's gaze darted around the group before she turned back to the minstrel. "The owner of the Cedar Apple wishes to speak to you, actually."

Leaning more heavily against the barrel, Vilo folded his arms. "This hardly seems like a day to ask for my services."

"He has something of yours. At least, he believes it belongs to all of you."

"Is that so?" Michael growled. "Did he ask for all of us specifically, or as many as were with the minstrel?"

"Shh," Lazarus cautioned, stepping forward. "What is this thing that belongs to a group of homeless men?"

"You search for it now, but I am to tell you it will be discarded if you do not all come to talk to the tavern keeper."

"It's a trap," Tevin muttered, shaking his head. In another corner, Raymond shifted.

Lazarus looked toward the hunter before turning back to the girl. "Until you came to us, you did not know how few of us there would be. How could your master make such a demand? What if only our minstrel went?" He shrugged. "What if we're not searching for anything?"

The girl nervously glanced at each of them in turn. As she again met the fisherman's gaze, a little of her courage seemed to return. "If you care for your missing item, your minstrel will come, at least. We wish to make a deal with you, but with the soldiers on the move, none of us have much time."

While Lazarus and Vilo appraised the girl, Raymond softly stepped up beside Michael. "We'll find our own safe road," he whispered. "Make sure they have what they say they do, whole. If not, fly back swiftly. We may be discovered."

With a nod, Michael checked to make sure the girl would not see, then transformed and took to the skies.

In the end, Lazarus decided most of them should disperse into the city. They had probably spent too long sitting there as a group as it was. Eight men, including Vilo, Raymond and himself, would go speak to the Cedar Apple's owner. Their group would be few enough to avoid suspicion from the soldiers, but large enough to escape a trap if needed.

On command, the small party crept down the well-trodden path to the mountainside tavern. The girl, who had introduced herself as Abby, opened the side door and hastily beckoned them into the kitchens.

An older woman greeted them with a nod as Abby closed the door behind them. "Five of you may follow our girl," the woman said. "But the rest of you must wait here. Abby, it's the seventh room down the hall."

The girl nodded. Trading glances with Lazarus, Raymond asked, "Any five will do?"

"Any five." The strength of the woman's gaze was reminiscent of Matalaide, at her least patient.

No one said anything more. Raymond, Lazarus, Vilo, Tevin and Thomas stepped forward.

Abby led them to a small, plain door. Opening it revealed a tight, dark stairway winding around on itself. Without lighting a candle, the girl started upward. "Shh," she warned as she disappeared into the blackness. "There are dignitaries in the upstairs rooms."

"Here?" Tevin asked.

"They are stuck until more of the snow melts."

In the dark, they filed upward, coming to a landing at the end of a dim hallway. As softly as they could, they tiptoed down to the seventh door on the left. There, Abby knocked.

"What do you want?" a rough voice demanded from inside, followed by the sound of footsteps.

"It's Abby," the girl said. The door opened. Standing behind it was a man built much like Lazarus, although shorter, who hustled them in and quickly shut the door behind them.

The alarming click of the lock was lessened by the sight of Arnacin's motionless form on the bed. Still, Raymond searched the rafters with his gaze. Their red eagle perched atop a high dresser, so still that only those looking for him would have noticed. How he had slipped into that window-less room was anyone's guess, but he was there—the Isfullen's extra protection.

"I thought the owner wished to speak to us." Vilo's question brought Raymond's attention back to the man who had allowed them entry.

"I do."

Vilo appraised the man. "You're not the innkeeper to whom I spoke last month."

"I'm the new owner," the man said. "Vincent. Now, I believe you are connected with that instigator." He jerked his head in the bed's direction.

"What did you do to him?" Raymond demanded.

With a sneer, Vincent growled, "We saved him, stupidly enough. His heart wasn't beating when we pulled him in, but we were able to start it again. His very presence endangers everyone here though. So..." He looked pointedly at Vilo. "How much is he worth to you?"

A frozen stillness settled on the room as the handful of Isfullen studied the man. "What do you want?" Raymond asked after a moment. "You ought to know we own nothing of value."

Vincent stared back, his eyes narrowing. Finally, he rubbed his chin. "We might as well say it. We lack trust in you and you lack trust in us. So... I'll start. Your friend was found buried in the snow with a rope tied around his wrist. *Naturally*, Abby recognized him as the minstrel's friend." To the side, Abby blushed.

Brushing her reaction away with an impatient gesture, the new innkeeper continued, "It was obvious he was in trouble, and in trouble with the regent. Today has only proven that."

"Yet you hid him?" Lazarus asked politely.

Again rubbing his chin, Vincent shrugged. "How successfully is your rebellion going?"

Everyone, including the eagle, turned to Lazarus. The fisherman exhaled, took his cap off and ran his fingers through his hair. Then, with a preparatory breath, he replaced the cap. "I think you put too much stock in rumors. We, at least, have no rebellion. What the rest of the city is planning due to our presence is a different matter."

"Is that so?" Smiling slightly, the new owner nodded. "Then why is Castle Dalacort in a panic to catch the new 'rebel leader'? To our knowledge, they are still turning over every floorboard in search of him. And anyone who still has any sense is trying to evacuate, as long as they think they can make it to the next city at all."

When no one replied, Vincent looked back at Arnacin. "Or are you saying he has no connection with you?"

Lazarus puffed a sigh in defeat. "You know he is a friend of ours, but we are not looking for a rebellion."

Turning to the girl standing beside them, the innkeeper asked, "Abby, how many of them did you find?"

"I think there are a couple hundred men. There were at least a hundred in that alleyway."

"A couple hundred?" Vincent's grin made Raymond feel like a mouse faced with an adder. "A couple hundred, and you're not starting a rebellion. You would not be so insane as to keep such numbers in this city unless you had a mission. Or do I speak to the wrong man? Is there someone else to whom I should take my offer?"

Lazarus shook his head, yet said nothing.

Studying him, Vincent whispered, "Know this—you need us. But if you remain unwilling to admit it, very well. Take your chances."

"What are you offering that we so need?"

"Shelter and food."

"Really?" Vilo muttered. "Suddenly so generous?"

"Did you forget your friend still lives?" the owner exclaimed. "Go see for yourself. We even woke him once, to make sure the danger to him was passed—although I doubt he was actually alert. Don't scoff, or our consideration could instantly change."

Lazarus and Vilo remained where they stood, keeping by the door should they need to escape. The other three approached the bed. Arnacin's breathing was regular, and though his hair, clumped against the pillow, was still crusted with mud, someone had sponged most of the dirt off his face. It might have been the room's lighting or the lack of grime emphasizing his black hair, or the new clean shirt, but he appeared deathly pale. Still, his breathing was indeed regular and his fingers were warm to the touch.

Raymond realized everyone was now watching him. Meeting Lazarus's gaze, he tilted his head slightly in question. The fisherman merely nodded. Taking that as permission to choose the next action, Raymond sighed.

Vincent was glancing between them warily. Regarding the innkeeper in turn, Raymond folded his arms. "What little nugget do you take out of this?"

The innkeeper shrugged. "A chance for freedom, if you win. I like the idea of a rebellion."

"You must be insane if you think we're fooled by that," Vilo spoke up. "The danger to you if a rebellion makes your tavern its base is immense. And important couriers and nobility often stop here. So, if you please, be honest."

"Very well, minstrel. You know I am not the old owner. I was, in fact, a slave. This nice, fortified, out-of-the-way tavern, however, allowed more..." He paused, sucking on his teeth. "...*opportunities* than other locations. For instance, the unfortunate death of our master. We want your rebellion to continue spreading alarm, thereby covering our former master's odd disappearance."

Chapter 10

THE CEDAR APPLE'S PRICE

A SHUDDER PASSED THROUGH RAYMOND as he thought of the implications of Vincent's words. No one moved for a moment, and the hunter tried not to picture what the inn's staff had done with the body to conceal it from the searchers that had just been there. What might hide even now beneath their feet or in the walls?

For that matter, there was no promise that an uncaught murderer would not strike again.

At last, Vincent shrugged. "Look, you can't refuse. The duke is sure to keep extra patrols on the streets until he finds the threat he's looking for, and that's not one person. He searches for a rebellion. Any group of people found loitering will be seen as suspicious. Every act of compassion will be seen as an attempt to buy supporters. The city will soon be paved in blood, mark my words. If you won't hide, yours will join the stream."

Hesitantly, he offered his hand. "What say you? Our food, warmth and shelter in exchange for your group's continued aggravation of the regent?"

Vilo and Lazarus shared a glance. Then, after a moment, they nodded. Raymond also inclined his head, and the fisherman took the proffered hand. "Very well, but I warn you—betrayal will go the worse for you. We have ways of making sure of that."

If they did, Raymond had no idea what they were. True, they had an enchantress on their side, but who knew what she would or would not do?

Vincent nodded thoughtfully, drawing back. "We will heat some water. After food and a bath, you will likely feel restored."

Arnacin was roused by pain pounding in his temples, and he pressed the back of his hand against his forehead.

The flap of wings and a gust of wind brought the islander to full consciousness. He jerked away from the sound. Michael had settled on the headboard, his long talons digging into the wood. Above, a red canopy was draped over the bed's frame.

In alarm, Arnacin pushed himself to his elbows. He made it no farther, however. The room seemed to pitch, and his stomach complained. "Michael," he moaned. "What happened?"

A flutter spoke of the eagle's relocation. Then, the bed sank under the boy's weight. "The Cedar Apple offered us a deal. Raymond only just left to help move barrels from the cellar."

"What deal?" The islander's traitorous breath caught for a second. When Michael tried to push him back against the pillows, he resisted, seizing the boy's arm. Yet he lacked strength, and Michael's gentle pressure won. Still, he asked, "A cellar?"

Michael was silent for a moment. That was all it took for Arnacin to know his fears were real. His heart rate increased. The air thickened around them. Only the enchanter's piercing copper eyes kept him aware of time and space. He must have looked petrified.

"The Cedar Apple has offered their food and shelter," Michael said, "in exchange for our continued distraction of their government and its powers. Their cellar is big enough for all of us and will allow us to come and go without passing any of the public spaces."

Arnacin shook his head. "No! Not a cellar!"

The owners would shove all the Isfullen in and lock the door. Without much effort on Arieh's part, the Isfullen would die in a tomb and all would be lost.

"Arnacin," Michael snapped in warning. Only then did the islander realize he was gasping and the boy's fingers were turning blue from the vise-like grip on his arm. As Arnacin released him, the boy said soothingly, "We discussed every-thing. None of us trusts them either, but we made what precautions we could. Besides, many of the tavern staff are clearly sympathetic to our situation. It will be hard for them to work against each other."

"I can't—"

"You must." There was no room for argument in the enchanter's tone. "Just as Vilo must stay out in the streets for the next few weeks, regardless of the danger. He is too well known, but since his relation to you is not certain, only his disappearance at the same time will reveal that connec-tion. Without it, no one will turn in their minstrel.

"You, on the other hand, must not appear again." Michael lightly shook the islander's shoulder, blending reprimand and comfort. "Nor can you stay here, if you were going to suggest it. This is a main corridor for those staying overnight at the inn. A stream of food and water going in and out of your room would look suspicious, and you cannot risk being seen. For your sake, I hope you can stay put so I can make sure no one attacks Vilo when he goes out."

Muttering an apology, Arnacin pushed his fist into his forehead. Somehow, he had to be sane. Somehow. Sane, while locked in a cellar.

Over the next two weeks, most of the Isfullen stayed hidden. The few that went out brought back reports that the duke was hanging anyone he even slightly suspected, especially among the homeless. Charity became a precursor to execution. No one could speak softly together or in groups without grief.

In turn, most people with shelter stayed in until they had no other choice. When they did need to step out, figures flitted with heads down, alone and silent through the streets, to accomplish the most urgent tasks, then returned home.

Vilo was forced to accept pay for his music, although it brought less money and patrons to the taverns than it had. After a week, the Cedar Apple, which served the various Evfel messengers and saw no such decrease in paying customers, allowed the minstrel to stay for a week to perform for them. A room and one meal a day was their offer. He could keep whatever the patrons gave him as additional recompense.

Exhausted from tramping the streets in the cold, he agreed. Although the Isfullen dared not interact with him during that time, many felt soothed by his music as it distantly floated down to their hole.

Meanwhile, illness attacked Arnacin. He had curled up in a corner of the cellar, hardly eating, barely talking, and never sleeping. Then, on the third week of their disappearance, high fevers came.

"He just doesn't *want* to live," Michael grumbled, sitting beside Raymond while they watched Arnacin twitch in delirium.

"We need him to," Raymond whispered, pulling the blanket higher over his sick friend. "He knows that."

Michael said nothing.

It took two days for the fever to break, and another five for Arnacin to recover any sort of real strength. Raymond resolved never to let it happen again. Arnacin *would* eat and sleep, whether he wanted to or not.

As was the tradition in Ansky, the birthday of the current Maxwell king, or their heir apparent, was their New Year celebration. The Dalacorts left it alone, at least for the time being, and the locals, though they swore their hatred of the prince, were glad for any reason to hold a winter party in the Sky Haven.

Many people had eaten less for days to stockpile food for the merrymaking. Now, despite being a group of mostly women, children and old men, they filled the center of the cleared floor with dance. They used their voices, a couple of glasses, and an overturned bucket as instruments.

The few girls who hoped for a male partner either picked their little brothers, cajoled their aging fathers, or loitered around with an occasional glance at Max, standing behind the counter. He had made himself the designated fire tender, tidier and attendant if needed, but he had retreated into shyness. Now, he stood politely listening to the chatter of two girls, but his usual easy laugh was missing.

Watching him, Taylor Magree wondered if he had discovered one reason his assistant was so good with animals—crowds intimidated him.

As a dance ended, someone lifted a tankard high. "To our beloved Prince Maxwell on his seventeenth birthday! May he die tomorrow!" With a cheer, tankards clanked together. Behind many laughing and happy faces, Max stayed in the background, fidgeting with his fingers.

"It is treason to drink to that," someone said.

Turning back to the group, Taylor sighed, "Martin, our king is Wilber Dalacort. What difference does it make?"

Martin did not look at him, his own gaze fixed on Max. Softly, he growled, "Phillip was not just my king, Taylor. He was my friend, and I will not betray him by drinking to his son's death!"

Beside him, his wife, Christina, placed her hand on his arm. "Enough of this. Start the dancing. We may not be young, but I can still dance a jig that leaves all you men breathless."

Laughing, a younger girl asked, "But can you leave me breathless?"

"And what about Max?" another maiden piped up. "He is too young to lose his breath during a jig."

"The only man to be so," Christina laughed. "Well, someone, start the music again. The challenge is on."

As Christina issued her challenge, one of the girls, who had introduced herself as Tanya, plucked at Evan's sleeve. "Come. Will you dance this one?"

"Oh," he sighed, "very well. I'll warn you now though, I make a terrible partner."

Tanya laughed. "Just listen for the instructions. This is easy enough for toddlers, and if you turn the wrong way at first because you forget your left and right, you can fix that easily. No one cares."

He knew she was right, so he lined up within the circle with the others.

Amid that fast dance, as partners kept changing, he found himself briefly with the middle-aged Christina. "You are too quiet, Max," she whispered, but he had no time to answer as they swung past each other, hooking arms with the next partner and then changing again.

When Evan was finally able to slip out, however, Christina joined him against the counter, holding her chest as she gasped for air. "They were supposed to lose their breath before you, remember?" the prince laughed.

Christina shook her head, still panting. "They can win. Oh, I have not danced like that for years."

"I thought you held these every year?"

She sighed, her breathing calming as she did. "This time of year has always made me sad. I never feel like dancing." She shrugged. "This is the birthday of our prince. Each cele-bration just serves to remind me, I held him for his fifth and thus failed him. Had I been able to care for him and his siblings better twelve years ago, Wilber would never have stolen him, and I..."

Uncomfortably, Evan patted her arm as she faltered. Try as he might, he could not drag any memory of that winter forth. He only recalled the hazy image of some plain wood walls surrounding the door that Wilber walked through late the next spring. Yet, Christina was sure to remember better than he did, and if she truly had cared for him when he was five, there was no telling if she recognized him. Instead of continuing to pursue that dangerous subject, the prince asked, "Yet, tonight is different?"

The lady pushed herself off the counter. "It was an excuse this time."

"To stop a political debate?"

Christina hesitantly appraised him. "You now know my reason for protesting the toast. May I ask yours?"

Blood rushed through Evan's ears. Digging his fingers into the counter's edge, he licked his lips and shrugged. "I come from a foreign place. Taylor has told me a little about the problems with your prince, but in reality, he is unknown to me. Why should I curse a stranger?"

The lady's blue eyes narrowed briefly. Then she nodded. "You are very wise, Max, not to let others' feelings sway your own."

Yet as she walked away, Evan suspected there was more to what she thought. Shivering, he slipped into the kitchen.

"It's a lost cause," Wolflin grumbled, tromping into the Cedar Apple's cellar. "Everyone is too frightened to be even the slightest bit honest. They've been smiling like toads and saying they're blissfully happy for weeks." Plopping onto the stone floor by Lazarus, he rubbed his hands over his grizzled face. "This whole thing's pointless."

"I've said that from the beginning," Michael muttered, folding his arms. "But of course, no one listens to me."

Sighing, the fisherman patted Wolflin's shoulder. "We had to try. If nothing changes by the time spring—"

The door swung open, rendering them all silent. There stood a small cloaked figure, her curls blown about her face.

"Carrie!" Michael exclaimed, pushing himself off the wall.

"How did you find us?" Tevin asked, even as someone else said, "What happened?"

Nodding in greeting, Carrie soothingly replied, "Everything is well. Evan has fully recovered." She said nothing about how she had known where to go, but for anyone who knew Lisya, it was a silly question.

A large sigh of relief passed throughout the cellar until she added, "He is helping the Anskonian townsfolk."

Now, hundreds of protests echoed around the cavernous cellar. In the commotion, Michael exclaimed, "Oh, I am needed everywhere! Carrie, go back and drag that... that..." Suddenly, *fool*, *imbecile* and like words were completely inadequate. "Drag that *prince* into the Ice Woods."

Although laughter danced in her eyes, Carrie simply asked, "How is it here?"

Lazarus rubbed his creased brow. "Do us one favor, Carrie. Go back and tell Evan that as things stand, we have no access to Evfel. Fear and greed are their only motivators. Although some have suggested we try to use that, we don't know if he wants us to do so. Otherwise, we lack the resources and power to achieve anything more. Ask him if he wants us to continue or if we should return to Ansky in the spring, when it is safe to travel."

Though the enchantress's daughter gave a slight nod, she continued standing there, waiting. Tevin was the first to budge, nudging Arnacin in the ribs while the younger islander sat curled into a corner. "I'm sure you can tell her what happened."

Arnacin only curled up tighter, muttering, "No, I can't."

"But you used to be the best storyteller on the island," Vilo reminded him. Raymond snorted nearby.

"That was before I learned the value of silence."

A brief laugh escaped Carrie, causing Michael to glance at her. Very rarely did he actually hear her laugh. She must have found the islander anything but silent.

Pushing that thought away, Michael stepped over to his sister. Malachi, James and Thomas also approached. "Come on," Michael whispered. "I will give you more of a report as we walk. Most of these humans are incapable of enduring a summary without dying on the spot."

His sister's eyes danced at him. But wrapping an arm around Malachi, she stepped out with the twins. Michael shut the door behind them.

"Felleno has been our only successful connection," Michael sighed. Lisya's children had wandered down the trail from Arieh until it branched off in the lower region of the mountain. There, they took a less-used road while they caught their sister up on the past months. "He has become all but one of us, since he also must hide. Not so much as Arnacin, but still, the Cedar Apple's sanctuary is good for him, and his knowledge of Arieh and its people has been informative at least, if disheartening."

"If nothing changes," James whispered, "I fear Evan is lost, Carrie. Ansky is too strong, *and* they wait for him there. Evfel will never riot. They look out for themselves over everything else, including their own freedom."

Carrie had said nothing while her brothers talked. Now, as they turned back to the Cedar Apple, the path glinting in the sunset and winding away below them, she nodded. "I will tell Evan."

Michael stopped her. "Carrie, just tell him the facts, without speaking of the Isfullen's despair. He has to make a plan with some hope of success."

With a submissive nod, she transformed into a doe. But before she could leave, Michael touched her shoulder. "Should you not rest first?"

The deer's long lashes blinked at him, but she gave no other response.

"Look, Carrie," he sighed. "I can at least glide on the air currents. You clearly were cheated when the only thing you can effortlessly change into is a helpless-looking doe."

He knew that, inwardly, she was laughing at him, but outwardly, there was still no reaction. "Are you sure you would rather not learn more of your skills, at least until you figure out how to transport to a location or to fly?"

A shudder finally moved the doe's flanks, but nodding her head, she simply sprang north toward Ansky.

Endless days. No air. Darkness.

Lying there gasping, Arnacin tried to focus on the peaceful, even breaths of the sleepers nearby. It was odd that they slumbered without struggling to breathe—or maybe his fear was tricking his body.

Never mind. He was done. Pushing himself to his feet, Arnacin fled over his companions, through the cellar entrance, up the stairs, and into the kitchen. Yet even that room was an enclosed space, so he jerked open the door into the stable. Finally, he stopped, his chest heaving in the fresh, freezing air blowing through the cave's mouth.

As his heart rate slowed, he rested his back against the uneven rock wall. There, at least, he knew what was imaginary and what was real. Still, looking at the starlight blazing off the snow only feet away, he felt his heart clench with a desire to continue his flight away from those close corridors. If he froze to death, it would be a relief.

His weight was shifting in obedience to that compulsion when the sound of soft footsteps in the kitchen stopped him. With a sigh, he pulled his cloaks closer to protect against the cold—or rather, to hide his own darkness.

Unsurprisingly, it was Raymond who entered the stables. Shutting the door behind him, he appraised his friend and then leaned against the wall in silence.

Arnacin turned back to the view outside and the wind that rustled the hay around the cave mouth. No lanterns were lit inside, leaving dust motes to flicker beneath the moonlight reflecting off the snow. Steam rose from the horses' nostrils, curling into downward shafts of light. Due to the cold, Evfel stabled all their steeds five to a stall, and even the animals knew better than to squabble.

"What plagues you, Arnacin?" Raymond softly prodded in the gentle quiet.

With a quick jerk, Arnacin shook his head.

"I think you should voice it. It will heal better."

With a sardonic grin, Arnacin said, "Is that an order, Raymond? I thought you knew that wouldn't work."

Raymond laughed slightly. "You must have been eleven before I actually stopped giving you direct commands. Before then, you were far too impetuous for me not to try."

The sensation of sunlight and contentedness prickled in the back of Arnacin's memory, but try as he might, it never took shape. He shrugged. "I can't imagine it was ever a real war. Weren't we both quieter than that?"

In the silence that followed, he felt Raymond studying him. As he met that probing gaze, the hunter shook his head. "Do you really have no memory of it? Sometimes, I think you only know your own past from other people's stories of it."

Arnacin dropped his gaze, shifting uncomfortably, but Raymond's sigh saved him from answering. "No," the hunter admitted. "I can't remember a time we actually fought. It seemed you and Charlotte sometimes did nothing but argue, but you were closer in age."

With a slight nod, Arnacin pulled Michael's cloak over his nose, returning them to silence.

This time, it lasted only a moment. "Arnacin, what's in the cellar?"

Shuddering, the younger islander sighed. "The truth is, I can't speak of it, Raymond. If I try... I'll lose even the small bit of sanity I have left. I relive those moments enough without slowing down to retell them."

Arnacin shook his head, then continued. "I'm not sane, Raymond. Lately, I don't even know reality from imagination." With a small puff of amusement, he added, "And poor Michael's witnessed that firsthand."

Compressing his lips, Raymond patted his friend's back in sympathy.

In the relative quiet of the Sky Haven's common room, Taylor sighed. "Another blizzard, Max. Is this our third?"

Once again sitting across the table from the owner, Evan smiled. "You know Ansky, Taylor. At least seven blizzards will strike before it decides spring should come."

Sighing, the innkeeper pushed himself to his feet. "We should sleep, unless you can think of anything else we need to do?"

Evan shook his head, then rested his chin in his hand. After wishing the man good night, he added, "Of course, we can always stand guard in case the roof falls in from all the snow."

"Not my roof," Taylor called back from the stairs.

"It can happen. Even the wooden roof of the south t—" He quickly cut himself off before uttering the word *tower*. "Strong roofs have collapsed before now."

Taylor showed no sign of noticing the idiotic mistake, mumbling as he disappeared, "Well, if it does happen, I just hope it kills me in the process. There is no money to fix it."

Split between self-condemnation and amusement, Evan pressed his forehead into his palm. The sound of wind rushing through the door caused him to jerk upright. Carrie stood leaning against the doorframe, white and shivering.

Instantly, the prince was beside her. After forcing the door closed, he gently pulled her into the kitchen and set a chair for her near the fireplace. "Evan," she forced out. He shushed her, starting a fire in the hearth and hanging a pot of water over it.

Lisya's family did not touch meat. Knowing that, Evan brought out a block of cheese and a hunk of bread. "Eat something first."

He had no doubt she was quite content staying quiet and would do so forever if she could. As he pulled up a chair beside her, however, she exhaled.

"Duke Reginold has been hanging anyone he finds even slightly suspicious, so the citizens are all desperately supportive of their government right now. Even an act of charity is seen as a reason for investigation. Lazarus wishes to know if you would like them to return in the spring."

Her words felt like a barrage of water. There were so many details to consider, but no context. Skipping over the more humorous thought that she made for an interesting and unexpected courier, Evan voiced his second and more pressing concern. "Are the Isfullen safe in Arieh?"

Carrie nodded once, but offered nothing more.

"Have they found somewhere to hide if necessary?"

Another nod. She watched him as if waiting, seeming to expect him to understand the rest, yet... Was she even coming with word from Evfel, or was it her mother who knew these things?

"Did you actually go to Evfel?"

Carrie remained silent as the fire popped, and Evan's gaze was drawn to it. Had he sent the Isfullen into a country already in the bloody aftermath of a rebellion or was this the workings of the Isfullen? If someone had just tried to overthrow the government and failed, there would not be another opening for some time. Arieh would be extra watchful, and the people would remain too afraid to do anything.

Yet Ansky was running out of time. If Wilber's attention could not be diverted, and if Ansky so vehemently despised Evan himself, the Isfullen would have lost their chance before they had even started.

The Dalacorts had their empire. Evan had given it to them.

A light touch on his shoulder brought him back from the depths of the fire. Carrie watched him, her lips pressed together.

Smiling slightly, the prince asked, "Do you know if any of the islanders think there might be an opening?"

The enchantress's gaze dropped to the table. Evan had the distinct impression that he asked something the Isfullen wished to keep secret. Finally, she whispered, "They think it will only grow worse. Reginold hunts for Arnacin, in particular."

Exhaling, Evan ran a hand over his face. "By that, I guess you mean the Isfullen began their own uprising, and it has failed."

Instead of answering, Carrie tensed, turning toward the doorway into the common room. The prince heard nothing above the howl of the wind outside, but there was no doubt her senses were acute.

Hastily, Evan asked, "Do you have a way to return home t—?"

He broke off as two people came through the door. "Martin! Christina! Are you all right?"

He started to stand, although Martin shooed him to sit back down. "We are fine, Max. This storm just gives us extra cover so we could have an actual conversation."

Having stood anyway, Evan took a step back and glanced over at Carrie, who had also risen to her feet. "What conversation needs such discretion?"

The couple followed his glance to the young enchantress and they paused. "A friend of yours?" Martin asked.

When Evan merely stared, his heart beating fast, Christina approached. Anything that Carrie herself felt was shrouded behind her usual composed watchfulness, always ready for the worst, still seemingly never alarmed.

Yet Christina answered the question for them. "Of course you are a friend, my dear. Both of your silences and your sudden appearance during a blizzard says it all." As the lady neared, she placed a hand on Evan's shoulder. "We were wondering if there was anything we could do for you."

His fingers shook on the back of his chair. "What do you mean?"

Christina laughed gently as she moved past him to remove the pot of water from where it boiled over the fire. "Evan, you might as well be honest. You are obviously aware we know."

"Evan?" Despite the futility, he still tried. There was nothing else he could think to say. "Why did you call me that?"

"Evan." Martin's soft command froze the prince in place. "Return to your seat."

When the prince remained where he stood, Christina gently pried his fingers off his chair, turned it around, and pushed him into it. "Yes, Evan Maxwell. Did you not hear us say your father was our friend, and that we would never betray him by hating his son?"

"Not in so many words, no." Yet his reply was a mumble, caught between the blizzard and too-knowledgeable Anskonians.

After pulling out Carrie's chair for her and seeing her comply, Martin slid into the nearby seat. "If you wished to hide, Evan, your chosen nickname is too obvious, particularly when combined with your looks."

Meanwhile, Christina had quickly moved about Taylor's kitchen. Now, with four cups of tea steeping, she also settled herself. "Do you not remember we took care of you for eight months or so? Through the church's physicians, your father asked us to adopt you as he lay dying. But the church itself believed we could not teach you to rule some day the way you needed. Also, there was a lot of contention among the nobility. They feared the one raising you would use it to secure the throne for his own family. I took our friendship with your parents seriously, but could not stand against the will of the church. Like any biased mother, though, I never believed you were anything but a most wonderful prince."

"Yes," Martin admitted, "You had become such a part of our family that I have cursed the church ever since they asked the Dalacorts to raise you. However, we came to talk about what's going on right now." His eyes bored into Evan. "Even aside from the mysterious source of your food supply, there is also the peculiarity of your continued hiding. No one, not a soul, recognizes you. Yet we saw you just two summers ago. In the midst of islanders, there was the boy who promised to return, to accept his responsibility, who placed Radnor as regent—just for a time—so Wilber and his family could make preparations to leave."

As he stared down at his lap, the prince's only reply was silence. He felt their gazes, however, and had no good response.

Thankfully, Martin continued. "You might have aged some, but it seems ominous that not a single person besides us has called you out. I confess, there is something in your eyes, and your bronzed skin makes you look at least ten years older... But they not only fail to recognize you, they fail to recognize your resemblance to your parents and your mother's father.

"Truth be told, our nobility has long blended with Evfel's people. But like your grandfather, you have the compact frame of a true Anskonian. The texture and color of your hair is every inch your father's, your nose is reminiscent of your mother's, and so forth.

"Yet, again, no one notices any of this. How are you accomplishing that and the gifts? Or more importantly, why?"

"Why?" Slowly, Evan looked up. "Would you believe me if I answered it was because I care?"

While Christina nodded, Martin rubbed his scalp. "Let me go back," the older man sighed. "Everything Wilber pretended to confess made sense. It fit, but for one thing: you *did* steal his horse."

He paused, but when Evan didn't respond, he went on. "You never returned it, not even among the steeds you sent back from the island. Radnor attested to that, and worse. Oh, Evan, if you knew the harm Radnor caused... He never fumed while inside the castle. I think he feared to appear irresponsible in front of Evfel, not that he managed to hide it from them. Instead, he came to this inn with his woes and drinking, and wreaked havoc. He reminded all of Ansky of the stallion you stole and told everyone about the grass that came alive on the island to strangle most of them. What can any of us think after that?"

There was only one answer, one low breath of a word. "Indeed."

Yet Martin grabbed his shoulder. "No, Evan. I have no desire to put you on trial. I ask because you are my king. Yes, you are my king. For love of your father, if nothing else, you will always be my king."

Both Martin and Christina slid to the floor in subservience. Evan inhaled sharply, but there was nowhere to go. "Please don't."

Martin's mouth tightened briefly. "What happened, sire? While Wilber was confessing things, why did you say nothing about the events on the island? Why did you need untrustworthy islanders to back you instead of your own knights? I must honestly say, I cannot stand with you if you have done what logic seems to confirm you have. But I am begging you, reveal all or change."

The pop of the fire was the only sound for a moment. Then Evan sighed. "Come, drink your tea."

Although Martin and Christina both returned to their seats, they remained silent, the air tingling with anticipation. At last, the prince licked his lips. "The stallion, Darkfire, is not mine to take or return. He is a native of the Ice Woods. He came as a captive, yet he refused my attempt to set him free."

Neither husband nor wife interrupted while Evan relayed his wild story, always aware an enchantress shared the table with them—although he feared saying so, for her sake. When he faltered, Carrie placed her hand on his forearm, a reminder of her unconditional support.

Two hours had passed before he finished, leaving untold only Carrie's relationship to the woods. No one spoke. In the silence, the prince held his breath as his heart raced again.

Then Christina pushed herself to her feet. "Let us think on it, Evan. Will you join us for supper tomorrow?"

"I'm not sure, but can you travel safely home in this?" Evan asked, also standing.

Martin nodded. "It is only four steps away. If we keep our hand on the wall of the tavern, we can easily reach out and touch our home."

"Then, may I ask if you can give Carrie a place to stay for the night?"

Suddenly glancing at the girl, Christina gasped, "Of course! You are so quiet, dear. I almost forgot you were there. Any friend of Max is welcome, and I can see how another traveler, at this time in the middle of winter, would look funny."

"It would indeed." In parting, Martin clapped Evan on the shoulder. "Stay safe. You are under the shadow of the ax for as long as you remain."

Since Taylor was happy to excuse someone he swore worked much too hard, and since the sun had come out, Evan trudged through the deep snow to the cottage next door. Over a meal of bread, eggs and cheese, Martin, Christina and Evan discussed the choices facing Ansky and its option of rulers: either Wilber, Evan or Prince Andrew. Carrie, who had stayed with them the night before, nodded occasionally, but as usual, kept her thoughts to herself.

Like the prince's conversation with Carrie the night before, they came to no solutions. Wilber had the people on his side.

The truth of that was almost too hard to swallow. Tapping his fingers on the table, Evan sighed. "At this point, I find myself wondering if Andrew could possibly make a good king."

"I doubt it," Christina huffed. "From all I have heard, he was born spoiled and continues to be so. The only change is in the edge of coldness he picked up after Queen Lorene vanished. Mark my words, he will become a worse ruler than his father. His death sentences will come as unconsidered whims instead of ambitious plots."

"I'm sorry."

"There is no reason you should feel responsible. Lorene pampered him, and Wilber did the true raising, training him in the traditions of the Evfelian kings. That is all there is to it."

Yet Evan shook his head. "I have seen Andrew hiding among the hunting dogs, as gentle with them as I was with the horses. And when I saw him like that, I despised him. There was the first time I remember seeing him, for example. He was learning to walk, one little hand nestled inside his father's and the other in his mother's. I must have been six or seven, but I saw the pride and love in his parents' faces, the excitement in his. And I remember feeling cold and hollow, then the desire to scream and trample that boy right there. I slunk away instead.

"It never changed, though. He had everything I lacked, everything I craved. We have not met for the past two years. I do not know what he is like now, but in the past year I've wondered if he only returned what I gave him from the beginning, if I also created that spiteful beast."

Martin sighed. "There is no way to know what might have been, Evan, but I also doubt Andrew can now be—"

Carrie shot to her feet, alarm showing in her face. "Evan! Guards are banging on doors!"

"How do you know?" Martin asked.

"Trust her!" Evan leapt to his feet, throwing his cloak around his shoulders. "Do you have a back door?"

Christina also jumped up, while her husband cleared the table where the prince had sat. "Here," she said, grabbing a floorboard and shoving it aside to reveal a small hole. "Our cellar. I apologize for the size, but it is far better than walking into a guard on the streets."

He dropped into the small hole. As the board fell back into place, he heard a sharp rap.

All movement stopped. Slowly, Martin's footsteps—they were too heavy for a lady—approached the door. It creaked on its hinges, then a determined clumping echoed over Evan's head.

"We are taking one tenth of the food from every building for our troops," said a commanding voice. Then, dropping a little, it added, "We hear you have it somehow."

"Oh," Christina's voice fluttered. "Take a look."

"Thank you." The commanding voice accompanied the thunk of shod feet as the speaker started toward the indicated place. There was only one step, however, before those heavy shoes squeaked in a sharp turn. "You! Are you not an islander?"

Evan's heart stilled. For a second, no sound stirred the place. Then the tromping continued toward the center of the floor. "Your clothes are in their style! Are you an islander?"

"Leave her alone," Martin snapped. "Do you think a girl like her would entangle herself with their sort?"

"Where did you obtain your clothes?"

There was a slap, followed by a gasp, soft and pained. As Evan pictured the soldier harming her, he felt his blood boil.

"My mother," the young enchantress gasped in her musical voice. In the dark, the prince cringed: Carrie's voice, like her mother's, was beyond mortal ability, filled with the song of her thoughts and able to paint pictures of her feelings in another. Thankfully, this time, it was diluted, like the hush of an alert forest. Evan could only hope that was enough.

"Your mother?" the commanding voice pressed.

"She made it."

"In the island fashion?" There was no answer, but the now coldly commanding voice asked, "Are you a spy?"

"I warn you, leave her alone," Martin again interrupted. "As a man, it is my duty to protect her."

"You better not, or all three of you will find yourselves in a cell! As a man, your responsibility should be to your wife first!" The only sound that followed was the dragging feet. Yet, unlike with most maidens, Carrie never screamed. She simply struggled, though Evan knew she was tiny, no match for the man dragging her out the door. At least, not unless she revealed her true nature.

Martin's footsteps thudded against the floor. Then there came the whacking sound of a fist impacting skin and muscle. "Carrie, go!" Martin shouted.

There was no sound of running footsteps, yet it swiftly became clear that the girl had obeyed the order when the commander called out, "Guards! Catch that maiden! And arrest this couple for harboring spies." Feet clanked over.

"Sir! The maiden is gone!" A distant voice called. "She vanished around a corner!"

"Vanished?"

"There was no one there."

"Nothing living at all?"

"Just a deer bounding over the snow."

"Search every corner! She cannot travel fast once outside the lee of the buildings."

"Sir, her tracks disappeared where the doe's imprints began."

For just a second, there was silence, then the commander hissed. "Sorcery! Take these two, and burn the house down."

"No!" Christina shrieked, echoing Evan's racing heart.

Unintelligible shouts and thudding feet sounded, presumably starting the fire. There wasn't much time to escape. Hopefully, nothing blocked the floorboard from above, yet movement too early would just bring more danger to everyone.

As something clunked and hissed across the floor and embers began drifting down, Evan buried his nose in his cloak. Smoke started to fill the cellar and footsteps dashed overhead to the door.

Until the fire blocked the soldiers' view into the house, however, it was too risky to shift the floorboard. The prince had one deadly chance to time it right.

Heat and smoke consumed the air in that hole. Coughing, Evan forced himself to count another ten seconds. Then he shot to his feet, shoving his palms against the flaming wood above his head. To his relief, it shifted. Ignoring the cinders licking the floor's planks, he hauled himself up. The smoke was even heavier here, and his eyes burned along with his lungs.

Hearing a loud hiss above his head, he rolled aside just as a beam hit the ground beside him. No! It was between himself and the exit.

Snow thudded down with it. A great hiss of steam rose into the air, but the fire was already too hot to be quenched. That smallest potential respite was gone before it came.

Yet, through the hellish pop and crackle, a clarion call shook the air—high, clear and unmistakably Darkfire. That scared command forced Evan to push himself to a crouch as he contemplated his next move. If he leapt over the beam, he might fall right back down into the hole that waited unseen on the other side. But there was no other recourse. Darkness was already sweeping into the airless heat.

The prince leapt even as flames tried to grab him and his black cloak. One foot hit roasting wood, the other found the pit, bringing him slamming onto his knees. No air filled his lungs as he coughed and gasped in pain, yet he could not stop. Blind and swaying, he crawled forward—at least, he hoped it was forward.

Then, the ground changed to icy slush, and he slipped. Snow enveloped him as he crumpled. He had made it out. With that knowledge, darkness swooped over him.

Something bumped his shoulder, yet it was Darkfire's constant war cry that pulled him back to his senses. A doe stood over him, her breath blowing softly on his neck. Around them, Taylor and the other Anskonians had dashed into the streets, trying to contain the fire. Lightly armored men tried to ward off the huge stallion with lashing teeth and flying hooves quicker than the human eye. Martin and Christina stood to the side, released in the hubbub.

"Carrie," Evan gasped, painfully pushing himself to his feet. Although the wet snow soothed his blistered skin, it was not likely to make any difference other than stopping further damage. "Take everyone north."

"Darkfire says Wilber's men have surrounded the Ice Woods."

The prince shook his head. "They will all be arrested if they stay here." His voice was a rasp. "Just go. I'll distract them with Darkfire."

Somehow, the doe seemed skeptical. Regardless, she dashed up the snowy street that had been pressed down by the soldiers' supply sled. Truthfully, Evan was only hoping to stall long enough to allow the Anskonians to escape. There was none for him. The snow was too deep to run, and already, the castle drawbridge had been lowered. More men were streaming into the town.

A glimmer alongside Darkfire caught the prince's attention. Several bundles were carefully bound over the stallion's back, along with the silver and black sheath of Resplandecer. As quickly as he could, the prince dashed to Darkfire's side, ignoring the pain as he yanked out his sword.

Barely had he touched it before a cry sounded from the troops. They stood transfixed, staring up at the sky. Daring to follow their gaze, Evan saw a white flash skim the flames roaring from the remains of Martin and Christina's cottage. As it passed through, its formless body gathered some of the flames to it. Then, like a fiery projectile from a catapult, it dove over the troops, the blaze licking them as they ducked.

"Is that a dragon?" the prince croaked. "I thought they had all died."

"I have never seen a dragon," Darkfire muttered, "but that is certainly Lisya."

The enchantress's shapeless form brimming with fire hissed over the snow, melting it instantly. Then she whirled back, straight over the terrified troops as they dropped to the ground. She was clearing a path for escape.

"Come," Evan ordered. As Lisya's light form swooped once more, melting an even longer trail, Darkfire bent down to let the prince mount. Then, they shot past the troops, collecting the townsfolk and Carrie along the way and racing after the "dragon."

A furious, hate-filled cry followed them. "Maxwell!"

Chapter 11

Valoretta's Task

Somewhere above, a fiery winged creature guarded the flight of those fleeing from Ansky and led them forward. They were on an endless path of melted snow.

It was too hot. It was too cold. Evan was racked with shivers, and he sank into that pain. Darkfire's hooves pounded along. Wet ground squished beneath feet, wind whistled, and a loud panting filled the air.

Beams cracked and popped. Somewhere, people were screaming. The world spun.

Then, hands.

A gentle weight.

He was falling! But no, there were arms around him, carefully pulling him off Darkfire's moist back. After his initial alarm passed, he slipped off into the whirling darkness.

It was the presence—powerful and soothing—that roused him out of the deep blackness. He lay to the side in a small cave. Around a fire toward the center of the cavern, most of the Anskonians shrunk back—for there, filling the entryway, was the glowing, winged creature that had rescued him and the townsfolk. Its flames were extinguished, but steam rose from its now-solid body.

Everyone but Carrie and Darkfire had backed away as far as they could. The stallion himself was dwarfed by the size of their rescuer. Perhaps in an attempt not to alarm the Anskonians further, the enchantress did not change form, did not reveal that part of her. As her front claws stopped where Evan lay, steaming liquid rolled down her nose and splashed onto his blackened and split cheek.

A wonderful coolness seeped across his burning skin. His pain gradually receded, and as his body released itself from its hard toil, he drifted off to sleep.

Evan awoke sometime later to the sound of urgent whispers. Darkfire stood protectively above him while Martin, Christina and Taylor sat nearby around a pitiful fire. Beyond, Carrie guarded the cavern mouth.

As the prince shifted, Taylor turned. For just a moment, neither moved or spoke. Then, with a cautious glance toward Darkfire, the Sky Haven's owner slid closer. "You are looking much better, Max... So much so, I would think the journey was a dream. Do you care to explain yourself?"

Slowly, Evan pushed himself up, noticing that his clothes were not even burned. Yet he knew Taylor was not asking about that. "Would you have accepted the truth had I given it? I came to help because I knew it would be a hard winter for all of you, but in coming, I was told many wanted nothing more than to nail my carcass to a wall."

"Really?" a middle-aged man, Donall by name, scoffed. Wilber had deemed him unfit for fighting due to his badly twisted leg, but his infirmity did nothing to curb his hot temper and constant desire for action. He had been among the most verbose about "Prince Maxwell's crimes."

Warily, Evan watched Donall stomp nearer, yet Darkfire's firm leg pressed into the prince's back, warning the approaching Anskonian and tempering Evan's unease.

Donall halted his advance, but his glare did not soften any. Instead, his hands clenched. "Dare you deny that our homes are now ashes because of you. Anything that remained, confiscated. Drop your pitiful act. What do you really want?"

"Enough." The command startled them. Carrie approached from her earlier position, her deep eyes striking each of them. Yet again, it was not Carrie, not as Evan knew her. Gone was the quiet, reserved watchfulness. She was the enchantress revealed, if not with the radiating power of her mother when roused, then still with the untroubled authority of a being capable of ordering the world to yield. "The past is finished. You are here without lasting shelter, heat or food. The only discussion at the moment should be where you are going to go now to survive."

Everyone turned to look at Evan, waiting for his answer. "My reason for staying here is done. If you like, you may come with me to Evfel to join the others I sent to weaken that kingdom's strength from inside, but it is a hard journey. Alternatively, you could resettle in the mountain villages. Unless Wilber is overthrown, I have no power to restore your homes to you."

As expected, Martin and Christina volunteered to go with him. Their announcement hung in the air for a moment, then Taylor scratched his forehead. "I understand nothing, Max, but I will come with you. Perhaps you can explain things better to me along the way, but for right now, I trust in this: the man who came into my Sky Haven in a storm and scoffed at wanting a throne was not an act. He worked too hard, cared too much for every person and even every animal to be a fake. Perhaps some could argue that was all to trick us, but you did not remain in a burning house until it was almost too late to save yourself for an act. When I met that proud, yet also humble and wise, young man, I joked we could choose a lot worse for a king. Looking at him now, I still stand by those words. If he will accept the throne, I will follow him."

With a sorrowful smile, Evan bowed his head. "Thank you."

Donall had sworn to go as well, for the fight to regain the only home he would accept—Ansky proper. Others echoed his sentiment without the resentful tones against Evan. Still, many dispersed to the mountain villages. A frail older lady echoed Taylor's trusting statement instead and vowed to travel with her king until her homeland was restored. Despite Evan's protest and Carrie's attempt to dissuade her, she would not yield. The young enchantress submitted to her insistence first, yet required that the lady accept her cloak. After that, Evan acquiesced as well.

In the end, a small band of twenty-four set off for Evfel, meagerly supplied from several mountain villages. With Carrie to guide them, they took the little known high pass through the mountains since the gorge was, as ever in the winter, completely sealed off with ice.

Sharp wind and snow silenced the group during their travels over treacherous paths and sharp drops by day. It was also rare to speak by night in the shelters Carrie found for them. The weary travelers would take a small bite and fall asleep, except for those trusted enough to stand guard. As soon as dawn warmed the coldness around them a bit, they would set off again, Carrie in front and Evan with Darkfire taking up the rear. At times, the stallion would consent to allow the frailest of the travelers to ride on his back over the roughest stretches, and so they inched along.

A week and a half into their miserable journey, however, they were forced to find shelter early as the snow thickened too much for them to see their path. On that day, Carrie found them a shallow cavern, and, huddling in their damp cloaks, they waited. A contented snore from the elderly woman wearing Carrie's cloak broke the silence and little conversations drifted into the air.

Standing with Darkfire before the opening, Evan turned as Donall's voice rose in accusation. "Now that we have a break, you may tell us why we should trust someone who learned magic."

"I didn't learn any."

"Ha, then how did your appearance change so much until you were discovered?" As Donall's tone heated, Carrie stood, warning him again that the wilderness was no place for his lack of civility.

Glaring at the maiden, Donall retreated to the back of the cavern and threw himself down.

Evan shivered and pulled his cloak closer as he turned back to the curtain of snow falling outside.

"Beware, Evan," Carrie whispered. "He will not hold back from violence once we arrive at our destination."

"Remember, before leaving Ansky, he gave his word he would only fight against Wilber's men. How long do you think he can remain that angry anyway?"

The maiden shuddered. It was Darkfire who snorted, "Angry? He has told himself it is his duty to rekindle his wrath at every opportunity."

"More so," Carrie added, "he has convinced himself that justice dictates your death, and his exact promise was to 'only fight for Ansky.' I fear that means he will kill you for the sake of his country."

Shifting, Evan whispered, "Then he may have to take my life." As Darkfire stomped, he hastily continued, "If what you say is true, then I must assume he has convinced himself that I only did what I did to snare them, forcing them to become some sort of minions. The only thing that might prove him wrong is if I refuse to defend myself against death."

A small smile passed over Carrie's face, but she nodded in acceptance.

Darkfire, however, shook vehemently. "Who will return their homeland to them if you allow yourself to be killed? I should finish him here and then you need not worry about how they interpret your rationale."

Laughing, Evan sighed. "I think that would make it far worse. Please, leave me to take responsibility for my prior selfishness."

With one heavy puff, Darkfire bowed deeply. "Your servant, then."

"Never, Darkfire." Yet, curling up to rest a bit later beneath his friend's protective hooves, Evan could not shake the crawling sensation of unfriendly eyes watching him.

"You're growing too fast," Valoretta sighed, nabbing her escaping son as he shrieked in laughter. "Your father won't know you. But..." A groan slipped out as she hefted him. "It's time for you to rest."

Tenacius squirmed in protest, although his giggles continued.

"If you don't need a rest, I do. I don't have the energy to stay up for four hours in the middle of every night without napping during the afternoon."

Newton was already asleep, and Lorene had volunteered her newly acquired skill to make supper during the lull. Near Evfel's runaway queen, Talliaha sat at the table creating thread with a drop spindle.

"Valoretta." Lisya's soft call caused the Miran to turn. The enchantress stood in the doorway. Her skin was the gray tone it had been almost all winter. "May I speak to you in here after you have laid Tenacius down?"

With a small smile, Valoretta cradled her son against her shoulder. He quieted almost instantly, and she tucked him into bed and kissed his forehead. When the enchantress needed something, the children settled down without complaint.

As the Miran entered the back room, she noticed again the limpness of some of the plants. There was no mistaking the weariness of the woods' keeper. "How may I help, Lisya?" Her question brought a sigh, and she settled herself on the loom bench beside the enchantress. In that brief opening, she tried again. "Are you so tired because you are rethinking your past decisions? Right or wrong, you made the best choice you could at the time."

With a knowing smile, Lisya picked up her shuttle. "Spring is almost here."

A question seemed to hang in the air, and Valoretta nodded. "Has anything changed in Arieh?"

"Not yet, but tomorrow, Evan's group will arrive at the Cedar Apple. Yet, it is the lack of change that causes me to seek your opinion."

"Not that you don't already know it," the Miran quipped.

A small laugh escaped Lisya, yet her smile faded swiftly. "It is for you to decide whether you wish to do anything. Evan is not going to have an easy time in Evfel. Soon, they are going to be forced back here, back to Ansky. When that happens, they will have no choice but to attack the castle again. A spy placed there now might help them greatly when that battle comes."

"Why now?"

Lisya's shuttle flashed between the strands of cloth she was weaving. This fabric, unlike the material she usually crafted, shimmered beneath her fingers. "When the Isfullen use a piece of information that is to their advantage, Wilber must not suspect the spy. Therefore, the spy should be someone he is used to having around, someone who has insight into both the political and the tactical, and someone who has the time and skills to root out his weaknesses."

For a long moment, Valoretta was silent. She was tired of the quiet of the woods and desperately wished to do more for those out there. However...

"I'm a foreigner, Lisya. My voice alone will be all the evidence they need to condemn me as a liar."

The enchantress fully turned to her. "I can take it."

Involuntarily, Valoretta's fingers flew to her throat. "You would remove my voice? Forever?"

"I would never take it forever. But if you so desired, I could remove it when the wrong people might overhear, just until the war is over."

It was a terrifying thought, all the same. "Lisya," Valoretta finally said. "In all the world, you are the best spy. Why won't you do it?"

"I cannot leave the woods for long stretches at a time. Else it dies."

"And Tenacius? Who would take care of him while I was in Ansky?"

The enchantress's gaze pierced her. "Tenacius will gain you entrance where nothing else will, Valoretta. You are to take him. Because of him, your upbringing, and your lack of resemblance to my family or to an islander, you are the best spy available to the Isfullen."

Still, there was a concern. "No. I'm a queen, Lisya. Somehow, everyone seems to know that. How will that not seem suspicious? And if they suspect me, what will they do to Tenacius?"

"Under Ansky's rules, he is protected. They will make sure someone cares for him if something happens to you." She sighed. "Act the mute. It will help. Tenacius will help. Should the need arise, I will give them a story their minds cannot reject. And should they think you unlearned and incapable of speech, they may even say things in your presence that they believe cannot spread beyond their walls."

After Lisya assured her Tenacius would be safe no matter the outcome, Valoretta agreed to spy for the Isfullen. Yet when she placed her hand into that of the enchantress, she expected her voice to feel yanked out of her throat. Instead, a gentle warmth seeped briefly through her and then winked out.

Her hand flew to her neck. "That's it? You took it? I can still speak."

Lisya laughed. "It will disappear and return as needed. There is no cause to appear other than you truly are here."

When Valoretta asked how she could infiltrate the castle, the enchantress leaned over to her bureau and pulled out what appeared to be a pile of furs. "If you leave now, a path will open."

An hour later, Lisya left Valoretta at the slushy trail made by the constant travel of messengers from the Ice Wood's besiegers to Castle Ansky. The Miran tried to keep the furs wrapped around Tenacius. For the most part, he stayed still, clinging just as tightly to her as she was to him. Perhaps he was too cold to do anything else.

Thankfully, the enchantress had provided attire from Ansky's mountain villages, with fur leggings under ankle-length skirts. With the sun's warmth and the spring thaw, Valoretta's feet kept sinking several inches into the slush on the path, time and again. Without the protection, her legs would have been frozen by now.

She had just caught herself from stumbling with her son when the *squish, squish* of large feet came over the rise ahead. Her cry of warning came out as a garbled croak.

Then, a horse was sliding down the slope toward her, its feet slipping on the mushy, icy ground.

Someone screamed from atop the horse, but Valoretta suddenly could make no sound. There was nowhere to move off the path without climbing, and no time.

The horse's shoulder mushed into the wall of snow alongside the path, bringing it to a stop. Above the strong beast's chest, heaving an inch away from Valoretta's face, a well-dressed young man sat trembling, his own visage white beneath his red hair. "Are you all right?" he gasped.

Valoretta could only nod. Not a squeak of words slipped out.

Worry filled the rider's expression, and he dismounted, his eyes probing Tenacius for harm. "Can you speak?"

More slopping hoofbeats sounded over the rise. In moments, five galloping riders had pulled their steeds to a sliding stop at the top of the slope. "What happened, Your Highness?" one of the liveried guards asked, his brow furrowed.

The young man's expression closed. Without replying, he turned back to Valoretta. "It is insane to be traveling by foot at this time of year. Where are you going?"

Voiceless, the Miran shifted Tenacius to her hip so she could touch her throat. Hopefully, this was a recognizable sign for a mute person.

It must have meant something, because the young man's shoulders rose and fell in a sigh. "Do you have anywhere to go?"

She shook her head.

"Is the father coming?"

Another shake.

The royal's eyes cooled. "Did he run off?"

Valoretta felt her eyes grow wide at the assumption.

Again, an exhale escaped the young man as he rubbed the back of his head. "There is always room for more workers in the kitchen, doing the weaving, or as one of the general maids... That sort of thing." He held out his hand. "If you need a job and a place to stay..."

Behind them, the guards fidgeted, but no one voiced their thoughts. Clearly, this royal disapproved of anyone challenging his reasoning. He was the law, as far as he was concerned—a law that was offering help at the moment.

Slowly, Valoretta accepted his hand.

Despite Valoretta's unease being on the back of a horse and her concern that Tenacius would fall, he stayed still on the rest of their journey. The beast's original rider took the reins and slipped behind one of his companions for the ride back.

When they arrived, the young man told a courier to find someone named Clare. Then, he waited beside Valoretta until the requested lady arrived. "This is your new charge." He nodded in Valoretta's direction. "We found her on the road.

She is mute, but I am sure you can help her learn everything she might need to know to work here."

"Of course, Your Highness."

Once he had left, Clare turned to Valoretta and Tenacius with a smile. "I think we should begin with some food."

And so, in a cozy kitchen, the woman sat them down at a table near a fire and asked the head cook for some porridge. As he brought it, she joined them, longingly watching Valoretta feed Tenacius.

Shifting, Clare shook her head as if to clear away some thought. "I think you will like working here. All the servants are nice, usually patient—at least they have been exceptionally so with me this last year. I still feel useless, though, ever since I lost my job as handmaid to Queen Lorene." She paused. "That might be why Andrew charged me with you."

She fell silent, yet her words hung in the air. Between every spoonful of porridge she fed Tenacius, Valoretta looked up, her lips pressed together.

Clare laughed. "Such disbelief! Prince Andrew has more heart than anyone accredits to him. Yes, he can be arrogant and thoughtless, but I have seen him..." She broke off, absently running her fingers along the wooden edge of the table as if trying to smooth it. "He loved his brother." Her tone was a whisper of sadness.

There was no need to ask what had happened. A laughing, blond-haired boy rose in Valoretta's imagination. His very nature was happy, with a giddy bounce that even her content Tenacius could not rival. Little Newton was a brother anyone would love and be heartsick to lose. She had seen the pain of that family rift in Lorene's fervent need to busy herself, and in her long moments of distraction.

"Anyway," Clare sighed, yanking them both back to the moment. "Is there any way you can reveal your name?"

Valoretta looked down, shaking her head.

Regardless, the maid pressed, "Could you make images to represent it? I mean, is it a flower, or..."

The Miran pressed her lips together and Clare sighed. "I guess... Would you care if I made one up? What about Agatigold? After your hair color, with its red like an agate and yellow like gold? It is so pretty."

With a small smile, Valoretta dipped her chin in acceptance.

"Then Agatigold it is." With a laugh, Clare wiped Tenacius's oatmeal face. "And you are still young enough to do without one." He gurgled at her. "Yes, I love your smile. How about you let us know what you want your name to be when you can form actual words?"

His sole response was to slap the table.

Arnacin had learned a new method of survival. Movement kept his dark imaginings weaker. So he would pace in small circles, particularly through the night. When that no longer controlled the visions, he snuck back into the stables. Michael clacked his beak whenever he saw the islander leave the cellar, but nothing else worked. Even as it was, he felt exhausted, drained by the battle against himself.

Although existing that way was not tenable, he had long become used to doing so. It was the continual containment that bothered him. If some people thought prolonged exposure to a fear would kill it, then either they were wrong or it had just failed in his case.

Most likely, Raymond was right. Only healing could bring healing, as hopeless as that sounded. Only a sense of his heart's wholeness could remove the intense pull of his past.

The cellar door swung open; its creak sharp over the slumbering sound of hundreds of Isfullen. Arnacin's hand dropped to his side, yet his fingers closed on thin air.

Silently cursing himself for trying to grab a blade that remained aboard his ship many leagues away, he remembered Michael was sleeping in the kitchen rafters anyway. No person posing any threat would be able to come down.

Those thoughts flashed by in a split second. Then Carrie walked in carrying a small candle. Isfullen were shooting to their feet, and with exclamations of surprise, a press of twenty or more weary-looking people followed the enchantress's daughter inside. Michael fluttered in over their heads, transforming on the floor by Lazarus, near the back of the room.

The last person through the door, however, earned all the expletives from a clamor of voices. "Evan! How did you get here?"

Yet Evan had no chance to respond. Just as he shut the door, a middle-aged man who had just walked in punched him in the jaw. "Now, we have arrived."

Pushing forward, Arnacin grabbed Lazarus's arm as the fisherman began to shove himself through the crowd. "Let Evan deal with it."

"They have no right!" Michael's low growl caused Arnacin to sigh.

"What if they harm him?" Lazarus protested.

"Leave them," Arnacin insisted. "I have no idea what they need answered, but if we stop Evan from responding, the trouble will only brew and we will soon have an inferno."

As if sensing he was speaking from experience, both Michael and the fisherman relented, but the enchanter's eyes glinted as dangerously as the talons he often bore.

Evan made no move to defend himself as his attacker stepped closer. "Answer! You caused the burning of our homes back in Ansky, tricked us into taking you in. That was after you betrayed our trust in the first place by treasuring that horse above our protection!" The man jabbed his hand in Carrie's direction. "And she repeatedly tells us to keep our peace until we reach safety because it is too cold and we need you to come here. I think that was a lie anyway. She was the one to lead us here."

In his pause, Evan whispered, "I was trying to help."

"Ha, with magic?"

"I already told you, I never learned magic."

"No, you make others do it for you! What was that beast that healed you from your justly earned burns? Either way, you deserve to be strangled to death right here."

His hand shot out, seizing Evan by the throat. Before anyone else could move, Michael transformed, a bolt of red feathers streaking forward.

"Let go." Michael's growl resounded from all corners of the room. People pressed in, cutting off Arnacin's view, yet he heard Evan gasp as he was released. In the following silence, Michael spoke again. "If you are incapable of understanding our magic comes naturally, you may leave."

"Where are you?" the man demanded. "Is this more sorcery?"

"Ha. Sorcery? The enchantress of the Ice Woods has offered friendship and our natural talent. Do you think evil would risk itself to rescue your pitiful hides? I personally would leave you to die, you small-minded—"

"Michael," Evan's soft voice commanded the boy. "Donall, I could tell you the entire story, but you are not ready to listen. Yet, please answer me. With the power you have witnessed, and which you accuse me of using, why would I even need your support? You have seen what you call the beast—the height, the power in every inch, the strength in those claws. And she came to heal me, to make sure we stayed warm through the journey we were forced to take. You knew I was dead from the burns and the smoke damage, but there are no marks of it at all now. With that power, all of Elcan would have fallen to me. Those that refused to bow would be consumed. So why is the battle over thrones still continuing?"

No one answered.

As Evan pushed out of the tight cluster, Lazarus embraced him. Beside them, Arnacin dipped his chin in respect. That was his only greeting as the other Isfullen pushed forward.

Quincy was not appeased by the story of why their prince had brought back a young mother and her child. It was too innocent, too perfect. As a mute, if she truly was one, she could never impart the story of her beginnings for them to discover or prove. She had come out of nowhere, and there was no reason for her to be traveling south at this time of year. Around him, the servants, knights and guards were speculating about her leaving an abusive husband. That suggestion was, in fact, quickly gaining strength, and the more they thought about it, the less anyone believed there might be anything odd in her journey.

Without any specific suspicions, Quincy asked a maid to watch her for the night and pay attention for any sign she could actually speak. By morning, the maid informed him the mother was most definitely mute. Even when she was lulling her son to sleep in a silent corridor by night, she only hissed through her teeth in imitation of a soothing shush and gurgled a bit, as if wishing to hum. The maid, once a mother to young children herself, added that if Agatigold had been able to soothe her child, she would have—something would have slipped out naturally.

Nodding, Quincy thanked the maid. Yet, long after she had left, he remained standing with his foot on the chair seat, leaning his weight on his thigh. It was not until one of the men who had ridden out with the prince the other day asked what was troubling him that Quincy responded, "Do you not find it convenient?"

"What, my lord?"

"This Agatigold, as Clare now calls her. She travels south at such an odd time of year, when all Ansky has fled northward."

"If her husband deserted her..."

"Yes, but there would be other villagers to help. They make sure to care for widows and orphans. Even if her husband still lived, if she was in need, that should not be cause for them to act differently."

"Maybe she had no desire to stay after that."

"You are very trusting, Irwin."

The knight shrugged. "I see no reason to be otherwise. Agatigold is a delicate, thin creature, cursed with a want of speech, beautiful, timid around men... She completely lacks the face for duplicity."

Quincy snorted. "Yes, which is another concern. In the midst of this war comes this delicate creature, and she runs directly into Prince Andrew, no less. Yes, our prince is shrewd. However, there are things that can make him blind in this case: his softness for the wretched, for one, and for two, a lone woman with a young son, deserted by her husband. In his pain over his mother's betrayal, he would never think to leave her out in the cold."

"Maxwell obviously does not know of Andrew's compassion. They spent too many years hating each other for it to be otherwise."

"Perhaps." Quincy slowly nodded. "It may depend on where Queen Lorene hid herself, considering we never found their bodies."

"My lord, regardless of how convenient it is, if she is incapable of speech and never learned to read or write, how can she communicate? Although I have heard of some mutes creating their own way through gestures, I have never seen it here."

"Does she not know how to read?"

Irwin sighed. "Who would teach her? But never mind. There are ways to test her. Have Clare attempt to communicate with her. There would be nothing suspicious about that. Then, have someone watch Agatigold's eyes closely while Clare writes the words, 'You spy for Maxwell. Leave now while you can.' It would appear to Agatigold that Clare was trying to rescue her, not test her. If there is absolutely no reaction to those words, not even a flicker, it will be obvious she is incapable of reading."

Contemplatively, the lord nodded. "It is as good a plan as we have, Irwin."

After pushing the last two rows into place on the loom, Valoretta paused to stretch her aching neck. By her feet, Tenacius played contentedly with the loose yarn.

"Agatigold." The call caused the Miran to look up at Clare, approaching her with some water. "You can take a break if you need one." She smiled. "Ansky has been charged by the Evfelians for treating servants with young like royalty, but we women know. Your back always hurts more. You never seem to sleep enough, and so forth. Take a break. Play with your son."

Following her own advice, the maid bent down to Tenacius's level and brushed his black mop. "Have you learned to call your mother yet?" The toddler simply shook the ball of yarn happily, and Clare sighed in disappointment.

Looking back up at Valoretta, she asked, "Are you sure you never learned to read and write?" Before the Miran could reply, Clare shot to her feet. "Come! Let me show you. Maybe you know more than you think. We must try something!"

Scooping Tenacius into her arms, Valoretta followed Clare to the hearth, against which a man was leaning while sewing. Brushing some ashes across the flagstones, Clare pushed her finger through it to create letters. Each letter was familiar, yet despite training Arnacin to read Miran, Valoretta had never thought to learn his language, and she bit her bottom lip as Clare continued rubbing in those letters. She paused between what Valoretta guessed to be words and then smoothed the makeshift slate out to begin another.

After a little while, Clare sighed, smoothing away the last rubbing. "I guess it's futile. What do we do, Agatigold? How did your husband communicate?" Her eyes darkened. "Or did he not care about conversation?"

Reddening, Valoretta pulled Tenacius closer. Yes, she knew those types of men. She knew them only too well. The idea she would be weak enough to actually marry one was humiliating—to say nothing of how the question insulted Arnacin.

As she rubbed her nose against her son's cheek, however, she felt Clare's hand on her arm. "Sorry." From the maid's tone, Valoretta could tell she was not apologizing for asking, but because she thought she knew the reason for the blush.

Quickly, the Miran looked away from Clare, straight into the gaze of the man leaning against the fireplace.

He was studying her intently, and she involuntarily took a step back. For just a minute, she saw her Miran captors, snaring her with their gaze as they pushed her against the walls or onto the floor.

As Tenacius protested in her tight grasp, she forced herself to breathe. To her surprise, the man bowed and excused himself.

"Is she capable of writing messages?" Quincy demanded as soon as his spy returned.

"No, my lord. Although she did seem to make an effort to understand, Clare's message clearly had no meaning to her." Sadness filled the spy's gaze. "She was abused, though. I saw it in her eyes when she noticed my expression. I almost wonder if she was married to her supposed husband or if she was a slave."

Quincy snorted. "It would not be the first time such a disgusting thing happened." He shrugged. "That aside, we must keep ourselves from jumping to conclusions."

"My lord, Ansky rules that such acts are punishable by hanging—"

Quickly, the lord waved a hand. "*If* that is what happened, she could never testify and, therefore, her husband—" The manservant's mouth opened, and Quincy held up his hand. "Since there is no way for her to communicate otherwise, except by answering some very intrusive questions, we must assume it was her husband that abused her... At least until and unless we meet the brute himself and rip a confession from him."

Bowing, the spy cracked his knuckles. "He would never make it to the gallows if I had my say."

"I think you are too quickly attached to this girl."

The spy grinned. "You know I have a weakness for the vulnerable."

Shaking his head with a small smile, Quincy thanked the manservant.

Whether to escape Evan's presence or to help the Isfullen, the Anskonians dispersed into Arieh during the day. He, however, stayed in the darkness with Arnacin. Although the prince mostly slept through the first week, by its end, even he could not hide his restlessness.

"You don't like this cellar?" Arnacin dared to ask.

If Evan noticed the slight mocking, he showed no sign. Instead, he shrugged. "I never cared much for the indoors. After a while, I feel locked up." He shook his head with a sardonic grin. "And I constantly try to keep that feeling."

"What do you mean?"

"I grew up avoiding the throne, Arnacin." Evan's words came out in a guilty sigh. "It might as well be a cage at the end of the great hall. I did picture bars there. So, I ignored Wilber's actions. Nothing, not even if he burned the valley from end to end, could make me lock myself inside that thing. Or so I thought." His brilliant blue eyes fixed themselves on the islander. "I realized how much I was betraying my people when Malachi made me aware of what Ansky's future would be under Wilber."

Raymond's insistence that Evan was incapable of becoming corrupt echoed in the back of Arnacin's mind. Hastily, he turned away. The cellar fell into silence, except for the whisper of his pacing feet.

"And you also hate this cellar?" Evan's question was more of a statement.

Arnacin halted mid-step. He paused only for a moment before shrugging and continuing to pace. "I grew up on the mountain. Mostly, indoors were for sleeping."

He doubted he had fooled the prince into thinking he was unaffected by his confinement. Yet, all Evan asked was, "Were you also a wood nymph?"

Slowing, Arnacin pictured the woods of the island. A black-haired girl nearly danced alongside her sheep in the changing shadows of the trees. Her feet barely touched the ground. Noiseless, she shifted so much with the light that no one could say whether she danced or the light did it for her.

"No." He shoved those images away. "I was a shepherd..." Honestly, why did he answer at all?

Yet again, the other gently pressed forward, continuing the sentence. "Turned?"

In the pause that followed, Arnacin wanted the prince to finish that sentence. Ages had passed during which he had accepted everyone else's darker titles for him. In a way, he had even found a pleasing comfort in them. Everyone's fear had been a sort of safety, an assurance he still held some high ground. Yet, even as the word "wraith" hung on his tongue, he could not voice it.

As the silence dragged on, however, Arnacin finally asked, in a tone deeper than usual, "How did you make her think you were a friend?"

"Your wood nymph?" Evan's gaze grew distant. Wish as he might, Arnacin could not probe the images racing past it.

With a sigh, the prince looked down. "I think it was the other way around. It just happened. I apologize—"

"Don't." For Arnacin's cold heart, those words of death could not be spoken. Charlotte was naught but a shadow flitting across dreams and thoughts.

Still uneasy with Andrew's new charge, Quincy requested leave from the king to seek her background. Once he received it, he went to find the potential spy. He located Agatigold in the kitchens, feeding her son. Pausing, he again took note of the way she sat, her spine straight even as she leaned forward to wipe mush off her son's nose with her apron.

Perhaps the lord was mistaken, but he thought he saw power behind her fear when he looked her in the eyes, a power marked ever more clearly by her stance. It was time to find out.

"Come. You are to ride with me."

Although she looked up, the usual wariness in her gaze, not until Quincy lifted the toddler from his place in the center of the table did she shoot to her feet. Her arms rose to retrieve her child, her mouth forming an outspoken protest. If he was ever convinced she truly was mute, it was then, as she only gurgled slightly.

"Clare will take care of him. Never fear." His attempt to spark some slip in her disguise failed as she drew back, seemingly realizing his intention. Still, he had no need to drag her anywhere as he left the kitchens with her complaining, wriggling son in his arms.

Gently but firmly, Quincy deposited the child with Clare. "We will be gone for a few days. Take care of him."

Her brow furrowed, Clare nodded, accepting the boy.

With his hands free, the lord firmly grasped Agatigold's arm. "Please come without any struggle. I have no intention of harming you, but it is time to test your story for certain."

Glancing once more at her son, the mother followed.

Quincy planned to take the girl through the mountain villages of Ansky. Had she lived there, someone would recognize her—many people, in fact. Assuming everyone in her town would react to her presence, he walked his steed through each new place, with the girl sitting in front of him. Should that fail, he would take her door to door.

He had no need to fear. They were entering the tenth town when large groups of people halted their work, watching them ride by. In the lord's arms, the girl trembled as one man left his carving stool and disappeared inside a shop.

Halting, Quincy waited. Sure enough, a different man soon came back out, black-haired and bull-shouldered. "Found her, did you?" that man growled, tromping toward them as the girl drew back, her skin pale.

Valoretta struggled vainly as hardened hands seized her thigh and yanked her off the horse.

Shaking her, the angry man demanded, "What did you do with my son, you ungrateful wretch?"

The Miran's heart skipped. His son? Was he talking about Tenacius? That made no sense.

Even as those questions raced through her thoughts, an echo of the enchantress's words allowed her to breathe. *Should the need arise, I will give them a story their minds cannot reject.* Lisya must have known the town and asked them to play a part for Valoretta's benefit.

Quincy coughed above them. "Is he not also *her* son?"

"She still made off with Peter!" He shook Valoretta by the arm. "Your son or not, bring him back!" The man's palm slapped her cheek with a crack, yet she felt no impact. "You hear!"

Jumping off the back of his steed, Quincy grabbed the man's arm, pulling him away from Valoretta. "Not only is she not going to bring you young Peter, she is permanently leaving here herself. I came with her only to answer some of my questions."

The man wrenched his arm free, although he backed away from Valoretta by a step. "And who are you to steal my wife?"

"A lord of Ansky. There are some who want you strung up."

Sticking his chin out, the man again seized Valoretta by her bicep and hauled her behind him. Oblivious to her pulling against his grip, he furrowed his brow. "And I think you are a thief. Your horse and fancy trappings might just as easily have been stolen from a real knight!"

Quincy's eyes followed the Miran's struggle, yet he made no move this time to free her. "I can bring forces here to make sure you are apprehended. Ansky laws are very clear on the repercussions of such mistreatment, and it seems to me..." He again glanced at Valoretta. "You have taken advantage of your wife's inability to speak."

"Since she is incapable, as you say, no one can charge me and no one here would say anything. Do you see any bruises on her? How do you know she has not fallen in love with some other swine and tried to run to him? I could very well be the victim here. If you charge me of anything, either Ansky lacks the honor it claims or you are naught but a liar."

Quincy's glare hardened. "Then I am a better one than you." So saying, the lord punched the man in the face. As he staggered back, Quincy advanced with another hard blow.

Valoretta scampered aside.

The man's eyes reddened. He struck back, but the lord, the better trained of the two, ducked. "If. Anyone. Thinks. You. Innocent. Let. Them. Come." Quincy pronounced between jabs. "Your. Neighbors. Will. Know. How. Much. Or. Little. You. Are. Victimized."

Although villagers had gathered around to watch, no one moved to stop Quincy, even the man's shop hand. Some shook their heads, while others tsked, but none seemed to care. And no one heard Valoretta's gurgled protests.

As the fight continued, the Miran gasped, her hand covering her mouth. Was this a village that knew Lisya? She was letting them down, if so. Quincy was either going to beat the man to death or hang him once he was subdued enough to confess to anything the lord demanded. No one would act like this for payment, however handsome.

A warm presence settled on the Miran's shoulder. *Never fear,* the words whispered through her mind. *This whole town is an apparition. Did you feel him strike you?* A ruffled, white crow perched on Valoretta's shoulder, its beak clacking as its orange eyes watched the fight. *Nothing less will lay Quincy's suspicions to rest, and he will feel every impact.*

The tight knot in Valoretta's stomach eased, yet her hand still trembled as she brought it up to lift the albino bird off her shoulder, preferring to see the enchantress's eyes.

Quincy didn't halt until his victim was gasping in a heap on the ground. "Are you ready to cooperate?"

Panting, the man groaned.

"Very well. I will start with a simple question. What is the girl's name?"

The man's face scrunched up in pain. Blood trickled from the side of his face into his mouth. "Helel."

"Good. How long has she been mute?"

"Since birth."

"Does she have any other family?"

A shake of the head.

Leaning close, Quincy asked, "Is there a monk about who teaches reading and writing? Or is there someone who learned from one and can teach others?"

The man looked up; his brow furrowed. "You want to teach her to communicate? Women are better off not knowing."

Valoretta shot a glare at the crow, perched on her wrist, and an impish look appeared on its face. *What can you expect from a man who thinks so little of his wife?*

Quincy had no patience, however. "Answer the question."

"No. Happy?"

"Thank you." The lord grabbed the man's shirt under his chin. "Now. Was it your abuse that caused your wife to flee?"

Spitting blood and saliva, the man tried to pull Quincy's hand off his shirt. "This is coercion, not a fair trial."

Quincy's tone dropped to a threatening whisper. "The only thing your words will do is determine the length and pain of your execution. I am certain enough of the answer that I feel no shame in hanging you, but I can at least offer you a stool... or not."

The man trembled. "As in, you can snap my neck or strangle me?"

"You decide. Answer."

In the expectant pause, Valoretta grabbed the lord's arm, shaking her head.

Pushing his hair out of his face, Quincy turned to the Miran. His gaze stopped suddenly on the crow, then traveled to Valoretta's face. "You want this worm spared?"

She nodded. Fake or not, she had seen too many bodies in her time. Moreover, this crime was entirely imagined.

A low grumble came from the villagers—dissenting that he might live. Yet, Quincy only paid attention to Valoretta in that moment, searching for an explanation.

Finally, he turned back to the culprit. "Answer." He ignored the protesting tug on his sleeve as he hauled the man up. "Have you abused her?"

Trembling, all fight fled from the man's face. "Yes. She never wanted to lie with me, even after marriage. I gave her a home and shelter when I saw her unnatural connection with animals, and still she gave me nothing."

Quincy dropped him with a thump and turned to the crowd. "Is it so unusual that someone isolated by a lack of communication can woo any animal over time?"

A general rustle of shifting feet responded. No one volunteered a thought, however.

The lord turned back to Valoretta. "For your compassion, I will let him live. May he learn from it."

To her surprise, he ran a cautious finger along the crow's downy head without shuddering. Valoretta dared not look up to see if he felt the same warmth in the enchantress's touch as she did. Flapping its wings, the crow squawked once and took to the skies.

Coldness whispered down the Miran's spine as the enchantress departed, yet Quincy held out his hand. "Come, Agatigold. Leave the name Helel behind with this town. Our prince himself welcomes you to a better life."

Trembling from the tension, she accepted his hand.

As Valoretta moved more firmly into castle life, her place there was secured, although Tenacius's restlessness kept the servants awake every night. Eventually, they made a bed for her and her son in the weaving room. And if the Miran wandered the moonlit hallways with her son, no one thought anything of it. However, it was not while walking the empty corridors and hearing snatches of conversation drifting from rooms that she gathered her first bit of real information. It was while she was scrubbing the floor in the great hall.

"Maxwell must be in one of the Anskonian mountain villages." The voice emerged from the hallway right before Wilber, Andrew and Quincy entered the great hall. "Their Ice Woods have been surrounded almost all—" The king's sentence broke off.

"Agatigold is incapable of communicating anything, sire." Quincy confirmed Valoretta's guess that she was the cause of the abrupt silence. "No need to send her away. Nothing she knows can travel anywhere."

"You are sure?"

This time, it was Andrew who answered. "Completely."

Valoretta pressed her lips together, scrubbing harder.

Wilber waved his hand dismissively. "Knowing he could not have gone back into the Ice Woods and that we have searched the villages since the thaw began, where did Maxwell go?"

"Could they have gone back to the northern island?" Andrew asked.

"Summos Valley would tell us."

"But, by raft?"

There was no response from Wilber. After a moment, Quincy spoke up. "They might have fled to Evfel, sire. The troops in the mountain villages report no sign of them, and it was a good fifty people traveling. That is somewhat hard to miss."

Wilber rubbed his palms together in thought. "The pass was already iced over when Maxwell fled the town. If they took to the mountains, perhaps... But that is a dangerous, cold route. With the strength of the wind, the thin trails and gullies, our ancestors always thought it impossible. And, before we even ask *how*, what about *why*? Why would they go to Evfel?"

"To meet up with those they sent ahead," Andrew whispered, his eyes distant. "Remember the sightings of the eagle last autumn, and how some were saying they thought he had left?"

"Yes," Wilber muttered. "But how would they not die trying?"

Quincy shrugged. "He does use magic."

"Lord Quincy." The king turned sharply to his lord. "Do you not think it odd that Maxwell has yet to use his alliance directly against us?"

Andrew huffed. "We know he would if he could."

"No. We have seen a dragon, a maiden that turns into a deer, the Ice Woods's abyss growing outward and later shrinking back. Maxwell escaped mysteriously from execution and later survived his fall out of our keep. He is fully capable of destroying everyone, yet he toys with us. Why?"

No one answered.

At last, Wilber tapped his cheek. "Back to the topic of Evfel. What can he gain there that he does not already have here?"

For a minute, no one volunteered an answer. Then Andrew asked, "Could he be trying to convince us he is in Evfel, so we send a large party of men over there, leaving Castle Ansky more open to attack?"

Silence fell, as they contemplated the question. Ironically, they stood in the room with someone who knew that answer.

"If they are there," Wilber finally said, "Duke Reginold may have heard something, something he might have even written in his winter report. Did I read anything that seemed like it could be driven by Maxwell?"

He turned to his lord. "Go, Quincy. Ask Duke Reginold if everything seems well, besides the escaped prisoner they think too small to hunt down and the troublemaker that stopped being a troublemaker. If not..." He paused. "If it appears Maxwell has hidden even a small force there, let Reginold know he is to starve the city out. Make every-one know their own lives are at stake if they dare to harbor those criminals."

Valoretta could not control her gasp, but a horrified question from Andrew covered the sound. "The duke is to starve all of them?"

"Do not fear. Someone will know if there are such people there, and that person will be wise enough to do as asked. It may be a harsh action, but it will not kill anyone, and it will force Maxwell into the open."

"But... what if he is not there?"

"If there is reason to suspect revolt, only then will the food and water be withheld. But if they surrender a dangerous instigator, Reginold's orders will be to restore the food and water—at least until more trouble arises."

Her heart pounding, Valoretta hastily ducked her head, returning to her work. She had no one to tell. Only Lisya could alert the Isfullen now.

Chapter 12

Reginold's Attack

With someone else always present in the cellar, Arnacin found his need to escape into the stables decrease. Still, he paced through the silence with feverish steps. If his count could be trusted, a month had passed since the Anskonians had joined them.

"Arnacin." Evan's call brought the islander to a stop right before the cellar exit. The prince sat huddled beneath his black cloak, his appearance sickly due to his long seclusion. "What keeps you here?"

The islander paused. Had he actually heard such an illogical question? Perhaps it was insanity that now imagined those words, yet Arnacin nodded toward the ceiling anyway. "They'll have me strung up in moments if I leave."

Laughing slightly, Evan shifted beneath his cloak. "No, I meant in Evfel. Spring is here. You can easily travel all the way back home if you want. Your help here has become futile. If you so desire, I will send Michael to tell your mother to return home with Valoretta and Tenacius. You can meet them along the way."

Arnacin stood frozen to the spot. "What type of king are you?"

There was no reaction from Evan. Serenely, he waited.

"You are near to losing this war, Evan. I don't think I need to tell you that. What would possess you to release the only man you have with any skill, particularly when that man has not made such a request? No king with any brains would do so, good or bad."

The hint of a smile wrinkled those eyes. "Oh, you have more skills than the other Isfullen? You never said so."

"You know better." Arnacin's whisper was a broken sigh of defeat.

The prince's gaze dropped to the islander's fraying shirt, the one that had used to mark him as Miran nobility. Yet, when Evan spoke, he said nothing about that shirt's once-fine quality. "I will never force anyone into something they loathe to do. Any sacrifice of the self must be given willingly. The ruler who commands one to make that sacrifice in the name of the greater good never knew goodness."

His eyes again pierced the islander. "You are trying to make that sacrifice, but instead, you are eating your heart away in order to do what you loathe."

Before Arnacin could protest, Evan insisted, "You owe me nothing, and the truth is, your home is safe no matter the outcome of this struggle. Your loyalty to your islander friends and family is commendable, but I think they would also want you to return home. Arieh has marked you as a threat. Therefore, you are incapable of helping in this fight. Find somewhere you can live, heart and soul."

Evan's gentle order echoed Valoretta's plea from two winters ago for him to go back home alone. For her sake, Arnacin had not listened. Had he left her, he would never have found peace anyway.

Perhaps contentment was something he was forever doomed to lack. His diminished self-worth would haunt any freedom he found away from rulers, wars, greed and bloodshed. Again and again, he could only slam a metaphorical door on that beloved independence. He was forced to remain a slave to his conscientiousness.

With a sigh, he joined the prince near the far wall and slid down against the stones. Instead of answering, he threw the challenge back. "Your heart doesn't seem to be in this, either."

"It is. At least, in certain ways. I am their king. My life and death are theirs, and any other action on my part is betrayal. I want to serve them. I want desperately to serve them. Contentment is sometimes a fickle thing."

The islander did not doubt the combination of life *and* death had been purposeful. If, in the end, the Anskonians called for their king's blood and hanged him, Evan had given them his permission beforehand. His one mission was to make sure their bondage to Evfel was over first.

That night, Arnacin slept. To make sure he would not hit anyone with a thrashing arm or leg if he were to drift into disturbed dreams, he found an open spot on the floor. However, the creaking of the door some time later yanked him from an unexpectedly deep slumber.

Through it stepped Abby, her cheeks flushed. "You must leave! All of you! Now!"

"What's happened?" Tevin, the closest to the door, sat up.

"They're taking everyone's food. They'll be here in a moment. You mustn't be found."

"Can we stop them?"

Abby hastily shook her head. "Go! There isn't time. They're arresting anyone who resists."

Barely had anyone moved before Abby halted them. "Wait! You might be spotted." After receiving many impatient looks, she added, "Upstairs, there is a secret door to the tunnels. This tavern used to be the guardhouse for a mine. We don't know the ways or where they go, but maybe you could escape through them with some food."

As she spoke, Arnacin felt the air thickening, a pressure against his chest. "No!" The word ripped itself from his throat. Everyone turned to him, staring, and some of the sensation dissipated. Lowering his gaze, he whispered, "Anything but that."

It was Evan who rescued him from potential scrutiny by taking charge. "Hurry! Everyone, into the city. Arnacin, Darkfire is at the edge of the woods. Stay with him until we can come back tomorrow morning. The soldiers should be done pillaging by then."

No one questioned the prince. Some looked in favor of Abby's suggestion, but even so, they quietly obeyed. Behind everyone else, Arnacin filed upstairs and outside. While the rest of the Isfullen turned up the trail to the city, he raced downhill.

Warm sunlight followed his flight. Little tufts of grass and wildflowers nodded in the crags, greeting him as he rushed by. Then, there was the air, the wonderful breeze of spring. Instead of fear, elation coursed through him. At last, he was free.

Once he was within the shadow of the woods, a dark form broke from the trees. The islander froze.

"What is happening?" Darkfire asked, his voice low and throaty.

"They are purging the city of food."

Darkfire tossed his head, nodding southeast. "That is not all. Look." Horses and carts stood by as men dug a deep trench not an eighth of a mile away. "They have been at it all night."

Thankfully, the diggers seemed too absorbed to notice them.

"Deeper," Arnacin hissed. "Whatever they're doing, they'll spot us eventually if we don't put more trees between us."

Without a word, the stallion passed into the thicker foliage, darkness swallowing him as if it was one with his powerful body. The islander followed, trusting Darkfire's knowledge of the forest.

In silence, they walked ever farther into the woods until they reached a little glade. There, Arnacin settled along the edge.

Watching the sunlight streaming down, creating a thin yellowish mist, the islander sighed. "It must be nicer to be staying out here."

Darkfire snorted above him. "If you like spending days on end where the only other living things are dumber than the beasts on Enchantress Island."

"Are they actually less intelligent out here?"

"Yours are still animals, of course, but they have also picked up something of the mound. Their senses can tell you things. Not here. These animals can only impart the crudest of emotions."

Smiling, Arnacin quipped, "I wouldn't think loneliness would bother someone like you."

"It does when you are used to companionship."

"Is Evan a good companion?"

The stallion puffed. "He understands animals better than I do, and he is as wild as the green grass of the valley."

Seeing again the proud, untamable spirit in Darkfire's eyes, Arnacin drew his knees closer. "How did you meet Evan? Doesn't the herd stay in the Ice Woods?"

"Not I." Darkfire's words came out in a huff of self-reproach. "When I was a colt, my father constantly warned us foals never to leave the Ice Woods. It was very dangerous, he told me, but I was adventurous, arrogant. I knew all of the Ice Woods, and I wanted to see new things.

"Shortly after I became herd stallion, I took my chance. No one could prevent me, although I kept my intentions a secret.

"Slipping off, I left the woods and discovered blue skies." The stallion shook his head, but the motion had the feeling of exuberance from a good memory. "Oh, I had never seen blue skies, and the grass—rich, soft, warm and, I found, delicious.

I was certain nothing dangerous existed, and I returned to the Ice Woods elated.

"Although Lisya warned me, I continued to return to the valley day after day, exploring farther and farther. Then, one day, I saw stones rising from the ground. It did not exude warmth like Lisya's cottage. After looking at it for a moment, I turned back toward the woods, but the watchmen in that fortress must have seen me. Honestly, they must have seen me days before, because I found my way barred by riders. They even released a stallion toward me."

Darkfire paused, and his gaze returned to the islander sitting on the ground by his feet. "It should have meant nothing; my herd never attacks each other. But with that beast, I felt a challenge to my kingship. As they had hoped, their loosed animal distracted me.

"Instead of fleeing, I let them catch me, to throw ropes around my feet, neck and nose. When hobbling my front two legs did nothing to subdue me, they tied the back two together and forced me into their fortress."

The stallion shuddered. "The next days were terrible, but I had yet to realize how bad it could become. They left me tied in a tiny box stall, my legs still bound and a rope on each side to keep my head still. Yet, in training, they used soft words and repetition. On a dumb animal, it would have worked, but not with me.

"They would slide onto my back and sit there patiently to accustom me to their presence and weight. When I tossed my head in protest, they would whisper soft words and stroke my neck. Lisya had warned me never to let anyone outside the woods know I could think and speak, so I attempted to use my head's movement to make my displeasure known.

"One day, however, I could bear it no longer. Despite not having enough balance if I tried to buck while hobbled, I threw a tamer over my head, and consequently, fell forward on top of him. In my wrath, I tried to regain my feet and crushed him to death.

"After that, they gave me to a man in the Calmar Mountains known for taming the untamable beasts. There, I realized what horrors I had missed. This man released me inside a pen with walls so high I thought they could compete with those of the fortress itself. He followed after me with a long, knotted rope. Unless I ran around him, he flicked it against me constantly, ceaselessly. If I slowed at all or tried to run at him, it burned through my shoulders, flanks and chest.

"He kept me going, intent on running me into the ground. I refused to allow him to win. Inwardly, my thoughts had changed. In that moment, freedom was insignificant. Revenge alone existed. Only once it had been satisfied—against him and all who dared touch me—would I flee to freedom."

Though Arnacin shifted uncomfortably, he said nothing. Even more discomforting than the story was the ease with which Darkfire told it. The islander did not think he himself could ever heal enough to admit such things, but the stallion obviously had beneath Evan's hand. Or was it more than the prince who had healed those wounds?

Likely aware of Arnacin's turmoil, but leaving him to his silence, Darkfire continued. "Again and again, I lunged at him, yet he was equally cunning and skillful. At last, I collapsed in blood, sweat and pain.

"I can only assume he thought he had me broken. At least, he took great pains to restore my health. But even as weak as I was, I fought. Then, just when I had regained my strength, he handed me off to knights from Castle Ansky, claiming I was a gift for Wilber.

"Again, I was hobbled like before, and those men shoved what I have since learned was a war bridle into my mouth and around my nose."

At Arnacin's confused glance, Darkfire shuddered. "It is a rope they can continually tighten until it cuts into the flesh.

Still, no matter how hard they yanked it, I refused to yield as they dragged me across the valley. Eventually, they tied my head to my foreleg using the war bridle. As each hobbled step yanked the rope tighter, I surrendered for a time, concentrating on coordinating my nose's movement to my gait in order to stop the rope from cutting all the way through my skin.

"When we finally entered the confines of Castle Ansky, they released all but the ropes around my neck, and I attacked."

"Was Evan there? What did he do?" Arnacin asked.

A grin crinkled the scars along the stallion's nose. "Nothing, except prevent anyone from abusing me. Throughout the following days, all he did was insist I stop starving myself. I ignored him, and the first chance I had, I launched myself at him." Darkfire's voice quieted in thought. "Lorene rescued him, but it was his reaction that made me pause. I had broken a bone in his shoulder, and although I could tell the pain was intense, nearly rendering him unconscious, he never cursed me once. He just kept whispering comfort to me.

"I found I could no longer attack him. And in that partial surrender, I learned many things about him and myself. He never had been interested in taming an animal, but befr—"

Darkfire stopped abruptly, his nose raised to the breeze. "Come," the stallion said after a moment. "We must go east. Follow every step. There are still bogs at this end, although they are not as common as those on the other side of the river, Death Mirror."

"What is it?" the islander asked, rising to his feet.

"They are setting fire to the woods."

Feeling the softness of the dirt beneath his soles with a sudden acuteness, Arnacin paused. "It can't go very far when most of the wood is still wet, though, can it?"

Darkfire tossed his head. "More than one group is out there. Beyond that, I cannot say."

Sometime later, the stallion again halted, his head raised to the wind. After a moment, he bent to his knees, and Arnacin felt his heart stop. "It spreads faster than it should," Darkfire warned. "Climb on."

The islander instead took a step backward, but the stallion's eyes glinted. "Do not think I want you on my back, but I have no desire to become trapped in a furious forest fire. Safety in the Calmar Mountains is still some distance away, and you must come."

"I can run my—"

"Do not be absurd." That broke through Arnacin's hesitation. Even apart from his dislike for riding, he could not treat the stallion like a beast of burden. Still, Darkfire's reasoning was sound. Slipping on, the islander tightly wrapped the stallion's mane around his hands as Darkfire lurched upright and took off so fast Arnacin gasped.

Contrary to the islander's expectations, the stallion's pace never slowed from that initial burst. He showed no signs of tiring, either, even though the intense speed caused tears to streak from Arnacin's eyes. Instead, it seemed they were traveling faster with each passing second. The islander could hardly breathe.

However, Darkfire was fleeing for their lives. Only when a few sparks blew into a spruce tree they were passing did the islander fully realize how dangerous it would be to slow down.

Smoke was covering the skies, flames cracking around them, when Darkfire splashed into a river, plunging into its depths as he swam across. The feet of the Calmar Mountains lay on the far shore. Upon reaching it, the stallion wearily trotted out of the current. He paused only briefly before starting the ascent to safety. Dusk was bearing down on them.

Looking back as they climbed ever higher above the tree line, Arnacin spotted crowds backlit by the blazing woods.

"There are thousands," he breathed in horror as he watched them guiding the fire.

Although he did not stop moving his feet forward, Darkfire's head hung low and he coughed hoarsely. "Evfel is very large, and its people are greedy. If Evfel's duke paid people for this task, he could acquire any number of helpers."

"Without paying anyone anything of great worth, you can be sure of that."

Picking a spot with a clear view, the stallion stopped at last. As darkness came upon them, the two surveyed the devastation below. The forest had been cut down north of the Death Mirror to stop the fire from spreading farther, yet the extent to which the government had been willing to inflict damage just to starve out rebellion chilled the islander.

"They must have started preparing yesterday, or even the day before," the stallion panted.

Yet, watching that blaze, the islander felt another thought boil inside. "There was no need for the fire. They could have blocked the path and stopped anyone from living off the woods that way."

Darkfire only snorted his agreement. It took no intelligence to realize the duke wanted to horrify all of Evfel with this display of power. Arieh would suffer for years even if it did surrender.

"Arnacin!" The worried cry echoed around the Cedar Apple's cellar when the islander returned early the next morning. "What happened to the woods? We saw smoke and fire below!"

Too exhausted to answer everyone, Arnacin broke free of the welcoming arms to find Evan. "Darkfire has moved to the mountains. The woods are destroyed, burned and cut down, five leagues beyond the river, Death Mirror."

Weariness showed in the prince's posture. It took a moment for him to reply, and even that was merely a silent nod. When

Arnacin shifted, Evan finally asked, "How far away is the nearest point of the Sambrad Montis river, by your reckoning?"

"On foot, from the only descent off this mountain? Perhaps two days. Your stallion can reach it in a few hours, naturally."

With a small smile of pride in his companion, the prince nodded, yet his next words showed nothing of that emotion. "They confiscated or destroyed even our means of collecting water. Every bucket, waterskin and jar, not to mention anything we could use to reopen the collapsed wells, is gone. The Cedar Apple has saved a fair quantity of their beverages in the secret passages, but without food, I fear the effects of the alcohol. And the city has nothing at all."

"We'll figure it out in the morning," Raymond whispered. His hoarse voice reminded Arnacin that they had likely not drunk any water for an entire day, unlike Darkfire and himself.

"It *is* morning, Raymond," Tevin joked, equally hoarse.

When Raymond only gave him a long-suffering look, however, Lazarus sighed. "Raymond's right. We all need to rest. After some sleep has restored our minds a bit, we'll discuss it then."

No one argued. Bone-weary, Arnacin knew not even a single dream would bother his sleep. Yet, as he settled on the floor beside Raymond, his thoughts kept turning. Softly, he whispered after a moment, "You just stood aside and let them take it all? I'm glad I wasn't here. I couldn't have witnessed it without..." He bit back the words *killing some of them* and instead added "acting."

"Yes," Raymond muttered bitterly. "With all the people *acting*, I wouldn't be surprised if half the city's dead or in prison. We even lost Donall due to him defying them. He nearly said something about Evan as well, but... he didn't. I can't say I'll miss him, but I'm glad he made the choice he did in the end."

When Arnacin remained silent, Raymond added, "They hung hundreds of protesters today, including a witch."

That sparked a reaction from Arnacin. "A witch?"

"Someone asked a witch to curse the duke for them. They caught her in the midst of her incantation, and *still* she denied it." Raymond was silent for a moment. Then, he mused, "I don't see how anyone can accuse Lisya of being a witch. She's nothing akin to one. This witch was hysterical, and her eyes were rolling like those of a terrified horse. She had no power, Arnacin. Either the source of her ability betrayed her in the last moment, or she made it all up."

"I wouldn't doubt she could curse people," Arnacin whispered. "Mediums are dangerous, after all." A moment later, a thought occurred to him. "What possessed you to watch all those hangings, anyway?"

"I don't think there was a street that didn't have someone hanged on it. They were just sticking stakes in the ground with crossbars and executing people right outside their doors. There wasn't anything to do unless you wished to be killed or hauled off with them. Evan tried the only possible option to retrieve some of the supplies—theft—and was nearly caught trying."

"The idiot," Arnacin scoffed, causing his friend to choke.

"Michael said those exact words when he heard about it. But he added that even if they didn't know what Evan looked like, not everyone carries a black scabbard at their sides, even if it is covered by a cloak."

"Nor is it empty. What exactly was he trying to do?"

"Steal some of the food off the carts while they were trundling back up to the castle. I think the only reason they left him there was because he didn't succeed and backed away submissively." Raymond puffed in amusement. "Evan may be cunning in certain things, but he's a terrible thief."

Although Arnacin grinned, he had no time to think of a reply. Someone kicked him in the shin, grumbling, "Stop talking, you two. You're keeping us awake."

Rolling onto his side, Raymond whispered into his friend's ear. "If we were sleeping, we might hear that our *breathing* would keep them awake. Their thirst will do so all on its own."

Arnacin smothered his laugh with his arm, but nevertheless fell silent.

Chapter 13

Starvation

Early the next morning, Evan asked Michael to scout for a means of stealing back supplies. Grumbling, the eagle obeyed. He returned a few hours later while the prince was discussing their options with Lazarus and Vilo in the kitchen.

Transforming in front of them, the enchanter nodded a short greeting before giving his report. "There is no other entrance to the castle a group of us could use other than the main gate. A few people are trying to dig out their wells again with their hands, but the collapse goes deep, and their labor is only making them succumb to thirst faster. The loss of blood from their cuts makes them weaker. Most of the people just sit around looking miserable."

He hesitated, then sighed. "There are also large groups searching the city."

"Why?" Vilo asked.

"Signs are everywhere saying if the city delivers you and any instigators to the duke, the food and water will be returned. They give a vague description of you underneath the announcement."

All three turned to Evan—not that he knew how he was supposed to feel. He had expected that to be the reason behind the confiscation in the first place. No one, no matter how much of a fool, would so threaten one's entire populace unless it was believed death would be unnecessary and no other bribe would work.

In the silence, Lazarus reminded them, "We might not die of thirst. The Cedar Apple stores most of its liquids in the mine shafts. However, if anyone realizes we are not thirsting like everyone else, soldiers may come and hang all of us. Except for the risks associated with how stealthily we now need to move, having something to drink could help us reach a new destination."

In that case, the Isfullen would need to take the people of the Cedar Apple with them, as well as the Anskonians. Between the number of people and their wide range of ages, it would never take them a mere two days to reach the Sambrad Montis. It would take them four. If they even tried, they would leave a trail of fallen. The way over the mountains in the winter had been hard enough, and they'd had all the supplies they needed.

At last, Evan asked, "What if I died or was still in the mountains? What does their duke think to gain, besides everyone's death, when there is no proof I am here? They have never even met me to know what I look like. Yesterday proved that!"

In the brief silence, the others glanced at each other, then shrugged.

Evan shook his head. "If everyone here dies, Duke Reginold loses everything. He will have to import food from other places or enslave more people to work the fields below. It will make Arieh vulnerable. Does none of that matter to him?"

"Not that it will do us any good," Michael grumbled. "That is the future, after we are all dead." His eyes glinted. "But if I kill them all in their beds and steal the provisions back little bits at a time..."

"Murder?" Evan pushed away from the table. "How will that help do anything but brand us as monsters?"

Folding his arms, Michael jutted his chin out. "You might not say it, but we all know the rivers are too far away. Anwae could help, but you could never convince the Evfelians to reconsider their folly where it concerns her."

The prince stepped back. "Thank you, everyone, for your thoughts and advice. Give me some time to think about it."

"You don't have much of that, Evan," Lazarus warned. "If we don't move on some plan soon, many won't be able to move at all. It's already been a day since we had any water."

The prince's only acknowledgment was a nod.

Evan's decision was not made any easier by the elderly Anskonian woman who approached him on the way back down to the cellar. In her quavering voice, she begged him to take those who had the strength to flee and leave for another town. She knew those like herself would need to stay behind, but she said, "Ansky's rightful king must live. For all of Elcan, you must live, Prince Maxwell."

Patting her hand, Evan continued down the stairs. There was nothing private about the cellar, but he plopped down in an unclaimed spot and tugged his cloak, blanket-like, around his shoulders.

He only had two choices, as far as he was concerned—take the woman's advice or reveal himself to some mob and see if the duke knew how to keep his word. The first option only seemed to serve himself. Even the townsfolk of Ansky would die here before he could return with a sufficient force to use Arieh's weakness against it.

Yet the second option would give Wilber dominion over Elcan for decades, if not longer. He would toss the freedom of Ansky away and leave the keys of hope with Lorene and her second son.

While Evan sat there silently in turmoil, the crawling sensation of watching eyes came over him, causing him to turn.

Arnacin stood against the back wall, regarding him while talking with Raymond and Tevin.

After meeting that gaze, the prince turned back around, trying not to move too hastily. A small shudder ran down his spine, however.

While on the island, Lazarus had once compared Evan's eyes to Lisya's, but there was far more of the enchanter in Arnacin's, he was sure. Different, yes—calculating instead of accepting, shrewd more than omniscient, with that light accompanying a victorious grin when a word or movement proved his guess correct. He had the same piercing eyes as Michael, but with knowledge that far surpassed the enchanter. Arnacin was rarely wrong, but it was imperative he not guess Evan's thoughts this time.

The more the prince considered, the more the second option seemed the better. He had once told Charlotte he would never be the sort of king who let others suffer while he escaped, even if it was so the battle might be won sometime in the future. Rethinking his logic did nothing to sway his conviction, but he could hardly say that, considering it now meant his surrender.

He was just standing when Lazarus and Vilo entered the cellar. "What do you want us to do, Max?" the fisherman softly asked.

Freezing, Evan racked his brain for any excuse to slip outside alone. "I was just going to ask Darkfire his opinion before deciding. I know how little time we have, but he might have a new perspective, and I..." He shrugged, biting his tongue at the lie.

"Evan." The soft call came from Arnacin. "Don't go alone."

He knew. And what could be said to that? After a brief pause, Evan said, "I need to be alone for a moment." He looked up to meet the islander's gaze and noticed that glint, that all-knowing craftiness.

"Raymond would not interrupt your thoughts. You could forget he was there."

Compressing his lips, Evan turned back toward the door. "Raymond does not need to be out in the noon sun. At the moment, I need to be."

There was only the softest whisper of movement before he felt Arnacin's hand on his arm. Even though the islander was only a few inches taller than himself, Evan had to raise his chin to meet the other's eyes. Forget the eyes of an enchanter—this was a dragon, delighting in its own cleverness while its prey squirmed from feeble lies. The prince shuddered slightly, pulling away.

Quietly enough that only Evan could hear, Arnacin asked, "Did you forget Darkfire moved to the mountains? I think not." He did not wait for an answer, instead stepping through the door and holding it open.

That action was an order, in its own way. For only a second, the prince refused, remaining firmly where he stood. Then he surrendered and followed. As he did, Arnacin said, "Michael, go tell Darkfire we will meet him where the trail opens up."

Michael folded his arms, immovable. Feeling like a captive, Evan nodded reluctantly at the islander's request. Huffing, the enchanter transformed, and his red wings beat the air over their heads.

As Michael flew by, Arnacin shut the cellar door with a snap. He continued to wait, though the dragon was gone from his eyes. Sighing, Evan turned up the stairs. Only once they were outside and he had closed the kitchen door behind him did he turn on the black shadow of the islander. "So you know what I was thinking. Do you see any alternatives? Should I desert them, including those I dragged here from Ansky because I destroyed their homes?"

Despite the prince's flash of anger, Arnacin merely smiled with that same knowing darkness. "Raise the city in rebellion."

Evan paled, but Arnacin insisted. "The duke made his worst mistake when he took away their food and water. Their hatred has likely never been stronger, and with nothing to lose, they will all fight the castle with glee."

"They are dying of starvation. By the time we've formulated a plan, they will be far too weak to fight!"

"Hatred is a powerful weapon. It can make even the sickest man rise from his deathbed to kill."

Clearly, those words came from experience. Evan found himself wondering to what reaches of the world Charlotte's brother had gone. He quickly shoved those horrified thoughts away. "I refuse to use such hatred, even if it is strong enough to win."

Sighing, Arnacin looked away. As he did, he appeared to shrink back into his previous human form, with his own uncertainties and fears. "Evan, your death won't rescue them—"

"Reginold cannot afford to lie. Arieh will collapse."

"But without you, all of Elcan will collapse."

"There are people who can take up the banner. Newton is in the Ice Woods."

"Unless Andrew dies, Newton will never have the right to the throne. And even were it otherwise, he's still a Dalacort."

"I trust Lisya. In her home, he will be partially raised by her."

Arnacin's gaze flicked to him, then quickly turned away. While waiting for an answer, Evan started down the path. He would return to the city when he could, but they needed to stop loitering around the Cedar Apple's kitchen door.

Following along, the islander whispered, "I don't trust kings, Evan. I may be ready to trust you, but not anyone else. I don't think I'm alone in that thought, either. Elcan needs *you*. Therefore, you must attack in two days."

"Such a move is suicide! If you are right, the result would be worse than words could describe. I cannot encourage such hatred for any mission."

"We must try." When Evan stopped walking, folding his arms, Arnacin sighed. "Look, if your Creator... Since your Creator cares, you will win anyway."

"That would be testing providence! I've done that! I left Wilber in the Creator's hands and look where it has led!" The prince flung out his arm to encompass the whole city above them.

Arnacin also stopped, mimicking the prince's stance. "Evan, you will lead this battle, or I'll have you bound and gagged in the cellar."

The threat was said in a conversational tone, yet the prince felt his eyes blaze and his back straighten. The words *Try it* clung to his tongue. He bit them back, however, knowing Arnacin's words were an idle threat. He doubted the islander himself thought otherwise. All Evan had to do was enter the city, and his surrender was assured.

However... as long as they knew he still lived, the Isfullen would stop at nothing to rescue him. Unless he had enough of a head start that they would know him to be dead, they would reveal themselves in an effort to save him before it was too late. Once they did, the food and water would never be returned.

Unless Arnacin was never able to warn them either.

The air seemed to still in those few seconds as both studied each other. Given the choice between Arnacin's death and thousands of others, the decision appeared plain. It hung above them like a vulture, waiting, as the prince's arm dropped back to his side. His fingers unconsciously closed around the hilt of Resplandecer. Any sensible, responsible king would act when one life threatened an entire nation.

Arnacin made no move. No hint of flight shone in his eyes. He had voiced the depths of his convictions through his idle threat and was surrendering the final choice—and his own life—to the prince.

The tense moment slipped by. Evan looked away, slowly uncurling his fingers from the sword. Instead, he whispered, "You are not going to give me much choice, are you?"

Although Evan had never even seen Arnacin tense, the islander's muscles visibly relaxed and he smiled innocently. "Of course, you have a choice. You have the choice to agree willingly or unwillingly. This battle will occur, though."

Half-teasingly, Evan tried one last time, "May I remind you that I am king?"

The islander's smile only grew more wicked. "That is exactly why you don't have a choice." For a minute, Arnacin also fell silent as they resumed their walk. Then, he softly admitted, "I was once a king's personal counselor. Of course, he banished me for doing what I am doing now."

Looking askance at his companion, Evan asked, "Did you think I would do the same?"

Slowly, the islander shook his head. "You have shown time and again that you allow certain types of challengers... But you don't insist you would never punish someone for disagreeing with you."

"I hate that type of defense. If my actions cannot speak for themselves, assuring benevolence would make a liar of me."

With a contemplative nod, Arnacin turned back to the path ahead. After ten silent steps, he spoke up, "Evan... What is your decision?"

A minute passed, during which the prince studied his companion. How relieved part of him was at the thought that someone might stop him, that he was free from whatever horrible death awaited him if he surrendered. And yet...

"I can't, Arnacin," he finally sighed. "I cannot be made to have everyone here slaughtered willingly, and however you look at it, that will be what happens. Can you? Truly? Are you so hard that you do not care about your own side anymore? How can you even push for this?"

Arnacin stared at the ground. At last, he whispered, "To do otherwise is to surrender." He quickly continued, as Evan opened his mouth, "There is still a chance we can win. We need to take it."

Sadly, the prince shook his head. Arnacin insisted, "Evan, I'm serious. I'm not asking you to slaughter them willingly; I'm forcing you to take that chance. And if you don't, for understandable reasons, I will." He halted—his next words pained. "I must... We can't live wondering what would have happened if we had only taken that last chance, so the choice I'm asking of you is: are you willing or unwilling to lead?"

Unsure whether to smile in hopeless sympathy or strike the islander, Evan groaned. "Willing." He could not silence the mental whisper calling him a selfish weakling for surrendering, but outwardly, he only joked, "If you will not allow me to stop your suicide, I can at least rescue you from poorly made plans."

The islander grinned.

Once Arnacin and Evan returned from their meeting with Darkfire, the Isfullen spent the rest of the day spreading word of the uprising. Although almost everyone leapt to volunteer, some demanded to know the whereabouts of "Maxwell."

The first time Evan heard that response, he nodded grimly; this was but one problem with Arnacin's plan. Yet, the islander did not appear troubled. When the first defiant citizen asked about the prince's hideaway, Arnacin simply took a step closer, saying in a low and deadly tone, "You may think you can threaten us by informing the castle of our plans, but you should know better. If you made your intentions known to the people, they would never allow you to make it to the castle alive. On the other hand, assuming you kept your traitorous intentions silent until after you had informed the authorities..."

Arnacin trailed off, but like a mouse caught before a snake, the man stood transfixed by the islander's smile.

"Can you not guess?" the islander pressed. "With the entire city fighting for their very lives, thousands of desperate people, that fat army from the castle will never stand a chance." He paused for a minute to let his words sink in, then added, "And even if the uprising was squashed, where would that leave you? You are no more than a slave to Evfel. Never will you be anything else. In succeeding once at forcing you to do their will, they will feed you morsels from their hands and keep you begging for more. Whenever they want something from you, they will again remove your food and water.

"You have a chance that will never come again, a chance for every single person in Arieh to rise and eliminate their masters, to take a stand for their own freedom with a desperation that won't be quenched. Their lives and deepest desires depend on it, and you can be certain, when the castle is alerted, Arieh's citizens will be the victors on the battlefield, throwing off their shackles for all time. Your only options are to die enslaved or take a stand for yourself."

No one, not even Evan said anything in the following silence. Yet, by the end of the day, after having toured the city to discover their strengths and weaknesses in the upcoming battle, the prince felt his despair turn to fury against the islander.

He managed to control his seething thoughts until he pulled Arnacin into a private room off of the Cedar Apple's kitchen late that night. "Do you realize what we are doing? Not only are you turning them all into senseless, hateful fiends in order to win, you have condemned them to death regardless!"

The islander did not look at him, his gaze instead fixed on a spot on the wall as he shook his head slightly. "You could have chosen not to do this."

"Through murder only!"

A sigh moved Arnacin's shoulders. "You know why I acted as I did."

Unfortunately, Evan did. Moving into the islander's line of sight, he relented. "It is done, Arnacin. There is no going back. Hundreds of city folk are depending on us to make a plan to win back their supplies. What do we do now?"

Slowly, those indigo eyes warily focused on him. "About what?"

"Even ignoring the problems that stem from relying on their hatred, have you not thought that there is no access to Castle Dalacort unless they first lower their gates? And the soldiers will have no reason to do so once they see the uprising. They have all the food, so it is impossible to lay siege and force them out. The city would starve while trying, and even if we laid enough bait for them to engage, we will be trapped against walls and in alleys, where movement is restricted."

"If you can find something to convince them to leave their fortress, you can use the city to your advantage by placing archers on many of the rooftops."

"Yes, but how do we convince them to come out in the first place?"

"I can't think of what to do, Evan," Arnacin sighed. His voice dropped. "At least, not here."

Cocking his head in confusion, the prince studied the oddly pale islander. "What is here?"

"The entrance to the mines." His words were barely audible as he nodded toward the far wall.

Reminded of the islander's reaction to the suggestion they hide in the tunnels, Evan licked his lips in caution. "Why do they scare you?"

A sharp breath passed through the islander and a shudder shook his shoulders as his gaze returned to the room. His irises seemed to darken to black as they focused on the prince, but he said nothing for a long moment. Finally, he sighed. "You have internal scars yourself, Evan. Do they not torment you?"

"In what way?"

"In your dreams, in your waking moments..." Arnacin's words were coming faster now. "Do you ever forget where you are as those scars become your fearful reality?"

Evan's first reaction was to shake his head in horror, yet he knew the islander had opened a portion of his heart. Softly, the prince admitted, "Not in the way yours torment you, obviously. I doubt it has anything to do with my strength or experiences, though."

Arnacin merely looked away, and Evan whispered sadly, "You already know of my fear of the throne, of my guilt and terror of betraying all who rely on me. Yes, it keeps me awake. But I admit most of my nightmares left when I submitted to my calling. There is something healing in knowing you are where you always belong—"

"Rain!" cried a voice from the kitchens, followed by pounding feet. "It's pouring!"

Indeed, to say it was raining was an understatement. Leaving the Cedar Apple, the Isfullen had barely scrambled up the slippery path to the city when Evan looked back and saw a torrent of water gushing off the cliff the inn was built into and swiftly flowing down the trail. Until the downpour abated, they were trapped in the city—but in the rain, being trapped was hardly a concern.

By cupping their hands, they could drink their fill. Evan tilted his face to the sky, allowing the heavy, cold drops to smack against his cheeks.

"Find any containers, or thick fabric!" Malachi's voice rose above the wind and the splatter of rain. "A cloak, a blanket! Let it soak in the rain and then knot it. It will take much longer to dry, and you can keep using it for a little water after the rain passes!"

In the blackness, Malachi was just visible, handing a soaked cloak to a lady who tightly held the hands of two children. She shook her head. "That is yours!"

As she released the hand of her oldest child to shove the cloak back toward its owner, Evan wondered if Malachi's suggestion would even work with Lisya's cloaks, which were, after all, waterproof. He stopped at that thought. *Lisya's cloaks were waterproof.*

"Quick!" the prince called to the nearest Isfullen as he stripped off his own cloak. "Raymond, help me tie this into a bag! The rest of you, find Lisya's children and have them do the same!"

His urgent commands were instantly obeyed. As he had hoped, the cloaks proved able to catch the rain as if they were giant waterskins. Some of the city's inhabitants lent pieces of string to tie off the six makeshift bags.

It was Raymond who said, "We'll win this war, Evan. Even the skies are in your favor."

The rain stopped early the next morning. With thirst quenched and water bags locked in the Cedar Apple's pantry beneath Michael's guarding talons, the Isfullen slept well for a few hours. Evan woke first.

Realistically, their water supply would be finished within an hour if they gave some to the entire city—to say nothing of the lack of food. Again, they might make it to the nearest city, Grand-sire, or the woods without dying, but evacuating would hardly go unnoticed. Reginold would likely notify Grand-sire to ambush them.

Was it possible to take Grand-sire instead? No. If they did that, women and children would be caught on the battlefield.

Sighing, Evan threw his arm across his face.

Raymond stirred beside him. "What is it?" the hunter asked, pushing himself up.

Feigning ignorance would never work. Sitting, the prince pulled his knees toward himself. "I am deliberating."

With a puff of amusement, Raymond placed a hand on the prince's shoulder. "Evan, I'm sure you didn't choose this battle without thoroughly thinking everything through."

Arnacin lay on the opposite side of Raymond. As Evan's guilty glance landed on the black-haired islander, the prince felt his blood smolder. Watchful eyes regarded him in return, but neither spoke of their debate.

Raymond either failed to notice their feud or pretended to. He simply asked, "Do you think we can attack tonight? We don't have much more time."

"First thing tomorrow morning." Evan sighed. "I do not want the attack to go on after dark, and I have no doubt this will be a long struggle." Taking a preparatory breath, he met Raymond's gaze. "If you are willing, gather all the city folk who are eager to take a stand and start blockading the northernmost streets with anything you can find. Leave the main street, Lion's Heart, open. We shall try to draw the attack that way.

"Send the other Isfullen to find every makeshift weapon they can: brooms, shovels, butcher knives, anything. We'll gather in the Black Print tonight to distribute some water."

Nodding, Raymond pushed himself to his feet. "Will there be room for our bows?"

"Our archers will be positioned on the rooftops, which is why I want the battle to be north, toward the back of the city and out of range of the castle archers."

"And you're sure they'll come to us?"

"That is my task today." Glancing at Arnacin, Evan whispered, "I would greatly appreciate your assistance."

A grim smile crossed Arnacin's face. Then, sighing, he rose.

With the entire tavern left to the staff, the Isfullen had free range of the place. Evan decided to use one of the upper rooms with a window overlooking the road.

Pulling a gilded chair from the table, the prince dropped wearily into it. For a moment, he let his thoughts wander over the mountainous view outside.

Arnacin walked around the table to lean against the window frame. "Their rooms of finery," the islander scoffed, bringing Evan back to the present. "For the rich and the powerful. Stupid men don't realize their vanity kills them."

"What do you mean?" Evan asked, ignoring Arnacin's dark undertones.

"These windows are open to the air, aside from the wooden shutters, and the walls are uneven, vertical rock. That would never stop certain thieves or assassins. They'd scale the rock like a ladder, unhinge the shutter..." He shrugged. "The back rooms are more secure being built deeper into the mountain, but without the light and the view, they are not as exquisite. And so, for their vanity are the wealthy attacked."

Evan shook his head. "You are incorrigible!"

Turning, Arnacin met his gaze, a thin smile on his lips, half wickedly clever, half guilty. When he said nothing, however, the prince pulled them back to the point. "No matter how I look at it, Arnacin, I doubt Reginold will send anyone until we are near death. Then, he will reap all that he desires, unless it appears we're in no immediate danger of dying."

Leaving his position next to the window, the islander slid into the chair opposite the prince and rested his elbows on the table. "What lie would convince him of that?"

"It is the popular opinion that I play with magic and make pacts with the devil." For just a moment, Evan's tone cooled. "Considering where you have taken this battle with my assent, there may be truth to that."

Arnacin sighed. "Are you thinking of claiming the rain was requested by you?"

"Actually," Evan laughed, "I *had* prayed for it. But I dread to use that course. I hoped you could think of another."

Leaning back in his chair, the islander nodded. "So you want me to think not of a real plan, but of something to satisfy your unhappy conscience? Odd that you picked me, Evan. You should know I only think in the corrupt. I never voiced my idea of how to upend Arieh when you first asked us to come here. I could have gone alone with Michael. In a few months, we could have discovered all the political feuds and then launched an attack. One murder in the right place with seemingly the right culprit, and Evfel's strength would devolve into fighting each other. That is the sort of plan I make."

"I know better than to believe you 'only think in the corrupt.' I also know you have a very shrewd mind, and therefore, I consider it natural to ask you if you can think of another plan. If you cannot, I realize you have a gift for terrifying people through words alone, and I would like you to help me write a note for Reginold."

The islander did not move.

Leaning forward, the prince tried again. "Arnacin, I do apologize. I know you acted the only way you could, and I agreed. My frustration these past few days is far from fair..." There were no words to describe the turmoil in his heart. Putting his head in his hand, he moaned, "I have failed them already by choosing battle over surrender. Of course, it is equally probable this is just the outcome of my failure to take responsibility long before." He shook his head. "But then, taking the whole thing to be my doing is likely complete arrogance."

Amazingly, Arnacin laughed. "Evan, just accept this as the only way right now and go with it. When you acquire your throne, you will be a great king." He paused. Dropping his gaze, he added, "Those other fears, which you label failure and arrogance in turn, I consider no more than any leader feels."

Shrugging, he changed topics. "However, as to that note, I am a terrible liar myself."

"Are you so when writing?" Evan asked. "I also am a terrible liar, but the difference comes in the time to plan, and in that there is no face to belie the words on parchment."

"Then know I agree: fear is the only way to draw them out at the time of our choosing."

So, retrieving parchment and ink readily available in all the Cedar Apple's best rooms, they eventually wrote:

Reginold,

Do you think you can gain your wishes by starving the king's people? As for myself, your intended victim, I am not so snared, nor starved. The mighty storm the other day was no accident, I can assure you.

Continue on the path you now take and the rain will come again, in greater force. With it, my people can drink and then travel to feed in other places in Evfel while you continue to punish your own people. What will you do when you must inform your liege that you have destroyed his kingdom rather than killed the true king of Ansky?

I think it unnecessary that I even ask you. You are likely aware of the populace's rage, and you fear to open your gates until they lie dead. Since they are not dying, it will instead be you suffering to the point of death.

I also warn you that any troops upon which you call will never reach you alive. We have secured your city for you. They will be slaughtered on the road.

Ansky is, as always, a believer in giving opponents a chance. So, instead of describing the ghastly vision of starvation lurking before you, I offer an opportunity for you to achieve your king's desires honestly and rescue your hide. Meet my army in Arieh's streets tomorrow morning. Whoever wins this battle is fairly chosen by a higher order. May the best side win.

Respectfully yours,

Prince Evan Maxwell, King of Ansky, friend and ally of Enchantress Island and the Ice Woods, and Protector of Cyra.

Arnacin favored describing the ghastly vision of starvation, but Evan refused that suggestion.

So it was that they entered the city and asked where the highest window lay. They were informed they could use the orphanage, which had relocated to the castle after the removal of the city's vittles. From there, Arnacin released the note into the arm of one of the guards on the castle's parapet. With grim satisfaction, the islander returned to the street with Evan.

Most of the Isfullen gathered at the Black Print before the battle, while Lazarus and Carrie took charge of the water distribution that night and Evan looked to last-minute preparations. Michael, he sent to call Darkfire to Arieh. Raymond was placed in charge of taking the twins and Malachi out for more archery practice.

Although the prince had opposed allowing Lisya's boys on the streets themselves, they had refused to evacuate with the women, children and elderly to the relative safety of the Cedar Apple. Strangely, Raymond had supported the twins, saying they were, after all, fourteen. To Evan's further amazement, Arnacin had agreed with his childhood friend. By the time the prince had consented to the twins' request to stay, he lacked the strength to deny Malachi his wish, even if it was likely the boy had no idea what it was he truly asked for.

Evan was about to add he would like Arnacin to place everyone in position that very night when the islander asked him, "Have you made arrangements to counter Reginold's plans?"

Vilo looked askance at the younger islander. "As if he should know what Reginold will do."

Without looking away from Evan, Arnacin added, "What he is *likely* to do."

"Is that not rather presumptuous of you?" The minstrel's words were a verbal dig.

With a silent laugh, Evan saw the exasperation in the islander's expression.

Arnacin's gaze dropped to the floor. "If you make plans to counter as many of his potential moves as you can conceive, you have a better chance of succeeding." It was almost an unwilling confession.

Vilo laughed. "Now, where would a shepherd learn that?"

Laying a hand on the minstrel's arm, the prince interrupted the comradery. "Reginold's most likely move will be to try to manipulate the entire battle into Lion's Heart, where his greater numbers will overpower us. Therefore, the bulk of our archers—otherwise known as you islanders—must assemble on the rooftops lining that street. I aim to let them think they can win easily by standing at the end of it. With Darkfire, I will not be missed. If they instead move into the narrow streets and try to slip around, the blockades will be there to slow them."

Almost as an afterthought, Evan asked, "Are there enough archers to place one alongside every blockade?"

Sighing, Vilo rubbed the back of his neck. "There are neither enough archers nor enough arrows. You are going to need to pick the areas where they're most likely to advance and leave it at that, particularly if you intend to place many of us along Lion's Heart."

These words only validated Evan's fears. But looking to Arnacin, the prince asked, "Will you take charge of placing everyone? I intend to take Darkfire and ask the woodsmen if they have any extra weapons to spare, and perhaps a little food and water—although I doubt I will gather enough to give these men any actual sustenance before the battle. After the duke burned part of the forest, I presume the woodsmen will be angry enough to lend their support. But unfortunately, only Darkfire can reach them quickly enough to fortify our resources. They could never make it here themselves in time to serve as additional troops."

"You shouldn't go alone, Evan," Arnacin insisted.

Flashing an innocent smile, the prince shrugged. "It is too late to back out. You have no need to play prison guard now."

Those dark eyes cooled. "You know there are still those who feel it's better to kill you than attack Arieh. No other reason need exist to speak as I have."

Dropping his lighter manner, Evan said with a sigh, "All of you need to be here." He held up his hand as Arnacin opened his mouth. "No, please don't volunteer yourself or someone else. The more that go, the less room there is for supplies. Both Darkfire and I will be here in the morning. We must be there, at the end of Lion's Heart, together. And the last thing I want is for some castle guard to see someone else ride up on Darkfire and assume that, when it is a different person later, it is only because I set a trap and switched places with one of you. Considering they failed to notice me when they stole the food, I can only assume they have little idea what I look like."

As the islander started to protest, Vilo touched his shoulder. "He's right, Arnacin. Let him go. Darkfire is not a horse anyone would attack without power to back them."

"The stallion's not here yet, so Evan would be unprotected," came the instant retort.

"I will go." A soft voice caused all three to turn. Carrie stood only a few paces away, her now empty cloak back around her shoulders, wet though it was.

"You don't mean to say you will go instead?" Vilo asked.

"I can go with them as additional protection, and Darkfire need not bear me."

Glancing back toward Arnacin, Evan saw submission in those eyes, if not agreement. The prince nodded. "As you wish, Carrie. Come. We will meet Darkfire as he arrives."

Before they could leave, however, Tevin called out, "Evan."

Sighing, the prince turned back, but all the speaker did was to hold out his black cloak.

"You may want to use this tonight." Tevin glanced meaningfully at Evan's side, where the black scabbard hung with silver winding down it. "And you might want to cover your sword again."

"Honestly, the entire city has probably seen it by now since I donated my cloak to catch water," Evan remarked. Nevertheless, he accepted the returned garment with a smile and threw it around his shoulders. Any remaining dampness from the other night would soon dry—particularly in the wind Darkfire would create.

Patting Tevin's shoulder in gratitude, the prince escaped the tavern behind Carrie, sliding past the press of people. The line of city folk waiting for their share of water still stretched from the Black Print's door and around the first corner, so the twosome quickly slipped down a side street with more room and fewer eyes.

They had not gone far before Evan was suddenly grabbed from behind. An arm wrapped about his throat as a hand clamped over his mouth. The sound of scuffling beside him told him Carrie had also been attacked.

Chapter 14

The Vengeful Cry

INSTINCTIVELY, EVAN JABBED HIS RIGHT ELBOW back to strike under his attacker's ribcage. But his blow never landed, as even more hands seized his arms. Before he could act again, the arm around his throat tightened mercilessly.

A man's voice hissed beside the prince's ear. "Take his sword."

Struggling to draw breath, Evan felt someone push his cloak back, yet the movement stopped there. "It's not here," another voice whispered before a hand pressed his sword's hilt into his ribs. "Wait!" the same person exclaimed.

Even as the world darkened and Evan's chest protested from the lack of air, he tensed for his one chance.

A blinding flash burst through the evening dusk as the hand tried to draw his sword. Amid the startled gasps and cries, the men's grip on their captive loosened for a split second. Twisting around, the prince brought his fist directly beneath his first attacker's jaw, then yanked his sword out the rest of the way. To his eyes, it bore the hazy edges and dull colors that meant it was currently invisible to others, but as it lit the city before him, it solidified in his hands.

There was no other action needed. With cries of terror, his attackers fled, and he glanced over to make sure of Carrie's well-being. She stood in front of him as a doe, her body trembling. Beneath her front legs, blood oozed from a man's crushed skull.

"Carrie?" Evan whispered, concerned by the horror in those deep eyes.

Slowly, the deer raised her head. The prince sheathed his blade, then ran the back of his fingers down her velvety nose.

The deer's entire body shuddered violently, as if some spell had broken. Then she transformed back into the enchantress's daughter—but the horror on her face remained.

Sighing, the prince wrapped her in his arms, feeling what eyes could no longer see: that she still trembled. "Shh," he whispered, resting his chin atop the curly hair tucked against him. "You had to defend yourself, Carrie. Anything more was accidental."

Though she nodded, he felt her tears seep into the front of his shirt and she continued to hold him. Slowly, she checked her grief, straightening her small frame within his arms and resealing the doors that hid her thoughts and convinced people she was something other than herself—a bold and wise, if young, enchantress.

At last, she stepped back, and keeping one hand in hers and the other on his hilt, Evan led the way to where the stallion awaited them at the edge of the city.

Evan and Carrie returned on Darkfire just as dawn lit the horizon. Meeting them on the corner of Cliffside Street and Lion's Heart, Arnacin noted how Carrie was now riding, how Evan's shoulders sagged in weariness, and how pale both of them appeared. Even the stallion's head hung as he halted before the islander. Yet it was the prince who spoke first. "Carrie, return to the Cedar Apple and take care of the children as we discussed. Arnacin, gather some helpers and distribute these, please." He pulled various sacks off Darkfire's withers, handing them down as Michael flew to join them.

Smiling slightly at the prince, Arnacin remarked, "I probably should bind and gag you in the cellar anyway. You don't seem to have the energy to survive this."

With a smile of his own, weak though it was, Evan sighed. "Just hurry. The sun is already on its way."

Arnacin turned to leave with some of the sacks, then paused. Carrie was hastily cutting a seam of her cloak with her brother's knife. In moments, she pulled out a length of blue silk. With a glance toward Evan, whose attention was on the castle, Arnacin left.

Watching the sun climb ever upward, Duke Reginold sniffed. So this Evan Maxwell thought to challenge Arieh and all of Evfel with a handful of commoners. Magic or not, he had made his last mistake. Yet, as an eagle suddenly flashed into the sky bearing a long cloth of blue silk, a chill seemed to pass over the castle—even more so when the eagle attached it on the orphanage's flag pole and it was caught by the wind. A fiery horse with eyes ablaze fluttered there, while below a victorious cry filled the air.

"Do you know the location of their so-called king?" the duke asked his scout.

"He and his stallion have just stepped onto Lion's Heart, Your Grace."

"Then the fool has signed his own death warrant."

Arnacin had refused being positioned on a rooftop. Despite his role as an archer, he situated himself on the ground and ignored Raymond's concern about being in harm's way, knowing he could switch to a sword when his arrows ran out. Once Reginold's forces had located the archers, they would come in swarms to scale the walls. Ground cover was the archers' best defense, under those circumstances. Thus, finding a narrow alley in which the enemy could only advance one at a time, Arnacin waited with his bow at the foot of the rooftop stairs. There was only one drawback—he could not see an attack coming. Raymond kindly made up for that blindness from his spot on the roof.

"The castle gates just opened. Michael's dive signaled us."

"Are they already branching into the side streets, or are they taking Evan's bait?"

"They're that cocky." Raymond emphasized his grim smile by nocking an arrow to his bow. "They're driving straight for Evan."

Silence followed as they waited for the enemy to draw within range. The imagined tramp of many feet turned into a real one right before the islanders above Arnacin's head loosed their projectiles. Cries filled the air, angry ones mixing with those of the dying. Then, Darkfire's challenging call echoed from the mountain heights as the clang of engagement added to the din.

Still, Arnacin waited, his own arrow nocked and ready. Somewhere nearby, he knew, many groups of city dwellers also stood tense, listening. Then, the warning he'd been awaiting from Raymond came over the sound of a singing bow: "Evan's on Cliffside, but he's turned them back! They're filing onto the smaller streets!"

That message had barely finished when the first armored man appeared around the corner of the building before Arnacin. The islander's arrow embedded itself in the helmet's eye slit. His next felled the following man.

No one else was foolish enough to enter the alley. Despite the death raining on them from the rooftop archers, Reginold's men stood just out of Arnacin's range, sending a cover of crossbow bolts. The steps sheltered the islander from that attack until another group rounded the corner behind him.

"Arnacin!" The snapped warning gave the islander time to duck right before a bolt struck the step just above his head.

Yet another arrow forced him to leave the steps entirely, jumping into the crossfire.

He was saved only by his swift decision to rush the troops ambushing him, and by a sudden volley of arrows from the archers above, determined to cover him. Yet, even as Arnacin dropped to snatch a long knife off one of the bodies, Reginold's men gained the stairway.

Since Evan and Arnacin had positioned everyone to the west side of Lion's Heart, the easiest way for Reginold's forces to surround Evan's troops was to advance along Cliffside Street, running along the edge of the cliff. Evan and Darkfire had no trouble blocking that path, sending many an armored man over the knee-high wall running along portions of that road, where the houses, built to the very edge of the drop-off, did not protect anyone from a fall. More troops died by hooves or blade, adding another blockade, this one of bodies, to the web of smaller roads and alleys.

"Evan!" The scream came from above them.

Darkfire flinched, likely saving the prince as a bolt zipped behind his head to land in the stonework of the building beside them. Above them, Tevin shoved the bowman off the roof. Yet it was clear to Evan there were more of Reginold's forces up there. The islanders were defenseless.

Ever aware of the prince's tiniest nudges, Darkfire wheeled about, racing up the steps to help the rooftop archers. Now they had not only prevented any deaths on that roof but also acquired a higher vantage point on the battle. Unfortunately, that improved view showed they no longer had any solid defense across the rooftops. Some of the positions once held by their archers were strewn with bodies. On other roofs, furious skirmishes raged in attempts to keep the posts. On still others, armored men hunched with their crossbows, raining their bolts into the streets.

In their blockades below, men still attacked from behind their walls of overturned carts and beams, forcing the enemy back with an astonishing frenzy. Yet that strength would not hold under the fire of the forces conquering the rooftops. Already, some makeshift barriers were falling.

"Michael!" Evan called. "Signal the charge. They'll all die if they remain on the defensive!"

Trusting the eagle had heard him, he turned to the Isfullen around him. "Join the blockades. This part is over."

With that, he asked Darkfire to leap to the next roof where battle still raged. They needed to reclaim their perches.

Something was happening within the ranks of Arieh's citizenry. While the Isfullen's strength dwindled with their supply of arrows, their energy sapped by the growing press of their assailants, those of Arieh were increasing their attack. Fury turned their limbs to steel capable of blocking sword thrusts. Defiance in the face of death changed their weaponless fingers into claws that gouged out their enemies' eyes.

With inhuman strength, they snapped necks, ripped weapons from living hands, trampled wounded men to death, and surged forward, increasingly unstoppable as they continued. Caught in that press, Arnacin and Raymond could only rush forward with the mob or be trampled, like the dead. That rush drew them ever onward to the open bridge of Castle Dalacort, like a dragon blowing flames as it swooped down upon its prey.

Knights, infantry and crossbowmen fled back up the streets, their faces deathly white as the commoners—a writhing mass from the underworld—pursued them with relentless passion. Reginold could not move, a cry stuck in his throat. Maxwell was not lying about his dark powers, now gleefully winging across Arieh.

"Raise the drawbridge!" His order came out first as a strangled squeak, then as a scream. No one paused to question it. Every guard was already in the process of acting thus, with or without a royal order. Any of his men left out there were already dead anyway.

But the guards moved too late. A swarm of those tattered, skeletal figures from nightmare leapt for the rising bridge and hung onto the end in a furious effort to pull it back down with their own weight. For just a moment, everyone watched in frozen anticipation. Then something red streaked from the sky and the groaning chains snapped. The drawbridge thudded back to earth, crushing those caught beneath it, and the onslaught of creatures rushed across to stab at the wooden gates through the portcullis.

Reginold doubted even the sturdy oak would deflect the assault. His knees trembled. Then, the portcullis began to rise, and the duke's eyes fell on the black horse and rider standing in the middle of the road as hundreds of figures dashed around him. Did he control even the castle walls against their master?

The duke had no desire to discover the answer. "Guards! To me!" As he turned swiftly to the stairs, he commanded those stationed at the walls, "Do not let them inside! For the love of life!"

With that, he all but fled to the keep, knowing death chased him, laughing.

With a cry, Malachi fell amid the press of charging, enraged citizens. Unable to pick himself up, he curled into a ball, wrapping his arms about his head.

The wave of feet broke, however, as four black hooves set themselves down on each side of him. Malachi watched Darkfire snap his teeth at anyone approaching too close.

When the press slowed, the young Evfelian cautiously stood, accepting Evan's hand. Pulling Malachi up before him, the prince asked, "Are you hurt?"

"Bruised," the boy admitted, shivering. "Nothing is broken, though." Looking at Evan, he noticed the paleness of his rescuer's skin, the distance of his eyes as he watched the horde sweep by.

All the prince said, however, was, "Come. You're going to the Cedar Apple. There are still enemies in the city, but they have hidden themselves for now. Darkfire will know how to slip by them."

"Are you not needed to lead?"

A quick shake of the head, little more than a spasm, was Evan's sole response. Only after Darkfire had turned onto the trail winding down past the Cedar Apple did Evan whisper, "There is no leading them, not by any human, at least. In our stupidity, we've unleashed something that should never have been let loose."

Malachi shivered in reply.

There was indeed no controlling that mob. All the Isfullen could do was be dragged along into Castle Dalacort's outer bailey. There, a few escaped to the battlements, where they helped Michael dispose of the archers on the outer ward, while others loosed arrows at the castle archers shooting from the inner ward. If the Isfullen missed any, they at least drew the fire away from the people filling the outer ward.

After an hour of slaughter on both sides, the knights retreated into the inner ward, leaving their remaining archers to be cut down. For just a minute, all was still once Evan's forces held the outer bailey, yet a massive wall stood between them and Reginold's men.

Then, Michael plunged into the inner ward's archers with a cry that rent the skies. His eagle scream reignited the mob's energy and hatred. With a resounding crash, they bodily threw themselves against the inner gate.

"Thanks, Michael," Raymond grumbled, standing on the outer battlements. "We could have starved them out at this point. Most of the food they took is stored out here."

"We don't know how long that would take." Arnacin sighed beside him. "If we don't finish this today, they'll be able to call in reinforcements. Michael did what he had to."

Despite his words, however, he appeared no more eager to help the angry horde's renewed attack. As no enemies were firing upon them, he simply watched for a moment, then began yanking arrows out of bodies, finding those that could be reused.

Sighing, Raymond followed suit. His empty quiver needed refilling anyway.

He wasn't sure how long they toiled at the task, keeping half their attention on the battle, but their respite was ended abruptly by a renewed shout. Below, the horde was dashing eastward along the inner wall.

Soon, Michael flitted overhead from that direction. "There are recessed steps inside the well! I killed one of Reginold's men trying to escape that way!"

"Is it a passage?" Raymond asked. Yet the eagle was already beating toward the other Isfullen, who stood guard and waited for enemy archers to stick their heads over the inner ramparts.

Shrugging, Raymond turned to Arnacin. "We had best see for ourselves."

Yet, his friend stood as if transfixed, watching the dissipating crowd. Soon, the sound of renewed fighting rose from inside the inner bailey. Somehow, the maddened citizens had bypassed the castle's last defense.

"Come on!" With those words, Raymond sprinted to the nearest stairs in the tower. As he reached the bottom, he heard Arnacin trudging behind.

They reached the well just as the last of Arieh's citizens disappeared inside of it. With the other Isfullen behind him, Raymond looked into its gaping hole. Despite the inky blackness, which only grew thicker the farther it sunk, the piercing rays of evening light struck the wall inside of the well. Three recessed steps were visible four feet down from the top, circling its interior. Yet from the darkness below, echoes of the horde's vengefully excited shouts and pounding feet rebounded.

Raising his eyebrows questioningly, Raymond looked at the other Isfullen, now gathered around the well. His gaze stopped on Arnacin, whose face was so pale it appeared to shine in the late sun. Yet at the hunter's glance, his friend nodded for him to continue.

With a preparatory breath, Raymond slipped into the well, his feet finding firm purchase in the first foothold. In the quiet, the soft drip of moisture hitting the water far below echoed eerily. The well was not wide. Cautiously, the hunter started down, noticing how still the air was the farther down he went.

In another few moments, he heard panting and the soft scraping of more feet coming over the top. Waiting for his eyes to become accustomed to the dark, Raymond did not look back to see the source of the gasping breaths. It was an Isfullen, for no other could have snuck past the group around the top of the well. With that assurance, he continued downward, one careful step at a time.

At the twentieth step, his feet sank into water. For a second, he paused, his hands finding thin air. Was the passage underwater? Yet the echoes of battle coming from it spurred him forward.

He was knee-deep in water when his feet reached the dirt path. As he walked, keeping one hand on the wall, it gradually slanted upward. No sooner had he emerged from the pool than his feet hit something soft. A body lay there. From the clinking of metal when he stumbled into it, it was obviously a castle guard. Even the narrowness of the tunnel, which forced men to advance one at a time, had not thwarted the mob's hideous strength.

As Raymond traveled forward, he found more bodies. He even tripped over one with a small cry of surprise. Arnacin anxiously whispered his name, helping him back to his feet with a shaky grip. Neither said anything, however, instead starting forward with caution.

Without further incident, the Isfullen emerged from the corpse-filled darkness into a pantry. Only a few feet away, the door was smashed outward, its wood hacked and splintered. Through the gaping opening, hundreds of bodies were strewn across the inner bailey. Only a few were city folk. Beyond, knights, archers and guards were retreating into the keep, the mob pressing against them.

Sidestepping to allow the other Isfullen to join the battle, Raymond turned to Arnacin. His friend's color had only slightly improved, and there was a distance in his eyes as he stared at a trampled corpse lying at a grotesque angle on top of the smashed door.

After a second, Arnacin breathed, "We should find the duke before they do."

Shrugging, Raymond replied, "You lead."

Chapter 15

Death Trap

ACCOMPANIED BY JAMES AND THOMAS, Vilo was the last to go through the passage. The minstrel cast a glance at the many kegs filling the room as he emerged into the pantry. "Why don't you two find out what's in here? I doubt this is all the supplies, but there's a good start here."

Vilo had no need to add that he wanted to keep the twins out of the rest of the bloodletting. Their starved and exhausted faces lit up, and they nearly threw themselves at the kegs. Momentarily, the minstrel wondered if he should press on to rejoin the other islanders battling in the keep, but watching the two, he decided against it. If the enemy broke through their attack, the boys would be cut down for sure.

Therefore, Vilo exhaled in exhaustion and took a watchful stance by the shattered door. Around them, the room slowly dimmed as the daylight gave way to evening.

The battle had dispersed through the immense castle. A trail of corpses marked the passing of the mob. Other corridors swarmed with armed men. Knowing they would never beat the horde to their goal by following the same trail, Raymond and Arnacin took the hallways with the fewest bodies. They were met with fierce resistance from the duke's patrols, but the two islanders' progress was efficient and deadly.

With a blade plucked from a guard who could use it no more, Arnacin would block the attackers' advance while Raymond shot arrows through their eyes. Never once did the hunter strike Arnacin by mistake.

Despite the younger islander's familiarity with fortresses, Castle Dalacort was monstrous in size, and the search for the duke was like a run through waist-high water. As they neared their goal, up a tower, they were forced to follow the sounds of battle and a trail of the dead.

In the doorway of the topmost room, they froze. Duke Reginold's decapitated body lay in a puddle of crimson that pooled across the floor. One monster was still stomping on his corpse. Long stripes covered the mauled remains.

Nor was that wrath appeased with slaughter. Around the room, men clawed at the walls, ripped wooden beams off the ceiling, and tore at anything their eyes fell upon.

Raymond turned away, touching his friend's arm to signal they should leave. It took a few seconds for Arnacin to respond. Used to his own hate-filled reactions, he had taken anger's full power for granted. There was no stopping it now. Hopefully, the horde's senses would seep back with the end of the battle, but there was nothing more for the islanders to do. Beaten, they turned away.

For ten minutes, they shuffled along in silence until they were joined by Lazarus on the castle's third floor. Now in the fisherman's company, Raymond asked, "Arnacin, why did you want to find the duke before the attackers?"

Without looking up from the flagstones beneath their feet, Arnacin muttered, "I didn't want to see that, not if I could stop it."

"I'm glad, Arnacin," Lazarus whispered. Two chins shot upward while four eyes fixed on him. He smiled faintly. "I was beginning to fear you had indeed lost your heart. It's good to hear you can still feel empathy, even for a cruel tyrant."

Arnacin lowered his gaze back to the floor. Minutes passed as they walked in silence. Then he whispered, "What heart, Larry? I murdered it long ago."

Although Arnacin was quiet when the Isfullen returned to give their report to Evan, the prince never once said the islander should have known better than to goad people's hatred. Looking around the dark, body-strewn street on which they were gathered, he sighed. "It's over, then. Arieh has fallen."

"Do you want us to distribute the food?" Lazarus asked. "The twins and Vilo have already begun."

"No. Wait until we know everyone has returned to their own minds. Before then, it will be too dangerous. Michael said most of you drank water before leaving the castle?"

When they nodded, Evan softly commanded them, "Have a bite to eat and then rest while we wait."

"I doubt we have time to stop," Michael spoke up. "I saw a bunch of men escape toward Grand-sire. Beyond doubt, they will raise a force to retake Arieh."

"Michael," Evan paused before continuing, "there is nothing we can currently do, and everyone needs the rest. If there is to be battle, and I agree more is coming, we must be physically able to defend ourselves."

Bowing, Michael withdrew into the shadows.

The mob calmed by the time darkness came, but after some food and water, they turned to torching the castle. Evan feared Arieh could become a stronghold against its citizenry once again, and no one disagreed.

Using catapults and battering rams from the castle, the Isfullen breached the weakest parts of Castle Dalacort to ensure opposing forces could not use it against the city again.

Once done, Evan's forces retreated to the Cedar Apple while the castle fires died. There, the prince pulled Lazarus, Michael and Arnacin aside, along with Martin and Vincent, to discuss the next step.

"Men are already gathering in Grand-sire," Michael informed them. "I doubt any of those from Castle Dalacort have reached them yet, but the smoke probably alerted them."

"What if we sneak out now?" Lazarus asked. "We've hampered Evfel's ability to retake Arieh and probably created enough confusion and fear to annihilate their usefulness to Wilber in holding Ansky."

Slowly, Evan shook his head. "There are too many Isfullen to sneak out. For now, we must defend our position here."

Vincent crossed his arms. "We of Arieh aided your attack on Castle Dalacort because we doubted they would eagerly return our supplies when they could keep us licking morsels from their hands. We have what we need now and those who might have noticed the Ceder Apple's change of ownership are no more. I say you leave now. We won't support you further. I think we've all done enough."

Michael blinked. "Are you not worried about them coming to slaughter you as punishment?"

"They are after you, not us," Vincent snorted. "Why would they slaughter their helpless workforce? They need us to rebuild everything that was destroyed."

Evan sighed. "What you say makes sense, but they will see us leaving unless we can find a passage out. I was guarding the drawbridge after taking Malachi to the Cedar Apple. Not a soul left that way, so they must have another exit. If they think we are trapped here, it will be all the better. Once we are gone, Vincent, you pretend meekness, surrender and say we kept you confined while we defended the city from them."

With that, the prince turned to the enchanter. "Michael, will you find the escape route for us? You can explore that mountain face like no one else."

Michael crossed his arms. "Now, I suppose?"

"The sooner you start, the sooner it will be found."

The boy obeyed with his usual sound of dissent. As he left, Evan turned back to the others. "In the meantime, we must have a plan to defend ourselves."

An hour later, Martin and Vincent departed to begin their preparations. Once they left, Lazarus asked Evan, "After we escape, where do you wish to go? Should we pick another place in Evfel to infiltrate?"

"For what, Lazarus?" Evan sighed. "I had two objectives when I sent you here: one, to potentially raise some extra support, and two, that any turmoil in Evfel would cause Wilber to send a large party to quash the uprising, leaving Ansky weaker for us. He never did. At this point, he is more likely to seal off the eastern end of the gorge to stop us returning should he hear of what transpired and wait until the masses of Evfel properly overrun our smaller numbers."

The fisherman sat back, shaking his head. "Then we have to escape in time to beat any messengers back to Ansky. If Wilber sends men to blockade the gorge, that is still fewer men in Castle Ansky, as long as we are already on that side."

"I'm afraid that's not your worst danger," Arnacin spoke up. "Anyone Evfel sends will ultimately strengthen Ansky against us. We don't have the forces to attack now, and we will have even fewer in comparison then."

"How many men do you think Evfel will send?" Lazarus asked.

Arnacin shrugged. "A large enough force to combat attack. They don't know what happened here or if their enemy is all in Arieh. I think they will be prepared for an ambush, which gives Wilber a couple score more men in Ansky at least."

Rubbing his forehead, Evan nodded. "My fears exactly. No, we cannot allow them through the gorge while we live."

After warning Arieh's citizenry of the coming attack from Grand-sire and leaving them under the battle training of the islanders, Evan left the city to where its trail branched off into many different roads heading farther down the mountain. There, turning to his stallion, he softly requested, "Darkfire, I wish you to lead the horses we stole from the castle into the Elcan Woods. Hide them there for when we join you. This road must be closed, and I doubt our exit will allow for horses. Yet without them, our opportunity for escape shall end. Wilber would cut off the gorge before we can arrive."

Faithfully, the stallion bowed his head.

After gathering the Cedar Apple's staff to help him, Evan tacked up the three hundred steeds they had pillaged from Castle Dalacort. Once he made sure the horses' reins would not catch on anything or trip them up, the prince approached Darkfire.

"Reach the cover of the woods before Grand-sire mobilizes, or I fear they will come after you," the prince whispered in parting.

Dipping his head, Darkfire sounded a commanding neigh. None of the horses challenged his right as the herd stallion, each one turning. Within seconds, they were all galloping behind him.

Sadly, Evan watched them thunder down the path. Once the last tail disappeared, he turned back to the taverners. "Find stones, large and small. We are closing the road."

Taking James, who had helped Vilo pillage the castle armory, Evan went to inventory the many weapons they had gained. "They were crossbowmen, not real archers," the prince commented. Looking at the number of bows they had assembled, all of extremely fine quality, he added, "Yet they had all these."

An examination of the swords proved them to be of similar quality. Their glinting edges easily drew blood, and their balance was perfect.

"And we are pitched against Evfel," James said faintly, staring at the cool metal of a blade shining under the sun.

Smiling slightly, Evan touched the boy's shoulder. "Nothing has changed from yesterday, save that we are better nourished. Now, come. These weapons are needed."

Arieh lay still that night, yet at the top of that dark, soundless mountain, men hunkered down beside arrow-slit blockades of stone, sealing the entrance to the Cedar Apple's stable and barring the path. Catapults sat ready on the heights. Archers lined the edge of the city, staring down into the blackness below them, bows bent, waiting for the attack Arieh's citizens knew was coming. Had not Michael reported late that evening that, as he searched the mountainside, he had spotted an army from Grand-sire marching toward Arieh?

As the moon died in the darkness of early morning, Michael dropped onto Evan's shoulder. "They are here," the eagle whispered.

As planned, the prince drew Resplandecer and, in response to its blazing light, fires burst to life along the heights. Before the truly unprepared enemy could move, Arieh's catapults launched flaming stones into their midst.

With a cry of fury, the enemy charged up the path leading to the city, only to find again Arieh was several steps ahead of them, having formed a corner of death from the Cedar Apple stable's entrance and a wall a few feet farther along the path. Arrows flew from two sides out of invisible holes in impenetrable walls of what seemed like fallen stone while more arrows rained down from the ridge to join the death trap.

With a growing resentful respect toward Ansky's rightful heir, Grand-sire's army retreated off the path and began setting ladders against the cliff. Holding shields above their heads, they started the climb. Some ladders were flung backward by the defenders, bearing their occupants to their deaths; others fell to raining rubble. Still others of Grand-sire's army succeeded in reaching the heights. Footmen leapt into the city, cutting down the archers in their way with ease.

They did not get far, however, before they were blinded by a light as piercing as sunlight in a dark hole. Before they could realize their danger, some were cut through and others stumbled off the cliff, taking more ladders down with them.

Instantly, the blaze disappeared, but the Grand-sire army had already called a retreat. They would wait for the morning and set up a strategically placed camp.

As soon as the army retreated, Evan sent half the city's defenders to rest, remaining on guard with the other half on the slim chance Grand-sire would try again. When dawn arrived without further attack, the defenders' training continued. The prince again sent Michael to search for Castle Dalacort's escape tunnels.

Inside the orphanage's large courtyard, Evan went to train the few unoccupied Isfullen in the art of swordplay. Since they had nothing to use but the highly dangerous blades confiscated from the castle, they were forced to proceed at a much slower pace than the prince would have wished, yet learn they must. Evan thus spent the day carefully correcting stances, hand positions and parries. Over and over, he felt he was repeating the same things: Loosen your grip; slow your movements; play to the speed of the attack, not to the speed of fear; do not swing up if the attack is downward; parry down and out; and so on.

Fortunately, the islanders had a natural grace that aided their learning. Without a doubt, the villagers from around

Alleluia Lake progressed the fastest, thanks to Evan's training in other forms of hand-to-hand combat almost two years ago. After a couple of hours with the first group, he switched them out for other Isfullen and began all over again.

No more attacks came that day, thankfully, although Tevin informed the prince that Grand-sire's army was growing. Michael still had not returned when night fell.

Finally stepping back outside to check on their sentries, the prince felt some of his strength return at the feel of the relatively unhindered night breeze on his face. Weary as he was, the stars blazing above seemed to lend him support. On the other hand, while a word or light touch from the prince would give the men new strength and courage, it drained him of energy all the more.

When Evan joined Arnacin after finishing his patrol of the night watch, the islander asked, "Do you have any idea how we're going to slip through that growing mass if we don't escape soon?"

"If we do not escape before all routes north are blocked, Arnacin, then we have lost," Evan replied with a slight bite in his tone. His companion wisely stayed silent, instead running his fingers absently along his bowstring while his keen eyes kept watch on the dark shadows far below.

After another minute of silence, during which Evan also stared thoughtfully out over the view, Arnacin inquired indifferently, "How are the Isfullen progressing?"

"Not fast enough, but the less I say on that, the better," the prince admitted, casting a quick sideways glance at the islander. Arnacin's only response was a shrug. Slowly exhaling, Evan returned to the previous subject. "I am sure you know, Arnacin, that this was a doomed war long before the Isfullen entered Arieh. But we still need to hope, for whatever it may be worth."

Now it was Arnacin's turn to look askance at his companion. Yet he said nothing, turning once again to his watch with silence. All the same, Evan noticed the dark head was now angled toward the Calmar Mountains in the distance, not on the army below.

When the prince started to leave, the islander softly inquired, "Evan, what is it that you find worth this fight and these uncertainties? If you are hoping to restore Elcan to a peaceful land, it will never happen. That time is dead, and there is no making it rise from the past. You fight for a dream."

Turning to look back over his shoulder, the prince whispered, "I do not fight for the world, Arnacin, but for my Creator. Yet if you say good will never come again, I cannot agree. No, it will never be what it was before, but for as long as the world lasts, hope returns. If just to give strength to the upright, it returns for a short time."

He received no response and, briefly rejoining the islander, he whispered, "We are charged to press on, Arnacin, not because we are told what will happen when we do, but because we are here to do the best we can in the short time given us. At least we know in the end which side will win, whether we succeed or not."

Arnacin finally turned to the prince. "Which side is that?"

Letting his breath out slowly, Evan replied, "The side with the most strength, naturally. Is that not the general rule of warfare?"

"Yet you do not say if that is the good or bad side."

Smiling grimly, the prince nodded toward the view. "Are the mountains beautiful and the air sweet? Are the stars bright and the light soft? Look at the power and mind that succeeded in creating those things, keeping those things, and then tell me which side shall win."

Again, there came no answer.

Midafternoon of the next day came before a spear rose out of the castle ruins, marking the place where Michael had found the entrance to the escape route. As inconspicuously as several of the Isfullen could, they began trickling there to help clear the tunnel hole from above.

Evan closeted himself with Martin, Taylor and Vincent, whom he was preparing to leave in command until the time came for their own escape. To them, he gave as many plans as he could before departing to continue with the Isfullen's training.

It was not until the next day, however, that anything unprecedented happened. Arnacin finally had some spare time to join the other Isfullen practicing their swordsmanship. No one could miss the look of challenge between the prince and the onetime king's counselor as some of the Isfullen entered the courtyard. Despite Evan's suspicion that the islander was the one other person in the city who had fully mastered swordplay, he challenged the other Isfullen first.

All the same, he could not fail to notice, even from across the room, Arnacin's perfect stance and balance. If Evan was thankful for one thing, it was that the islander was not trying too hard to disguise his skill. Finally, Evan allowed himself to pass from Raymond to the hunter's companion.

"If I aim for your left shoulder?" the prince inquired. There was no need to fix positioning or grip. Almost as if he was bored, the islander's blade came up to block the stated attack, that challenging light glinting in his eyes. "The right side of your neck?" With the same unconcern, the blade moved perfectly.

Evan continued in that fashion for two more exercises. At last, Arnacin caved. "All right, I know a thing or two about the art."

"Really?" Evan grinned. "In that case, think you can prevent me from stabbing you?"

If possible, the islander stood even taller, dipping his chin. "Can you prevent *me* from stabbing *you*?"

The prince's smile widened. As he knew, Arnacin never boasted needlessly. Unsheathing Resplandecer, he stepped back to allow the islander the first strike.

That may have been a mistake. When Arnacin moved, it was sudden and unexpected, but seemingly slow, so smooth was it. The islander's blade almost grazed Evan's shoulder before he hastily blocked it.

Barely a clash sounded as Arnacin's tip moved with the new direction and then came down. Turning that stroke aside, Evan backstepped fast to give himself a second. One breath, and he shortened the space between them again, half-prepared for the other's tactics. As it continued, the duel grew in ferocity. Each tested the other, wide grins on both their faces.

For a good half-hour, they must have continued, up and down stairs, back and forth. The only sound to be heard was the ringing of their blades.

Though neither combatant was yet close to victory, Evan called a halt, smiling through his panting breaths. "We are wasting time. I plan to leave tonight, and still we are unprepared." He paused to draw more air, then nodded his respect. "One thing you have in your favor: you are smooth enough to alter everyone's timing to their peril."

Arnacin laughed, leaning on his knees. "Yes, but that doesn't help any against you. You're lightning fast." A wince slipped through. "I thought I would surely win."

Laughter erupted around them.

"It's true. Suddenly, Resplandecer's there, and one must scramble to block it in time."

Shaking his head, Evan slid his sword away. "If you were scrambling, you fooled me. Anyway, now that you allowed yourself to be exposed as a master swordsman, do you intend to hide it again?"

Hopelessly, the islander hung his head, his breath a puff of amusement. Yet, slowly straightening, he shook his head.

"Go see to the escape hole and the defenses, Evan. I can take charge of this task."

The Isfullen did not escape that night, since their exit was not yet clear. Instead, Evan joined the diggers after checking once again on the watch. If he was more demanding, it was because he knew time was running out.

Michael had already warned the prince five more Evfelian armies were marching toward Arieh from the closest cities and castles, with even more coming behind. Not only would the Isfullen be outnumbered and crushed beneath the waves, they only had a short amount of time until messengers arrived in Ansky.

Indeed, the next night, as the Isfullen finished breaking through to the tunnel, Evfel's army pulled their catapults forward. Before the defenders of the city even realized the danger, rocks smashed into them or flew past them to hit walls and shower them with stone and wood.

When the ground shook, Evan had been telling their minstrel, "We broke through, Vilo. When you can, slip back to the castle ruins. Michael awaits us there." He turned in alarm just as a boulder crashed into the wall beside them. Shards flew against his skull.

His knees collapsed beneath him and spots of white burst through his vision. A cry flowed through the ensuing blackness, then the sensation that he was being lifted. Darkness thickened as he tried to rouse himself.

The prince was lying on a cobbled surface with the sound of a large crowd shifting around. "Evan," a familiar voice said. Michael was kneeling beside him. "You have the worst tendency to land yourself in trouble."

"Never mind." With every muscle protesting, the prince rolled onto his knees, glad of Michael's hand on his shoulder. "Did the attack break through?"

"No," Vilo answered. "Raymond's leading the defense for now. The rest of us came here."

It took a moment for Evan to realize "here" was the orphanage courtyard. Those who had been practicing their swordplay under Arnacin stood around him, blades still in hand. When the prince didn't respond, Tevin asked the obvious. "If we're under attack, what are we going to do? We can't leave the people of Arieh while we slink off."

"You must." The statement came from Martin as he pushed forward. He bowed to Evan. "Begging your pardon, but you are the target, my king. You must leave with your fighting men before they bury us all beneath dirt and stones. We have no hope if you stay. And we who are poor in battle must remain here, lest we endanger you when you face Evfel's troops. As you know, they are headed even now for Ansky."

It could not really be argued. Yet there was always a drawback. "Who will defend you?" Evan asked. "Evfel already floods the hills below us. Once they take the heights, they are sure to seek vengeance if they cannot find us and so realize you were the ones defending the city."

"And Carrie and Malachi were to stay here!" James protested.

Evan glanced at Martin, who sagged. "Even Evfel is ruled by some principles," the bold Anskonian replied. "If they seek retribution, they will kill men, not women and children. Those, they are more likely to force into rebuilding what we have torn down. But there is no alternative."

The prince stirred at that. "Yes, there is. I remain."

There were several coughs around the courtyard. Martin shook his head. "My dear prince, I know what is at stake, but should you not leave, day may never come for any of us. Go now, and we shall manage the best we can here. That is all anyone can do."

As Evan took Michael's hand to help him to his feet, he relented. "As you wish, Martin. Find Raymond and swap places with him. But give us two days if you are able. Then surrender, saying we just escaped and none of you were fighting. Perhaps, if you appear meek enough, you may avoid their vengeance."

Martin bowed. "If you wish it, so shall we do."

"Believe me," Michael hissed, his voice echoing through the rough tunnel the three hundred Isfullen were shuffling through, "The next time you ask me to spend three days scouting endless passages, or however long it was—I say it was more, but Raymond insists it was three—in a pitch-black hole, burrowing for air, I shall quit without further ado. I warn you now."

Evan hid his smile by looking away from the boy. The torch-light made the walls curving only an inch above their heads appear to flicker. Many of the islanders—taller in general than men of Elcan—had to duck their heads or stoop to go through. Spiders scampered out of their way, almost blinking at the sudden glow, and many webs were disturbed, although the first surprised and sharp inhales upon meeting them in the face had long since passed.

"I ran through millions of cobwebs on the way in," Michael continued. "My wings felt like someone had tied every single feather to another. I am sure you have no idea of the complete discomfort of that."

"No, I am sure I do not." Despite his best attempts, Evan's voice cracked with laughter.

Michael glared at him. "For someone who never asks anything of anyone that he would not do himself, I should say that stretched the line."

"I do not happen to have wings..."

"Exactly. Yet you continue to ask me to use mine."

"You could always go back home, and I would cease."

All the boy could say after a minute of glaring was "Humph."

But when Evan glanced over his shoulder, his grin vanished. Raymond's brow was furrowed, his lips pressed together in a mix of concern and stubbornness or just in the knowledge that he would achieve nothing by speaking. Beside him, Arnacin walked a bit more stooped than necessary, a hand pressed to his shoulder. His eyes were glazed, his face pale and sweaty. Now that Evan noticed, he could also hear the gasping echo of every one of the islander's breaths, quieter than the hum of escaping beetles and drips of moisture.

"Arnacin," the prince softly called. He had to repeat the name more loudly before the islander stirred, shuddering.

Dropping his hand back to his side, Arnacin met Michael, Evan and Raymond's worried faces, then looked away. "The air is stuffy down here."

"The passage broadens before we reach the opening." Michael shrugged. "A few more yards, and even you giants shall be able to stand upright."

Although Lazarus's distinctive snort sounded from farther back, Arnacin gave no sign of hearing it. A couple of minutes later, the ceiling rose by a few feet as a small flight of steps took them deeper into the mountain. Where before, two people abreast would almost scrape the walls, five men could now descend side by side.

Evan could breathe more freely in the larger space. Yet when he glanced back to see if it helped Arnacin, he noted the same glazed look in the light of their torches. There was a difference, however. Walking more erect, the islander had pulled his green cloak closed about himself and yet he visibly trembled.

As Evan turned back to their path, he briefly caught Raymond's eye. Neither said anything, yet if they were not thinking the same thoughts, it was probably close. Arnacin's reactions were not physical. Perhaps only Evan was thinking of a possible answer, though, if Arnacin had not confided even in his family. *Do you ever forget where you are as those scars become your fearful reality?* the islander had asked in response to Evan's question about the mines. It took very little to realize what was happening, and Evan had no wish to know the details.

After what seemed like a lifetime, but was only one night, the light of sky blotted out the Isfullen's torchlight. Rounding the last corner, they arrived at the opening—a thin crack in the southern cliff face, invisible to an observer's sight because of the angle of the shadows about it, save for the long rope that hung from the entrance and disappeared into the grayness far below.

Dawn was just peeking over the mountains across from the opening, and they shivered in the cold. Frigid or not, Evan thought it a blessing after the warmth of his exertion and the damp sweat trickling down his shoulder blades. Nor did he think he was alone in his opinion. Beside him, color was seeping back into Arnacin's face.

They had all agreed before escaping Arieh that Arnacin would descend first and guard the bottom in case of an attack. Michael had assured them then there was only a thin path winding alongside the gully carved by the Sambrad Montis river below and no one of Arieh was nearby, but both Arnacin and Evan had felt the precaution of having a skilled swordsman on guard was needed.

Should no one be looking for them, the gully provided cover while they walked past the armies camped on the mountain slopes. By the time the river drew level with the ground again to the north, the Isfullen would intersect the recent trenches dug by the Evfelians surrounding the Elcan Woods.

They had to climb down first, however, and Arnacin hardly seemed ready for the descent. As if reading the prince's glance, the islander sat on the edge by the rope, saying, "You're to guard the back in case we were followed, remember."

Evan suspected Michael and Arnacin had agreed to the plan only to avoid him being caught alone in an ambush. Still, there was nothing he could say. Instead, he watched as the islander grasped the rope and started down. Beside them, Michael transformed and spread his wings.

Slowly, Arnacin's green hood was lost to sight as he continued to descend, carefully rappelling off the cliff. As the next islander sat by the edge, Michael launched into the sky, soaring down to keep watch on the climbers.

A couple hours later, the Isfullen stood in a long line pressed against the cliff. The river rushed by their feet, splashing them with spray. There was barely space to turn around, but as Evan touched the ground, he carefully slid about to face Michael where the enchanter fluttered behind his head. "Will you take this rope back to the tunnel entrance and inform Darkfire we are on our way? Ask him to meet us in the trench nearest the river. And after you are finished with that, fly back to Arieh and assist for three days. We will meet you in the gorge after you have seen to the defenders' safety."

Michael dipped his beak and took off with the rope. As the eagle disappeared from sight, Evan nodded toward Vilo, who stood in front of him—a silent confirmation that they could begin moving. That nod took another moment to travel up the line before they were able to take even a step. As they started off, the prince pulled his hood up against the cold and the sting of the water. It would have been surprising for even Michael to see the line of cloaked figures slowly moving in the gray mist of the river.

Horses stamped the dirt around Darkfire, futilely nosing the ground for food. Under the cover of darkness, they had eaten along the river, but for hours, they had been waiting in that barren trench at the stallion's command. Now noon was growing old, and Darkfire shifted in concern.

His ears pricked. Many feet were approaching along the riverside. It took another minute before the first cloaked figure appeared, trudging around the corner into the trench. That green-shrouded figure stepped aside to allow the rest to pass, and gratefully, they left their single-file line and filled the area, each stopping somewhere along the dirt walls.

Evan was the last to round the corner. Unlike the others, he hardly paused, except as he passed Darkfire. There, he slowed to run his fingers through the stallion's thick, tangled mane before silently moving on. Each step came with a tremor of exhaustion, but he kept going. They would mount once they were out of the trench and farther away from the enemy.

Heads down, the Isfullen fell back into step behind him. Darkfire waited until the last man had passed before nipping his charges into movement. Then Raymond and Lazarus joined him, guarding the rear.

For another few minutes, they trudged forward in silence, until Darkfire shook his head as if chasing away a fly. In this case, the annoyance was unavoidable. "I notice Evan is carrying the full burden of your kings—to stand when no one else can, to hope when none exists, and to give even when dry. I fear he is indeed dry right now."

"Aye," Raymond grunted as he stumbled forward. "Yet he keeps us moving. In all honesty, I don't think any of us have the heart to continue right now."

Lazarus nodded, even his strong shoulders hunched in fatigue. "I think you speak correctly. Even our unconquerable Arnacin shows signs of continuing only because of Evan. He froze before he entered the escape tunnels, and only after a glance at Evan did he descend those steps."

"I must admit, I didn't notice," Raymond sighed.

Chapter 16

Failure

IN THE EARLY EVENING, the Isfullen reached the woods.
There, they dug a ramp out of the trench. The darkness
was lengthening around them as they gained the level ground,
but Evan dared not stop. He wearily pulled himself onto
Darkfire and watched everyone mount horses, some alone,
others sharing. As soon as they were situated, they started
northward once more.

With Darkfire now leading and no need to walk on his
own, Evan slipped into sleep, the movement of the stallion
providing a soothing motion as the nighttime swallowed them.

The sensation suddenly stopped. Jerking upright, the
prince blinked. The sky was tinged with gray. "Is it morning?"

Darkfire snorted. "Early evening. The animals need to stop
for a bit." In Evan's bewildered silence, the stallion blew. "You
slept through the day. It was only one night and day, though.
Never fear."

With the slowness of the dimwitted, Evan looked around
the woods. Some islanders were nodding in their saddles.
Others shakily slid off their mounts, stretched and sank to
the firm ground. "Has anyone eaten anything?"

Something resembling a laugh emitted from Darkfire. "You
are the only one with the skill to sleep on the back of running

muscles. They shared a bite this afternoon, when I allowed the animals to slow for a bit. We have not stopped, though. The beasts need some food themselves now."

Nodding, Evan let his head drop onto the stallion's withers. "How long a break, do you think?"

"Give them four hours, Evan. You need it as much as they do." Carefully, Darkfire tucked his legs beneath himself. "You should also have some sustenance."

Lazarus approached as the prince's feet touched the carpet of dead leaves. "What would you like us to do, Max?"

"Rest?"

The fisherman laughed, playfully pushing the prince's shoulder. "Wake up, Evan. We need you. Do you want us to set a watch? For how long? How many men? Do those men swap out before we move again?"

Sighing, Evan allowed Lazarus to help him to his feet. "Have everyone eat another snack and then sleep for a bit. I would like five men to stand guard for two hours, then swap for another two. But if I am the only one who has had any real sleep, I can keep watch alone for four hours."

Lazarus appraised him for a bit, then nodded. "We'll see who's up for what." He departed and then returned a few minutes later with the news that Arnacin, Raymond, Thomas and himself had agreed to take watch for the full four hours. Although Evan mentally winced at Thomas's name, knowing the boy needed his sleep, he permitted it. Who was he to say otherwise, when he felt so spent himself but still intended to be the fifth watchman?

And so, those five built a small fire while the rest of the Isfullen settled in to sleep. Four of them faced away from the light, except for Arnacin, who withdrew slightly. As Evan sat on the ground with his head propped on his hand and knees, however, all he had to do was look up and catch the flicker of firelight in the eyes of the islander, whose silhouette merged with the tree against which he leaned. Not far away, Darkfire also walked among the horses, sleepless.

With a sigh, Raymond pushed himself to his feet. "Someone better think of a story or something, or I won't be awake for long."

"How are you supposed to keep watch, which includes listening to the night sounds, when someone's talking?" Laughter tinged Arnacin's voice.

"Did I say anything about speaking loudly? I'll hear the forest sounds better over someone's voice than while asleep."

Thomas laughed and Evan quickly grabbed the boy's knee in warning. Forest sounds aside, it would be terrible if they woke the exhausted Isfullen before it was time.

"Oh," Lazarus sighed. "Give me a minute. I might think of something to keep you awake."

A full minute passed in silence. Then Thomas rolled onto his stomach. "Well?"

"I can't think of anything."

"Larry," Arnacin jokingly admonished. "*You* can't think of anything?"

"Oh hush, you little gloating dragon..." Lazarus trailed off as Arnacin's eyes glittered in the dark. He then took a breath. "All right. A dragon."

"What about them?" Thomas asked. "They all died."

"Did they now? We may never know."

"Why not?"

Evan fondly shook his head at how easily the boy bit at the storyteller's ruse. Yet he agreed. It was an interesting question—assuming the fisherman had not simply invented it for the sake of a story.

"I am glad you asked." Lazarus coughed. "The dragons were a strange race. An egg could take several hundred years to incubate, yet even when it was ready to hatch, the baby could hibernate indefinitely until it sensed someone it wished to bind itself to. It would then not hatch until its chosen partner touched it. Once hatched, its companion was a companion for life.

"Now, dragons mostly bonded with other dragons. But their milder cousins, the wyverns, were not unknown to claim enchanters as their companions. Many of the dragons considered the wyverns weak for it. The enchanters used their wyverns as beasts of burden and saw both them and the dragons as animals without the intelligence they themselves possessed. Yet as far as the dragons were concerned, the only difference between them was in the seven large stones the enchanters used to see all possible futures."

Thomas's head rose off his folded arms. "How?"

"I am just telling you the story as I heard it." Lazarus shrugged. "None of the enchanters could completely manipulate the future to fulfill their desires, however, because there were so many trying to do the same thing. Yet, if there had ever been just one, that enchanter could have dominated the universe."

A shudder passed through Evan, and he noticed he could not see the flicker of firelight in Arnacin's eyes anymore—although he thought he heard a sharp inhale from where the islander stood.

Lazarus hardly paused. "The stones built more contention between the dragons and the enchanters. Why did the enchanters feel they had a right to them? Since they shared them among themselves, surely it was only bigotry that kept those orbs from the dragons.

"So, the dragons pretended to make plots against themselves, hoping to hide their plans from the enchanters and their peace-loving cousins, the wyverns. Then, in a sudden attack, the dragons stole all the seeing stones and disappeared from their homeland.

"It took a couple of centuries for the enchanters to track down the dragons and send a small group to take their revenge. Had the dragons cared to use the stones like the enchanters had, they might have seen the attack coming, but it seems they never foresaw it. Perhaps they lacked the patience to sift through many futures like the enchanters had, or perhaps they thought the small group insignificant and easily vanquished. The only thing known for certain is that they were all destroyed.

"But... no one knows if there are any dragon eggs hidden in this world, and if there are, how many?"

After a fortnight of travel, the Isfullen reached the gorge. Its crack loomed before them as the horses trotted forward. An eagle circled above.

Straightening on Darkfire's back, Evan held out his arm invitingly, in the likelihood it was Michael.

As the prince expected, the eagle plummeted. Powerful wings beat the air, and Michael's talons wrapped around the offered perch, clinging to it without piercing the skin. "The Evfelian force is two days behind. My guess is three thousand fighting men."

Evan bit the inside of his cheek. "First, how are things in Arieh?"

The eagle clacked his beak. "You know how to make enemies." Michael smiled as the prince exhaled. "Vincent spun them such lies about the people's victimhood under 'the Isfullen,' Evfel will never know the truth, not for a hundred years. It worked, though. No one was harmed, and they are decently cared for, although the city was burned to make sure no one was hiding. The talk is that Evfel will take them to where the damage starts and reconstruct from there."

"Will Carrie be able to help them escape?"

"Probably not everyone, but most. Quite a few of Arieh's people feel you betrayed them when they discovered your disappearance. And as to Arnacin's promises of freedom..."

"Yes." Despite that one word, Evan squashed his agreement with their anger. The islander had manipulated all of them. Providence help the Isfullen keep their word, despite the rashness of what had been promised just for the sake of sparking flames. "Forget that. We have to keep going or no one will be free."

Michael shook his feathers. "My point is that they would rather kill you than help. But Carrie told me she would at least leave with the Anskonians."

"I suppose we must accept that as it is. Have you found a path to the top of the gorge?"

"Not far from here, yes. They must have been chiseled on both sides at one point by Evfel, probably to ambush Ansky if they ever made it this deeply westward."

The cliffs rising above their heads seemed to become more ominous with that information. Evan shuddered slightly. "Thankfully, that war never happened or Evfel might be prepared for our tactics now." Asking Darkfire to turn around, the prince found his quarry on the horse behind them. He was very glad he had not given vent to his empathy for Arieh's furious people. "Arnacin, will you keep fifty here to enter after the Evfelian troops? I will give you your choice of men, but leave the best archers with me."

The islander consented. To hide better among the trees, his chosen group dismounted, leaving the horses with the prince's force.

As those still mounted followed Michael into the gorge, Evan turned back to Arnacin. "Stay hidden until the Evfelians pass by, then close in behind them. If all goes well, we will not need to face three thousand of them."

Arnacin spent half of the first day securing places to hide fifty men where the forest touched the gorge. Then, he made the men drill their sword skills. When it grew dark, he assigned some to sentry duty amid the underbrush. They would continue a rotation of resting and guarding throughout the next day until Michael returned to warn them of the Evfelians' approach.

Only Michael asked why Arnacin did not include himself in the rotation. "Are you not going to sleep? I can keep watch if you are concerned. I probably see better than any of you anyway."

With a grim smile, Arnacin glanced at the boy. "Islanders see well enough in the dark, and even if it doesn't help anyone else, staying awake gives me something to do."

"Hmm." With that, Michael settled himself beside the islander against the tree trunk. "Better eyesight must be one of the gifts. Do you need to sleep much?"

"What?"

"Anwae felt called to Elcan, but your island has always been home for her—your village especially. A strain of enchanter blood was left there. Some might not consider those alterations gifts, but..."

"What were the gifts?" Arnacin kept his tone casual. "Has she talked about this?"

"You sound suspicious. There is nothing criminal in it, nor was it fully purposeful. She has not talked about it, but she has talked about your island, and the rest I have come to know. Your lives are longer than some. Aging comes more slowly. Yes, it comes, but have you noticed that at some seventy-odd years, your mother shows only a little of her age? She tires more easily, and her hair is streaked with silver, but it remains mostly black. For what she does, she is very energetic."

"You don't think that's natural?"

"Yes, natural to an island that was exposed to our magic for hundreds of years. You might find, Arnacin, that in some ways you are indeed not human, and your family—with the strongest determination to remain in the mountain's woods— is the most affected. No, you are not like us, but perhaps you are as isolated among humans as your home is from theirs—islanders from Enchantress Island, a different race of people. You may find that even Evan, Malachi, James and Thomas are altered."

Shifting uncomfortably, Arnacin changed the topic. "Is Evan well situated in the gorge?"

"As well as he can be. He has twenty-five archers on each clifftop, and the rest of the men are blockading the gorge. I doubt humans could make a better plan."

"You, of course, could do better."

"Well…" Michael's grin seemed to light the night.

Arnacin did not smile back.

As predicted by Michael, Evfel's troops arrived within two days, tens of hundreds of footmen and around twenty horsemen. Up in a tree, with Michael perched on a branch by his elbow, Arnacin watched them all pass beneath him, a terrible flood washing through the Isfullen's hideaway. "Why so many? And why so few horses? They're not just reporting with that crowd, and if they wished for reinforcements from Ansky, they would travel lighter and faster. All of them should be mounted."

Michael's feathers rose around his head. "How many places do you think I can be at one time? All I heard was they needed a strong force in case of 'the Isfullen's magical attacks.' If there are any other reasons for their actions, I am incapable of revealing them."

Quiet as their interchange had been, Arnacin dared not continue it.

It took a full twenty minutes for that mass to disappear into the gorge. Even then, Arnacin waited another half-hour before he signaled his group to close in behind them. Moving now should put them just beyond the Evfelians' sight.

Stepping into the gorge, Arnacin could still see the forces in the distance. Hopefully, the same could not be said in reverse. Yet, he could not keep his blockade back any farther. They needed to be there when the clash of sides came.

So passed the afternoon—Arnacin's small group trailing the large force of marching Evfelians. He saw the narrow paths leading to the clifftops, hidden except to an astute observer, and then they passed by. There was no sign of Evan's blockade.

In mounting concern, Arnacin looked for Michael, but of course, the enchanter had flown on to report to the prince. There was no way to ask him if something had happened.

Perhaps there was an even narrower section of the gorge that forced the Evfelians to pass through only two at a time? Arnacin had no recollection of such a place, but considering the manner of his travel through it the first time—head down, heart hammering, thoughts in disarrayed turmoil—he doubted he would remember anyway.

Ignoring the questioning looks thrown his way—as if he should know what was going on—the islander kept them moving forward. Michael would surely have told them if something had gone wrong. They could only keep going and trust that what they expected to happen would eventually happen.

Dusk was falling when the eagle returned with word. "The Evfelians are only an hour or so away from the collision point. Have you had any water or food today?"

A snort sounded behind Arnacin. Somehow, he managed not to react. "Someone failed to mention how far ahead Evan's blockade is, so no, not really."

"Then take some now while you follow me. And stay invisible until then." With that, Michael rose back into the open skies.

"So much for an apology," one of the islanders muttered. It was hard to distinguish which one.

The screams started when complete darkness fell. Behind that sound came the softer whoosh of arrows. Shouts of anger followed, thumps and groans of the falling, then running, clumping booted feet. That last sound echoed off the gorge walls, drowning out all else but the cries.

Arnacin quietly increased his men's pace. Soon, they passed over the arrow-struck bodies of Evfelians and their horses and fanned out toward the cliff walls to avoid arm's reach of any of the fallen. Ahead, the clash of metal rose. The front line of the enemy had met with Evan's blockade. The hail of arrows continued, never missing.

Stopping his men twenty paces behind the last of the Evfelians, Arnacin lined them up into a blockade and waited for that inevitable moment when the enemy would turn around. Minutes later, they did.

Arnacin winced as the first Evfelian hurtled blindly into his sword, all the weight driving into his right shoulder. That was just the initial blow. Although most of the islander's strokes went unblocked as he cut through the back of Evfel's forces, there was danger in fighting practically blind assailants. He knew about the risk of fighting amateurs; this was likely akin. The Evfelians' attacks were wild, jerky and unpredictable—spasmodic blows that came out of nowhere.

As Arnacin lopped off one opponent's head, someone stumbled into his back. He allowed himself to roll onto his knees and noted it was an Evfelian who had collided with him. Lurching back up, he drove his sword through the man's shoulder blades.

And with the impact of his thrust, his injured right shoulder ignited in sharp pain that sparked upward to his neck. He bit his tongue hard to keep from crying out and sacrificed his skill to use his left hand. Good thing he could see so well in the dark. His left normally could not be trusted in a fray of this size. Sadly, however, the Evfelians' thrashing had taken its toll too early.

Even if they were mostly blind, the Evfelians' far greater numbers wore on the relatively few Isfullen. Arnacin knew from the empty spaces behind him that his blockade had shattered. When exactly it had happened was anyone's guess, but the islanders were no longer a solid wall.

Not long after, he found himself by Evan. It was strange to see the prince still had Resplandecer sheathed in favor of another blade. But it made sense—the light of Lisya's sword could undo the Isfullen's advantage.

Stranger still, however, Evan's attacks always went against the Evfelians, never mistaking an islander for the enemy. "So, it's not just us," Arnacin commented. "You can also see in the dark."

Evan dispatched the Evfelian before him with an exhausted huff. "What do you call seeing?"

"Clearly, you know who to attack."

"That's obvious. They move erratically. You islanders move as smoothly as if it were daylight. Therefore, you are all the more invisible in the darkness."

In silence, together, they hacked, slashed and stabbed. No, Evan's skill was nothing like it was by day. Still, he was doing remarkably well for a native of Elcan. Arnacin only needed to dispatch one or two foes for him in the flood of enemies.

"How many are still here?" the prince asked after a little while.

"Of us?"

"Them."

"I haven't had the time to count."

"And I can only see moving shapes a few feet in front of me. I assume we are all mixed in a bunch. You were on the opposite side."

Arnacin shrugged. "More or less. I know they're escaping back west, toward Evfel."

"No," Evan gasped, driving harder into the mass of Evfelians. "Not escaping. They want the archers!"

It had been easy for the archers on the clifftops to continue their barrage against the Evfelians, even after the two sides clashed below. The magnitude of those thousands packed into the gorge had kept the center a clear mark. Raymond designated ten of his archers to target any Evfelian that broke through to the east, while the rest of his charges continued to thin the pack in the center.

Against all those thousands, the archers ran out of arrows after a couple of hours. He hung onto his last one, afraid that if he used it, something desperate would happen later, and it would not go well. And so they watched helplessly as the ranks broke below and the Isfullen merged into the mass of Evfelians. Michael rose from the fray and plummeted right back down, marking Evan's place by slaughtering those behind and to the sides of him.

Then the eagle shot upward again. Instead of circling, he continued upward to land at Raymond's feet on the southern clifftop. "Evan thinks the Evfelians are headed for you. How many have gone back west?"

Raymond shook his head. "We've been watching the east."

"Well, kill them!"

Typical Michael.

"Those going west? We're out of arrows."

All of Michael's feathers bristled, forming an irritated mane about his sparking eyes and clacking beak. Yet, without a word, he launched off the cliff.

Raymond turned back to his archers. "Who feels the most confident with a sword?"

No one stepped forward.

After a moment, Tevin sighed. "What's your plan?"

"We need to meet them at the top of the trail. It's narrow there. They can only come up one at a time."

Tevin sighed again, but nodded.

By unspoken consent, anyone who still had an arrow passed the precious shafts to Raymond—five in all. With that, they set off back toward the path.

Dawn light split the gorge, its brightness screening the one side from the other as they came within view of the trail. The first Evfelians were almost at the top.

Raymond killed the first of them, giving Tevin time to step into position. The others drew their swords in readiness.

Tevin lacked the skill of the Evfelians, however, and their vision was no longer hindered by the dark. A swipe to the knee brought him down. Instantly, Raymond plunged his blade through the opponent's throat and stepped into the gap while his friend rolled aside.

Against the swordsmen, however, Raymond was not any more skilled. Even against a bone-weary aggressor, the hunter could not keep up. A sting shot across his arm, the first warning that the next stroke would likely mean the end of his defense, one way or the other.

"Evfel! To me! The horses are over here! Grab one and retreat!" That call saved Raymond and his archers from death. The Evfelian facing the hunter immediately backed away. Once at a safe distance, he charged back down the trail to join his comrades, fighting their way up the opposite cliff.

Shamefully, Raymond trembled in relief. He dropped down by Tevin.

"No, no," his friend protested. "It's just a scratch. Stop them from taking those horses!"

Easy for him to be heroic—he was incapable of moving. "Just a scratch." Snorting, Raymond ripped off the cleanest part of his undershirt and wrapped it snugly around Tevin's knee. "At least you're right. You'll probably survive."

As soon as the hunter had tucked the knot in, Tevin pushed his hand away. "Okay. It's wrapped. Stop them before they reach the horses. We didn't target theirs for nothing."

He had no more excuse to stay away from the battle, even though it would doubtless be a slaughter. Those Evfelians had trained for years, and most Isfullen would not stand against them for long.

Still, Raymond straightened and led his small group, except for Tevin, down to the gorge. Not to malign his friend's bravery—he had been the one to volunteer to block the top of the trail first, after all. It was just providence that kept him away now.

Below, Evan had arrived with the remaining Isfullen at the rear of the Evfelian force climbing the cliff path. Arnacin, seemingly unfatigued, guarded their rear. He was the only one, besides Evan and Michael, who was slaying the Evfelians as easily as they were dispatching the rest of the Isfullen.

At the front of the advance, Evan stumbled. Raymond jumped the last of the trail onto the prince's opponent. At the same time, red wings plummeted. Ripping his talons through the Evfelian's throat, Michael then rose back upward, crimson rain splattering in his wake.

Raymond took a breath, rose and turned with Evan toward the next Evfelian trying to push through them. Time blurred with each opponent's stroke. One came there, then there, then there. Location, hour, light and people all vanished into a desperate blur of slashing, stabbing blades.

A sharp whinny stilled Raymond, stilling them all. A horse and rider thundered down the path toward them, running over everyone in its way.

Raymond dodged. Not one, but a stampede of mounted horses rushed by. The Evfelians were escaping, with little anyone on foot could do.

One horse in the rear bucked. Evan had leapt behind the Evfelian rider. In the tussle on its back, the beast shied. Then Evan fell off. The winner kicked his mount into a run down the cleared gorge even as the prince rolled back to his feet.

But that horse never joined the rest. A lithe figure jumped in front of it and plunged his sword into its chest. Hooves thrashed briefly above his black head, yet he moved aside too quickly for a strike to land.

As the rider disengaged from the dying animal, Evan grabbed a fallen sword and ran the Evfelian through. The rest of those on horseback had escaped. He let the blade drop to the ground. Thousands of bodies stretched around them and far out of sight.

The Isfullen had barely taken a breath before the call came.

"Evan!" Thomas was running down the northern trail. "Come quickly! It's Lazarus!"

Any remaining color in the prince's face vanished. He stumbled up the path behind the boy.

His heart beating fast, Raymond followed the two. He could hear feet pounding behind.

At the top of the cliff, Lazarus lay in Vilo's arms. The fisherman's side was sliced open and his skin held the pallor of death. James and Darkfire stood nearby, the boy twisting the hem of his shirt in his hands.

Evan sank down by the fisherman. "Lazarus?"

Weakly, those green eyes fluttered. Even more weakly, a bloody hand rose to the prince's arm. "There's no healing it, Max. I am glad... I am..."

"Shh." Evan squeezed his hand. "I refuse to say goodbye, Lazarus. I can't."

A slight smile crossed the fisherman's face. "Then say... until then. I am glad to... have served you, my king. Know that."

Evan nodded quickly, closing his eyes as tears welled beneath his lashes. "I would beg you to stay, but there's no point, is there?"

When no response came, the prince squeezed those strong fingers. It was not until the fisherman took his last rasping breath that Evan leaned forward, kissing his friend on the forehead. "Until then, Lazarus."

Chapter 17

Heart and Soul

In the Ice Woods, Talliaha had asked to help with the weaving. Now sitting at the loom behind the enchantress's closed door, she watched as Lisya paced back and forth, agitation present in every abrupt turn. Yet the island's lady dared not remind the enchantress of her presence. Looking back at her work, Talliaha shook her head in resignation.

But then, as if the enchantress had reached some decision, she strode over to a large white stone sitting atop the dresser. Spreading her fingers, she placed her hand over the orb. From its depths, a light appeared, flickering faintly. Contrary to expectations, the enchantress did not gaze into it, but instead closed her eyes.

Talliaha half rose from her bench. "Lisya." She stopped herself. In that instant, all traces of age vanished from the enchantress. Carrie had confided in Talliaha that, just a few months ago, the enchantress's hair had been thin and colorless, her height had diminished by several inches. Even when the islanders had first come to the Ice Woods, though the enchantress's hair had been silver and her height was as it always had been, her skin had still been lined.

Even those signs of age had now vanished. A tall enchantress with hair the color of an autumn forest stood there, her skin as smooth as water, her breath gasping.

Before Talliaha could move again, light burst from the stone. A vortex of color shot along the floor, then upward like a forest fire. She thumped back onto the bench and jerked her legs up beside her, yet there was no searing heat.

The stone glowing beneath the enchantress's fingers was shifting—flattening, stretching and splitting.

A rainbow of light abruptly shot across the stones by Valoretta's feet in the weaving room. Following it to the castle window, she pushed through the crowd of white-faced servants blocking her view. There, she felt her breath catch. Bright dancing light filled the sky to the north, where the Ice Woods lay. The valley shone purple and emerald green, blue and yellow waving between them.

"It has come," a lady at Valoretta's elbow declared. "The Ice Woods are about to attack."

"With those colors?" another asked. "I thought the skies would return to black."

"What is that, if not an announcement of attack?"

No one answered. They just watched in horrified fascination until the light vanished as suddenly as it had burst into the sky.

With a last gasp, Lisya crumpled to the floor. The rainbow of flames disappeared.

"Lisya!" Talliaha rushed to the enchantress's side. Rolling the heap of auburn waves and fabric into her arms, the lady seized the unusually frail wrist. Beneath her squeezing fingers, she felt the slight beat of a pulse, yet the enchantress did not stir. "Lisya, what did you do?"

No response came. She could hardly expect one, but she continued to sit there for a second more, cradling the enchantress in her arms. Lisya was not sick or injured. Whatever had caused her to collapse was magical, and Talliaha had no knowledge to treat that.

A quick survey of the room caused her to pause. The stone was no more. Two radiant crowns now rested atop the dresser, glinting softly in the light emanating from their white depths. Their beauty mesmerized her. One was designed for a queen and one for a king.

Carefully, Talliaha inched out from under the enchantress. She went to the door and flung it open. "Lorene! Help!"

In the main room, Lorene set her son on the floor. As she entered the back chamber, her eyes fixed on Lisya and widened. "That cannot be the enchantress."

"It is."

"I thought nothing could harm her."

Talliaha sighed. "Please, help me carry her to the fireside. Hopefully, some water and warmth will rouse her."

Soon, they had wrapped the enchantress in blankets by the fireplace. Newton now sat against her, patting her shoulder.

"Lisya." Talliaha sighed with relief when the enchantress stirred sometime later. "What did you do?"

In a weak and tired voice, the enchantress said, "I won."

Lorene's gaze flicked back over Lisya's red hair. "What battle were you fighting?"

"The internal battle." Slowly rising, the enchantress accepted the water Talliaha passed her. "That stone allowed me to see all futures. Through it, I could know each of the events and choices that led to every turn and course in the world. I could dissect the very roots of an occurrence and turn them to my will. Now, with no one else who could see as I do, it would be easy."

Talliaha studied the table's wood grain beneath her fingers. Glancing up, she saw the horror on Lorene's face and sympathized. Her own stomach twisted.

Sighing, Lisya dipped her chin. "Yes, such was the treasure that took my kind to the peak of Mount Jade, now Enchantress Island. My homeland owned seven such large stones, and the dragons took each one. The only way to destroy them is to shatter or change them. I altered this one forever. Now, though it will still show me futures, it can only hint at possible outcomes."

"Your kind obviously did not see everything." Lorene's confusion was apparent in her expression.

A sad smile crossed Lisya's face. "Our destruction was because of too many gods, Lorene. Even evil has a hierarchy for a reason. We did not, and so we tripped over each other."

"Any large stone gives you such ability?" Lorene's face had turned ashen.

"Not all. Ones like that are made from the depths of the earth and hol—" Cutting herself off, the enchantress dropped her gaze to her cup.

"Surely, though," Talliaha finally spoke, "the stone could not kill you for destroying it."

"It was the battle against myself that nearly killed me, Talliaha, not the stone. From the moment I touched it, I was in the realm of absolute knowledge. You must know what such possibility does."

Slowly, Talliaha nodded wordlessly. It was Lorene who asked, "But if you could see all outcomes, why are you so convinced it would be wrong?"

Lisya's gaze remained on the table. "Only love has the wisdom to dictate such things. Love alone would grant mortals their own choice, and therefore, only love can save them. I fear I would merely create a mirage of peace and life by enslaving all minds to my will."

Darkness covered the gorge, apart from the fires flickering here and there. Around one such blaze, Evan sat silently beside Vilo, Arnacin, Raymond, Michael, James and Thomas. Darkfire lay behind him, his side pressed against the prince's back and his head arched toward the flames, deep eyes glinting in the light.

"How many Evfelians escaped, do you think?" Thomas finally asked, shivering beneath his cloak.

Vilo chucked a twig into the fire. "Too many."

No one else responded, and Evan sighed. "We were never going to win this fight. I wish I had never started the battle. The town of Ansky is burned to the ground, Arieh and the island turned to ash. Even if we win, I will never be able to give Elcan's people the freedom they want, or the peace. Changes in governments are traumatic, as a rule. Maybe…" He shook his head.

"You are overtired, Evan," Michael scoffed. "You should sleep. We will hear more sane things afterward."

Although the prince smiled slightly, he continued to stare into the fire. What was hope? They had lost too many, while Castle Ansky was strengthened and Evfel was easy for Wilber to reconquer.

Raymond reached out to slap Evan's shoulder. "You must continue, or all these deaths—among the people of Ansky, Arieh and more—will be in vain. And it's not about you succeeding or not in giving them freedom. It's about you trying."

The silence stretched, filled only with the crackle of the fire and the whir of insects. At last, Evan said, "I bet the Evfelians have no idea how many they have left, either."

"You're thinking something."

"I could slip inside the group."

Everyone turned to the prince. "For what purpose?" Michael exclaimed.

"Our only chance of winning now is to sway Ansky's loyalty back to the Maxwells. I am the reason they lack it. Only I can change it."

"You would never have time," Arnacin spoke up. "You do need someone to reason with Ansky's men, but it must be done by someone other than yourself."

"And who would do that? I know those men and—"

"And they know you. You'll be executed before you can say a word. One of us should go."

"Not one of you could ever pose as a knight from..." As Evan's gaze met Arnacin's, he trailed off. The islander's eyes danced in the flickering firelight. Softly, the prince whispered, "Yes, there is another possibility. But only one."

It was somewhat comical how everyone turned to face Arnacin, sitting on the opposite side of the fire. Some waited expectantly, others appeared skeptical. Raymond's face was carefully masked.

"Is that a request, Evan?" Arnacin asked after a moment.

"You know otherwise. But it was your suggestion, was it not?" When the other gave no reply, Evan added, "This choice is yours alone, Arnacin. I have already said my piece. Your accent is close enough, with some managing. If you can do it, you are our only other possibility of catching the Evfelian force. Darkfire can take either of us there. Then, in the dark, he can buck the rider off and return here without anyone realizing the truth."

For a moment, the islander said nothing. No one interrupted his thoughts. Then, with a sigh, he said, "All right, I'll go. You know my skills anyway."

"Only to a degree, Arnacin." Evan climbed to his feet. "You better move fast, then. Darkfire will take you to the forces once you change into Evfelian garments."

Though Raymond left the fire to help his friend find clothing from the bodies scattered nearby, only Arnacin joined Evan and Darkfire twenty minutes later as they stood outside the borders of their camp. From the unmasked authority in his poise to the sword and belt he was buckling over his tabard, Arnacin appeared every inch nobility.

Hiding his laughter, Evan knelt to allow the islander a step from his upper leg onto the stallion's high back. "Are you completely sure you want it this way?"

Ignoring the gesture, Arnacin fiddled with his belt a moment longer than necessary. Finally looking up, he sighed, "I don't see that either of us really has a choice."

"Do not," the prince reminded as he stood back up. "Watch your accent and choice of words. If there is one thing that will betray you, it is your native speech."

With a chortle, Arnacin slipped something over his head and held it out for the prince to take. "My accent no longer sounds like an islander."

"But your verbiage will still mark you as a foreigner."

The object was a many-spoked wheel with a glass-encased arrow that swayed back and forth as it moved. Evan closed his fingers over it and then helped the islander onto Darkfire's high back.

Gesturing to the item, Arnacin said, "I promised Valoretta the compass would come back to her."

Evan nodded.

"I will try to be back by noon," the stallion promised, yet the prince's hand stayed in his mane.

Looking up at Arnacin, Evan asked, "I apologize if I am being intrusive, but... did you abdicate?"

"From what?"

"Valoretta is a queen."

Arnacin sighed. "If you ask that to determine whether I have the will needed to go in your stead, I would answer that it hardly matters. You cannot go."

"Yet?"

The islander fidgeted. "I married Valoretta only after her kingdom fell. There were men hunting her in order to benefit their own thrones."

"Did marriage protect her so much?"

"When she had a fatherless child on the way, yes."

Evan's eyes widened slightly. "Tenacius is not yours?"

"I honestly don't know." Arnacin's confession was a low breath, his head lowered. "Where we were, no one else could have given him his black hair except me, but... we have had no such interactions. I know there's no way to believe that, but it's the truth. While I could say he's not mine and I adopted him, or invent a story in which our marriage contract required a child to make it legal, I can't. I can't look friends and family in the eyes and say any of those things."

"That is why I believe you, Arnacin. And I am sure your family would never doubt you either."

The islander only continued smoothing the thick mane in his fingers.

Patting Darkfire's neck, Evan stepped back. "Take care."

"You refused to answer back there if you had the will to see this through," Darkfire rumbled. Yet his stride remained long, his pace enough to keep Arnacin tucked into his mane just to breathe. "I believe I know the answer, but for you to do this, you must also."

When the islander remained silent, the stallion slowed to a canter. Sitting upright, Arnacin protested, "Are you going to catch the Evfelians at this speed?"

"In your words, 'it hardly matters.' You must know the answer because there is no way you will win other people to Evan's cause if you waver yourself, and we all know you will be caught eventually. You are a warhorse among shaggy ponies, a king among the uneducated, and an islander among Evfelians. Do not think you will hide forever. What will your answer be when they catch you?"

A shudder passed through the islander. "What answer do you want?"

Darkfire's breathing heaved beneath the islander's knees. "Ansky will ask—*demand*—to know if you are willing to trust and support Evan Maxwell at the cost of everything you hold dear. If you waver, they will never 'see reason,' as you put it before."

For a long moment, Arnacin didn't reply. At last, he said, "I have no answer, Darkfire. I know you already surrendered much, but did you know you would before the moment you were forced to action? I have never given anyone, even long before I..." He stopped himself, then said, "before everything, the type of loyalty and trust you are suggesting. Not even the Creator."

Darkfire's great head dipped. "Yet, you must know what you agreed to. Are you so convinced of your own cunning to think you will escape?"

Licking his lips, Arnacin admitted, "I just know the one who goes can't be Evan, and someone must try."

"Then I will leave it to you and your Creator." With that, the stallion again increased his speed, and Arnacin ducked back out of the wind.

In the darkness of the early morning, Arnacin and Darkfire caught their quarry, still making their way out of the gorge. Even so, the stallion's breathing was unhindered. His gallop was more silent than that of many a horse, without the clomp and clap of hard hooves. As the pair caught up with the host of a few hundred riders, the night breeze blew the men's words back toward them. "Do you think we might be running into a trap instead of away from one?"

"How many men do you think they have?"

"Practicality aside, they are witches and they appeared back *there* suddenly. I thought they were surrounded in Arieh."

As Darkfire joined the last rider, the Evfelian turned to Arnacin. "Well? Am I the only one who thinks we should send a scout?"

"No, I think that is very shrewd advice," the islander commented, matching their accents.

Satisfied, the Evfelian nodded sharply before increasing his steed's pace to catch the men in the front. Left in the back, Arnacin leaned closer to Darkfire's ear. "They were traveling more quickly than we reckoned."

"Yes," the stallion puffed softly, his voice the more dangerous of the two if overheard. "We still have enough dark to make our act convincing."

"Particularly if you and I volunteer as scouts." To make things more difficult, conversation had to be kept to a minimum, and Arnacin could not communicate secretly with the stallion, unlike Evan.

When those ahead stopped a few moments later, Darkfire pushed forward without prompting. Men were asking about the reason for the halt. The response from the apparent commander was, "We need someone to volunteer to scout ahead. He must have a good horse too."

"My horse is hardly tired," Arnacin spoke up. This time, the crowd parted for Darkfire. "How far should I go before reporting back?"

"See if there is anything first. Come back either way. If your horse remains up to it, keep returning after every two leagues. If we are walking into a trap, we will have to decide what to do then. Whatever you do, watch the shadows. Maxwell's men have proven incredibly shifty."

It was probably a good thing the darkness hid Arnacin's smile as he nodded. "Yes, I will carefully watch each shadow. Should two of us go for extra protection?"

"Two will never sneak up on them if they are there. Go. And hurry, or Maxwell's men might catch up."

"Two leagues," Arnacin agreed as Darkfire's muscles tensed. With that, they set off at a lope.

"It might be unbelievable if I dump you in the first round," the stallion said once they were at a safe distance. "Will you agree to two?"

"Can you make eight leagues at a normal horse's pace before the dawn?"

The stallion's abdomen filled with air and shrank with a huff. "Not at their pace, no. Therefore, you will need to play along more. When we return to them, I will prance a bit before I throw you. Once they pick you up, tell them I was restless all the way back. Hint that perhaps I sensed something from the Ice Woods or their people."

"That will make them think there is an attack ahead. But if you sensed danger, you would not run toward the valley. Yet that's where you need to go before you return to Evan, so you can slip past the Evfelians after they turn toward Castle Ansky."

"Do you have any better ideas?"

"Yes. Let them assume what they will. I will tell them you were nervous on the way back, but I fear if I play it up too much, it will seem too perfect—or full of holes."

"It is," was the stallion's only reply.

Even before the pair saw the Evfelian riders, Darkfire began to shift, prancing nervously on his feet and sliding away from Arnacin's hand on his neck. Then, as the islander heard the Evfelians and saw them approach, the stallion's prance turned to scared bucks.

Almost instantly, the riders kicked their mounts into a gallop in an attempt to reach the supposedly frightened horse, but Darkfire never gave them time to near. After bucking, he reared. On the stallion, the sensation was like riding something shooting out of the ground, growing ever upward. On his back legs, Darkfire was over eleven feet tall.

Arnacin let himself slip. With a crack, his head slammed into the dirt. His stomach heaved in nausea, and then he sensed a hand on his arm, but he never felt its owner help him stand.

Sunlight streamed over Arnacin's face. Wincing, he turned his head away from the light and instantly regretted the movement as his skull complained.

"Was there anything ahead?" a deep Evfelian voice asked as something bumped the islander's shoulder.

An agile-looking Evfelian held out a waterskin expectantly. The force had apparently stopped until they knew what lay ahead, letting their tired horses rest and graze.

Slowly sitting up, Arnacin accepted the skin but refrained from drinking. "Nothing, but the horse was skittish all the way back."

"Do you think it sensed something?"

"Would they be that invisible? I find it more likely that my unease affected him."

"Perhaps you are right. We have to chance it, anyway, or run out of food and water." The Evfelian held out his hand. "Not that we have wasted this break. We finally had enough time to greet each other. You missed our introductions, but I am Erik of West Fryah."

"Arnacin," the islander muttered, nevertheless shaking the Evfelian's hand.

Erik's gaze dropped to the lion on the tabard Arnacin had stolen. "Of Arieh?"

"I came from there, yes."

"I think you are the last one from Arieh. The rest apparently fell to Maxwell's troops."

Shrugging, Arnacin pushed himself to his feet. "I have that fortune, it seems. Who is in charge now?"

"Lord Andon still lives, remember? He asked for the scout last night."

The only way the islander could cover for that was to shrug and allow his hand to go to the back of his still throbbing head.

"Your memory will come back," Erik laughed. "That was a hard fall, but I will go inform everyone of your report. Then, you may ride with me. We failed to catch your horse and, to be honest, your answer is the same as ours. We saw and heard nothing while we chased that stallion. I am sorry about its loss. That was a powerful steed, but that was why the rest were just not up to catching it."

It took the Evfelians three more days to leave the gorge behind, and another one to reach Castle Ansky, which was guarded by hundreds of soldiers. Cold crept over Arnacin as he entered beneath the towering portcullis and heard the gate close behind him. Luck or providence had been with him in removing all the men from Arieh in the contingent, but here in Ansky, he had helped lead the islanders in the attack to rescue Evan. There was every chance someone would recognize him.

Wilber stood on the keep steps as the Evfelian troops fanned into the inner ward. At the front of the host, the lanky Lord Andon was the first to dismount, bowing before his king. "Sire, I have the most unfortunate news—Evan Maxwell has taken Arieh and Duke Reginold is dead."

Although the king's face darkened, he waited for the lord to continue. "We had hoped to bring the news that he is besieged in the remains of the city, perhaps even now killed, but he and his forces instead waited for us in the gorge. We bring two hundred and forty-one of the three thousand that left Evfel to do your bidding."

Almost as one, the Evfelians dismounted and bent to one knee. With no other option, Arnacin followed suit, if a second after them. He was the first to stand again when Wilber motioned for them to rise.

"Do you know where the prince is now, Lord Andon?"

"We were not ambushed again after that first attack, but all things considered, I cannot say whether he remains in the gorge or in Evfel."

"Very well." With those words, the king turned back up the steps. "Come make a full report. Lord Quincy will see to the men."

Quincy appeared from the keep; he clearly had not been that far away. Despite the muttered complaints about an Anskonian lord commanding them, none of the assembled men argued when he stopped before them.

"You will find, gentlemen," the lord said, "that Ansky is very capable despite its rough appearance. That said, our knights have a barracks to themselves, but it is not a palace. If you would be so kind as to regroup into knights and footmen, we will lead you to a place where you may clean up, rest and eat something."

In irritable silence, the men began shifting as stablehands took their horses. Some footmen mockingly placed themselves among the knights to see if Quincy could tell the difference. The Anskonian lord ignored the obvious ploy to trick him, though his eyes darkened a bit more.

Yet when Arnacin, properly dressed as a footman, joined the lower ranks, Quincy studied him. The islander dared not shift under that gaze.

The Anskonian walked toward him. "You are a footman?"

"You can hardly think otherwise. Evfel's knights know how to dress. Perhaps your sloppiness goes to show how little skill Anskonian lords possess." Snickers followed, particularly from the few footmen among the group of knights.

Quincy remained impassive. "It was not Ansky that lost its capital to an army seventy times or more its weaker."

The snickers instantly silenced, yet Arnacin grinned.

"And yes, I know the difference. I ask because you have the bearing of one with authority—much more than any footman I have ever met."

"Perhaps Duke Reginold refused to trust me with more."

"Perhaps, indeed." Turning to the group at large, Quincy announced, "And any others who want to lie about their rank, you can dilute your knights' skill or pretend idiocy as you wish. I care not."

The Evfelians sullenly straightened out and allowed themselves to be led to their proper quarters. Even as they dispersed, Arnacin could feel Quincy's gaze on him.

Two days later, Lord Andon was ordered back out, along with most of the Evfelian knights, to relieve those posted around the Ice Woods. Of that, Quincy was quite glad. The new footmen, however, remained in the castle—which meant the one called Arnacin stayed. To the Anskonian lord's amusement, he was not the only one with an interest in the footman from Arieh.

Spotting Andrew on the inner parapet as the Evfelian footmen watched their companions leave, Quincy asked, "What causes you to be here today, my prince?"

With a glare, Andrew quipped, "You have no standing to order me back to those books."

"I had no intention of doing so. I merely noticed your furrowed brow."

With an uncharacteristic sigh, the prince asked, "How do you think Evan...?"

When Andrew's pause grew long, Quincy shrugged. "You probably know more than I do on that matter. He is your cousin."

"Huh. He was never a cousin of mine." They fell into companionable silence. Abruptly, Andrew asked, "Who is the black-haired footman?"

Pouncing on the subject, Quincy replied, "Arnacin? The one who looks like he could lead a country?"

"Exactly. From which part of Evfel did he come?"

"Arieh. He refuses to say why Reginold would keep him a footman. Are the knights there not also picked by skill?"

"You should know. Our kings themselves are picked by skill." With a sly look that spoke of cunning if not strength, Andrew continued, "Is there a chance he is not from Arieh?"

Below them, a footman named Erik slapped the man in question on the back to turn him toward their barracks. Quincy shook his head. "If not... either all those men are not who they claim to be or he is an inconceivable actor. They all believe him, and considering how little he blends in as a footman, I do not believe he is being false."

"Yet it is impossible for a footman to learn... that kind of authority. A footman is required to learn the opposite, to lose all independence and take orders without a flicker of disagreement. As the first ones on a battlefield, a lack of unity would see them cut down in seconds."

Lowering his voice, Quincy asked, "Do you know what sort of games your father's duke might have played? Would he take a footman and train him for... whatever he might decide?"

"Like what? A personal assassin, which is what he resembles?"

Quincy just stared at the boy, waiting for him to answer himself.

After a moment, Andrew shrugged. "Reginold was a coward, but an ambitious one. That is as much as I know about him. If this Arnacin was personally his, then to whom is he now loyal?"

"I might know a way to test that, if his skill is actually up to the challenge."

"How?"

"If your father asks him to train Ansky's footmen, what then? I certainly lack the time, yet the king wants them readied."

"How would you know he would do it properly?"

"Since a certain prince has the eyes of a hawk, I will pretend I have no idea where he is when his instructor comes looking."

Laughter shone in Andrew's smile. "Sometimes, Quincy, you make a great lord."

After the first day of rest, during which Arnacin actually did very little, the Evfelian footmen were written into the guard shift rotation. When not on duty, they were expected to practice their skills with Ansky's conscripted footmen. Despite it being almost two years since they had been hauled away from their homes to build Ansky's defense, their fighting skills remained terrible.

Arnacin spent his free time watching instead of participating. After the second day of that, Erik stepped aside from their mock quarterstave bouts. "Arnacin, come join us!"

"Why? You slaughter the Anskonians just fine without me."

"Then help them if you are so sporting. It might be better if we broke up the groups, anyway, and had some skill on both sides."

For a minute, the islander only contemplated the Anskonians, his head tilted to one side. With a sigh, he put aside the knife he had been sharpening and picked up one of the weapons they were using in their practice.

Warily, the Anskonians opened a place for him among their ranks. Arnacin waved them to the sides. "All right, leave me to be your front defense if you are able. But keep them away from my sides, or I will be no help to you at all. Perhaps we can break through to the other side of their ranks."

The bout ended fast and badly. The Anskonian to Arnacin's right brought his stave up to block an attack and lurched sideways, ramming the end of his weapon into the islander's ribs.

Gasping in pain, Arnacin forced himself to hold the defense until he felt the same thing happen on his left side. That made him collapse into a panting ball on the ground. "That is it," he puffed. "From now on, Ansky is on its own."

The footman to his right turned a deep red, while the Evfelians laughed. "Why do you think we keep to ourselves?

We love our ribs too much." Even Arnacin had to laugh, although he cut it off, wincing in pain.

"Thank you all the same," the young Anskonian footman on his right muttered, extending his hand to help the islander up. "If it helps exact your revenge, I am Cyril. And yes, I know I am terrible."

As the sky reddened in the evening and the footmen turned to the task of seeing to their equipment, Cyril joined Arnacin on a barrack bench. "Are your ribs...? I mean, nothing was broken, was it?"

"If it was broken, you would know." When the Anskonian blushed, Arnacin laughed. "I think you might have more skill than you know."

"What makes you say that?"

"I only guess, but with how frequently you blush, I am inclined to think your problem is self-confidence and not a case of incompetence."

"Maybe. I am the youngest in a family of what was—" He quickly ducked his head back over his work.

For a minute, Arnacin left him alone—but only for a moment. "Are you keeping Ansky's secrets or your own?"

"I have no idea what you mean."

"Do not mistake me. I am not saying you *are* keeping any secrets. But I have noticed you all claim allegiance to the same king and then build walls around whether you are Evfelian or Anskonian. You are Wilber's, or you are not. That should be the only thing to define you now."

Cyril stared at him for a moment, his eyes narrowed. "You were the first to draw the line between us, on the day you arrived."

With a small smile, Arnacin shrugged. "Call it an opportunity. However, I never serve anyone unless I believe in their cause, and I would think a common goal with Evfel should unify you."

"You are sneaky."

"Why?"

"That is a dirty trick for discovering what I refused to say. Yes, we have the same goal currently, but is it not true that Evfelians stand for ambition? If they can walk over someone else, they will."

"Who did the trampling?" Arnacin muttered, not looking up from his work.

Blushing again, Cyril protested, "What happened this afternoon was an accident. But very well, I may be biased. You, at least, seem different from the other Evfelians."

"So, what was your family, if I may be so curious?"

"Part of the king's reserve. Ansky was criticized for many things—among them, our lack of security—but there were more precautions than anyone thought. We had a secret exit through the castle in case of attack, and to add to the attacker's confusion, they could have destroyed all the soldiers in the castle and then found the town itself was an army against them."

"Were all the townsfolk trained?"

"Most. Phillip trusted all of us."

Staring into the distance, Arnacin contemplated the kingdom so described. "What happened to that reserve?"

"Evan Maxwell abdicated and then ran into the arms of evil itself. What were we to do but join Wilber, heart and soul?"

"Have you?"

Cyril turned his head to scrutinize the islander. "Whether true or false, you should know there is only one answer I can give to an Evfelian."

"Yes," Arnacin murmured, but he let the subject drop.

As soon as darkness fell, most of those on the midnight watch went to bed—except for Arnacin, who stayed to see the stars come out one by one. Approaching footsteps caused him to turn. "The king wishes to speak to you," the messenger said, raising his torch higher.

For a minute, the islander remained where he sat. "Do you refer to the footmen in general, or just me?"

"You are Arnacin of Arieh, yes? He wants to see you."

His heart hammering, the islander nevertheless stood. "Let me grab my cloak, and I will come."

"It is a very warm night. After all, you are out here without it."

"It was a warm night," Arnacin mumbled.

Chapter 18

A Spy's Duty

S TEPPING INSIDE THE BARRACKS, Arnacin grabbed the brown, Evfelian, satin-lined cloak that, although unadorned, was still clearly that of a person of some means. Yet, it could never compete with the comfort of his thin green wool one that was likely burned among the Evfelian bodies in the gorge.

Still, the islander pulled those folds close as he and the messenger tromped across the night-covered ward. With each step closer to the keep, he told himself that if the king had discovered him, at least six knights would have come to escort him, not just one defenseless man. Of course, with all the security in readiness for the assumed attack from the Ice Woods, they could collect any number of guards.

As they neared the great hall itself, Arnacin's steps slowed of their own choosing. Had there been more elaborate stone-work, he might have had an excuse to linger, but Castle Ansky was, for the most part, unadorned stone—a humble fortress for protection and sanctuary, nothing more.

Three people awaited them inside the hall: Wilber, Quincy and a youth with dark red hair and the air of someone accustomed to others' immediate obedience.

Inclining his head in a partial bow, Arnacin asked, "You sent for me, Your Majesty?"

"Sire, if you will. It is less impersonal."

"Slightly."

The air grew still, as if both sides were waiting for something. At last, Wilber asked, "For what, if anything, did Reginold train you?"

For a long moment, Arnacin said nothing. Then, he softly dared, "Why do you wish to know... sire?"

The boy's gaze shot to the king, while Wilber himself scrutinized the islander through narrowed eyes. "The reason is irrelevant. What is the answer?"

Stopping his foot as it slid back, Arnacin muttered, "I was trained in..."

As if sensing the islander's fear, the king strode forward. Arnacin retreated six steps, hastily concluding, "Combat."

"Indeed. You also seem to have been trained in obedience, although yours appears a special case."

Arnacin's spine straightened, though his response was a hiss. "Yes. One could say I was trained in that."

"Very well. In which knightly skills were you not trained?"

"Anything to do with horses." It was a mistake to answer so, but thankfully, none of those there had seen him ride Darkfire.

"Were you trained as an assassin?"

"No. That is a trade I refuse to learn."

"Is that so? For what special purpose were you selected, then?"

Again, Arnacin paused, yet after a second, he whispered, "For whatever purpose suited. Sire. Anything I would do without debate."

"You were given too much freedom. Here, that is intolerable. Now, draw your blade."

It was no doubt a test, an order to see if Arnacin would yield to the soldier's rule and obey without understanding. For a moment, he stayed immobile. Then, with a sigh, he pulled his sword from its sheath.

With a twitch of his lips, Wilber folded his arms. The room went quiet, stretching out that moment of submission, tempting it. Clenching his jaw, the islander waited—but not without wishing the king would drop dead where he stood.

Although the silence seemed endless, it could only have lasted a minute before the boy stepped forward, drawing his blade.

"It is my desire to see how well you were trained," the king ordered.

"With live blades?" Arnacin asked, appraising the youth.

"Prince Andrew is quite capable of holding his own."

"What if I am not?"

Andrew only grinned, and the king commented, "Remember, you do not need to understand."

As his blood heated, the islander locked gazes with the youth and waited for that first twitch. If they wanted a demonstration, he could give them one, to the pride of Mira's swordmaster.

Andrew was not hasty himself, his gaze flicking over his opponent, taking in that easy stance still slightly disguised beneath the cloak, questioning that apparent lack of preparation. Then he moved smoothly—yet, even more smoothly, Arnacin turned aside and whacked the flat of his blade against the prince's young ribs.

With a small cry, either of surprise or injured pride, the prince pivoted. This time, the islander allowed him to engage, trading sword arms to do so. For five strokes, he permitted their mock fight. Then, once more switching hands, he slipped through the prince's defense and smacked his blade across the room.

To his credit, Andrew was barely breathing hard, yet his green eyes burned as he silently retrieved his sword and slid it away.

"Impressive," Wilber said in the following silence. "With that skill, you are in charge of training the Anskonian footmen." As the islander stiffened in alarm, the king continued, "Your reward for any sort of refusal is immediate death."

A minute passed. Then, with a slight bow, Arnacin whispered, "Yes, Your Majesty."

"Sire," the king corrected.

Snared, the islander allowed that word to hiss through his lips. "Sire."

With that, he was dismissed. No one needed to remind Arnacin to take six backward steps before turning and walking away. He saved his angry stride for after the great hall doors had closed behind him.

Early the next morning, Quincy came to the footmen's barracks to inform everyone that Arnacin was in charge of their training. Leaning against the outside wall, the islander ignored the glances thrown his way, just as he wished he could ignore the responsibility.

Before he left, the lord gave Arnacin a long stare. The islander, in return, began to give a dismissive salute. As his mind caught up with the completely alien gesture, though, he instead turned his fingers to scratch his forehead. Still, Quincy seemingly accepted that move as an acknowledgment and turned away. "You are to begin immediately."

"Understood."

All eyes turned to him. Cyril blushed as the islander regarded each of the Anskonian footmen in turn. Resentment filled some of the men's faces. That prompted action.

With a sigh, Arnacin shoved himself off the wall. "I will return. Practice as you will until then." There was one thing he knew; the Anskonian footmen had already formed terrible habits. He knew he had no patience to fight them, but there was only one alternative.

When he spotted a dark-haired boy of around ten hunched under yoked water buckets, Arnacin approached. "May I ask a favor?" When the boy halted, the islander continued, "Do you own a ball?"

"A ball?"

"Yes, the type used for fun when the work is past."

For a second, the boy regarded him. Then he nodded. "I do. Are you not too old for play?"

"In this case, not only am I not too old, but a whole bunch of other men are also young enough, though they know nothing of it now."

The boy's face brightened. "May I play? I will ask my mother if I may after delivering this water."

"I would hardly refuse you if your mother agrees."

"Wait here!" With a grin, the boy took off, water sloshing. Smiling himself, Arnacin waited.

After twenty minutes, the boy returned, a ball in his hands. "She said I could play!"

Involuntarily, Arnacin tousled the boy's hair. "Then you shall play, young sir, and you will probably make the rest look like fools."

Laughing, the boy tossed the islander his ball. "I am simply Onre, and I am never going to be a knight."

"And I am simply Arnacin. I hope never to be a knight." With Onre behind him, the islander turned back to the waiting footmen. "It is time, gentlemen, for a new game."

"What is this?" an Anskonian scoffed. "Lord Quincy ordered you to train us, not shame us with children's games."

With a wicked grin, Arnacin quipped, "Authority requires absolute obedience, remember? Your chosen king selected me for this task. I can do as I see fit."

No one argued. Arranging them in a circle, Arnacin designated each one with a number, told them they could only hold the ball for a second, then winged the first toss across the wide circle to footman number thirty-two.

Finding Andrew atop the inner curtain's northern tower, Quincy asked, "What do you think of Arnacin?" Below, the enormous circle of footmen burst into laughter as one man missed the ball and it bounced off his face.

"He is sneaky."

"Why do you say that?"

"I wondered if he was simply mocking the task at first, but their reflexes are already improving. No, he is teaching them coordination, speed and even strength of arm. See how far they heave that ball across to the next person?" Andrew spoke with an artificial growl.

"You sound like you wish to join them," Quincy surmised.

Andrew gave him a sideways glance, straightening slightly. "Never. Such games are not for princes."

Smiling, Quincy rested his elbows on the crenellation. "Perhaps not for princes of Evfel. The same is not true for our princes." He quieted as his words returned him to a lost past. As if to himself, he whispered, "I remember playing with two of them, alongside all the boys in this castle."

Andrew was staring at him with a mixture of disbelief and scorn, as if he knew Quincy was talking about Alexander and Evan Maxwell. With a sigh, the Anskonian lord admitted, "That was another world." Yet that memory pricked at his conscience, and he looked away from the Evfelian prince.

Andrew did not leave him time to reminisce. "Only because they had no dignity. I wonder that this Arnacin from Arieh also lacks any."

Quincy shrugged. "To my understanding, Evfelian peasants are peasants, able to play when they have time without fear of a lack of dignity. Your footmen all come from the streets or are plucked from their homes to become soldiers, I believe."

Andrew's gaze was closed. Yet seeing that expression that was impossible for most thirteen-year-olds, the Anskonian lord considered a life without a childhood. Although the prince hid that pain, his mere silence said everything.

"Your Highness," Quincy softly dared to ask, "would one moment of play destroy your reputation?"

Looking back at the disguised training below, Andrew squared his shoulders, but Quincy heard the small sigh that escaped from him.

In the midst of their game, Cyril pointed. "Agatigold could use some help!"

Turning around, Arnacin froze. There was a young woman by a tree, leaves blowing out of her apron as she tried to catch them. A toddler was playing with a few on the ground. Despite the plumpness of that black-haired child, the islander knew both. For four heartbeats, he could not be sure he was truly breathing, even as the Anskonian footmen were already rushing to help the mother gather her leaves.

Swallowing his alarm, Arnacin plucked one leaf from the ground and trailed the other men. The mother, her red hair shining gold in the sun, dimpled as he handed her the leaf. She would not look up at him, however, and he tried to keep his voice steady while he asked, "Do you use the leaves for a special medicine or tea?"

A grin grew on her face amid silent laughter, and she pulled out a fistful of leaves, knotted into the shape of what might have been an animal. Her glance at the boy clarified the purpose of the makeshift toy. Then she pulled out a leaf covered in charcoal scribbles. Around the edge, hiding simply as a decorative border, ran some words in the Miran alphabet, spelling in that country's ancient tongue: *My room is the second floor, sixth window over from the right, south side.*

Words escaped Arnacin, but he was saved when Cyril whacked his arm. "Are you one of those who loses their tongue around females? You have no need to fear. Agatigold is married."

"Married to whom?"

"You sound surprised she has a husband?" Laughter burst out. "Ninny, how else would she have a son?"

Even Valoretta laughed at Arnacin's confusion, albeit silently. The islander did the only thing he could think of—with a polite nod, he herded all the footmen back to their training. The words on the leaf told him enough—he was to climb into Valoretta's room by night, at the first chance he found.

For two weeks, Valoretta paced every night until she was too tired to wait any longer. By day, she noticed Arnacin had shifted from using games to train the footmen, although those still resumed at times, to using actual practice weapons. Already, the difference in their raw ability was astonishing, yet the islander apparently never found time to see her.

To be honest, she was staying inside the keep, taking care of her duties as a castle maid and a young mother. Yet, she could not prevent herself from watching out the windows when she was involved in any sedentary task, such as carding wool, which became a favorite pastime of hers.

After two weeks, however, as she rubbed Tenacius's back, the soft hiss of movement came from behind her. Gasping, she whirled.

A cloaked figure crouching by the window lowered his hood. As he slowly stood, the Miran ran to embrace him. She hardly cared whether he returned her affection. But to her joy, his arms folded about her waist and his cheek rested atop her head for one beautiful moment.

Pulling back, Arnacin asked, "What are you doing here, Valoretta?"

"What am I doing here? Lisya sent me in the spring to gather any useful information I could. Meanwhile, you're here training men into skilled fighters?"

Her islander glanced at the ground, but he did not explain yet, instead kneeling beside Tenacius's sleeping form. "I can't believe how round he's grown," he whispered, brushing black wisps off that peaceful face.

"If you think he's round, Arnacin, you haven't seen many toddlers. He has only enough weight to seem healthy."

Those dark blue eyes glittered impishly as the islander looked up at her. Yet he dropped his gaze back to his son, and pain again returned to his features. "The Isfullen are on the verge of losing, Valoretta. Ansky's chance to regain its freedom has all but vanished."

The Miran folded herself in beside him. "How many islanders were lost in the battle with Evfel?"

"There are only slightly over a hundred left, and the Ice Woods have been blocked to them since…"

"Early this spring," Valoretta finished. "I know. Lisya told me to leave while I could if I wished to help in this manner."

"You should have stayed."

Meeting his firm gaze, the Miran straightened. "The enchantress herself has removed most of the ways I could be discovered. To everyone's knowledge here, Agatigold is a mute, and Lisya herself introduced them to a nonexistent village with a nonexistent husband. They are firmly convinced I and my son, Peter, are from Ansky."

Looking down at the sleeping child, she whispered, "I'm afraid he'll only recognize Peter as his name. I don't even dare use his actual name at night, in case he starts speaking. Not that he's ever tried. He'll cry and make happy noises, but… Newton already had his own language when I left, and they aren't that far apart in age."

Arnacin took her hand. "Give him time. Will was also a very quiet child." His voice was barely a whisper, rising from hidden wells of loss, spoken just to soothe her. "He's only slightly older than twelve months."

Squeezing his hand, Valoretta reverted to the previous topic. "What does Evan think to gain by sending you here?"

Without looking up from Tenacius, Arnacin cocked his head slightly, as if spotting something for the first time. Yet it was more likely that "something" was his thoughts, visible to himself alone.

"What is it?" Valoretta asked at last.

"I don't know. I think it must have something to do with his love of freedom, or an outrageous trust in us..." He shrugged. "Twice now, we've been sent to do something without any orders for how to do it. Yet it's not with the same air as when... forces were sent into Melmoor."

Wincing at the reminder of how poorly things went in the Miran forest, Valoretta asked, "What did Evan want?"

"Someone to stir the independence of every Anskonian until they destroy Wilber's forces here. The only possible candidates for that task were myself and Evan."

Softly, Valoretta sighed. "Well, there is nothing our Black Phantom does better than divide."

Dark hair shadowed the islander's expression as his head lowered.

Instantly regretting those words, the Miran shook her head. "I'm sorry. I didn't... I should have kept that to myself. It's not even true, not in that way."

Instead of returning to the previous subject, Arnacin asked, "How did you manage to avoid the servants' dormitories?"

"Tenacius. This is the weaving room by day, but they gave me this pallet and blanket so he doesn't keep the other maids awake."

Arnacin returned to stroking his son's head. In his silence, Valoretta amended her previous statement. "There is nothing the Black Phantom does better than remind people of their freedom, of their sovereignty as individuals to choose right or wrong and change the world by doing so. I may wish he had more wisdom to mix with that virtue before, but I don't ever want him to change."

A grim twitch of the lips was the only response. After a moment, Arnacin stood. "I have to return."

Standing with him, Valoretta grabbed his arm. "Wait… please. I need to know: do you truly support Evan? You will act a part, live a lie, for him?"

"For him? I'm training men to kill him. That's how much I support him." Yet the islander's growl was habitual. Pulling his hood up, he sighed. "As king, Evan will return Ansky's freedom and restore its dignity. For that, I will give my support, yes."

"If Wilber finds out, you will hang in disgrace as a spy. Where is the righteousness in that deceit, particularly after training his men?" When he made no reply, she tried again. "Please, Arnacin. Stay the night. I act the mute by day to hide my foreign accent. Even if I didn't, we couldn't be seen around each other without raising suspicion."

"Suspicion of what? Cheating on your husband?"

Warily, Valoretta faced that sly grin. "Are you making fun of that lie? It wasn't funny when Lisya created it." He shook his head, and she reminded him, "You wouldn't laugh at people believing you dishonorable."

A sigh escaped him, and he turned back to her, lowering his voice. "I will never love honor, real honor, any less, Valoretta, but I learned long ago I don't have any. It's a lie to pretend otherwise. Yet, I wasn't even mocking that. I was just laughing at their gullibility."

Arnacin again turned to go, but the Miran took his hand. "Stay, please."

"I can't, Valoretta. They took me off night duty the day after I began training the footmen, but I'm still the one who reminds the guards when shifts change. I have to at least be there then, or they'll notice my absence." Snuffing the low candle, he returned to the window.

As he slid out, Valoretta caught his hand on the sill. Leaning over to where she knew he was, directly below her, she whispered, "At least promise me you'll be careful, even if it takes submission to be so."

At first, nothing but silence met her ears, though his hand did not shift. After a moment, he whispered, "As you wish, my lady." Then his hand pulled away as he started down.

Chapter 19

WILBER'S CHARGE

VOICES WERE FLOATING out of the footmen's barracks when Arnacin approached. Cyril's words carried above the others'. "I really doubt the islanders are magical. I still find it shocking that Arieh fell to Maxwell and his lot."

"What makes you so certain they used normal means and not magic?"

Arnacin stopped in the doorway, unnoticed.

The men, Evfelian and Anskonian alike, were sitting on and around three of the beds, with Cyril in the center as he threw up his hands in exclamation. "The reports of the knights—Sir Radnor, Lord Quincy himself, when you can convince him to confess. Wilber burned down the villages of Enchantress Island without any magical resistance."

"Ah, but the grass strangled men to death—our men, not theirs."

"Why only in that conflict? Why would they not defend their homes and families if they could do such a thing? And why did they not strangle the Anskonian knights, only the Evfelians? I know you think it insane, but what if the magic came from another source, not them?"

Before any response could come, Arnacin stepped forward. "You seem to be uninterested in sleep, so you will not mind that the midnight shift is about to begin."

Cyril jumped. "How long have you been standing there?"

"Long enough to discover you have been interrogating your betters about that island."

The footman turned red, yet he stood his ground. "Is it not good to know what Ansky is facing?" Cyril paused, studying the islander. "Arnacin, you were in Arieh when it fell. Did they win by magic? Is that how they managed the impossible?"

Pinching out the candlelight beside him, Arnacin stalled. At last, he said, "It was too long and brutal a battle for magic to have been involved."

Silence settled over the barracks. As men began leaving for their shifts, Cyril stepped up to the islander. "Will you tell me the details while I take my shift? You rarely sleep at night anyway."

"Why do you want them? One way or the other, you know Evan Maxwell is detestable, correct?"

"Yes, but I am curious."

"Very well. Perhaps you can tell me certain things yourself."

His gaze wary, the young footman nevertheless nodded.

Arnacin waited until the old watch returned to the barracks before joining Cyril on the wall. There, they patrolled slowly in silence. Finally, the footman dared ask, "Are you actually going to tell me the story, or are you just here to interrogate me about something else?"

Grinning despite himself, the islander shifted the weight of his cloak on his shoulders. "That depends. There are quite a few secrets in Arieh's story, and I hardly think we have any reason to trust each other that much."

"Oh? I think I told you some of my secrets within the first days of your arrival. It is only fair you also share some. We know many of yours already."

"Is that so?"

"Yes, you were privately selected and paid by Duke Reginold for his dirty work. You were to be his personal bodyguard when he stole the Evfelian throne. That is the secret, is it not?"

For another moment, Arnacin said nothing. Then he asked, "Are you really investigating the island because you wish to know your opponents?"

"Why should I not?"

"I must admit, I have wondered some things myself. Such as, why would you show that much support for your previous king, or any king for that matter? You never even met him. He fathered your prince and his sister married the king you refuse to admit you hate, but whom you all detest quite obviously."

"So, you are *that* type of person," Cyril sighed. "The one who lives for himself because there is no one worthy of serving. Of course, we will support a king. When there is no government, one creates a world where everyone preys on everyone else."

In the dark, Arnacin did not need to fear his involuntary grimace. It would not be noticed. "Perhaps, if you know so much, you could enlighten me. What makes you so certain of Phillip—a king you never knew? Would you still give him the same love, trust and respect after all this?"

With a sigh, Cyril turned back the other way. As Arnacin quietly followed him, the Anskonian shook his head. "With any other Evfelian, I would suspect a trap, but somehow... You are different, you know, with your sneaky training tactics, your strange patience, and even your... your invitation to the boy with the ball. Were circumstances different, you might even be... the type of Anskonian that lived under Phillip. That is the reason we never question him, you know. Anskonians were different. They were loving, fiercely independent, and yet..." He shrugged. "Just different. Only a free land, basking in the protection of a good king, can create that."

"But—"

Cyril again shook his head. "There is no but. It is a fact, proven perhaps by current events."

"I disagree. They say around here that your Evan Maxwell was a very compassionate boy and that a child never leaves his father's training if loved. Yet, I have found no reason for his demeanor to change. His aunt and uncle purportedly loved him too. Therefore, I must conclude either you are all lying to make your past more tantalizing or you have no reason to believe what you currently do. Not even the plague can so destroy the personality of a boy who is loved."

"Are you daring to suggest we have not seen what our very eyes tell us? Evan Maxwell has joined with the forces inside the Ice Woods. Whatever strange things are left unanswered, we know only evil lurks there."

As if drawn to it, both turned to the lighter patch of sky in the north, below which the dreaded woods lay. "Truly, it is a very beautiful, soft light by night," the islander dared whisper, sensing Cyril's fixed stare.

"Arnacin, you cannot be serious. We *know* the wickedness of the Ice Woods. They cannot be otherwise."

"I have one thing to say. In my experience, a gap in logic as large as the one in Evan Maxwell's story can mean only one thing—someone here, in this castle now, is lying. If I am to believe you about Maxwell's character before his disappearance, then I must assume Evan Maxwell was driven to his current actions. If that is the case, you may already be serving the evil you fear."

Cyril's gaze had withdrawn. He stared at his companion, his eyes searching in the dark yet never fixing on anything.

It occurred to Arnacin that while he could see almost as well as if it were daylight, he was an islander. Cyril could probably only see his silhouette.

Arnacin resisted the impulse to draw his hood up and deepen the blackness he was hiding within. Instead, he returned to the charge Cyril had set against him. "Perhaps that liar is a better one than today's Anskonians. At least that person is beyond the point of lying to his conscience. He knows he only serves himself." Crisply, he nodded. "May your watch be pleasant. Good night. I will satisfy your curiosity when you can satisfy mine."

The next morning, Quincy was instructed to teach Arnacin to ride. They were busy for hours, through the time the islander usually set aside for training his charges, yet the footmen kept themselves occupied without question.

Watching the riders below her window as she embroidered in the late afternoon, Valoretta smiled. While every movement from her islander showed irritation, his steed only blew out a long breath.

Again, the lord adjusted Arnacin's grip on the reins. It was clear to her that the islander had no wish to learn, yet Quincy and the horse had the patience of a mother.

"Agatigold," a voice giggled, causing Valoretta to resume her needlework. "You need to behave yourself, even if your husband is contemptible. That smile of yours is nearly adulterous." One of the maids approached. Leaning over the Miran, she began watching those in the yard herself.

Valoretta lightly kicked her.

With a laugh, the girl turned away. "I like Arnacin, but I am not in any danger of being smitten with him."

As soon as she left, the Miran stole another glance out the window. Quincy was bent toward Arnacin, speaking softly as they walked their horses in circles about the yard. Whatever he was saying, it had apparently changed the islander's refusal to learn. He was taking correction.

The next time she looked back up from her sewing, they were leaving the ward. Biting her lip, Valoretta returned to work.

"Can you now control the horse during a gallop?" Quincy asked, as they skirted the remains of the town and traveled east.

"How long are you going to make me circle the keep if I still lack the skill?" Arnacin asked in return.

"I am ordered to keep you in that saddle all night if I must. The king insists you learn the skills you need to become a knight. There will be a bit of this every day, as well as lessons in how to care for them."

"Very well." Arnacin kicked his steed, bending low. Beside him, Quincy pushed his reins forward, joining the race.

"I figured it had to have sunk in by now," Quincy laughed, spurring his steed on.

For a moment, Arnacin considered dropping behind and then returning to the castle just to escape the horse, but in the freedom of the open valley, he instead urged his mount faster, heading east. All the while, he let Quincy set the pace, trotting here and galloping there as they trailed over the wild grass of the valley, topped in evening's gold.

Then, the ocean came into view.

As his heart leapt into his throat, Arnacin hauled his steed to a stop. What had sounded like the wind was now revealed as the splash of the retreating tide. He halted for only a moment before its call drove him forward again—the call of his birth.

Ahead, Quincy slowed and looked back. "Arnacin, what is it? Are you that afraid of the water?"

Swallowing, the islander joined the lord, and they rode leisurely along the shore as the sky reddened. The sight, smell and sound brought with it memory upon memory of home, and Arnacin turned his gaze away. Thankfully, Quincy was watching the vibrantly red horizon instead of him.

That hissing wash of the waves on shore, that salty tang in the air, had been there every morning throughout his childhood—all those years with a father who worked hard, but loved his family enough to sacrifice every evening's rest to spend extra time with them, as if he knew how little of it he had; a mother with such loving patience that she gave her children the freedom to choose their own paths in life; a sister with the wisdom and wildness of a sprite, a nymph indeed; and a brother whose tiny face bore a mix of grief and laughter. All of it came back to him thanks to the sight of Ansky's shore. All of it sacrificed in folly.

At the very least, he was soon to rejoin them. He only had until Wilber discovered his ruse, and it wouldn't be long...

"I suppose Evfel could have a greater fear of the ocean than we do." Quincy's comment broke through Arnacin's visions of home. "Yes, Anskonians also fear it. We know the blackness that hides out there somewhere, the dragons that will bring it farther inland. Yet we also know the shore protects us. Here on the ocean, we have never seen the blackness. At least, Cyra says they have never seen it, and they guard the east."

He turned to the islander, who dared meet his gaze. "To be perfectly honest, Arnacin, we chose to walk the length of the Calmar Mountains rather than sail around the coast when the islanders destroyed the rails. So, yes... We also are afraid of the wild water. You do not need to look quite so pale, though."

There was only one thing to say—the opposite of his heart's yearning. "I would like to return now."

"You have learned the basics, Arnacin. Lead the way. Temperamental horses will come later."

And so they turned inland, though Arnacin refused to look back. The ocean was a thing of the past, as was his island. Long ago, it had disappeared with the setting sun.

Somehow, a month and a half had passed since Arnacin entered through Castle Ansky's portcullis, and no one seemed to suspect anything. Yet he was also aware that autumn was approaching, and wherever Evan had made his camp, it was unprotected from Elcan's harsh winters. Then again, even though some of the Anskonian footmen appeared more ready to discuss Wilber's qualities—or lack thereof—in private, they had made no real change in their stance on their rightful king. Pushing harder would benefit no one. Neither would training them, perhaps, but no other option presented itself.

Meanwhile, it was ever clearer that horses and the islander did not work together. Of course, Arnacin knew he had hardly tried, opposing Wilber's wishes any way he could. His impatience, to which the horses reacted, was one way he could prove to the Evfelian king he would never make a good knight, regardless of anyone's wishes.

Wilber's response to his quiet rebellion was to make him the master trainer's assistant when he was not drilling the footmen. The master trainer's approach was to keep him in the stables even through the night, except on "good days"— those when the horses somehow remained collected when the islander was with them.

Occasionally, Arnacin passed by Valoretta, going to or from the well, but other than a nod of greeting, they never interacted. Indeed, other than Cyril, who would frequently take breaks in the stables—albeit mainly to shake his head at the horses' dislike of the islander—most everyone left him alone unless they were working with him. At any rate, his isolation did nothing to assist his mission of persuading the footmen to see the truth about Evan and Wilber—not that Arnacin could have helped those obstinate people that much even if he had been around.

One day, Quincy entered the barn as the islander was struggling with a mare he was supposed to be wiping down. As the steed irritably swung her teeth at Arnacin, he thwacked her across the nose with his wet rag.

A laugh burst from the Anskonian lord as he grabbed the mare's head, soothingly stroking her nose. "The way you go about this task, one could wonder how you still live." His smile deepened into sympathy as he added, "This will not always be your responsibility—which could save your life—but Wilber insists his knights know every aspect of the field, even how to forge a weapon, should the need arise."

Sighing, Arnacin wrung out his rag. "That is very astute of him."

"A compliment from you?" With a cock of his head, Quincy regarded the islander.

"In that only." With that, Arnacin returned to flicking the rag over the mare's rump. Thankfully, she had quieted under the lord's hand and seemed to take no more notice of the islander's frustration.

"I have no understanding of you, Arnacin. What are you resisting? What did the duke teach you?" When the islander only shook his head, the lord released the mare. "I am to check on our camp by the Calmar Mountains or I would stay longer. But remember this, Arnacin: as a soldier of any type, you must trust your commander to know best and follow him without question, whatever he has in store for you, else you fail your duties."

Dropping his gaze, the islander muttered, "I know." A warm pat on his shoulder was all the reply Quincy made as he turned to his steed. Arnacin's thoughts were forced back to Mira and its fall while he quietly watched the lord ride away. That advice was not new, but despite knowing its truth, Wilber would never be the first to receive that respect from him. No, quite the opposite.

"Arnacin." Cyril's voice was followed by footsteps. Turning back around, the islander returned to his task. The footman stopped at his shoulder, patting the soothed mare's neck. "Have you heard the rumors, or are you just ignoring them out of obstinacy?"

"What rumors?"

Shaking his head, Cyril took the mare and led her into her stall. Once done stealing the horse, the footman folded his arms. "If you would learn this task, you might be rewarded with more than just knighthood."

Retrieving the mare's empty water bucket, Arnacin turned away. "In case you failed to notice, I am happy to be unrewarded."

Arnacin's leaving for the well did nothing to deter Cyril. "I understand why some of our Anskonian knights are grumbling about the possibility of you becoming a lord, but surely—"

Arnacin whirled on him. "Wilber would be a fool to try! He knows I will never agree. I have not once hid my opinion, and if he has a problem with that..." He paused briefly as Matalaide's words rose to mind from when Gwenre visited. With an impish grin, he lowered the bucket into the well. "He has not said so."

"Arnacin, be reasonable. It would be the best thing for your own sake. Land, money, authority—come on! Why is it any worse than how you are serving him now, training his men? Anyway, the Anskonian footmen think you should become one if the speculation proves more than rumor."

With a sigh, the islander turned back to the barn with the filled bucket. Hearing the footman still following him, he warned, "There are some things you must not ask. Hopefully, you will understand someday, but I cannot be the one to tell you."

Cyril seemed to content himself with that, although he stayed with Arnacin for several more hours.

"So why do you train us now with your left?" Erik asked Arnacin the next day, during practice. He planted his feet in a refusal to retreat into the barrack's wall under his instructor's steady advance. "Before this, you were using your right."

With a sly grin, the islander stepped back, allowing Erik to attack. "Maybe I used my right to demonstrate for your sakes, or perhaps this is better practice for me. You are still learning the basics, after all."

Pressing the attack, the footman hacked the air viciously. "Taunter. I am not." Puffing, he pushed Arnacin back.

Then he halted abruptly, his gaze fixed on something behind the islander. "Look out!"

Expecting a trick, Arnacin cautiously spared a glance over his shoulder—and instantly dropped his practice sword. Tenacius was scooting on hands and knees toward the shining shields and swords beneath the barrack's eaves, grinning as only a toddler could. Beyond him, Valoretta was striding toward them, but at the rate he was moving, Tenacius would beat her to his goal.

"Ho there." The islander plucked his son from the ground. "What interest could you have in those things?"

Instantly, Tenacius let loose a high wail, squirming and reaching for his mother. Arnacin silently passed him over. He only settled once she held him again, protected from the stranger. The toddler's pale blue eyes, so much like his mother's, stared warily back at Arnacin, every fine line of his small face Miran. Indeed, Tenacius was the prince and heir of Mira, even if he did not know it.

Valoretta was also watching the islander. With a silent nod, he turned back to the footmen. Only later did he find the reason for Tenacius's escape. By the well, charcoal drawings and scribbles decorated the stones. But alongside them was a message in the Miran script: *Come tonight.*

There was something in that order that forbade discussion. Something had caused concern.

Valoretta was waiting on her pallet beside her sleeping son, when Arnacin slipped through the window. "Arn—" The Miran paled, her hand shooting to the base of her throat, as he froze in the process of pulling off his hood. Her gaze meeting the islander's, she put a finger to her lips.

For another three seconds, not a sound stirred, either in the hall outside or in the room. Straining his ears, Arnacin thought he could hear the hiss of the single candle's melting wax beneath Tenacius's peaceful breaths, but there was nothing more.

Then, footsteps sounded down the corridor. Arnacin studied Valoretta anew while they waited for the safety to speak.

Slowly, the footsteps shuffled even farther away, passing the intersection of the corridors. Valoretta waited another few seconds before a small breath escaped her throat and she pushed herself to her feet.

"How did you know someone was approaching?" Arnacin asked.

Blushing, the Miran again placed her fingers against the base of her throat. "Lisya made it impossible for me to speak right before anyone dangerous comes within hearing range of my voice. When your name stuck in my throat, I knew."

Meeting her in the middle of the room, the islander lowered his voice anyway. "Why did you want to meet? What have you discovered?"

She also lowered her voice, stepping closer until she was looking up at him. "Wilber has been contemplating making you a lord."

As Arnacin opened his mouth, she clapped her hand over it. "No, listen. Don't make the mistake of scoffing. Everyone knows he doesn't trust you, but as far as he's aware, you're Evfelian. You already belong to him. You would commit treason by refusing."

Although she let her hand fall to his arm, she was not finished. "He knows you fear him, and he believes you are out for your own fortune, hence your assumed loyalty to Reginold. As far as he's concerned, you'll swear anything when you face death on one side and the right to property on the other. As long as he needs to eliminate his nephew, he might be willing to grant you a certain amount of authority."

Her hand on his arm trembled. Clasping it, Arnacin sighed. "He also knows I refuse to lie. I doubt—"

"Yes!" Vainly Valoretta tried to pull her hand away, but the islander gently kept his hold. Surrendering, the Miran lowered her gaze. "He knows, but that only gives him more cause to think the gamble's worth it. Don't give him that chance. I can't stand aside and watch him execute you. Yet, if I'm to protect Tenacius... Leave now, please. Return to Evan—"

Firmly, Arnacin shook his head. "No, Valoretta."

"Why? I know you'll refuse Wilber's order, and he'll have you killed as a traitor without ever learning the truth of why you're here."

For a long moment, the islander studied her pleading gaze. "Why, Valoretta?" he finally repeated. "If I flee, I mark myself as a spy."

"And what are you accomplishing that would make that so devastating? Arnacin, at the very least, Tenacius needs you! Think of him. He is yours, and anyone who knows anything knows that. It's his hair, his personality. He's determined and boisterous. I don't have that kind of energy. I have no idea how your mother did it. Fighting for Ansky's prince is one thing. Choosing to walk to the gallows for him is entirely different. Why would you?"

Dropping his gaze, Arnacin softly admitted, "Valoretta, you've seen Wilber. If Evan doesn't win, he will enslave all of Elcan—"

"That's Elcan, not the island. It's not your place to save nations. To think so is arrogance."

The rebuke stabbed at Arnacin, more so with the weight of Mira's collapse behind it. "If Evan is to win, he needs to conquer Wilber here. This castle's defenses must be weakened before he attacks. Honestly, I feel like I've strengthened Wilber more than crippled him, but a few Anskonians are beginning to doubt their past convictions. Should they brand me a spy, they will have little reason for that doubt. I will just appear to be a snake."

Valoretta's head dropped. "Then I can only pray Wilber chooses against making you a lord."

Squeezing her hands, Arnacin let his forehead rest against hers. "Mira, surely you understand?" There always was, always had to be, a higher calling, one that had caused her to condemn her people to starvation, had joined them in marriage, and was now tearing them apart. Without that calling, however, darkness would win. They both knew it.

Her chin rose in response, causing their noses to touch. As they stood there like that, the islander's heart quickened. It would be easy, so easy, to tilt his head just slightly...

Yet he quailed. Perhaps he feared it would thrust open his last shields and thereby consume her in all his darkness, or that it would not be fair now, not when they both knew what was to come. How he wished she would take the choice from him—but he knew she was waiting for him to signal he was ready. And of course, most likely, he never would.

The time to make their marriage more than words had passed. The dream that had only recently begun to glimmer was shrinking in the distance. As if sadly agreeing, Valoretta shifted and lightly kissed his cheek. Like the kiss she had given him back on Mira when he had told her he would share Cornyo's punishment for insubordination, it was her blessing as well as her farewell.

Arnacin shivered, stepping back. "Do pray, Valoretta," he whispered, drawing his hood up. "There are some things I can't choose to change."

For another four days, life in Castle Ansky continued for Arnacin as it had. Then, early on the fifth day, during one of those rare times when the islander slept, someone came right before the sun rose with a summons. Wilber again wanted Arnacin.

Sighing, the islander rolled over and yanked the blanket higher. "This early? He can wait."

"Arnacin!" Shaking the islander's arm, the messenger reminded him, "That is insubordination."

"I move in my own time." Nevertheless, Arnacin threw the blanket off and pulled his boots on before grabbing his cloak.

The messenger said no more, stepping carefully over pallets of sleeping men while the islander followed. Outside, rain had filled the yard with puddles and still dripped from the sky, drizzling but not yet finished.

Splashing through the ward, they hurried into the keep, where Arnacin took the lead into the throne room. Both Wilber and Quincy awaited him, the king of Evfel seated on the single throne on its stone dais.

His heart momentarily stopping, the islander bowed.

"You have learned horsemanship." There was no question in Wilber's tone. When Arnacin said nothing, the king nodded. "Good, then it is time for you to swear your loyalty as a lord of Evfel. After Prince Maxwell no longer threatens the peace, you will be given land over there."

The islander remained frozen where he stood. As Wilber rose, he took a step back. "My apologies, sire, but you ask the wrong man."

Those green eyes bored into Arnacin. "You never question your king. Accept this position or die."

In the following silence, Quincy coughed. His face red, he bowed out, as if to give them privacy. As the door closed behind the Anskonian lord, Wilber turned back to the islander, his voice low. "What is your choice, footman?"

Pale, Arnacin whispered, "Other than the threat of death for refusal, why should I agree?"

"Rather, why would you refuse? Idiocy? Warped training from Reginold? Whatever loyalty you once had to him, he is dead."

"I had none, but I never promised any to him. You are asking me to swear a loyalty I lack." Wilber's eyes gleamed and, steeling himself, Arnacin continued, "I give such loyalty only to kings I can trust, and I most certainly cannot trust you, who place yourself above all moral rules and pretend you are a god because you think you are strong enough to hold a throne."

For just a moment, the air itself seemed to still in anger. Then Wilber announced, "Then meet your death, treasonous worm."

Swiftly, Arnacin drew his sword, yet the hall stayed ominously still. Wilber only folded his arms, daring him to attack.

Backing warily toward the hall's eastern door, the islander strained his senses for any sign of the king's intentions. Quincy could be back through the main door with reinforcements at any moment, but hopefully, Arnacin could slip out before they caught him.

When he reached the door and yanked it open, however, twenty swordsmen rushed through—far more than Arnacin could handle on his own. Still, he retreated a step and then met them.

Thanks to a sidestep from the islander, the first attacker fell, but the next soldier's swing forced Arnacin to block it, biting his teeth against the jolt it caused to his right shoulder. He had used his right to spar with Evan; he would will it to last again.

Yet the sound of rushing feet from the main entrance meant his stubbornness was also useless. Resolutely, he held his defense anyway, but there was nothing he could do against the press behind him or against the strong fingers that clamped, twisting, over his sword arm. As he stifled a cry of pain, someone kicked him to the ground. Coarse ropes bit into his wrists as they were yanked behind him.

Having so restrained him, his attackers forced him once again before Wilber, this time on his knees. The king regarded him for a moment, then asked, "I assume your obstinacy derives from the old belief in a creator—most notably Ansky's belief."

Arnacin simply stared at the floor, and the king shrugged. "You mock my strength? I can tell you for certain that those of that religion are very weak."

The islander's head shot up, forgetting to control his diction. "When was the last time you willingly chose your own death over betrayal? Never. You're too cowardly, too concerned with your own skin. By your standards, I'm not the weak one."

One of the men pinning the islander cuffed him about the head, yet a cruel smile played about Wilber's face. "I'm not the weak one," the king mimicked his captive's foreign inflections. "Look around yourself, *islander*." Though Arnacin paled, Wilber continued, "King Phillip believed that nonsense, and it was his kingdom and family that was wrecked by plague. Your Evan Maxwell is left with an army that has to rely on a thief and spy to survive—I assume that is why you are here. And you? You might have escaped if you tried to attack me instead of running. But you, so holy, could never attack an unarmed man, could never attack first."

"Let me go, and I'll change that now," the islander growled.

With a humorless laugh, Wilber stepped closer. "I gather you are aware Evfel hangs criminals by hauling them up, never with a bucket or trap door? Instead, you die a slow death by strangulation."

Staring at the pale gray light hitting the floor, Arnacin whispered, "Naturally."

The king turned to Quincy. "Take him to one of the tower dungeons and make sure no one sees you. Go as inconspicuously as possible and do not breathe a word of this to anyone. As far as we know, Prince Maxwell still has that red-haired spy lurking about." He glanced back at Arnacin. "Unless you wish to lighten your struggle by telling us where he is?"

After a moment, Arnacin admitted, "I haven't seen him."

"Undoubtedly," Wilber scoffed. "Very well, Arnacin—if that is indeed your name—I will grant you a week to consider your lack of strength and prepare to meet your Creator."

"I only said I was strong by your standards."

Arnacin's muttered quip was ignored as Wilber beckoned Quincy forward. For a moment, the lord glanced between the prisoner and the hallway. Then he had Arnacin's hood pulled up, using the rest of the cloak to cover his bound wrists. As another precaution, he gagged the islander and had two men lead him to the dungeon, their arms across his shoulders as if they were a group of friends.

The dungeon was only reachable by a ladder thrust through the small trapdoor in the floor. Standing above it, the guards simply shoved their captive through the dark hole with a laugh.

Chapter 20

Gallows

WHILE THE AIR was still knocked out of Arnacin from the fall, his guards propped him against the wall and locked his wrists into manacles protruding from a stone four feet above the floor. Only then did they remove the gag, climb back up the ladder, and lock the trap door, sealing him into darkness.

Although it felt like years, not more than a few hours could have passed before a small man dressed in brown inched down the rungs. Once at the bottom, he adjusted the sack hanging across his shoulders while appraising the captive at his feet. The islander stared back, sightlessly.

Dipping his chin, the man unslung his sack. "I am here to see to your final needs."

Arnacin studied the man in the dim light. "I *need* to be released." His fear of hanging aside, there was Valoretta, Tenacius, his mother and even Evan to consider. Tenacius no longer recognized him. How could he die, then, without so much as an opportunity to mend that?

The man sadly shook his head. "That is beyond my authority to grant, but what I may give, I will." With that, he laid his hand on the condemned man's head, despite the jerk of resistance. "You tremble, son. There is no fear if you look to the Creator."

"If you obey Wilber, you hold little right to speak of Him."

"There is little help I may give if you so harden your heart."

Shaking his head, Arnacin still attempted in vain to dislodge the hand. "Then leave. I know the condition of my heart. At best, you're blind, and at worst, you're a faker. So why should I discuss it with you?"

The hand moved at last. "Prince Maxwell gathered an unyielding group. I think it a terrible loss that such conviction is so misguided."

His head lowering, the islander sighed. "Go."

His beaten appeal was again ignored as the man knelt to probe his legs. "I was told they dropped you down here. Did anything break?"

In answer, the islander folded his limbs under himself. With a gentle smile, the man turned his attention to his sack. "I gather not, then." Withdrawing a pair of scissors, he glanced back up. "Will you allow me to cut your hair?"

"What?"

"Those condemned to execution should be bareheaded before their Creator. Convicted females go with their hair down, without covering, and males go shorn. Simplicity helps when you leave this world to be judged by Him alone."

Staring at the shears in disbelief, Arnacin struggled to find an answer. At last, he asked, "For outward appearances, doesn't it make as much sense just to take my boots? It would be less time-consuming on your part, and equally humble looking."

"Your feet will need that protection down here." As the man stood, grabbing a clump of black hair, the islander reluctantly submitted. "It can be cold and wet in these dungeons."

"Since you make no protest against my death, why should you care?"

"Because we of Ansky detest torture."

"Then you are all fools. There's always torture for the condemned. At the very least, they will leave me to weaken from thirst during the week rather than risk coming down here regularly."

The cutting blades paused as the man stepped back to regard the prisoner. "Yes, we are aware of that. That is one of the reasons our abbot demanded the king allow this meeting. In Ansky, we can veto an execution if we feel something is wrong." Again rummaging in his sack, the man withdrew a flask. "Drink," he urged. Uncorking it, he placed it against the islander's tightly compressed lips. "You will want it in the following days."

Although Arnacin was fairly certain he would not, he relented. Either he was too tired of his own long battle to die his way or his burning desire to live was stronger than the knowledge that living only guaranteed his death by strangulation.

When the man returned to his shearing, silence settled for a few moments until he spoke. "There is one last thing our church does for the condemned." He waited, then when no response came, he asked, "Is there any family that will need support?"

"Why would you ask that of an islander?"

"Islanders are also people."

Yanking his head away, Arnacin looked up into those compassionate eyes. They, like the man's hair and clothes, were also brown. "Do you not know that if Evan Maxwell loses this war, you will have no contact with those islanders? They will burn the tracks behind them and forever deny Elcan's existence."

"I would ask, why should your islanders refrain from doing so regardless of whether Prince Maxwell wins? What did he promise them to win their favor?"

"He promised nothing. Although I wasn't there when they first pledged their support. They... believe in his cause."

Stepping back, the man studied the islander. "You sound sincere... Indeed, you are defending this claim even to death. However..." When Arnacin met his probing gaze, he shook his head. "Only a terrible power would have conquered Evfel's capital, and that is one thing you cannot argue."

"I don't. Arieh's own hatred of its slavers destroyed its defenses, not the Isfullen."

"And what, pray, fueled that hatred?"

Guiltily, the islander admitted, "I did. Not Evan. Arieh's citizens faced a slow death under a siege unless he surrendered. I refused to allow him to do that, but there was only one other option..."

Wordlessly, the man returned to his work. But in that wary silence, Arnacin whispered, "Yes, I've caved to darker forces more than once, but no one can fault Evan for that, nor... although most of Ansky would doubt it... the Ice Woods. Believe what you will."

"Very well, I will contemplate your words and pray for you."

"I don't want your prayers for me. Instead of wasting your time, pray for the truth to win."

"Your truth?"

"No, the only truth."

A day passed without Valoretta seeing any sign of Arnacin. That was not unusual. But after two days, and then three, her concern mounted.

The third night, Tenacius would not sleep. Perhaps he sensed his mother's distress as she walked him in circles in their room, bouncing him lightly to no avail. He cried and fussed almost without pause. There was nothing she could do about it, any more than she could soothe herself.

"Valoretta!" The call from behind her made the queen gasp in surprise and whirl toward the voice. A small, vibrantly red eagle sat on the windowsill, its head cocked as copper eyes regarded her warily.

Hesitatingly, she approached. "Michael?"

"What other bird would call your name?" the eagle quipped, opening its long wings to flap into the room. "The only words I want to hear right now are an explanation of why you are here."

Swiftly looking away, the queen kept her mouth shut. After a moment, with a slow exhale, she replied, "Your mother sent me months ago to gather information."

"Who does she think you'll inform?" The boy stood before her now, folding his arms.

"It so happens, does it not, that you're here."

"Fine," Michael huffed. "Then maybe you can help. Did Arnacin ever arrive here?"

His question exacerbated all her fears. "Is he not here? Have you looked for him already?"

Nodding thoughtfully, the enchantress's son stared at the wall for a moment. "So he was here. When was the last time you saw him?"

"In the afternoon, four days ago. Have you searched the dungeons?"

Copper eyes flicked up to meet her pleading gaze. "I gather you are not in a position to search yourself?" Valoretta compressed her lips, and the boy sighed. "Yes. I have searched everywhere, hence how I found you. I have listened to count-less conversations to try to discover something. Based on their discussions, I was beginning to think he never even came here, and I have told Evan as much. He sent me back. In fact, the little dictator told me to stay here until I could find proof, but it's as if Arnacin never existed at all—at least, it was until you reacted as you did."

Tenacius's fussing was growing worse, and Valoretta placed him on his pallet to wail away from her ear. "Did you listen to the footmen? He was there. Wilber ordered him to train them."

"Did he?" Michael's words were an accusation, and Valoretta lifted her chin.

"You may tell Evan his folly has aided his own enemy due to him being idiotic enough to send the man he did. You should know by now, Arnacin exudes authority. What king wouldn't use him? Moreover, as Evan's spy, what could Arnacin say to such an order?"

Michael's copper eyes glinted, though his head stayed lowered. "Your Arnacin volunteered. That was the only reason he was sent. However, I will concede your point. Is there anything else you know that could help before I report to Evan?"

"Wilber was going to make him a lord. When I warned him, he refused to flee in the concern that it would mark him as a spy, but we both knew he wouldn't make that pledge of allegiance. I don't know if Wilber ever acted on it, but I haven't seen or heard of Arnacin for over three days."

The boy's shoulders heaved with a sigh. He was silent a moment, and then asked, "Did Wilber need Arnacin's help as a lord? Is he lacking commanders?"

"Yes. When Wilber returned after the battle on the island, he announced that Evan had abdicated and given him Ansky. Since then, he's demoted the few nobles of Ansky to knighthood and called in a few select nobles from Evfel to govern the forts and mountain towns. Here, he only has Quincy, whom he overworks, honestly. I have the feeling he doesn't trust many people. He has some kind of leash on Quincy, and I guess he thought he could have a similar one on Arnacin. I've also heard that the policing in Evfel keeps many of the nobles over there occupied."

As she paused, Michael turned back into an eagle. "Anything else?"

"The only other thing that might help... There's a knight that refused to believe Evan abdicated."

"Klement." Michael nodded. "He has seen no more of Arnacin than you or I. And as far as his loyalty to Evan... Yes, he still refuses to yield to Wilber, but because of our help..."

He fluttered his wings pointedly. "He hardly trusts Evan enough to serve him, either."

As he hopped to the window, he commented, "You know, I think Klement and Arnacin would relate if they ever did meet." He dipped his beak. "I will be back tomorrow, somewhere. Thank you." With that, he flew off into the night.

He returned at dawn to ask her if anything had changed. When her answer was no, he disappeared. She did not see him again over the following days, yet she never doubted that somewhere an eagle was skulking.

An unexpected visit from Wilber shattered Arnacin's dream about trying to claw out of an airless tomb, this time with Valoretta and Tenacius sealed in beside him. Arnacin was grateful for the interruption, but as the king's cold green eyes pierced him, he wished he could turn invisible, or at least stop his feverish shivering and heal his cracked and bloody lips.

"Reality has broken your pride, I see," the king commented, daring to descend the last rung of the ladder and stand between the prisoner's feet.

Too weakened to respond or kick out, Arnacin merely stared at Wilber's knees, which were at eye level, his head propped against the crook of his arm. Secretly, he knew reality had changed nothing mentally, yet there was no point in saying so. Not yet.

Wilber used two fingers to force his captive's chin upward. "Do you care to live, or die less painfully? I will grant you one of these small mercies if you answer this: How many strong is Evan Maxwell's army?"

Arnacin attempted to pull away, but the king only grabbed hold of the islander's jaw, forcing eye contact. Losing that small fight, he continued in his lackluster state.

"I see. No answer?" Wilber's cruel gaze considered his captive, the cracked lips and the slight whistle in each labored breath. "Not even for some water?"

In his weakness, the small laugh at the back of Arnacin's mind never was vocalized, yet his lips twitched all the same. At this point, water was a means to prolong the agony. Of course, he would do nothing for such bait, even if he was inclined to yield.

Yet the king was shifting beyond the islander's line of vision. Then, a flask was shoved in Arnacin's mouth and liquid spilled down his throat. As he choked, Wilber released him at last.

When Arnacin stopped coughing, the king demanded, "What does the sorcerer who used his magic against Arieh look like? Can he be killed through normal means?"

"You're so certain it wasn't treachery?" the islander gasped. "A poisoned tongue can accomplish much without magic."

The shackles about his wrists yanked against the forward lurch of his body as Wilber kicked him in the ribs. Blood filled his mouth from biting his tongue. Forcing himself to breathe, Arnacin slowly straightened.

Wilber had stepped back to the ladder and slipped one arm through a rung as he watched the islander struggle. "Do I need to remind you? Your island has just sworn away their freedom to a king they think will honor their independence. Undoubtedly, you can see through lies."

Revived by the water, Arnacin grinned and his eyes glinted. "Assuredly."

The king paused, a flicker of uncertainty crossing his features. If he caught the intent behind that word, however, he disregarded it. "Is it too much to assume you understand that I will not only give you your freedom but your islanders' theirs in exchange for your assistance against Prince Maxwell?"

Shifting in pain, the islander leaned back against the stones behind him. "You are but one in a long line of worms who have slithered across my path. I have withstood every one. Dare you think yourself so unique?"

Wilber's eyes flashed. "Very well. You may think yourself worthy to be a king, but you will die the death of a wretch. As you deserve."

By the seventh day after Arnacin's disappearance, Valoretta decided to do some investigation of her own. Even if Michael had checked the dungeons, by helping in the kitchens at just the right time, she might be sent to the cells without suspicion, and they were a likely place for information about criminal activity. So, she left Tenacius under Clare's loving watch and went to scrub pots.

Sure enough, as Valoretta worked, the head cook called, "Agatigold," pausing with a wince as she placed a hand on her back. At the worried look she received, she waved her fingers in dismissal. "Please take this bowl down to Klement in the dungeons."

When Valoretta approached to take the clay vessel, the cook leaned forward to whisper in her ear. "I added a little more sustenance. The poor man is sick, and if this keeps up, they will never need to execute him. Not that I am hoping for that."

With a smile, Valoretta nodded. Yet before she could leave, the cook stopped her once again, grabbing a worn blanket from over a chair and placing it around the Miran's shoulders. "It is colder down there, with autumn on its way. Oh, one more thing"—again, she leaned closer—"Follow the jailer to the cell. He will know only a woman knows how to care for the sick. I have had other help do the same."

With a silent laugh, Valoretta pulled the shawl closer and gathered her skirt in her hand to climb the kitchen stairs to the main floor.

The jailer awaited her at the base of the stairs to the dungeon, but when he held out his hand to take the bowl, she pulled it closer to herself with a small smile. Sighing, the jailer turned, shifting through his keys. "You will dislike what you see, but if you insist."

Indeed, Klement was shivering in fever, even with the extra blanket someone had found for him. His gaunt cheeks were an angry red beneath the hair that straggled across them, his lips cracked and bleeding.

Michael had been right; even if there had been a whisper of Arnacin's disappearance down here, Klement would never know. Still, Valoretta's chest tightened in pity.

Seeing the Miran's hesitancy, the jailer shook his head. "You are in no danger of catching anything. He suffers the sickness of starvation, as well as whatever else happens to prisoners after a while. I should know."

With that assurance, Valoretta slipped inside, settling on the hard, cold floor beside the shivering prisoner. Although his eyes fluttered open as she slid her arm under him and positioned his head into the crook of her elbow, they were glazed with fever, the eyes of someone who sees temporarily, then instantly forgets.

It was difficult to make sure none of the pathetic soup was wasted, and the Miran saw why the cook thought only a woman would have the patience to do it. At last, she was able to free herself and gently place Klement's head back on the edge of the blanket. She paused as he moved weakly, his skeletal fingers sliding out from under the covers to squeeze her arm lightly in thanks.

Nodding, Valoretta left, wishing all the more for Arnacin's safety.

She was at the top of the stairs returning to the kitchen when she passed two maids muttering to each other. "Whatever they say, there are no islanders who could be... well, who could have Arnacin's authority. I think Wilber is lying again, or he made a mistake."

Valoretta froze.

"Shh. Whether you like it or not, Wilber is our king. And you cannot forget that islanders are witches. They could have more authority than any king if they so wanted."

The conversation moved beyond her hearing, yet for a second, the Miran remained on the top step, her heart pounding, unsure if she should follow them or continue to the kitchen. Those maids were clearly off to some task, and for all she knew, they had changed subjects.

One thing was clear—Arnacin was discovered. And if Michael was searching for him, then he clearly hadn't escaped.

Making up her mind, she dashed down the stairs to return the bowl. "Agatigold," the cook exclaimed as Valoretta rushed in. "What happened?" As the Miran mouthed Arnacin's name, the cook sighed. "Ah, word is circling. Wilber somehow managed to keep it secret until now, but no one can hide anything when there is about to be a hanging."

There was a moment's pause, broken only by the crack of the bowl breaking on the floor. No one moved to clean it. As Valoretta shook her head, the cook pursed her lips. "It appears he is one of Maxwell's men, here to... I have no idea what he could do here, honestly. But then again, I have no interest in the guile of warfare." Meeting the queen's pleading stare, she shook her head. "No, I refuse to tell you where they are going. You like Arnacin a little better than is good for you. Yes, I know all about the innocence of a young woman's heart, but the answer is still no."

Without waiting for more, Valoretta raced back up the stairs. One piece of information she had gleaned—they were taking Arnacin somewhere. Hopefully, they hanged their prisoners outside the castle. That way, Michael might already have heard about it, and the Isfullen could then ambush Wilber's troops.

She arrived on the outer keep stairs in time to see some armored brute kick Arnacin down the battlement steps. Quincy and a cart waited a few feet away. "Enough!" The lord's order snapped through the bailey as he bent to haul the crumpled islander back to his feet. "The king waits at the abbey!"

Other men in the cart shackled Arnacin to its floor by an iron collar about his neck. Valoretta hastily scanned the number of guards, the portcullis's entry tunnel, and the gatehouse. Before she could form any plan, she felt the heavy beat of wings stirring the air and whipping it against her head. "Just stall! Remember Tenacius!" A red streak shot over her head to the north. As the cart began to move, she rushed over, reaching for the horses' bridles.

"Move, woman!" the driver barked, yet she shook her head vehemently, hoping her eyes showed only beseeching fear. Someone grabbed her around her waist, hauling her aside, and she struggled against that grasp.

"Let her be, for just a moment." Quincy commanded with a sigh. "I doubt she understands why executions are necessary, considering her plea to spare the life of her husband."

Gratefully—though her eyes burned—Valoretta approached the side of the cart where Arnacin's head rested. Had he not been the stubborn man he was, chaining him in would be absurd for all the strength he seemed to possess. He lay at the bottom of the cart as if already dead, only his heaving chest suggesting otherwise.

Choking up slightly, Valoretta placed her hand against her true husband's hot and bleeding cheek. Bruises forming around fresh cuts informed her of the brutality of the men sent to fetch their prisoner. His raggedly cropped hair highlighted his injuries all the more.

Naturally, he kept his eyes closed. They both knew the potential danger to her if their gazes met. The Miran bit her lip, feeling the tightness of his jaw beneath her fingers, praying this would not be the last time they were together. Incapable of freeing him, she yearned to at least kiss him once, but she resisted that as well, forcing herself to breathe past the lump in her throat.

"We need to go now," someone growled, again seizing her around the waist. As she kicked her attacker, Quincy dismounted and put his hand on her shoulder. "Come on, Agatigold. This has to be done." With more gentleness than she would have expected, the lord scooped her up in his arms and turned toward the keep.

"Wait for me," he ordered his men.

For some reason, Valoretta allowed him to carry her away, though tears ran down her cheeks as she cried. There was nothing more she could do except pray she had given the Isfullen enough time to stop the execution.

Every bump of the cart's wheels caused extra pain to jolt through Arnacin. Yet, when an arm slid under his head and something pressed lightly against his mouth, he jerked into alertness.

Cyril was supporting him, offering a water jug. "Drink, Arnacin. It will soon be over, but it need not be that much torture."

After accepting a bit, the islander gasped, "Where is your anger?"

"I just cannot understand. Why did you pick Prince Maxwell?"

"You know," Arnacin rasped. "There's only one type of king I'd support, after all."

Shrill whinnies accompanied by a shout interrupted whatever else the footman was about to say. The cart abruptly halted between the charred beams scattered alongside the street. A short, hunched crone stood in their path, startled by their presence. Pulling his charger to the side, Quincy demanded, "The town of Ansky was destroyed by a fire, woman. Where are you going?"

"To find people with money who are not so superstitious as those in Summos Valley," the woman gasped, picking herself off the ground and brushing the ash off her dingy shawl. "Naturally, there is only the castle left." She eyed every one of the troop beadily, and Arnacin's breath caught at the quality of her seemingly omniscient eyes. "Is anyone unsure of their future?"

"Is that what you peddle?" Quincy coldly said. "You better turn straight back to wherever you learned how to deceive people for coin."

When he started to push his steed past her, she laughed. "No time to learn if you will live or die in the war against Maxwell, or even if he is on his way now?" Her nose went up in the air, and a hush went through the troop. "Very well, I shall not tell you."

With a quick shake of his head, Quincy ordered, "Out of the way, or we shall run you over. Should you not, you may be the next one on the gallows, considering what you pretend to know."

With that, he spurred the troop forward. Squawking, the soothsayer scurried to the side. Yet as they all passed, they heard her cackling, "Well, do not blame me when you are unprepared for what is coming."

The men and horses following the cart blocked Arnacin's view, and he did not see the lady again.

Without further delay, they reached the abbey, sitting slightly removed from what had been the outskirts of town, and rolled through a side gate in the wall. The slow pounding of a drum filled the yard as the black-hooded executioner neared the cart.

Shaking feverishly, Arnacin closed his eyes as that man bent over him. A hood masked the entire face, except for two slits for the eyes. Icy fingers unlocked the collar and the shackles around the islander's ankles, pulled the chain out from the rope binding his wrists, and hauled him onto the raised platform in the center of the yard.

Tripping over the wooden edge of the low gallows platform forced Arnacin's eyes open. Then, as the noose swung in the light breeze, its shifting shadow utterly unavoidable, he felt cold perspiration sliding down his back.

The drums stopped as a priest stepped forward, book in hand. Stopping before the condemned man, he sighed. "May God give you peace. As He instructed us to pray, 'Dear Father...'"

Arnacin locked his jaw as the priest rambled on, knowing there was a part of him, the part fueling his racing heart, that hoped the prayer would drag on forever...

Arnacin tensed as the long speech ended at last. Nevertheless, his blood heated when the priest concluded, "Arnacin of the northern island—if that is your true name—you have been found guilty by this court of witchcraft, rioting, murder, deceit and espionage. Do you yield to the ultimate judgment?"

The convict scanned the crowd of knights, footmen and monks for Wilber. Finding him standing front and center, their eyes locked momentarily, two cold, burning gazes in a motionless battle of wills. "Ask your king that," Arnacin finally voiced with all the bitter strength left to him.

The priest blinked for a second. Then, apparently not finding a suitable reply, he stepped back to allow the execution to begin. "May the Creator judge."

From nearby, the executioner unwound a long rope, binding Arnacin's ankles together, then his legs. As the islander had seen in Arieh, his arms were tightly pinned to his sides and the end of the rope was knotted at his shoulders.

If Arnacin's heart could have pounded any faster, it started doing so the second the executioner slipped the sack over his head. Then, when he felt the rope follow, he instinctively stopped breathing.

Chapter 21

The Eve of Battle

Darkfire's insane flight from the Isfullen encampment ended at the church. On its steps, his legs collapsed. Flung from the stallion's back, Evan and Vilo rolled to their feet as the red eagle flew over the abbey walls. While the minstrel dashed into the church, the prince turned back to Darkfire. Lying on the ground, his sides heaving and eyes rolling, the stallion weakly lifted his head. "Go rescue Arnacin."

Despite his worry, Evan obediently tore himself away and followed the sounds of Vilo's hurried feet up the bell tower steps, two at a time.

The top offered a clear view of the courtyard and gallows below, over which Michael was circling. There a figure dangled, capturing everyone's attention. Already, Vilo had an arrow nocked on his bow. Ever true, the minstrel's projectile shot through the taut rope of the gallows, dropping its victim with a thud. Grimly, the prince nodded as his own warning arrow landed half a second after at Wilber's feet and Michael dropped from the sky to perch protectively above the platform.

The onlookers turned to stare upward at the bell tower, frozen for just a moment. Naturally, Wilber regained his composure first. "Seize the archers!"

With a shout, knights charged forward.

"Stop!" the father cried. "You cannot defile the sanctuary with bloodshed!"

In response, a few knights turned back to the motionless heap on the platform, but a few more arrows landing at their feet brought them to a halt again. Above, the eagle's talons glinted a warning in the sun.

Wilber was never one to miss an opportunity, however. "Surrender," he shouted, staring at the top of the tower, "lest you anger the Creator in your dishonor to his house."

"Who ever asked if we cared!" Evan snapped, ignoring Vilo's wince.

A hush settled over the courtyard, but again, Wilber broke the silence. "See what *king* you inherited? He has no regard for your God at all. He plays with magic and defiles the church. That is what he has turned to."

"Just let me catch you," Vilo growled under his breath.

Raising his chin, Evan kept his lips sealed. Hot blood rushed through his ears.

On the ground, Wilber conversed softly with Quincy before turning back to look up at the tower. "Stay in the abbey like cowards for however long you want, but just try to leave." At his word, the troops started filing out to where Darkfire still lay before the church.

Knowing they would never allow the stallion to recover, Evan whirled. "Darkfire! Inside, now!"

There was little hope his order would be comprehended. That dark heap on the grass was not conscious enough to move, and even Arnacin was not likely to last if he still lived. The second the order left the prince's mouth, however, the stallion weakly scrambled to his feet. He ducked through the front doors of the church just as the first of Wilber's men passed through the side gate.

After checking on Darkfire and leaving Vilo to help him, Evan stepped into the courtyard within the abbey's enclave. With a few monks still around, Michael had not transformed. Instead, he remained atop the gallows' beam, his beady eyes missing nothing. No one dared approach, but as an eagle, he could do little for Arnacin below, whose every small gasp sounded strangled.

Ignoring those watching, the prince knelt and slipped the rope and sack off the islander, then sliced through the rest of his bonds with a dagger. Air slapped his face before Michael's talons bit painfully into his shoulder. "The beasts," the eagle hissed, his gaze fixed on Arnacin's cut and swollen face.

The islander himself seemed oblivious to their presence, his breathing as ragged and strained as before, his dark lashes closed in pain. "Come on, Arnacin," Evan whispered, carefully propping the other into a sitting position against his knee. "Breathe."

Shifting on the prince's shoulder, Michael spoke after a few moments. "Your uncle ordered us surrounded. Escape is very unlikely. If this church threatens us, what course of action do you desire?"

"One problem at a time, please. Keep watch for us, but I highly doubt any of these men will attack, despite how easily Wilber fools them."

As if to confirm his whisper, one of the monks drawing water from the nearby well stepped forward. "I think I can help, if you will permit me."

Evan's grip on Arnacin's shoulders tightened, yet the islander's intermittent gasps were not sounding any better and the prince knew the limit of his own skills. With a sigh, he nodded, joining Michael in scrutinizing every movement.

Placing a filled cup on the platform beside them, the monk placed his palms over the islander's chest. Pumping several times, he pressed and released. Arnacin's breathing slowly responded, evening out as his weight settled into Evan's arms in deeper unconsciousness.

"He should be all right," the monk stated.

"Why the sudden switch?" Evan demanded. "You meant to kill him."

"Do you not know your own land's beliefs, Prince Maxwell? If someone survives an execution, even if they were rescued by comrades, it means the culprit was meant to live. The judgment is not ours to give, after all." Brown eyes pierced the prince. "And in this case, his survival probably means something more." When no response came, he explained, "Some aspects of this are beyond comprehension to me, but... I think his continued life means our Creator is backing your reign, and I know Father Almec agrees."

"And where is the father?"

"Helping your friend wash the lather off the stallion and setting up a sleeping place in the stable." He picked up the cup, yet before he could give any to Arnacin, Michael launched himself off Evan's shoulder, snapping up some of the contents. "It *is* just water," the monk insisted.

After clacking his beak several times, the eagle nodded.

For a second, the monk just stared. "You train your eagle to be a cupbearer as well?"

"Not at all." Looking into the bird's copper gaze while the monk dribbled some water into Arnacin's mouth, Evan sighed. "All right, Michael. Please inform Valoretta he lives, then warn the Isfullen waiting in the Calmar Mountains to prepare for battle. I will join them before dawn."

With a glance at the monk, Michael dipped his beak. "How will you slip through Wilber's guard?"

As the monk gasped, Evan paused. When no further inter-ruption followed, he answered, "Once Darkfire has hopefully recovered, the darkness will hide his flight. Unfortunately, there is no more time. We must attack before the cold comes and leaves us without shelter."

Rushing wings signaled the eagle's departure.

"Michael!" Valoretta cried, her hand at her chest as the eagle landed on the window beside her. "Arnacin, is he—?"

"He lives," the bird soothed, his bright eyes watching as the Miran's weight sagged against a wall. "Wilber surrounded the abbey, so they are stuck within, but the father has granted them safety as long as they stay."

"For how long?"

"That is unknown, but Evan and Darkfire intend to run the blockade in order to lead the Isfullen to what should be the last battle. I have no doubt that, one way or the other, this will end here."

"He means to attack here? How?"

"That is sure to be worked out tomorrow."

"Tell the prince, then, there are a thousand fighting men here, and another thousand surrounding the Ice Woods. They also filled in the stable door with stone, so there is now only the gate entrance from the outer curtain into the inner. Finally, even if I tried to help by drugging their wells, there's a large cistern below that they use in times of siege. They may just drink from that without using the wells, sooner than expose their water bearers to the open baileys."

"They have what?"

"A cistern to collect rainwater. It's as large as the entire foundation of the keep, but I don't know if there's any drainage port. If I were to drug that water, it might never cleanse itself."

"Is that from the original building of the castle?"

"It's possible. To my understanding, Ansky was always more of a military fortress than a castle anyway. Although they didn't build the moat, they still designed the place to withstand sieges, with a secret escape route should they need to use it."

"Can the Anskonian footmen be counted now among Wilber's men?"

"No, he's confined them to the barracks almost as soon as they returned from the hanging. I didn't count them in the numbers."

The bird's head cocked. "Does the king fear Arnacin's influence? Perhaps I should ask, do you think they would fight for Evan? How many are there?"

"There are only fifty Anskonian footmen. As far as where their loyalty lies, I have the feeling even they don't know, but their disheartened state when they came back seems to have made Wilber uneasy. I only know they were solidly against their rightful king until this afternoon."

"Have you noticed anything that may be a weakness to Wilber? What about Quincy? Is he doubting his loyalty to the king?"

"He seems to be, as ever, for the king. If you capture Andrew, that might force Wilber to bargain. But, even that isn't a certainty. And I doubt Evan wants to use that tactic, even if he could."

Bowing, the eagle unfolded his wings. "Thank you for the information. If there is anything you notice to help us during the battle, sit in this window and I will come."

Arnacin's awakening from deep nothingness was almost like coming to life for the first time. Stars blazed in the sky above, yet for a moment, he had no memory and little comprehension of anything.

Then, the simmering pain made itself known. With his lungs that felt caved in, swallowing increased the torture. His first experimental shift caused blackness to sweep back over his awareness, but as best he could tell, it was brief. With an involuntary moan, he rolled onto his side and pushed himself halfway up to a seated position on shaking arms.

So propped, the islander dared not move farther as the wood platform of the gallows tilted, the edges growing hazy. Yet, the dark fabric an inch from his fingers caught his attention—too soft to be wool and too thick to be anything else. He weakly lifted his head. "Evan." His voice came out raspy and his clammy face heated under the watch of the prince's quiet blue eyes.

In compassion, Evan sat still at the edge of the platform wrapped in his black cloak, as if awaiting some signal from the islander. There was only one thing to say. "I'm sorry. The footmen are all trained."

"I know."

Arnacin stared at the prince warily until a sad smile passed over Evan's face. "What am I supposed to say, Arnacin? You did all you could, and more besides. You live, Darkfire will recover, and at the moment, that's all that matters."

Before the islander could think of a reply, Evan hugged him. Trembling, he returned that embrace. Somehow, friendship had broken through all the walls that should have made it impossible.

"Are you able to walk?" the prince asked, straightening. "The others are in the stable."

With the help of Evan, Arnacin pushed himself to the edge of the low platform, placed both feet on the ground, and stood. Once upright, he pulled away from the prince's support and stubbornly limped toward the stable.

Evan shook his head, grinning. "It's nice to know you live."

"Meaning what?"

"Your obstinacy may only be matched by Michael's—or Darkfire's, though his is different. I don't mean that as an insult."

Arnacin could only nod, with a small smile.

The barn was both compact and already largely full, with two cows, several goats, a few sheep, and multiple chickens. There were no stalls. Despite that, someone had made room for Darkfire. Or rather, it seemed, the stallion's aura had cleared out some extra space, judging by the stares he was receiving from a few goats and chickens as he dozed on his feet.

"Arnacin," the minstrel sighed as the islander and prince entered. "Thank the heavens you're alive."

Sinking painfully down by the doorframe, the islander accepted the cup Vilo handed to him. "I'm not sure I can share that sentiment at the moment."

"Then drink. Happiness will come later."

As Arnacin obeyed, Evan stepped past him to wake Darkfire gently. "Thank you," he whispered as that great head rose. "I should have been—"

"No, you were where you needed to be." The stallion shook his mane. "I had my rest. The run is over, without a shadow remaining."

The prince's lips compressed as his head lowered.

"What is it?" Darkfire asked.

"The Isfullen wait for us tonight."

"All four of us? I thought we were encircled by Wilber's men."

"Just you and me. We need to attack Castle Ansky before everyone connected to us dies. Are you able to run the blockade?"

"Evan," Arnacin protested. "You have less of everything now than last time you attacked Ansky, and Wilber has more. How do you even plan to succeed?"

Without turning around, the prince whispered, "We have no shelter, nor enough food for the winter, nor anywhere to go. If we delay the attack, we die—and not only the Isfullen, but all those that should be on their way here with Carrie. If changing that was as simple as surrendering, admitting Wilber won, I would. But he would execute all of you as criminals.

"I already told them to attack regardless of my presence, yet what type of king would I be if I stayed in safety while they went to war? As a king, I've been terrible. I need to start acting like one. I have to be out there with them if possible."

A chill crept over Arnacin as Darkfire dipped his head. "Then we should go now if it is dark enough," the stallion said.

Stepping forward from where he had been soothing a cow, the abbot nodded. "The moon has disappeared for the night. I will make sure all the courtyard lights are snuffed out—since it is the usual time, after our nightly prayers."

Arnacin yanked his legs out of the way as the abbot neared the doorway, yet the priest stopped there. "I do apologize you had to be our test. Know you are quite safe now. No harm will come to you."

Darkly appraising the abbot, Arnacin nodded. "Seeing as I'm apparently stuck here, that's nice to know." Whether he fully believed that was another story.

Silence followed. After a moment, the abbot stepped out and Vilo helped the islander up. Evan and Darkfire followed them into the darkened courtyard to where two monks stood watch over the north gate. Both appeared a bit surprised by the approaching group. "Father Almec, what is it?" one asked as the gray-haired abbot approached them ahead of the small band.

"Our prince must leave now. Please, extinguish all the torches." As the two hurried off, Almec turned to Evan with a bow. "I could offer one suggestion, Prince Maxwell. Would you and your forces dare take sanctuary within the abbey to winter instead of risking suicide? We have shelter and food, which we grow on our own. If there is any way we can convince the blockade to lift—"

"Father," Evan gently interrupted. "Even should we not deplete your resources, I doubt Wilber would let you keep your sanctuary under those circumstances. He would have the abbey burned down with the excuse you joined with demonic forces and were no longer a church."

"Then," taking his leave, Almec prayed, "may God go with you."

Resting against the nearest arcade pillar, Arnacin waited until the abbot was no longer within earshot. "Evan," he whispered. "I have something more to ask."

In sympathy, the prince placed his hand on the islander's shoulder. "Do you need to be the one to go?"

"No, I wouldn't be of help to them. I wish to know why you don't think yourself a true king."

Evan's hand dropped and his gaze turned to Darkfire, as if seeking an answer. Then, looking back, he sighed. "I agreed to become king only because I realized I... had little choice if I cared about anyone but myself. But I've constantly made poor decisions, watched the death toll rise, and..."

As he trailed miserably off, Arnacin reached for his arm. "You are a king, Evan. Now, this moment. You don't have 'to start acting like one.' Take responsibility, by all means. But I've known of too many decent kings who have fallen because they take on too much of it. They forget, or perhaps never knew, the universe was never theirs to control. Leave the consequences of choosing the right action where they belong. In the end, even a king is a man, like any other."

The prince embraced the islander. Then clapping him on the back, Evan said, "Take care of yourself, Arnacin. I would rather not hear that Vilo had to force you to live." From underneath his cloak, he withdrew the compass, its arrow spinning with the movement.

The islander grinned, accepting it back and slipping it over his head. "Why do you think that would be a problem?"

"I was stuck in a cellar with you for ages, remember?"

"You'll want to hurry, Evan," Vilo warned, stepping forward to give a hug of his own. "I'll take care of things on this end."

As Darkfire drew closer, the minstrel patted his nose with a grin. "Run fast, Darkfire."

"I ought to bite you."

Laughing, Evan slipped his fingers into the stallion's mane. "You only need to run for a little while. We have no desire to repeat this afternoon."

Comparing the height of the stallion to the lintel of the gate while Vilo helped the prince up, Arnacin warned, "You'll have to duck."

With a silent nod, Evan drew up his hood, shrouding himself in the darkness—a black rider on a dark horse in the moonless night. Vilo went to open the gate and even Arnacin himself could not hear the hoofbeats that followed. The hazy mass that was horse and rider slipped out, though, and the minstrel closed the portal.

The two islanders stood there, waiting for the warning shout from Wilber's men that meant Darkfire had been spotted, or worse, for cries of death.

Arnacin counted five heartbeats. Then a shout rang clearly over the walls. Feet thudded while metal hissed and bowstrings twanged. There was still no sound of Darkfire.

Concern spread across Vilo's face. "I'm going up to the tower. Do you want to come?"

"Go, Vilo. You can run."

The minstrel needed no explanation. Arnacin would never climb the stairs in time to see anything, even if he could face an interior at the moment and his heart did not still at the word *tower*. Instead, he waited outside, leaning against a pillar in the colonnade as angry shouts continued on the other side of the bolted door.

Although the two monks returned to their watch by the gate, ten minutes passed before Vilo returned from the tower with news. "They escaped. I didn't see them, but by the number of mounted men flying north and the lack of victorious shouts, we can be certain they made it."

"Did they make it without injury, though?"

Vilo's shoulders slumped a bit. "You need to rest, Arnacin. I myself need rest, and there is nothing more we can do."

Taking the islander's arm, he hauled him off the pillar. "Come on. There are blankets waiting for us in the stable."

Arnacin was too weak to protest.

A rapid gasping filled Vilo's sleepy awareness. Wooden beams stretched above his head as he opened his eyes. In alarm, he sat up. The sight of Arnacin, twisting in his sleep, with his rope burns, shorn hair, and bruised and swollen face, brought the minstrel's memory back. He was in the abbey's stable. Evan had left only hours before.

Clearly, however, Arnacin was suffering, and Vilo crawled over to him.

The younger islander's eyes flew open, fixing on the minstrel, but his heavy gasps remained unchanged.

"Breathe, Arnacin," Vilo whispered. "I can bring one of the brothers to see—"

Yet Arnacin only trembled. "Let me out."

"Out of where?"

"Here."

When Vilo attempted to feel the temperature of those flushed cheeks, the islander pulled away. "We're surrounded, Arnacin," he pleaded. Never had he imagined he would need to reason so with anyone in Talliaha's family, all of whom had been able to debate rationally with any adult from the age of five. "They'll shoot us the moment we try to leave."

Arnacin buried his face in his arms, but Vilo thought he heard him mutter, "Good." Other than the continued trembling and gasps, he remained still. Then, abruptly, Arnacin lurched to his feet, whirling in the direction of the door.

Paling, Vilo leapt after him, in no doubt as to where his sick companion was headed. "Arnacin, wait!"

But there was no stopping that insane flight, fleet and quiet as a running beast. Striving to catch up, Vilo hollered, "Help! Hurry!"

As Arnacin neared the side gate, the monks awoke where they had slept against it. Although the islander swerved, they caught him, but he fought against their hold, felling them all.

Vilo quickly joined them in pinning Arnacin to the ground, knowing he was unconsciously repeating his companion's name, praying for him to regain the sanity that had vanished without warning.

Newly lit torches illuminated the church steps, and Vilo heard a rush of feet. Someone firmly pushed him aside and seized Arnacin's upper arms. "Peace!" Almec commanded the struggling form beneath his hands. "In His house, you are in the Creator's presence!"

Or so they hoped. Vilo kept his mouth shut, yet a bit of Arnacin could be glimpsed through his panic as he scoffed, "With a gallows in the same yard, yes!"

Resting his head on one of the pillars of the colonnade, Vilo silently agreed. He stepped back as other monks arrived and one passed a flask to their father. While others helped keep Arnacin still, the father carefully trickled the flask's contents down his throat.

Within another few moments, Arnacin lay asleep, his breathing returning to normal. Everyone else bore faces as pale as ice under the torchlight.

It was a full minute before someone dared ask the question filling the air. "Is he possessed?"

Realizing the inquiry was directed at him, Vilo looked up from studying his companion's face. "No!" Despite his snapped insistence, he felt doubt chill his heart. Instead, he bit out, "Evan tells us you are Ansky's healers. While he's unconscious, I would like it if you examine him. Please."

With a sigh, Almec also looked up from Arnacin. "I hear your concern, young man. Yes, we will gladly help if we can. Some survivors of the gallows never fully recover, though their bodies appear to heal.

"As to why we would execute criminals within the same walls where we worship the Creator, that is simple—Ansky believes that closeness to God gives them a better chance to meet Him before their last breath. Yet, it is also because we believe our God is the only one who can rightly judge. After our law has passed judgment, then, it is only right to defer to the true judge here at the last."

Coolly nodding, Vilo knelt beside his companion. "I'm taking him back to the stable. Meet me there." With Arnacin over his shoulder, he stepped out of the circle of torchlight, noticing the sound and scent of dawn in the air.

True to their word, the monks soon came with a poultice, cloths and clean water. Although they did what they could, they would need to wait to know if there was any lasting damage.

Sunlight was twinkling into the stable when the brothers departed, leaving the minstrel to watch over his companion. They returned once to leave breakfast for their guests, but it was noon before Arnacin's eyelids began to flicker. His breathing again increased in speed, and Vilo tensed.

Although the islander jerked, ripping off the poultice wrapped about his neck and clenching it in his fist, he did not move again for another minute. Slowly, his breathing returned to normal.

After a moment, Vilo dared whisper, "Arnacin?"

"What?" came the beaten sound.

The minstrel had no words, unsure how to raise his question. As the silence stretched on, he finally spoke. "All that over...?"

Resting his arm over his eyes, Arnacin sighed. "I'm not sure what 'all that' is... But no, it goes back much further."

"So you don't remember this morning?"

He gave a slight shake of the head.

Vilo smiled grimly. For the sake of Arnacin's pride, he would refrain from retelling the story. However, he asked, "You didn't seem to have much fear of hanging while it happened?"

"What was the point? I told myself it would only last a few moments. Unfortunately, I lived."

"You can hardly complain, can you?"

The only response was the twitter of birds and the sound of beasts. Vilo waited. His thoughts had turned from wondering about Arnacin's secrets to the island and a childhood long lost. At length, Arnacin sighed, sitting up. "I'm sorry, Vilo."

"For what?"

Rubbing his hand over his face, the younger islander shrugged. "For whatever happened this morning."

"You don't need to apologize. I doubt you had any control over it."

"Not entirely, but I should know better than to sleep after something like that."

Shaking his head, Vilo touched his companion's arm. "You are sick and exhausted. You needed to sleep." With that thought, the minstrel climbed to his feet. "They brought breakfast, but you were still resting. I'm sure they'll make something fresh."

As he started to leave, however, Arnacin grabbed his arm. "No! Stay. Please."

Seeing how those fingers trembled, Vilo slowly resumed his seat. "You need to eat, Arnacin." At the minstrel's questioning gaze, his companion's eyes turned away. "What happened?"

Without answering, Arnacin rested his arms on his knees and dropped his chin on top of them. "Drugs leave you feeling so... dried out and defenseless," he mumbled.

"Have you been sick so often? Do you have that much experience with being drugged?"

A guarded stare met his gaze, no longer hiding but still unwilling to answer. Shrugging, Vilo relented. "Very well. I'll stay until you feel strong enough to defend yourself, should the need arise, but then you should eat the little bit that's here. It's obvious they starved you, and you need to take care of yourself."

It was evening before Valoretta heard the expected news. Clare rushed in, her face flushed, and found the Miran feeding Tenacius in the kitchen. "Agatigold, Maxwell's army is in the valley just beyond the town's ruins. The king has warned everyone to stay inside unless there is a specific reason to do otherwise."

When Valoretta simply stared at her, the maid held out her hand. "Come, you may see them from the keep's tower."

Hefting her son, the Miran followed Clare. Many stairsteps later, they exited onto the north tower under a brilliant red and purple dusk. A group of men and a single horse dotted the view just beyond the ruins of the town, preparing a small camp. Valoretta felt her breath catch. Arnacin had warned her about their lack of numbers, yet seeing it in reality was still chilling. If the Isfullen had half the men who had left the Ice Woods the previous fall, she would have been surprised.

As a sigh escaped her lips, Clare placed a hand on her shoulder. "We have nothing to worry about, except a bit of inconvenience. When they move in to attack, the king intends to send pigeons to alert our forces along the Ice Woods. That small band—Maxwell's Folly—will be cut down at last. Peace is within sight, Agatigold."

Little did Clare know. That insignificant force was Arnacin's kinsmen, and her heart stood with them as they chose to make a last stand for freedom rather than surrender, knowing their deaths were likely.

Instead of calming, her breathing began to race. It took her only a moment to realize why—Mira's end. She had lived through this before.

"Agatigold?"

Shaking her head, Valoretta pressed her cheek against Tenacius's brow, her reminder that someone would live according to Lisya's promise, even if everyone else died. There would be life. As she began to turn away from the sight so eerily reminiscent of her past, her gaze caught on the two figures in the church's bell tower.

Even at the size of her thumb, she recognized her islander leaning against the very edge of the roof's opening, also watching the Isfullen. Thankfully, Valoretta saw no archers along the walls below her, if they even had anything to make a shot so distant. Still, she could read weakness or defeat in his stance, in how his head rested against the archway as if it alone held him up.

If that bearing was due to frailty, he would do better to step away from the edge, although that was something his companion was likely watching. But she would have wagered his weariness was as much emotional as physical. He had lost everything except his islanders. And now, he was watching the eve of their destruction but incapable of so much as joining them. In fact, he likely hated himself for training the men fighting against them.

If nothing else, that hardened her resolve. Even if it permanently tainted it, she would drug the cistern. That was the only thing she had in her power to do. And if no one but the soldiers were allowed into the baileys, she knew where everyone would go to draw their water.

Chapter 22

The Final Drive

Despite Valoretta's resolve, one glance around the kitchen reminded her she hardly even knew what she needed to drug the water safely. Instead of guessing, she put Tenacius in bed and waited until the castle slept. Then she sat in the window, hoping Michael would indeed come.

She did not have long to wait. In the enchanter's rush to land, his wings slapped her face. Before she could speak, he transformed, cloaked and hooded in thick maroon. "The good news is that Evan says the cistern can drain into the underwater streams that feed these wells if the need arises. So, I brought you some of Anwae's plants. They create a gentler sleeping draught than those used by Anskonians." Holding out a vial, he slipped his cloak off. "I also brought you this."

"What good will that do me?"

"The water must be treated tonight. This will help you slip down there unseen."

"I will be seen anyway. Wilber put guards on the door. They know every water carrier, when they come in and when they leave."

An exasperated puff exited the boy's lips. "Very well. They expect me to still be around. Marks of my talons in their necks will not be a surprise."

Sighing, Valoretta folded her arms. "And so obvious, they'll know the water's dangerous to drink."

"Well, what is your idea? You just said the guards would recognize you."

"Yes, but I will draw the water first, before tainting the rest. Then, it will seem to be the next carrier who brings the drugs. Even if some of the men are drinking from the wells, those relieving them will take it from the cistern."

Michael shook his head. "If we lose—and by every bit of logic, we will—they will find the culprit and..." His frown deepened as her gaze traveled to her sleeping son. "Look, Anwae cannot help more than she has. I begged her already, but... she knows Ansky itself will murder the Isfullen if she does. I know it as well. Their fickleness and fear where it concerns us proves it. Yet, for that very reason, I also cannot spirit your son back to the Ice Woods if something happens to you."

For a long moment, Valoretta said nothing, her gaze fixed on Tenacius. At last, she stood. "Michael, someone must do it. As soon as you attack, Wilber will send pigeons to bring their other forces on your backs, and you have too few men already."

"All right," the boy huffed, holding out the cloak. "Put this on and show me where this door is. I will come back tomorrow and see if I can give them a reason to suspect magical means if they start investigating. Then I will kill those pigeons."

Throwing the floor-length cloak about her shoulders, the Miran paused as she again glanced at her son.

"He will be fine." Michael insisted. "He sleeps. But if you are that concerned about it..."

His eyes grew slightly distant. Abruptly, Lisya stood nearby, now ageless. "Go, I'm here for now. I can watch over him without discovery."

While Lisya settled herself by Tenacius, running her fingertips across his head, the Miran pulled her hood up with a grateful smile. Michael had already transformed, and he followed her into the corridors.

Only the soft whisper of cloth whipping over stones and the beat of wings filled the silence as Valoretta hurried them along shadowed corridors. Yet her ears strained after the slightest noise. At last, she spoke, realizing the loss of her voice would alert her far better than her ears of approach.

"Honestly, there's not any chance they won't know who did it. Tenacius shouldn't drink it, and therefore, neither should I."

"You better give it to him and yourself. It is perfectly safe. I told you, it is of Anwae's making."

"I—" Her voice broke off, and she pressed herself against the wall, listening for footsteps. Michael disappeared into the rafters, but they did not have long to wait. The crunching of boots came from far down the corridor, then a shadow appeared, coming their way.

As a guard came into view, Valoretta turned her face into her shoulder, letting her hood cover it and the shine of her eyes. Thankfully, he passed by without looking in her direction.

Above, the eagle's wings were tense, his talons gripping the beam as if to hurl himself off. His narrowed eyes and lowered head shouted his deadly intent should the man turn.

Yet the guard rounded the corner without paying her the slightest attention. After another minute, Valoretta's voice returned. "I have a hard time accepting that," she finished, before tugging her hood to make sure it was still in place and then whisking down the side stairs.

"I already said—"

"Just be sure to win, then, so there's no investigation." She stopped to look at the eagle landing on her shoulder. "You better win, Michael. Win for your chosen prince, for Arnacin, for the freedom of the island and Ansky, for Lorene's sacrifice, and for Tenacius. Win, by all that is sacred. I don't care how."

Copper eyes stared impassively at her. "You must win," she said, resuming their path. He took off again.

She led them down a long circular stairway. At a short landing, she pointed to two guards who stood before a thick wooden door. Michael alighted on her shoulder as she pressed herself against the wall just around the bend.

"This is the lower level," the eagle whispered. "Did they portion off part of the dungeon as a large pool? Or is the dungeon below it?"

Unable to speak so close to the guards, the Miran nodded.

Michael sighed. "All right, you may do it, but when you do, I will follow to make sure you are safe. When you are finished, you must have Tenacius drink it, along with yourself. You have the enchantress's word it will harm no one, no matter how small."

"I dislike all of her plan, Michael," Evan sighed, leaning against Darkfire's side with his arms folded. "Even supposing we win, what will it gain us? If the fighting men are still drawing water from the wells, none of them will sleep."

"She says someone brings water out to those preparing to replace the shift going off duty, and sometimes those that are leaving drink from the same buckets. Wilber has divided his forces into units of fifty men."

"Which means we might remove a hundred if two shifts drink from the cistern. That is still a very large risk for so few."

Michael threw his arms into the air. "You talk to her, then! But while you try, remember how many we stand against. A hundred might seem insignificant, yet fewer is fewer."

With a soft sigh, Evan nodded. "All right. She may do as she feels best. Little say I have anyway. Right before dawn, we are starting our attack on those surrounding the abbey, then moving on to the castle."

When Tenacius awoke that night at the usual time, Valoretta took him down to the kitchens. There, the head chef always put aside the imperfect breads and various scraps for servants and their children.

She did not have to wait long to put her plan in motion, however. Tenacius had eaten five bites when a tired moan came from the pantry where the head cook slept by night. A moment later, she emerged, scratching her arm.

At the sight of Valoretta, she put her hand to her chest. "Oh, Agatigold. God must have heard me tonight. My back has been giving me such trouble, and those water buckets are so heavy. No one wants to disrupt their rest to give the sentries water, so they left it to me, but would you be willing tonight? I can watch your son."

With a smile, Valoretta agreed to the request, while also suspecting it was not the cook's prayers that were being answered, at least not exclusively.

"Remember to refill the two kegs outside the cistern door while you are at it. With all the servants, we go through them so quickly." The cook picked up the two buckets and their yoke from the fireplace. "Will this be too heavy for you?"

At the moment, they were empty and easily carried. Too heavy or not, Valoretta would find a way.

Her footsteps sounded loud in the sleep-deadened corridors—if sleep, the castle inhabitants did. Most of them seemed to dismiss the Isfullen's impending attack as one would dismiss a mosquito. Slap it and the attack is over. Yet, in moments of silence, they would pace or sit, biting their nails. Some, if only a few, dared whisper, "But they are magic. Just one of theirs could win against our thousands. They did it in Arieh."

Regardless of their feigned unconcern, the sentries kept their watch with alert diligence.

One of the two posted guards opened the door to the cistern when he saw Valoretta approach down the flagstone staircase. Nodding a greeting, she paused by the two large water kegs standing nearby. "Our kegs," the head cook had called them. Perhaps they were used for the everyday tasks, now that the wells and cistern were mostly inaccessible. One was still full, the other half empty.

Once she stepped into the cistern room itself, the guard shut the door behind her. Two torches on either side of it lit the water, glistening at the foot of a stone slab before it dipped into the pool. Blackness blanketed the area beyond but for flickers here and there as the water caught the reflection of the flames.

It took six trips to replenish the partially empty keg. Then she filled both buckets and reattached them to their yoke. Once they were safely beside her, she paused, listening to the silence.

Water rippled softly where she had disturbed it, yet in the vast pool hidden above the dungeons, it remained eerily calm. The small pouch of powdered substance Michael had given her hardly seemed sufficient against that amount. Then again, Lisya had made the drug.

Pulling that pouch out from her belt, Valoretta opened it and emptied its contents into the cistern. She could only imagine its effect as it swirled into the water while she lifted the yoke onto her shoulders with a gurgled moan. Liquid sloshed over the sides of the buckets as she opened the door and staggered out. The weight of both of them pressed sharply into her neck. She had built enough muscle to carry one full bucket without trouble. Infuriatingly, however, she was now learning it was not enough.

With a laugh, one guard, still by the door, held up his hand. "You will not have any water to give to anyone if you continue as you are going. Here, let them wait and tell..." He caught himself. "Never mind. You are the mute."

He looked instead at his companion. "If we lock the door and I take the key with me, do you think anyone will mind if I help carry the water?"

His fellow guard shrugged. "If you go to that much trouble, you better refill the buckets after what she already spilled."

Valoretta's heart froze. Despite that, not a sign of nervousness touched her controlled expression, thanks to her political training. She only hiked her shoulders, as if in embarrassment.

The first guard sighed, "Stop. That is just mean. She has only spilled a little so far. Just lock up and pass me the key."

Once the door was safely secured and Valoretta was headed away with the guard, she could breathe more easily. No one would fall prey to the drugs yet, not until the next time someone came to draw water from the cistern. She only hoped they would send someone no one could ever believe to be guilty.

When at last she had delivered the night shift their water, returned the empty buckets and yoke to the kitchens, retrieved Tenacius from the head cook's patient care, and went back to her pallet, she fell almost instantly asleep. Thankfully, so for once did her son.

Morning began before dawn, as it usually did. The servants trooped down to the kitchen for their small breakfast, then dispersed to their various tasks. Valoretta could not help but note the small bowls of water taken for the sideboards of the nobility, the servants' cask of drinking water, the kettles put on the fire, and the sink filled with suds.

Mute as ever, she took her son to the weaving room that day where others had begun the morning's labor. It was there she heard the cry raised outside, just as the sun's streams of light shimmered through the window. Maxwell had begun the attack.

Everyone abandoned their tasks to rush to the closest north-facing window or viewpoint. Equally interested as the others, Valoretta swept up her son and followed the press. He snuggled into her shoulder, hiding his face. Sadly, there was no real protecting him from the alarm filling the air.

The Miran found an open window in a tower stairwell and peeked out at the conflict. Someone dashing past her cried, "They started their magic already! They have the gatehouse!"

Indeed, the drawbridge was down, although it looked like the portcullis still steadfastly barred the way. As for the gatehouse, men were dragging a few bodies out while others hurried in, sunlight glinting off their armor. It seemed no one could raise the bridge to halt the potential advance across their dry moat.

Beyond the castle walls, however, the Isfullen were exposed. Although they seemed to be out of range themselves, their arrows found the men along the walls, felling many. Still, it seemed impossible for them to approach, and the catapults hoisted up during the night posed a huge threat to the shifting group under their blue banner.

"Look!" a manservant cried, pointing to a flock of birds headed north from the castle. "I think pigeons are being sent to alert our men around the Ice Woods." As a lone eagle gave chase, he laughed. "Ha! Maxwell is trying to stop them, but I am sure even he knows there are too many for one bird to kill."

A sigh of relief came from a maid nearby. "We should have their support in another few hours."

"So you are afraid," a young man next to her goaded.

As others laughed at her, the girl pointed to where bodies lay scattered among the rubble of Ansky's town—the remains of Wilber's small force from around the abbey. "Clearly, Maxwell has been moving by night, and I see no evidence of islander bodies there. Every form shines with glinting armor."

The chamberlain came by, whisking all the servants back to their tasks. "The battle is not our affair. We need some of you to see to the wounded. The rest of you, go back to what you were doing. Those fighting will still need food and so forth. Weavers, make as many bandages as you can today, please."

With moans and sighs, the loiterers returned to work, but Valoretta, like many others, often found excuses to pass by windows and check on the battle. Everyone around her spoke endlessly about the progress of the combat outside.

"Wilber has stopped our catapults. Maxwell's men are just using the stones as cover while they approach the castle."

"Have they found out what is wrong with the drawbridge?"

"The rope was cut. Men are working on replacing it."

"Did they find the one who murdered our guards in the gatehouse last night?"

"I think we know who did that—that red-haired spy. And no, he still has not turned up."

After a while, someone alerted them that the Isfullen had crossed the drawbridge. Grabbing fresh bandages to take to the injured, Valoretta passed by a window, Tenacius on her hip and the bucket of cloths in her free hand. Outside, steaming vats sat along the battlements over the gatehouse tunnel. Each had a fire under it heating the contents within. As she watched Wilber's forces ducking behind the walls, they tipped the vats over the slanted flagstones beneath their feet. Steaming, discolored liquid poured out, seeping over the stones and disappearing down unseen cracks—murder holes. Valoretta held her breath.

A sharp, angry challenge from a horse rent the air, and the doors from the tunnel into the outer ward boomed under heavy blows. The wood splintered. That stallion the Isfullen called Darkfire burst through, head whipping and eyes blazing with power and fury, the very essence of his name.

Shivering at the sight, Valoretta watched as islanders streamed into the outer ward behind him. No one seemed to have been injured by the boiling attack, although that stood to reason. This was the home of Evan Maxwell. He would have known how to avoid the dangers of the murder holes and arranged his troops to stand in safe areas. The burning liquid might have splashed the stallion a bit, considering his wrath, but even he did not appear to be injured.

"Agatigold!" The call came from Clare, and Valoretta turned to see her sweeping down the corridor with a pile of bloody rags. "Are those more bandages for us in your bucket? Please hurry."

Startled, the Miran did as requested.

Midday came. The next water shift passed, and with the servants' kegs refilled, all the water in the castle became contaminated. Valoretta avoided drinking any until her son started requesting water. She sighed. Lisya had said it was safe, and the enchantress had never failed anyone. So, they both drank of the water.

Meanwhile, Evan had the portcullis closed and the draw-bridge pulled up behind him, blocking off the riders coming from the north. The islanders found better cover in the buildings and shops in the outer ward, yet they were still surrounded and likely tiring.

Just as Tenacius drifted off to sleep on the pallet by his mother's feet, the chamberlain entered the weaving room. He also had the slight shuffle of the sleepy. "Wilber is giving up the outer ward. He called in those from the outer case-ment. We have fresh men"—He hid a yawn behind his hand as he leaned back against the wall—"lined up."

Again, the chamberlain shook his head, as if to clear his thoughts. Blinking, he looked around the room at everyone, their movements slow, some of their heads nodding.

"No." The chamberlain pushed himself off the wall. "This is some spell. I must warn..." His voice faltered as he lurched away.

Valoretta turned back to the window, watching for the islanders' movements. Nothing. Sounds from some of the captured buildings suggested a new plan was in the making to cross the outer ward, but for now, the two sides seemed at an impasse.

Drowsiness stole over Valoretta. Unconcerned by her list-less stage, she slumped to the floor, leaning her head against the windowsill, and slowly rubbed her son's back. Just before her eyelids closed, she saw Quincy and three other men enter the inner ward's gatehouse.

With rising incredulity, Wilber watched from one of the inner curtain's guard towers as most of the crossbowmen on the ramparts sagged. Maxwell's spy was truly everywhere!

Feet pounded up the tower steps, and the king turned. A knight emerged into the light, gasping. "Sire, the servants are all asleep, the cistern guards, and our reserves! No one can wake them."

"Who still stands?"

"Your knights. It was the men who came in from the outer ward that realized everyone slept. When we saw the plight of the cistern guards, we gave those men who withdrew wine instead and ordered them to stay away from the water." The knight shook his head. "Oh, and it appears those sleeping along your ramparts were the relief. None of those who fought all morning have had any difficulty besides some expected weariness."

Wilber allowed himself a flicker of concern. "And the prince?"

"Still observing the battle from the keep with his tutor."

There was no time for emotion. "Pull the drugged crossbowmen off the walls and fill the holes with knights. When those islanders cross the bailey, let's hope that the number of quarrels will be more important than the amount of skill behind the aim."

Bowing, the knight left to relay Wilber's orders.

It was not long before the first islanders appeared in the bailey, a small, makeshift box of moving barrel staves held as shields before, above and to the sides of a tight cluster of men. Behind that square, Maxwell's black horse broke from the doorway of the cooper shop into the outer stable while a human figure ducked from one shop entrance into another.

As those few islanders scurried across the outer ward, two-thirds of the crossbow bolts went wide. The final third could not penetrate their defense. Although quarrels stuck out, the wood the islanders were using was reinforced.

He should have strangled Evan Maxwell long ago. Smacking his fist against the crenellation in front of him, Wilber swallowed every other sign of fury. He might be mostly alone, but there were still a few soldiers waiting to deliver his messages.

No matter. Once that supposed king of Ansky and his forces were through the inner gate, if they even made it past its portcullis, Wilber's knights, fresh and long-trained in sword play, would finish them all.

But then, dozens of horses from the captured stable charged across the outer ward driven by that loathsome stallion. Meanwhile, many of his crossbowmen, leaning over the wall to fire on the shielded islanders approaching the inner portcullis, screamed as arrows from the outer ward's buildings were buried in their necks.

As a second box of staves moved into the open, Wilber realized how shrewd the islanders were under Maxwell. Not a quarrel hit the second trundling box. They had taken out the last of his expert crossbowmen. That second group of Isfullen, watching from doorways, had carefully noted which men were the most skilled. While the first group served as bait, they used what arrows they had to eliminate the largest threat to them.

Wilber could no longer restrain his scream of anger. He whirled on the three waiting messengers and indicated the youngest. "Tell Lord Quincy to position a company of men just inside the gatehouse tunnel and then have the portcullis raised. They have had their games playing on their strength in archery. Let them face our superior men-at-arms."

Wilber felt as if the world was holding its breath. Quincy waited at the gates with three hundred knights and footmen. At any moment, the Isfullen would appear and be slaughtered.

The king checked his sword, preparing to join the end of the battle. Below, the doors shook.

In that moment, Quincy moved, drawing his blade and driving it into the knight standing next to him. About a hundred men around him instantly followed suit, killing those beside them.

Betrayal! It took just a moment for Wilber's loyal men to act. Then, with a roar of fury, they launched themselves at the traitors—including, of course, Arnacin's footmen.

Wilber hastened down the tower's steps, forcing himself not to ponder what had caused Quincy's change in loyalty. For the moment, he could only accept it had happened and deal with it.

Emerging back into the sunlight on the battlements, the king paused to observe the chaos that had erupted below in the short time it took for him to run down the stairs. Maxwell's small army had entered the fray while Wilber's knights were still struggling with identifying whom to attack.

One crossbowman, cocking his weapon near the tower's doorway, remarked, "That stallion is demonically intelligent." He nodded toward Maxwell's beast as it herded the horses about the inner ward so they trampled the knights trying to reach the struggle by the gates. To make matters worse, some of the horses plunging into the fray were war-trained. They kicked through obstacles instead of shying around them, particularly with that beast driving them on—that beast who Wilber suspected communicated in their own language, yet with the sophistry of a human.

"Have you tried sending a shaft through it?"

"I wasted two quarrels trying already. It moves much too quickly, like..." Yet he clearly could not think of a comparison. No real need, anyway. They both knew the stallion was from the Ice Woods. It merely looked like a horse. Thanks to Quincy, Wilber's forces were undeniably, inexplicably, losing. They had only moments to regain control before they were completely crushed.

"Do you know how to ride?" Wilber asked.

"No."

"Find five knights you can drag away from the skirmish and tell them to mount. I want those horses herded back around that stallion. Use them to push it into the king's stable."

"Sire," the soldier acknowledged, hurrying away.

The king ran to the stable. There, the stablehands struggled to soothe their charges.

"Saddle five of the strongest war horses!" Wilber commanded. "Then loose the rest to run alongside. When that is done, climb into the loft with snares ready to trap the stallion." With the short amount of time they had left, the king assisted, sliding bridles over the animals' heads.

In twenty minutes, the knights-turned-herders kicked their steeds into motion, running the remaining horses from the stable before themselves in hopes that a greater number of steeds would more quickly redirect the beast's stampeding chargers.

Readying himself, Wilber found the master trainer's long whip.

The moment the stallion dashed under the stable's entrance, horses blocking its escape, Wilber attacked with his chosen instrument. Dark burning eyes fixed themselves on the king, standing alone. Despite the whip lashing its chest, the beast charged him without flinching. Yet that helped Wilber guide it deeper into the stable and toward the men in the loft.

Retreating bit by bit, the king's back hit the wall. Perfectly smooth hooves rose above his head. He felt his heart race for just a moment before the thing opened its jaws, no doubt to snap his neck. That instant, a noose dropped through those plunging teeth and tightened behind the ears, jerking the beast off balance. Another closed about its mouth.

By ensnaring the beast, and with the extra coaxing of the whip, they managed to haul it onto its back feet, suspended with ropes by its front hooves and head. Angry breaths snorted from its nostrils, but continuing to fight would cause it serious harm. No one doubted it fully realized that.

Marveling yet again at the power of his subdued opponent, Wilber knew he would have to plunge a knife into its shoulder. Before that, however, he used the stall walls to climb onto its high back. As he had long ago, before Maxwell took off with it, he felt the thrill of conquering such a beast, of holding its will in his hands. This indeed was what strength felt like—being master of even the most powerful.

Having proved his control over the stallion in its last moment, he took out his knife and tauntingly slid it over the beast's blood-streaked, angrily quivering neck. He then flipped the weapon over, aiming its point just behind the stallion's shoulder blade.

Chapter 23

For King and Country

"WILBER!" Authority rang in that call.

A swordsman stood in the doorway, gore running down his white blade, his black cloak just falling into place around him after his swift entrance into the stable. A bit more scrutiny caused a skip in Wilber's breathing. "Evan Maxwell."

The prince had changed almost beyond recognition in just a year and a half. Haggardly thin now, with the hollow look of sleeplessness about his eyes, he appeared far older than his age. Add in the anger in his expression and the cuts from the long battle, and he looked not only capable but deadly.

As Wilber had known long ago—but refused to admit—this was no Phillip Maxwell. He now faced a true king. Such a king required fair combat. The only question was, who would win the crown in that moment? In the silence of the stable, it appeared as if every other living soul had retreated. Slowly, Wilber returned his knife to its sheath, slid off the beast's back, and retrieved his sword.

Prince Maxwell remained where he stood, waiting as Wilber cautiously approached. He knew his nephew's anger, had cultivated it even, yet this was not the same. Despite his advantage as the fresher combatant, his heart pounded traitorously. While he would not be fooled has he had been the last time he faced Maxwell, something told him the other would not need trickery again.

With the speed of a striking serpent, the prince swung as soon as Wilber came into range. Hastily, the king retreated, his blade clashing against the other's only by instinct.

Clash! Ring! Clash! This was a battle to the death. Despite all the king's attempts to gain the offensive, Prince Maxwell was always one step ahead—panting perhaps, but unstoppable.

Instead, the parlay continued—block, retreat, block, stand ground, block, block, retreat. Wilber began to gasp for air, and unlike his opponent, he could not continue battling at this speed for long. Or perhaps this was Prince Maxwell's pace when slowed by exhaustion. That thought alone caused the king's mouth to dry.

As if mocking him, the prince retreated two steps, giving them both a chance to breathe. In fury, Wilber lunged. Yet, his sword went spinning away as Prince Maxwell blocked the attack.

A clatter of something bouncing against the flagstones sounded behind the prince. Although the king could see there was no one there, the prince clearly thought otherwise, spinning toward what he must have thought was a new attacker. Wilber took the moment offered him. Grabbing his knife, he lunged.

Several things happened at once. A sharp warning came from the stallion, still held by ropes. Too quickly to believe, the prince pivoted back and his blade sliced into Wilber's neck.

Whatever happened to the thrust of his knife, the king never knew. The last thing he saw was the stone Andrew had thrown as a distraction, innocently lying a few feet away.

A cry of horrified denial filled the air as Wilber fell, his head landing by Evan's foot. For just a moment, the prince thought it might have come from him, but that idea vanished as soon as it flitted through his mind.

He whirled back to the doorway, from where the sound had actually come. A young man of about thirteen stared at him, eyes wide—Andrew. In that second, the younger prince's expression was filled with shock. Then he spun and raced away.

Sighing, Evan turned back to Darkfire and quickly sliced through the ropes, freeing him. With a scream of fury, the stallion launched himself through the door, his gait slightly off. The prince merely nodded to the stablehands peering fearfully down at him, then left. Unfortunately, the battle was not over yet.

Outside, a knight rushed forward with his sword drawn at the sight of Evan. Yet voices rose from the blackness of the open stable doors. "Wilber is dead! Fly!"

The knight, in the midst of raising his sword to attack, stepped back. A look almost of relief passed his face. Carefully, he tossed his sword to the ground and raised his hands in surrender.

Throughout the ward, Wilber's men were following the knight's example. Hardly had the wonderful sound of silence filled the air, however, before a scream rose by the gate. One of the knights crumpled.

"Farewell, traitor!" With that, Andrew dropped a crossbow and kicked a horse to flight beneath the portcullis and over the drawbridge.

With a bellow of challenge, Darkfire gave chase, while other Isfullen raced to recapture the gatehouse from whomever the Dalacort prince had placed there. Most likely, Andrew's sacrificial supporters were not many, and they would be easily overtaken once he escaped.

Shaking his head in weariness, Evan approached the fallen knight, lying face-down on the ground. Two men gently lifted the wounded man to prop him up against their knees, avoiding the shaft of a crossbow bolt that protruded from his

back. As they removed the knight's helm, the prince slowed...
It was Quincy.

"Prince Maxwell," the knight croaked, weakly lifting his hand. "Forgive me. I—" He winced in pain before a grim smile tightened the corners of his mouth. "For sure, Andrew has good aim when he so desires."

Kneeling beside Wilber's lord, Evan put a hand on the man's shoulder. "Someone will look at it. Try not to move in the meantime."

"No. No. Listen. I knew... I knew Wilber was corrupt, regardless of how I felt about you. I wanted the position I could earn beneath him and was ready to seize it at any cost, including the freedom and life of my country." He coughed up blood, yet weakly shook aside suggestions to not exert himself. "It took your Arnacin. His words and actions haunted me. Somehow, more than all the things... I had witnessed... and heard..." Again he trailed off, his gasps slowing. Evan squeezed his shoulder, as the knight breathed his last.

"As far as it is up to me, Quincy, I forgive you." Perhaps more astonishing than the lord's awakening was the fact the prince meant those words. Even though Quincy was a traitor, not just to Evan, but to his entire country, every word of forgiveness was sincere.

From the church's bell tower, there was no longer anything to see to the south once the fighting moved off the castle's battlements. Sighing, Vilo glanced over at Arnacin. The younger islander was unstringing his bow with an air of resignation.

"Oh, Arnacin... It's for the best that we used all our arrows on the pigeons." The minstrel lightly patted his companion's shoulder. He had unstrung his own bow and leaned it against the wall long ago. "We'd most likely break sanctuary if we killed a single one of that party down there." He gestured to the hundreds of mounted men who had thundered by a few moments earlier only to find the Isfullen already inside the castle and the entrance closed and locked.

A slight, ironic smile flickered over Arnacin's face, a clear sign to those who knew him that he could not make himself care. Which was another reason Vilo was glad he had stayed after the Isfullen had removed the guards around the abbey. Arnacin was not well enough to fight, but he took confinement poorly indeed. Any sensible person as badly treated as the younger islander would be asleep, waking only to eat. Not so with him. The only support he had accepted was water.

Shaking his head, the minstrel settled himself on the stone floor with a groan as the younger islander kept watch.

"Vilo!" Arnacin's tone brought the minstrel leaping back to his weary feet.

The castle's drawbridge was lowering. Even before it settled into place at the opposite guard tower, a mounted rider charged over the decreasing gap. As soon as he was across, the bridge began rising again as a dark horse shot up its planks.

"That second horse isn't going to make the jump," Vilo said. "It will crack its head on the tower if it tries."

Arnacin drew his lips in thoughtfully, but there was no time to say whether he agreed or not.

The first steed exited the guard tower and sharply pivoted to the east. Wilber's recently arrived forces, standing about nearby, backed their horses away in confusion. Seeming to come to their senses, however, they wheeled their mounts to the northwest and raced away toward Evfel.

The dark horse leapt from the tip of the drawbridge, already level with the roof of the tower. Truly, it plummeted more than jumped. Then it emerged from the entrance, limping every third giant step.

It also turned to the east, far less sharply than the other horse and stretched out into a gallop, a streak of black. "That's Darkfire!" Vilo gasped.

"I know." Not a tremor of surprise or alarm sounded in Arnacin's voice. "The rider being pursued is Prince Andrew."

"Andrew flees the battle? What type of coward leaves in the thick of things?"

"No. Andrew would never flee as long as Wilber lived. He's far too protective of his father. However, I noticed Evan wasn't with Darkfire."

"What do you mean?"

Arnacin shrugged. "With Wilber dead, Andrew becomes the next contender. Evan either decided to let his cousin escape if Darkfire doesn't catch him, or..."

"What? You think there's a possibility he's dead?" When there was no response, Vilo shook his head. "No. With Evan dead, Andrew would be able to secure an empire for Evfel once and for all. I doubt he would toss it all aside just because his father died."

Arnacin stayed silent. Honestly, with how many thoughts he divulged, he was more secrets than flesh and blood now.

An equine scream drifted back to them on the breeze, and Vilo shuddered. It was not hard to picture Darkfire chasing anyone down, salivating with blood and foam, murder in his eyes. "Darkfire is wonderful with Evan, but it must be something out of a nightmare to be in Andrew's place right now. I almost hope he does escape."

Vilo's ruminations ended as a blue standard rose into the sky above Castle Ansky. Gazing at the fiery horse on its silk background snapping in the breeze, Vilo felt tears prick at his eyes. They had won.

Evan was king of Ansky...

Talliaha herself met Arnacin and Vilo at the castle gates when they walked over. Throwing her arms about her son, she wilted in relief.

"When did you arrive?" Arnacin asked without moving to pull away.

"I arrived with Lisya, Lorene and Newton just a few minutes ago."

Stepping back, she took in Arnacin's battered face. "What happened?"

When her son just glanced down, Vilo answered, "They tried to hang him. As you can see, another few days and he'll be fine."

Talliaha's face whitened. With a mixture of impishness and conciliation, Arnacin shrugged. "It wasn't the first time."

His mother gasped. Her hand went to her chest. "Arnacin, at my age, you can't say things like that. In the past or not, my heart will stop for good."

Despite the prickle of guilt and sadness, the islander could not control his grin. Instead, he again wrapped his arms around her. "I'm here, and I live."

At that moment, the sound of running feet filled the gateway, and Arnacin looked up just as Valoretta threw herself into his arms. Ignoring the shadows of people dancing toward them along the barbican walls, he buried his face in his wife's shoulder.

Cool fingers touched his temple, and he started. That slight jump was his only movement, however, for at that gentle touch, warmth seeped through his aching body. The knot of pain in his chest that still lingered after the hanging disappeared. His hot skin eased, and he felt the weight of longer hair on his scalp.

As he looked up into Lisya's eyes, she smiled almost shyly and turned back to the keep. Behind her, Michael held Tenacius, who was reaching his short arms out toward his grandmother.

Laughing, Talliaha accepted him. He cooed in reply as he settled happily onto her hip. It only made sense that while Arnacin was in Evfel, the toddler had built a stronger attachment to his grandmother than to the father he seemed not to recognize. As a hollow feeling replaced the previous knot in his chest, Arnacin sighed, glad for the comforting warmth of

Valoretta, still tucked against him as she also watched their son with a sad smile.

The rest of the day was spent treating wounds and burying the dead. To the men of Elcan, Evan offered freedom to make their own way in life—to return to Evfel or live among the people in Ansky. Those who wanted to remain soldiers beneath the blue standard of the dark horse were welcome, but not if they doubted its worth. Sadly, Erik and a score of other Evfelian footman had refused to betray their king and country with Quincy during the battle and so had been killed. Sir Klement was moved from the dungeons to a bed, where Lisya administered her own medicines.

Shortly after dusk, Darkfire returned with word that Andrew had leapt from his horse, leaving it to its own devices, and dashed onto the boat of a Cyran fisherman, right before fainting. Alarmed by the fiery stallion, the fisherman himself had rowed with all urgency back to Cyra, the prince in the bottom of his boat. With no stamina left for swimming, Darkfire had stood on the shoreline and reared in warning.

"Well," Evan sighed. "I wish him a contented life for as long as he stays there." Carefully patting the stallion's shoulder, the prince nodded to the stables. "Go rest. Have some water if you are cool enough. I'll find Lisya to look at your wounds."

"Such injuries have healed before," Darkfire huffed.

Ignoring the rebuttal, Evan entered the keep.

Lisya was still with Klement when the prince arrived. "He will take nothing from me, Evan," she whispered. "Perhaps more importantly, he has been told much concerning you. You should be the one to help him."

Evan settled beside the enchantress on the edge of the sickbed. She passed the prince a cup and then rose, retreating a short distance away.

Hesitantly, Evan turned to Klement's sleeping form. At his touch, the knight's eyes snapped open, his fear obvious despite his weakness. "Prince Maxwell," he mumbled as the alarm in his gaze faded to a withdrawn wariness.

"Don't speak," Evan sighed. "Just drink."

The knight glanced over at Lisya. "She made it, did she not?" When the prince only pulled the cup back, running his thumb over the rim, Klement closed his eyes. "Then I must not drink it."

"I am certain you will feel better."

"That is not the same as truly healing. Besides"—Klement weakly shook his head—"it will do you no good if I heal. I am sworn to my Creator." Once more, his gaze opened to study Evan. "Tell me, honestly, Prince Maxwell—if you are even capable of truth—did you give yourself to demons?"

"No!" Pricked and tired, Evan stood. "I am not asking for your assistance, *sir*, with whatever kingdom Ansky has become, and I have already released your compatriots to go their own way, wherever they may choose. I refuse to accept anyone's false support. Swear fealty if you believe in the new Ansky, otherwise leave." He exhaled, reining in his irate fatigue. "I demand only one thing."

Again, the prince lowered himself onto the edge of the bed. "Speak with Lisya yourself." He took one of Klement's hands and wrapped his frail fingers around the cup. "She is not human, not a being capable of judging as we would judge ourselves. Please do not let your biases or a limited understanding of what your Creator can do taint your conversation with her."

With that, he slid away. "I leave every other choice to you. And thank you. You have already served Ansky more than enough for any man." Bowing, he absented himself.

Night closed over Ansky, forcing most activity to cease. Though Arnacin would have stayed awake with the few still setting the castle to rights after the battle, Talliaha and Raymond advised him to rest. As Valoretta led him to the weaving room, where her small pallet still awaited her, the islander asked, "Are you able to sleep well with me nearby? Or would you prefer I slept across the room?"

"Tenacius's warm body has been curled against me for over a year. I've grown accustomed to it." The Miran took his hand with a loving squeeze. "I doubt you'll be as close as he is anyway."

With a faint smile, Arnacin agreed.

Once Tenacius was asleep between them, however, the two remained awake while Valoretta told Arnacin about her part in the battle.

"Were you not afraid to be unconscious when they discovered your crime?" Arnacin whispered, his head pillowed on his arm as he lay on the flagstones with his cloak beneath him.

Lowering her gaze to their son, the dethroned queen gently ran her fingers through his silken hair. "Yes. But if I hadn't been, they would have known beyond a doubt I was the one responsible. I resisted, but I needed to drink it. Lisya *had* promised no ill effects from the drug itself, for either me or Tenacius." She shuddered. "Thankfully, we were both safe and healthy when Lisya and Michael woke us."

Meeting Arnacin's wan smile, Valoretta reached out to touch his arm. "Your breathing's ragged."

With a sigh, the islander pulled out of her reach, well aware of his trembling. "Yes. Wilber nearly strangled me to death."

"Lisya healed everything he did, right?"

"Yes, but when did the physical heal the emotional in these matters?"

"I was just thinking that physical pain would act as a trigger for... all such memories. So without that, hopefully, things like what happened in Mira are not as powerful. I'm sure that's why Lisya healed you so quickly. Usually, she assists, but allows healing to come a bit more naturally." In his silence, she studied him. "Blood ties can be a stain. I wish I could undo my father's—"

Placing his hand over hers where it lay on the stones beside him, Arnacin soothed her. "There's a point at which you can only be responsible for your own actions. You should rest while Tenacius sleeps."

Tenacius woke three hours later, his light blue eyes blinking open and fixing on Arnacin's quiet gaze. Softly, the islander rolled to his feet. "Come on, Geno," he whispered the endearment for his son. "I'm awake anyway."

Thankfully, the boy did not complain as his father carefully lifted him from his mother's side. Valoretta sleepily twitched her blanket higher, but otherwise did not stir. With a smile, the islander straightened the cover around her, then took his son to the kitchens for a bread roll before they headed outside.

Clouds scuttled across the star-strewn sky, twisting in the wind while the grass of Castle Ansky's inner bailey flickered with the motion of the heavens. Yet, it was the light from the king's stable that drew the islander down the keep's steps and across the bailey.

Darkfire lay sleeping, stretched out in the largest stall while Evan sat knotting his mane to keep it off his slashed neck and shoulders. A soft blanket lay underneath them, undoubtedly to keep the hay off the stallion's other injured side.

Looking up as islander and son entered, the latter sucking on his bread, Evan smiled despite the exhaustion lining his face. "I see Lisya worked a much faster healing on you."

Arnacin shrugged. "Didn't she help Darkfire?"

"Yes, she did. Her fallyo leaf will have removed all evidence of Wilber's abuse by the time he wakes in the morning."

Setting Tenacius in the hay, Arnacin settled himself against the wall. "Yet you're concerned?"

Evan did not answer at first, instead watching Tenacius crawl over to him. The boy held out his soggy bread, causing the prince to chuckle. "After all of your complaining, Tenacius, when your father tried to hold you yesterday afternoon, if you remember me from the Ice Woods, I think you just want to make your father jealous. For shame."

"Honestly," Arnacin murmured as Evan graciously accepted the roll into his hand, if not his mouth. "It was probably just the wrong moment, considering how easily contented he is. But it would be odd if he remembers you. How much time did you spend with him before you left for Ansky last year?"

"Two months at most." As Tenacius continued to pull himself into the prince's lap, Evan's gaze met the islander's. "And if this is memory, he is sure to remember you, no matter what. He has no other midnight playmate. We all just told him to go back to bed, except when Lisya rescued us and took a turn."

Arnacin responded with a twitch of a smile. Again, he noted the prince's face, lined with weariness and more. He could guess their causes, so instead, he asked, "What keeps you up tonight? After all that, you should rest for at least one night."

Sighing, Evan dropped his gaze back to the boy, now energetically beating his arm. "Andrew escaped."

"I heard. Considering his loyalty to his father, I doubt Lorene is wrong—he will be back, blood on his mind."

"Yes, and when I said I had no intention of chasing him, Father Almec advised I marry fast."

"What political brilliance." Arnacin could not help but scoff.

With a brief glance, Evan grinned at him. "Lisya took it further." He paused before continuing. "She suggested... if Carrie consents, we pretend she is a foreign princess through whom an alliance will be made when we wed. A complete sham, of course, but one that might work."

"Did you agree?" The islander's tone was soft with compassion.

Evan shrugged. "Even if we disregard Andrew, there is Evfel. Right now, it lacks a ruler and that may keep them busy. For now. If Ansky remains as weak as it is currently, Evfel's lords may quickly align with each other to take us out of the challenge once and for all, and then start their battles over finding the strongest man for their throne afterward. If they think another kingdom has promised military support if we need it, it could slow them down long enough for us to reinstate a trustworthy government in Evfel for them."

"Do you think Carrie is the best woman to become queen of Ansky, and possibly Elcan itself?"

"Am I best to become king?" Yet, Evan's smile drifted into seriousness. "If no one had been suggested, if I just had to choose someone now... I think I would choose Carrie. Beneath all her quietly alert qualities, I have seen her deep insight, her courage, and her ability to listen. She has the servant's heart that Ansky needs, but also the will and discernment to command when necessary.

"And if I have to marry, which I think I must in order to lead Ansky effectively, I think in time, I could grow to love her like I should." The prince laughed. "I already know she will never be a nag, or manipulative, or any of those common complaints about some women."

Arnacin snorted. "Oh, you're just salting a wound, aren't you?"

"Not that I know." Yet the reply held an impish tone.

Smiling himself, the islander nodded. "Good. We were discussing the threats to Ansky. If you are able to completely take Evfel, does Lorene think she can control it until Newton is old enough to take the throne or does she wish to win Andrew back somehow?"

"She doubts she can say anything to Andrew, and she fears taking her land back for herself or Newton. If it reforms under the Dalacorts, she believes Andrew will have more of an opening to retake Evfel and use it for revenge. She has decided instead to stay here and back Ansky."

"She has such a high opinion of her son."

"To his understanding, his mother betrayed him and his father was murdered. And he was taught how to react to events by his father. Someone else might be able to heal him, but no one here is likely to breech his wall of pain."

"In short, you think his unofficial exile to Cyra might be the best option he has."

"The only alternative would be confronting Andrew, with the potential outcome mirroring the second chance I gave his father." Evan's troubled eyes finally met Arnacin's. "I've hated him for years, him and his father. My cousin loved nothing more than tormenting me. But I've realized that, as with my aunt's dislike, I helped create our mutual hatred. If I'm honest with myself, I know I hated him before he was nasty, because he had parents that loved him. I can't go back to fix things, but if I can spare him, I have to."

"Your reclaimed kingdom's a little weak right now for such a gamble," Arnacin warned. "Are there even any nobility you're able to trust? Do you intend to strip the titles of those you can't?"

"I would remove all of them. I don't feel I can depend on a single one. Perhaps Martin can become one, but Ansky itself is in ruins, and as for defenders, there are few to none. In fact, my history with the Ice Woods means there are even fewer who are willing to support me. Klement, for example. When he was conscious enough to recognize anyone, he just stared at me with distrust—fear, even. Yet, at one time, he would have been among the first to swear allegiance. Not anymore. He finally agreed to speak with Lisya. In the end, he promised to reconsider his previous conclusions. For most Anskonians, though, I've joined with witches and demons, as far as they are concerned."

Dropping his gaze, the islander plucked at the hay beside him. "I'm sorry."

"None of us can do anything about it, Arnacin. Some of this war came before either of us was even born. I do think it will force Lisya away much faster than she would otherwise go."

"She's leaving? To where?"

"Home, to the Creator. Enchanters choose their own moment of departure if they're not killed beforehand. I cannot say she should stay here. She deserves to go, yet..."

"Her children. Malachi's only twelve, and Michael wanted to learn from her. Certainly, he shouldn't teach himself."

"She feels the purpose for which she was called to stay is finished, and her presence endangers her family more than it helps them at this point. The youngest three will have a home here, and Michael was the only one who could have delayed her departure since Carrie never wished to delve deeper into her power. Yet he decided not to tempt himself."

"I guess that's that, then. Her race is run, and if ever anyone has won, it is her."

"Indeed," Evan softly agreed before adding, more to himself, "I almost wish mine were as well."

"Evan," Arnacin sighed, "somehow, Ansky will heal under your reign. Yes, I'm sure there will be strife and discontentment. You'll be a hero one day and their archenemy the next. If a sickness or blight comes, it will somehow be your fault. That's human nature.

"But those you take the time to know personally will all come to your support, even the wary ones, if you continue to serve them with all your commitment, love and wisdom. You'll see."

Carrie, Malachi, Felleno and the Anskonian survivors of the battle of Arieh arrived late the following night. While Evan greeted them all—including Martin, Christina and Taylor—in the outer bailey, Vilo gathered the islanders into the empty great hall. "With everyone here, Evan has most of the numbers he needs for defense. That means we'll be leaving for home soon."

A somber silence filled the hall, more than Arnacin would have expected for such an announcement unless they all knew what Evan was trying to keep from them—that without help,

Ansky was still lost. It took Valoretta, however, to ask, "Does that not make you happy? It's your home."

Tevin shrugged. "I'm just waiting to see what Vilo really wants. There has to be something more than telling us it's time to return, right?"

With a small smile, the minstrel fiddled with the cuff of his sleeve. "Yes, I'm wondering if the island should also swear allegiance to Evan."

A loud silence answered as all eyes stared at Vilo. At last, Arnacin shifted. "I thought you had. Matalaide said you had a king. Isn't Evan who she meant?"

"Yes," Raymond answered. "But no. He hasn't asked for our allegiance, and in words, we've never given it. In fact, Evan doesn't want us to give it."

"Why would we?" Tevin asked.

Again, as if he had already discussed it with Vilo in private, Raymond answered, "Because the island needs that accountability. Already, some have noticed our conscience has slipped. Realize that if Lisya's name hadn't been raised when Evan came, most of us would've sent him straight back here and told Wilber we had done so."

"Isn't that just common sense?"

"No, it's the act of those purposely cutting off the world, a dismissive crowd of prigs."

Amid the guilty whispers that followed, Vilo spoke. "Or we could form an alliance of some kind. Having that accountability wouldn't really change our own freedom. We know Evan will leave us to ourselves, but there will always be that reminder."

"I can add something," Talliaha whispered. "We actually aren't as free as we pretend. Long ago, we claimed a queen—unofficially perhaps, but we did. It was she who has chosen Evan as her successor, and I know she plans to leave soon. She feels her time is here. She's just seeing to a few things before she says goodbye."

"Then I guess the decision has already been made," Tevin sighed. "Our queen has spoken."

Vilo shook his head. "She never was that sort of queen. Naturally, I think those at home should be part of our decision, but if we're in agreement here, it will help. Do we swear our fealty to the king of Elcan or unite ourselves more fully?"

Little by little, muttered agreements to forming an alliance filled the air while Arnacin looked away.

Talliaha only nodded. "Then I'm sure the rest will agree when you return."

Both Raymond and Arnacin stared at her. It was the hunter who repeated what she had said. "'When *you* return?' Are you not coming?"

"I know Evan will need help, particularly with Lisya's departure."

"Then I must also stay," Raymond quietly said.

"I'll not gainsay your choice," was all Talliaha's reply. Arnacin had nothing to say as Valoretta's hand found his.

As the Isfullen broke for the night, Arnacin slowly trudged behind everyone else. He looked up as Talliaha slipped her arm through his. "Walk with me," she whispered.

On his opposite side, Valoretta smiled softly and dropped back. In silence, mother and son strolled to her room. As they shut the door behind themselves, Arnacin released his mother's arm. Curtains had been pulled across the windows. Shivering slightly, Talliaha bent to the cold hearth.

"Mother," Arnacin softly protested, joining her. "Allow me."

Nodding, she settled into the nearby chair, pulling blankets around her shoulders while he started the fire. Once he finished, however, she faintly requested, "Open the windows, please, Arnacin. The night is warm enough, and my bones are content by the fire."

Warily, Arnacin glanced at her, but she only sighed. "You're as white as a newborn lamb. You need some fresh air."

With hidden relief, her son complied, pushing the heavy curtains aside and allowing the windows to swing free. A cool fall breeze hit his face. His shoulders relaxed. For a moment, he allowed himself to rest against the window frame, but then he turned back to Talliaha. "What did you want to talk about, Mother?"

Smiling softly, the lady patted the arm of her chair. "Come here, Arnacin." Once he joined her, sitting on the floor beside her and resting his arm on her knees, she sadly patted his hand. "You were not happy with the decision. I want you to know, Arnacin, I will go back to the island if you wish. I don't have my entire life before me anymore."

"You said you felt you had to stay."

Talliaha shrugged. "I promised Evan I would stay if he needed me, and I confess I don't care to return to the ghosts back home. But the biggest deciding factor was that I thought... I thought you would want to."

Barely swallowing his scorn, Arnacin demanded, "Why would I want to?"

"If you've forgotten, I haven't. You yearned to go to sea to find something that would challenge every fiber of your honor, day by day, second by second... Something that would take every part of you—your wisdom, sacrifice, health. When lying on your deathbed, you wanted to know it had been worth it, that you had succeeded, and that you deserved the treasures of the afterworld."

"That will never happen." Arnacin could no longer control his scoffing tone.

"No, it won't. No one wise ever thinks so. Regardless, I believe you were given those burning desires for a reason, and that you have found that reason."

"Yes, it's called 'be careful what you wish for.'"

"Arnacin," Talliaha gently admonished. "Do you believe that? Do you not see the connection? All that's pulled, cajoled and led you here, preparing you along the way?" She sighed. "Do you not see how everything's aligned with that one burning desire with which you were born? Elcan and Evan are your answer, I believe."

When Arnacin only drew a shaky breath instead of replying, she kissed the top of his head. Straightening again, she asked, "What do you wish for now?"

Staring at the floor, her son painfully mumbled, "I want Charlotte and Will back. I want Father back. I want to return to a time when I didn't know that I could only gain what I once wanted through war and millions of wrong choices, without the possibility of a right one, and that there is no such thing as an honorable person."

Silently, his mother stroked his hand as she stared into the fire. Then, as if reading the answer in the flames, she asked, "If you were able to set time back, would you?"

For a long moment, Arnacin was silent, thinking of Evan, of Valoretta and Tenacius, of Darkfire, and of Evan's desires for Elcan. At last, he whispered, "No. I would forever be restless with the need to give more, and in hatred for myself that I lacked the courage to do so. They say in other places, 'Some are born to die for king and country.' I guess I'm one of them."

Softly, Talliaha whispered, "Then take this opportunity you've been given, my dear son. It was created for you by someone who loves you beyond all your imaginings."

In Abbot Almec's role as the head of the local church, he advised Evan to marry immediately to ensure a little more safety against possible attack. Ansky would crown both king and queen at once. Before their coronation, Valoretta helped write a document of alliance between a foreign kingdom and Ansky, an alliance allegedly made through the marriage of their daughter to the king of Ansky. This was affirmed by two royal seals, one of the Crane and the other of the Stallion. With that document sealed within the abbey's records, Evan and Carrie were married and during the ceremony she took the name Gwendolyn.

On that night, between wedding and coronation, Arnacin leaned against the parapet of the castle's middle tower after most had already fallen asleep. Above, the stars stabbed the autumn sky with holes of light. He did not turn when Valoretta joined him.

"Are you truly ready to yield to a king, Arnacin?" she softly asked, leaning her elbows on the parapet.

Glancing at her, the islander's gaze halted on the strands of her hair hanging over her folded arms, long once again. Thoughtfully wrapping the closest strand around his finger, he sighed. "Are you?"

"No. I'm a queen... I didn't think I had any of that pride left until I watched Carrie these last few days." She smiled slightly. "But what does that matter? Your Creator has ordained that part of my life is over and calls me toward another. Indeed, Elcan has risen and even the remnant of Mira yields to its power, as our seer warned." A silent sigh, visible only in the movement of her shoulders, escaped her. "Yet, I've submitted to Him repeatedly during my time here, so I should be willing to hand even that last remnant over."

Looking up at the sky, she added, "I wish it were that simple."

"Well, you've answered your own question, then—I wish it were that simple."

For a moment, neither spoke. Then Valoretta laughed softly. "I could ask why we're not used to it, with all we've been forced to leave, never to know again."

"And gained, I suppose."

The Miran stilled. "Have you gained, Arnacin? With a wife and son to whom you're enslaved? With honor such a harsh master?"

Fully turning to Valoretta, the islander protested, "Enslaved? Do you think honor alone could have forced me to act as I did?"

"Didn't it?"

A guilty smile crossed his face. "You've asked me if I knew you loved me. Don't you know the same?"

"That you love me?" Valoretta's face was pale under the starlight as she stared up at him, probing. Then, she turned away. "You've never mentioned it."

"But you do know."

"As what? A sister?"

Unable to hide his grin, Arnacin shook his head in exasperation. "Yes, and weren't you desperately envious of Charlotte?"

"Well, that's different. I'm not your sister."

Instead of answering, Arnacin kissed her lips. As they parted, he rested his forehead against hers. "I never said you were."

A smile lighting her entire face, Valoretta leaned forward again. Never had one kiss meant so much to a scarred soul.

THANKS FOR READING *The Final Drive*. If you've enjoyed reading this book, please leave a review on your favorite review site. It helps me reach readers who might enjoy more of my books.

Acknowledgments

L IKE THE CHARACTERS, *The Final Drive* marks the end of a chapter in my life and the beginning of a new one. Before the page is turned, however, there are many people who have made this chapter possible, who must be mentioned once again before embarking on the next stage:

My parents, who allowed me time to explore and dream. Dad, for your supportive pride in us. Mom, for staying up late with me to puzzle over sentences and for being my schoolteacher from the beginning.

My grandparents, who let me stay with them while I wrote the original draft of *The Final Drive*. At the time, no one even told me Valoretta existed; I was just meeting Arnacin himself. I was writing the climax of this book when I first began to realize his secrets were so deep and intriguing that he eclipsed Evan and I needed to do something about that. Some seasoned writers advised me to kill our islander off! Instead, I joined Raymond in trying to pull background out of a sealed tomb.

It was then I met Valoretta, and thanks to her queenly grace and openness, the story of *The Savage War* slowly came forth. I am glad that with her portions of the story revealed, Arnacin relented, as much as he ever does. Otherwise, the Black Phantom Chronicles could never have been.

I also could not have made it this far without Emerald Lake Books. To them, a huge thank you is due. They've put up with a very independent ambassador for Arnacin and Valoretta's story. Thank you for believing in this series enough to stick through it with me.

To my local Barnes and Noble, whose workers have all supported Arnacin, Valoretta and myself, bending backwards to keep the series stocked when ordering the first book through the regular channels became impossible, and for being one of the most enthusiastic street-teams an author could find.

To my first writing friends and editors, you helped turn a dyslexic novice into a writer and opened doors to ever greater opportunities.

To those who will listen when I come apart or feel the extreme isolation that too many authors know from time to time, who will give their support, prayers and understanding.

To the endorsers and beta readers of the series, who have been willing to read this epic in a limited amount of time.

To the readers, who have shown such love (and the frustration born of care) to our ever-unbending Arnacin and informed me that Valoretta is of the strongest females ever known.

To the Florida Authors and Publishers Association and Realm Makers, for the opportunities you give authors.

And to so many others who have come in and out, uniquely participating to make *The Final Drive* a reality.

Thank you.

About the Author

Esther Wallace lives in Connecticut. When she's not writing, she's working for her local bookstore or illustrating for her clients and her own written works. Her award-winning series, The Black Phantom Chronicles, carries such themes as she is passionate about—themes of heroism, strong females, healing, true love, and independence. In her leisure time, she might be found at a Renaissance Faire, hiking the East Coast's green mountains, or, when she's able, with a horse. You can find out more about Esther at theblackphantomchronicles.com.

Esther enjoys hearing from her readers. If you'd like to contact her or invite her to your next book club meeting, visit emeraldlakebooks.com/wallace.

For more great books, please visit us at
emeraldlakebooks.com.